KU-610-341

THE
MYSTERY
OF
FOUR

SAM BLAKE

CORVUS

First published in Great Britain in 2023 by Corvus, an imprint of
Atlantic Books Ltd.

Copyright © Sam Blake, 2023

The moral right of Sam Blake to be identified as the author of this
work has been asserted by her in accordance with the Copyright,
Designs and Patents Act of 1988.

All rights reserved. No part of this publication may be reproduced,
stored in a retrieval system, or transmitted in any form or by any
means, electronic, mechanical, photocopying, recording, or otherwise,
without the prior permission of both the copyright owner and the above
publisher of this book.

This novel is entirely a work of fiction. The names, characters and
incidents portrayed in it are the work of the author's imagination. Any
resemblance to actual persons, living or dead, events or localities, is
entirely coincidental.

10 9 8 7 6 5 4 3 2 1

A CIP catalogue record for this book is available from the British Library.

Paperback ISBN: 978 1 83895 300 3
E-book ISBN: 978 1 83895 299 0

Printed and bound by CPI (UK) Ltd, Croydon CR0 4YY

Corvus
An imprint of Atlantic Books Ltd
Ormond House
26–27 Boswell Street
London
WC1N 3JZ

www.atlantic-books.co.uk

MIX
Paper | Supporting
responsible forestry
FSC® C171272

For Sam and his cat (the real Merlin)

The tall bluish purple flowering aconite, also known as Jupiter's helm, monkshood, wolfsbane, devil's helmet or queen of poisons, comes from a group of over 250 species of flowering plants belonging to the Ranunculaceae family .

Highly poisonous, growing to an elegant metre in height, Aconitum is native to Europe where it is extensively cultivated. Often used by florists, Aconitum's deep blue hue and flower-clustered stems makes it a particularly appealing perennial for ornamental gardens. Flowering from May to October, it has won many awards, such as the Royal Horticultural Society's Award of Garden Merit. The roots and tubers are traditionally used to treat muscle-bone illness, paralysis due to stroke and other ailments.

There is a narrow margin of safety between a therapeutic and a deadly dose.

Prologue

ALMOST MIDNIGHT. The garden is ink-black, as though it's been washed with a brush, details of marble statues and sweeping steps picked out by the weak moonlight.

Below, a bronze fountain cast in the likeness of Apollo splashes water into the lake, disturbing the stillness of the hour. Accompanied by the distant scream of a fox, the hoot of an owl, the night sounds meld into backdrop for what is to come.

"The stars move still, time runs, the clock will strike."

Skirting the high granite wall, careful footsteps crunch on the gravel to the end of the path where towering gates stand open, wrought-iron flourishes picked out with golden ivy leaves, visible even in the darkness.

Now cutting across the neatly mown grass in front of the glasshouses, and through another set of matching gates.

Beyond, a series of round rose beds and square ponds are linked like gems in a necklace along the formal Rose Walk, leading to the wishing well and the yew maze. On either side, crowded flower beds wait for the morning sunshine, their scent heavy, trapped between high walls covered in more roses, their stems entwined, thick with thorns.

A black shape slips into the foliage unseen, green eyes watching.

Almost there. This will be the last trip.

It's been a long journey, the planning detailed, but there's been a lot of time for that. Now, the last act will be easy.

The water in the ponds is deathly still, the fragrance of roses and buddleia heavy in the night air.

Just before the last set of gates, tucked into the corner, is the Poison Garden. Fenced in to keep the unsuspecting public safe, the brass sign is dull without the sun to light it. Stepping onto the bone-dry earth, trowel ready, the tall purple-flowered stems are hard to see, buried deep in the shrubbery. But it is the roots that are the most potent, dried and ground to a lethal powder.

Watching her suffering as she slowly succumbs will be poetry indeed.

Glancing up, windows mirror-like in the darkness, the house is quiet now. As if it's waiting.

Waiting to see what happens.

Because it's all about to happen.

"The time is come."

THURSDAY

Chapter 1

'I'M SORRY, JUST run that past me again?' Tess Morgan turned up the speaker on her phone and ran her hands into her bubbly chestnut curls, narrowing her eyes, as if it would help her better understand the man who had just called.

And possibly ruined her life.

Wherever he was, she could hear traffic, the pip of a pedestrian crossing. He had a strong Northern Irish accent, but that didn't mean anything.

'I wanted to talk to you about Eoin Doyle. We've received some information about the disappearance of Fidelma Hoey. I believe Doyle works for you?'

'And you are again?'

'Jerry Lynch, *Daily News*.'

The *Daily News* was an Irish national tabloid – as her best friend Genevieve's eternally elegant mother Clarissa put it so aptly, a rag she wouldn't clean her shoes on. Getting a call from them was never going to be good. Tess cleared her throat.

'Eoin doesn't work for me, I don't really know him at all. I mean I know *of* him, but only what I've heard.'

'I had information that he was involved in the restoration of Kilfenora House. You *do* own Kilfenora House?'

'Yes, yes I do.' Tess paused for a moment, thinking hard. 'It's possible he was working for one of the contractors – maybe? I'd have to check. I didn't employ him personally.'

'I did wonder about that, given that you live alone.'

Tess wasn't sure if she was more surprised by his tone or the fact he was implying knowledge of her domestic arrangements. Either way it was creepy.

'I'm sorry?'

'Eoin Doyle has been connected to the disappearance of several women over the past ten years. They all lived alone.'

Tess tried to catch her thoughts and process what he was saying. Eoin Doyle lived in the village, had done all his life. He had a conviction for assaulting his ex-wife, she knew about that, and there had been rumours about the guards being interested in his activities around the times various women had disappeared in Wicklow. According to local gossip, Doyle maintained that he'd just been in the wrong place at the wrong time – albeit on more than one occasion.

Enough times for him to be taken in for questioning, but not enough to land him in court.

Although that *could* have had less to do with his innocence and more to do with the fact that the missing women's bodies had never been found. The Gardai kept denying that a serial killer might be at work, but it was in all the papers that they'd launched a single investigation into what had been dubbed the 'Radio Snatcher' disappearances, and were drawing links between them.

But what the hell had this got to do with Kilfenora?

'I'm sorry . . . Jerry, is it? I'm still not clear how this relates to me.'

'We've had a tip-off that there might be an area of interest to the Gardai on the edge of the Kilfenora estate.'

Tess looked blindly out of her office window, barely focusing on the tiny front garden and its riot of summer colour. Across the lane Clarissa's black cat Merlin skulked around the wide stable yard entrance, keeping to the shade of the granite walls. Tess squinted, trying to make sense of what Lynch was saying. *What was an area of interest?*

'You're going to have to spell it out for me, I'm still not following.'

'A body, Ms Morgan. We've had a tip-off that one of the women Eoin Doyle is thought to have been involved with has been buried in a place called Fury Hill. I believe that's on your property.'

For once, Tess was lost for words.

Chapter 2

*H*OW COULD THERE *be a body on Kilfenora land?*
    Pulling her cheery bright red front door closed behind her, not feeling in the slightest bit bright or cheery, Tess headed down the tiled path that bisected the front garden of the Butler's Lodge. There was a welcome breeze today, albeit slight, the scent of lavender strong as she pulled open the wrought-iron gate, the sounds of excited children drifting up from the direction of the wishing well.

They had eight days to go before the official opening weekend, when the newly restored Tudor manor with its now tamed gardens would be officially thrown open to the public, and the past two and a half years of sweat, occasional tears and many sleepless nights would finally come to fruition.

Unless, of course, the entire place was covered in crime scene tape and the drive blocked by news camera vans.

Tess felt herself wincing at the thought. The apparently inexplicable disappearances of several women from their homes was one of the biggest ongoing news stories in the country. The last one had been eight years ago, but every year since, their stories had been revisited by the press. And the local gossips in The Cross Keys.

Walking across the dusty lane that divided her cottage from the back entrance to Kilfenora House, Tess felt as if she had brain freeze. Lynch's words were caught in a loop in her head, a loop that was getting tighter and tighter the more she thought about it, and was starting to hurt.

How on earth could this be happening now?

Ever since she'd bought what was left of Kilfenora House and moved in to renovate it, the part of her mind that was constantly on media alert had been looking for press angles and photo opportunities. The opening weekend – with the vintage car rally, a craft and farmers' market, and the stage production of *Doctor Faustus* that they were putting on in the ballroom – was carefully engineered to hit as much of the speciality press as possible, as well as catch national coverage.

But a body on her land? The thought of a killer who targeted single women being anywhere near her property – even eight years ago – filled her with dread, personally and professionally. Kilfenora House was set in a huge estate, and despite the alarm system, it had occurred to Tess more than once that it would take the guards at least twenty minutes to get here from the nearest station if she hit the panic button. Twenty minutes during which anything could happen.

Tess could feel her heart rate increase at the thought. And if that wasn't enough, if the press got hold of this news, now, the week before the opening, she'd be besieged for all the wrong reasons.

As her bank manager was constantly reminding her, there was a lot riding on this weekend being a success. More than a lot, in fact. Pretty much every last penny. As well as friendships and the livelihoods of half the village.

None of them could afford for this weekend to be a flop.

The press was crucial in the mix, but this really wasn't the sort of coverage she'd had in mind at all. She needed people to come to Kilfenora to spend money and see the house in all its refurbished glory, to bring their children and their grannies to see the gardens; not to take selfies at a crime scene – assuming they weren't frightened into staying away in the first place.

And more to the point, why had a reporter called her and not the Gardai themselves?

Tess was still only half concentrating as she reached the shade of the broad stone arch that spanned the entrance to the cobbled stable yard.

It was even hotter today than it had been earlier in the week. The tiny part of her mind not panicking about bodies was thankful that at least they had the weather on their side. Although, as of twenty minutes ago, and Lynch's phone call, the weather suddenly seemed a lot less significant.

Glancing at her clipboard but barely seeing today's checklist, Tess mentally took a deep breath, fighting the growing black hole of fear that was manifesting somewhere deep in her stomach. *She needed more information.* Then she could worry about it properly – or, more precisely, try and look for a solution.

She could be totally overreacting.

Genevieve, still her best friend after all these years, had been saying since their first day in senior school that she overthought things. And Tess knew she was exhausted, to say nothing of the fact that she hadn't been feeling at all well recently. She needed to be sensible; now was *not* the time to panic. Although parking the maelstrom of dread making her already queasy stomach roll, was a lot easier said than done.

As soon as she'd ended the call with Lynch, Tess had phoned the local Garda station to find out what the real story was, only to be met with bafflement. Which did give her some hope that it was all a big mistake, a tabloid journalist making a story out of nothing. But as she'd ended the call to the guards, another thought had hit her and made her feel worse, if that was possible.

Could this 'tip-off' be something to do with the creep who had trolled her on Twitter and Instagram for so long? Part of her had been waiting for something to happen – maybe this was it?

The trolling had started soon after the first newspaper report that she'd bought the house, and had gone on for almost two years. Vitriol about her, and how Kilfenora would become a penance, how she'd regret returning to Ireland. She'd laughed at it at first, but it had gradually got more frightening: about how she'd get her comeuppance; how she'd pay for 'it', whatever 'it' was.

She'd ended up ignoring her mentions, but the whole point of using social media as a way to build the Kilfenora name was engagement. Then, six months ago, when the TV restoration show had launched, it had become even worse, taking a step up from being abusive and menacing, to plain terrifying. Every time she blocked one account, another appeared in its place.

Twitter was predictably useless and the guards couldn't do anything because the tweets were worded so carefully. Which made the whole thing worse – whoever it was, was clearly intelligent. It had been Gen who had finally persuaded her to come off social media completely, finding her a media student to take over scheduling, showing followers that the accounts were all managed externally. Just to be on the safe side, Gen had made the village Facebook private at the same time.

And it had all stopped. Just like that. Overnight.

Which proved that it was personal.

Had whoever it was found a new way to attack her now, by tipping off a journalist with some sort of crazy story that could end up ruining her?

Chapter 3

'*H*OLD MY HAND.'
     A strident voice cut through Tess's turbulent thoughts and made her falter, suddenly aware of the dizzying heat of the sun on her back. Closing her eyes, she fought the images she knew would come.

The chill of the concrete, the oily darkness.

The sirens.

'*Hold my hand.*'

'Won't!'

The child's scream of temper brought Tess crashing back to the present, the edge of her clipboard cutting into her ribs where she'd gripped it unconsciously. *Christ, today was the day that just kept on giving. What had she done to deserve all this?*

'What did I say before we came, Starlight? No ice cream if you are going to misbehave.' The sound of the mother's voice filled the empty stable yard like nails on a blackboard.

Turning to the pair, Tess took a steadying breath, and forced a smile on to her face. There were times when she deserved an Oscar for her acting skills.

'I'm afraid this area is closed to the public at the moment. The ice cream van is beside the fountain on the front drive, this area is only open at weekends.'

The woman looked her up and down haughtily and pulled her rose-gold designer handbag up her arm.

'Well, the signposting is very bad. I must say it to the owner.'

Tess was tempted to say, 'You're looking at her,' but bit it back. The woman probably expected someone grand, grey-haired, dressed in tweeds with a spaniel at her heels. A slight thirty-one-year-old with her wildly curly bobbed hair now scraped into a ponytail and in need of a wash, wearing a creased Repeal T-shirt and ripped jeans, didn't fit the picture at all.

'Mummy!' The miniature Disney princess tugged hard on her sky-blue tulle skirt, her face red. 'Ice cream.' *Ice* came out 'Ith'.

With the politest smile she could muster, Tess pointed through the pedestrian arch behind them. She really had no idea how people ended up wandering around the back of the house during the week. It would be different after this weekend, when they'd be open seven days. But today was Thursday and the tea rooms were currently only open at weekends. The signs were perfectly clear.

There were times she was sure people did it on purpose, curious to see the latest development.

With the receding click of the mother's heels, Tess drew in a deep breath, trying to steady her nerves, a waft of lavender from the borders outside the walls reaching her. *God, it was hot.* She'd slapped on factor 50 after her shower this morning, but she'd need to stay in the shade or she'd end up with a migraine to add to her problems.

If this body business really was real, and not some vicious rumour dreamed up by a social media lunatic, could she put the *Daily News* and its story-hungry reporter off until the week after next, after the opening? How would that look?

Tess felt the dark hole of worry in the middle of her stomach deepen at the thought. They had just over a week to go and all the media she'd landed would come together.

Towards the end of the six years she'd been working in Dubai she'd felt as if she was only marking time, waiting for the moment when she'd be able to come home and build a business for herself. And then Genevieve had sent her a picture of Kilfenora on an Instagram post advertising its auction, making a joke about them being neighbours again, and Tess hadn't been able to forget it.

She let out a sigh. Everything she'd done to date depended on this weekend being a success. Getting the TV people on board to follow the restoration work had been a huge coup, and they'd be back as the gates opened officially to make the final show; it was starting to feel as if the whole country would be watching to see how it all turned out. Somehow the restoration of Kilfenora House, with all its disasters and dramas, had become a symbol of national hope, with even the tabloids taking an interest, her every move, everyone told her, featuring on social media. Although thankfully speculation about her marital status, and how she'd ended up working in Dubai, seemed to be limited to the bar at The Cross Keys.

Now, after everything, if Jerry Lynch was to be believed, the country's most notorious suspected killer might have concealed a body somewhere on the estate. You really couldn't make it up.

Resuming her route across the courtyard, Tess felt her phone vibrate with a text at the exact moment that the heavy wooden door at the back of the house was flung open, and Laetitia O'Riordan appeared to fall out of it, clutching an imperial purple velvet cloak around her thin shoulders. She looked even paler than normal, but no less dramatic, her eyes wild as they alighted on Tess.

What the . . .?

It took Laetitia a moment to catch her breath and speak, a moment in which she gesticulated wildly, beckoning at Tess to follow her.

Tess looked at her quizzically. Of the three O'Riordan girls, Laetitia, or Tis, as she was known, was the artistic one, the one for whom getting up in the morning required a dramatic performance, and missing the bus was akin to a national disaster. Holding the door open, Laetitia pushed her long dark hair from her face as she finally found her words:

'Come, come, *quickly* – there's been a terrible accident.'

Chapter 4

GENEVIEVE FORTUNE LEANED forwards on the glass display counter at the back of her shop, and tapped her phone screen, her charm bracelet jangling against the glass as she moved. She glanced up as Facebook opened and, seeing that the pavement outside was empty, she clicked through to the Kilfenora Community Forum.

Genevieve shifted, her bum getting numb on the stool that her mother Clarissa had insisted on having upholstered in burgundy velvet, to fit with the 'aesthetic'. She'd been right, of course. She'd managed to bring her own inherent sense of style and the feeling of a London West End emporium to an Irish country antique shop by putting up the chandeliers and mirrors that had been gathering dust in the back room. When Gen's divorce had finally come through and she'd bought what would become Fortune Finds, her priority had been getting the apartment above it fit for her and Malachi to live in.

But then Clarissa brought a force of energy to everything she did. From walking every day to exercising in her home gym – *who even did that at over seventy?* – Clarissa was stronger and fitter than Gen would ever be. She was one of those tall, willowy types who never put on weight and was convinced that keeping her body fit would keep her mind sound. Her ongoing chess game with her mysterious partner, was, Gen was sure, another tactic to keep her thinking sharp.

And she needed all her faculties to look after Malachi – yesterday they'd been hiking; today they were having a quiet day, finishing baking the chocolate babka bread that required proving for hours. Gen had no idea how an eight-year-old was going to be able to wait a full day for it to be ready, but Clarissa had smiled at her knowingly as she'd got into her little Mercedes to get extra Nutella in Rockfield. She was the perfect granny in so many ways, *especially* now that she wasn't actually living with them, and she had her own cottage on the Kilfenora estate. Tess's arrival home and the purchase of Kilfenora had been a godsend in so many ways.

Gen reached for her mug, her bracelets chiming, and took a sip of her coffee. Opening the forum, she cringed again; the 'about' section had been Clarissa's idea, too, her tone typically strident:

This is YOUR village, get involved!

This is YOUR local forum for the village of Kilfenora and its townlands. Please respect other users, we will not tolerate any abusive posts, comments, bullying, or hate speech of any sort – anything of this nature will get an automatic ban. We support local business wherever we can, no negative comments please. If you have a problem, please resolve it privately. If you are not happy with the way this group is run, please consider leaving. The admins are voluntary and we are all too busy for debate.

Gen could hear Clarissa's voice. The day Genevieve had told her mother that she'd set up the forum, to get everyone together to stop the council taking down the ancient oaks bordering the main road into the village, Clarissa had insisted that the lines were drawn very clearly.

This is a private group. Only members can see who's in the group and what they post. Being part of this forum requires mutual trust. Authentic, expressive discussions are welcomed, but may also be sensitive and private. What's shared in the group should stay in the group.

Gen's face twitched into a smile. What was shared in the group was the main topic of conversation most nights at The Cross Keys. It was just as well it was private now.

Everyone is welcome once you follow the RULES. The admins give up their time on a voluntary basis to run this forum so we would ask that you respect other members – if they can follow the rules, so can you. If you don't like how the forum is run, please consider leaving. The rules are clear.

Well, that was true.
Before Genevieve could scroll down further, her phone pipped with a text – from Clarissa. Sometimes Gen felt as if she was watching her.

Have you heard from Tess? I'm worried about her overdoing it this week. Cxx

Gen sighed and tucked a long stray strand of sandy hair behind her ear. Clarissa must have said the same thing to her every day for the last month. She was right, of course; Tess was overdoing it, but she'd been planning this opening thing for so long, she was completely invested.

But both she and Clarissa had seen the strain on Tess's face increase as the grand opening came closer. Personally, Gen thought adding the whole play was just too much – there was no reason why a performance couldn't be put on in the ballroom in a month's time, but Aidan Gaunt had been very persuasive.

And as Clarissa had pointed out privately when he'd first approached Tess in January, he was after maximum exposure, which wasn't a bad thing for Kilfenora. When the *Country House Restoration* team returned to film their follow-up show, he'd get his moment in the spotlight.

Genevieve pursed her lips, chiding herself at being so critical. He *was* putting the production together for free, so he deserved the exposure, and he had written it. *But still* . . . His acting career to date seemed very patchy to her. According to the website she'd checked, he'd been an extra in a few things. According to him, he'd also done a lot of stage work.

He'd been pushing hard for Clarissa to get involved – hardly surprising, given her stage career and occasional foray on to the screen – but she hadn't been keen. She'd insisted that she was busy enough looking after Malachi, and she could add gloss and glamour to the production in lots of ways without showing the predominantly amateur cast up on stage, or clashing with Aidan over his production ideas. She'd keep an eye on proceedings but preferred to stay well back. She'd retired for a reason – and much as she loved Tess, reviving her career with an am-dram production really wasn't high on her list of priorities. Far from it.

Gen caught a movement outside the shop window and glanced up again as Mark Mulligan sauntered past in a T-shirt and long denim shorts, sporting a bright yellow pair of Crocs that made his tan appear even deeper than normal. He looked in and raised his hand in a mock salute as he continued past.

Gen grinned in acknowledgement, smiling inside at what she knew would have been Clarissa's look of horror had she been here. Clarissa Westmacott might be forward-thinking in many ways, but she firmly believed Crocs had been designed for the operating theatre and should stay there.

Not that Mark would be bothered by Clarissa's critique of his wardrobe – the reluctant landlord of The Cross Keys was one of the few people in Kilfenora who didn't care what anyone thought of him. In fact, there were times when Genevieve felt that Mark didn't really want to be here at all. Which was a shame, because he was one of the few residents who seemed grounded in common sense, with the added bonus of being very nice to look at.

In a quiet moment Gen had discovered that at thirty-four, not only did Mark own the pub, but he'd had a thriving business in Australia. Scrolling back far enough through his profile, she'd found a birthday post and been able to work out his age. He'd been with his late wife in the photo – a stunning brunette.

Before Gen could think more on Mark Mulligan, his mysterious past and the rugged charm he brought to the village, her phone pinged with a notification. Another forum post.

Carrie O'Connor
I heard Faustus is booked out – I wanted to get six tickets, any ideas?

Gen shook her head to herself. Why did people go on a forum to ask a question when it was faster just to google it? As she replied 'Try the Kilfenora House website' another post popped in:

Lou Lou O'Neill

does anyone know if Laetitia O'Riordan is still doing tarot? Friend wants to have a fortune telling party. Don't have her number.

Gen raised her eyebrows. Asking for a friend? Gen doubted it. Katie-Louise O'Neill had been drifting about for the past few months as if she was in love, repeatedly late when she was supposed to be opening up the shop on a Tuesday. She only did one day a week, giving Gen a chance to get into Dublin to the auctions, but she was becoming more ditsy as the summer progressed.

Genevieve strongly suspected that she was madly in love with Mark. She certainly never stopped talking about how he dropped into the shop to say hello whenever she was working. Which, given that he didn't seem to drop in when Gen was there, could have been a sign that he was interested in Katie-Lou, but Gen somehow doubted it. Katie-Lou just about managed the till on the days she was in the shop, but the poor girl hadn't been born with brains. She guessed that Katie-Lou had managed to misinterpret Mark's trips to the Spar or the post office as some sort of deliberate ploy to chat her up. Gen was pretty sure that Mark was the upfront type, that he wouldn't be messing about trying to engineer accidental meetings if he really wanted to talk to her.

Unless there was a side to Mark Mulligan that none of them knew about, of course.

Chapter 5

THE OUTSIDE DOOR slammed shut as Tess raced up the steep back staircase behind Laetitia, her Converse silent but her heart pounding. Whatever had happened, there hadn't been time to explain it, which meant it wasn't good.

There was already too-much-not-good happening today for Tess's liking. What could possibly have gone wrong now?

Today was the first full dress rehearsal, Aidan Gaunt's reimagining of *Doctor Faustus* finally coming together in full technical splendour. Teams had been working in the ballroom all week, getting the sound and lighting to Aidan's exact requirements. Half the village had been making costumes.

It was a modern version of the play, but Aidan had wanted to maintain the mystery of the original in its look and feel. Faustus was being portrayed as a social media star in black jeans and T-shirt who sold his soul to the devil of the internet – in return for unlimited riches, knowledge and power. Just about everyone else, including Mephostophilis, the Devil's messenger, had authentic costumes from 1616. It was the perfect play for the opening weekend, as Aidan had explained enthusiastically when they'd first spoken about it: the original house had been built in the same year that Christopher Marlowe had written the play.

On the stairs ahead of her, Laetitia's dark velvet cloak swirled over the worn stone treads as she paused at the top step long enough to check that Tess was still behind her. Yanking open the door into the cavernous ballroom, she shot through.

'I found her.' Laetitia's breathless announcement was more like a proclamation.

The door slammed behind them as Tess headed over to the elevated stage, her pace increasing as she registered the tension in the room. This wasn't just a Laetitia drama. Everyone was gathered in an anxious huddle in the middle of the stage, bending over, looking at something on the floor.

Or someone.

As Tess ran up the steps stage left, Megan, one of Laetitia's sisters, waved a mobile phone at her, her face pale.

'I've called an ambulance.'

Tess's mouth dried.

Megan clamped the phone to her ear as the cast parted. In the centre of their circle, Aidan was bending over someone.

Oh Christ.

'Can we stand back, give him some space?'

Still not believing her eyes, Tess motioned for everyone to take a step backwards. The circle opened like the tightly curled petals of a flower.

Beside Aidan, Faustus – village heart-throb Conor Kelly – was lying on his back, with what looked like a steel box with a high-wattage light inside it only inches from his head. A pool of blood was forming beneath his mop of dark curls, gleaming in the footlights, the shadows of his fellow players falling over him as they shifted anxiously.

Aidan's shoulders moved rhythmically as he pumped Conor's chest.

'What on earth happened?'

Kneeling opposite Aidan, young Liam answered for him. 'He had to do the new opening about six times, and when he got to swollen wings the lighting track came down right on top of him.'

Tess could feel her own heart accelerating. 'There's a defibrillator in the hall, beside reception.'

'I'll get it.'

Liam began to move before she'd even drawn a breath at the end of the sentence. The crowd parted as he ran straight for the main doors and staircase, his jump off the edge of the stage hardly breaking his stride.

Tess's heart swelled. He was only nineteen, was stage manager as well as doing the prompts, and utterly immersed in the production.

Aidan glanced over his shoulder.

'Have you ever done CPR?'

'Yes . . . yes.' Tess heard her voice cracking.

'Take over from me?'

Jesus Christ. For a moment Tess felt she was going to vomit, or faint – she wasn't sure which. *This couldn't be happening again.* They'd done CPR in school, but she'd never thought she'd have to use it twice in her lifetime. She could feel a surge of emotion, tears hot in her eyes. *The rain beginning to fall, icy cold on the back of her neck, the sirens.* But there wasn't time to panic now.

Falling to her knees beside him, she took several short breaths and focused on Aidan's hands moving rhythmically on Conor's chest as he counted her in. Then her mind went blank.

'What's the song?'

'"Staying Alive", Bee Gees. Guys, sing it with her.'

There was an awkward pause. Aidan looked up at the rest of the cast.

'Sing it – the timing, she needs the timing.'

It took them a moment but then someone started humming it, the group around her joining in as someone else in her peripheral vision found the words on their phone.

One hand on top of the other, she took over the compressions. Aidan sat on his heels, shaking out his arms. She had so many questions jumping around her head but didn't dare break her concentration to ask them now. The timing was vital. Around her, the voices began to trail off.

'Keep it going.' Aidan started singing with them, louder, giving them all direction and energy. She felt a surge of relief that he was here, that he was in charge. He was one of those natural leaders, the type of person people followed.

From somewhere behind her, Tess heard Megan's voice. 'They're sending the helicopter. They said another five minutes.'

Tess glanced at Aidan, his face remarkably calm. He must have done this before, too.

'Is that fast enough?'

He drew a breath between clenched teeth. 'I hope so.' He glanced at his watch. 'Just keep going, it's all we can do.' He turned to Megan. 'Ask them about the defib – will we go ahead with it?'

Megan had moved around to look at Conor. She nodded, her face pale against her glossy dark hair, but Tess was focusing on keeping the rhythm, fighting the panic attack that was threatening to overwhelm here. *Not now.* She just needed to keep going.

'Christ, I don't know how this happened.'

Out of the corner of her eye, Tess could see Aidan kneeling back, hands on his hips, his words mirroring her thoughts.

Was it an accident? Perhaps she was being paranoid, but with thoughts of the Twitter troll fresh in her mind, Tess sure hoped they weren't going to find out that someone had sabotaged the lights in an effort to stop the play.

Surely not.

Today was truly turning into the day from hell – *and Faustus thought he had problems.*

Before anyone could comment, the sound of running feet echoing in the main stairwell reached them and Liam arrived in the ballroom, racing across to the stage. From the thump and vibration on the boards, it sounded as if he'd jumped all four steps. A moment later Aidan was beside her, opening the defibrillator, ready to take over again, the pads from the machine ready in his hand as they heard the throb of helicopter blades overhead.

Chapter 6

LEANING BACK ON the counter in the kitchen of Clarissa's cottage, Genevieve bit her lip and looked out of the open door. Beyond it, Malachi was lying on the lawn in a pool of afternoon sunlight, concentrating fiercely on an action figure and a rocket. Every now and then they caught the sounds of explosions as the game became more dramatic.

'I still can't believe it. Did the paramedics give any clues as to how bad it is?' Genevieve anxiously ran one of her pendants along its chain.

Wiping down the plastic kitchen tablecloth with its cheerful purple spots, Clarissa glanced at her, her face creased in a frown. Her long grey hair was swept up into an elegant chignon, secured with a silver clip. She was still wearing her bright red apron, a C embroidered on the bib in gold thread, although it was now covered in floury handprints. The whole kitchen smelled divine, the chocolate babka bread they'd made cooling on top of the Aga, the end missing where the vital process of sampling had begun while it was still hot.

'I'd guess it's too soon to know. I only heard third-hand from one of the gardeners, so I've no more information than you, really. The gossipers on the forum probably have a better idea – half of them were there.'

Genevieve grimaced. 'What a thing to happen. I texted Tess to tell her I was closing up early and would be here if she needed me, but she's not replied yet. I don't want to call up to the Lodge in case she's in the middle of things.'

'Which I imagine she will be. Something like this needs to be managed carefully.'

Clarissa turned to pick up her sapphire ring from the kitchen window sill. She slipped it on and brought the vase of fresh cut flowers, that she'd moved for the baking, back to the middle of the table. Long elegant stems dripping with what looked like purple bells, they were the same colour as the polka dots on the table cloth. Clarissa always managed to have everything matching.

But Genevieve wasn't thinking about the flowers as she crossed her arms, her bangles jangling.

'I've had a bad feeling about this week for ages. That troll has been back on Twitter, and Facebook now. The young one who's running the accounts finds it hilarious, but really there's nothing funny at all about the sheer nastiness of it. I'm not going to tell Tess, by the way.' Gen looked hard at her mother. 'And don't you, either. Tess has just got so much riding on the success of the opening weekend, she doesn't need more worry. I know she's got huge experience in running events, but I don't think she's been sleeping. She really doesn't need to know her stalker is on the warpath again.' Genevieve could feel her own anxiety arcing in the warm air like electricity. 'God, as if a troll isn't bad enough, Conor's accident is just awful.'

Positioning the vase, Clarissa pursed her lips and gave the table a final wipe.

'What makes you think she's not sleeping? She must be exhausted by the time she hits her bed.'

She moved over beside Gen to rinse the cloth, folding it meticulously on the side of the white porcelain Belfast sink.

Genevieve grimaced. 'Just something she said the other day.'

Clarissa looked at her, her perfectly shaped eyebrows raised. 'Could you give me a clue? There's no point in hinting and not telling me.'

'I could be wrong.'

'I doubt it, you've known her a long time. Through thick and thin, as they say.'

'It's the thin I'm worried about.' Genevieve sighed. 'I called in on Tuesday after the auction. And she was just very quiet. When she's stressed the nightmares come back, and normally she takes tablets, but I'm guessing she doesn't want to so close to opening in case they affect her during the day. Once she gets through the weekend, it'll still be full on, but she can relax a bit.'

Clarissa picked up her reading glasses from the centre of the open cookery book she'd been using and hooked them onto the top of her apron. The lenses were half-moon-shaped, in plastic frames of an otherworldly green, not dissimilar to the colour of pond weed.

'What did she say?'

'It wasn't so much what she said, it was what she didn't say.' Glancing out of the door to make sure Malachi was still fully occupied, Gen moved away from the counter and pulled out one of the kitchen chairs. There was a dusting of flour on the seat. She brushed it off with her hand, shaking her head at the proffered cloth. A bit of flour was the least of her worries; her summer dresses were a flowing patchwork of florals and the flour wouldn't show. Sitting down, she continued. 'We went into the office so she could show me the maps of the estate and where everything is going to go. I mean, she's got it all worked out with military precision. I've never seen so many spreadsheets.'

Twisting behind her, Clarissa picked up a glass from the draining board and ran some water into it from the tap.

'Go on.'

Gen put her elbow on the table and rubbed her face with her hand. She was tired and it wasn't even the end of the week; she didn't know how Tess was coping.

'It stresses me just thinking about it, in all honesty. But you know that bowl she has, the Japanese *kintsugi* one?'

Clarissa took a sip of her water and, realising Genevieve had left her own glass on the counter, picked it up and put it in front of her on the table.

'That bowl is *such* a beautiful blue, the gold along the cracks just enhances it.'

Gen toyed with her glass. 'I know, but she was looking at it and she made a comment about how the Japanese are positive thinkers – how they can make something broken more beautiful by adding the gold to repair the cracks.'

Staring at the bubbles rising around the ice in her water, Gen paused.

'I'm so annoyed that I can't remember exactly what she said, but it was more *how* she said it. It really pulled me up. It was something like that despite the repairs, the cracks remain no matter how we try to disguise them, and that the gold can't take away the darkness inside the bowl.'

'That sounds a bit deep. What did you think she was talking about?'

Gen looked up at Clarissa and let out a loud sigh. 'Herself, of course. You know how long it took her to recover after the accident, what with running away to Dubai. I always felt she should have gone to the trial, to put everything to rest. Giving evidence by video link keeps you removed.'

'Perhaps that's what she needed – to stay removed. You didn't go.'

'I know. With Tess not being there, it didn't feel like my place. I wasn't there that night. Me being in the court wouldn't have helped anyone. You went with her parents for the sentencing. It was a parents' thing.'

Clarissa sighed. 'I ended up spending most of the trial in the ladies with Kieran's mum. I can see why people say attending is important for closure, but honestly I'm not sure it did her any good.'

'The judge giving that bastard Adam O'Donnell four years for the death of her son was the bit that didn't do her any good.'

Clarissa pursed her lips. 'You really think it's causing Tess trouble again now?'

'When something as traumatic as that happens, it never really leaves you.' Gen paused. 'What's worrying me now, is how she's going to cope with Conor's accident on top of everything else. And then there's this troll. The comments are getting more and more personal, apparently. I mean, what if he turns up at the house?'

Chapter 7

TESS REALISED HER hand was shaking as she reached across her kitchen table for her phone. Another text. Did this Jerry Lynch character have nothing else to do?

Once Conor had been stabilised and evacuated, she and Aidan had calmed everyone down, assuring them that all the lighting would be double-checked before any rehearsals continued. Then she'd sat down on the edge of the stage to take a few minutes to gather herself, conscious that her phone was hopping but unable to look at it. Right then, she only had so much headspace to deal with disaster, and it was all used up.

She was sure that they wouldn't hear anything about Conor and his injuries for at least a few hours, and there were things that had to be done before the day was out: Aidan needed to write an accident report; she needed to call the insurance company. And they both needed to decide what happened next.

And that was even before she started thinking about bodies again, or if something more sinister was going on. She mentally stopped herself. There wasn't anything much more sinister than having a serial killer hanging around the place. *What on earth was she thinking?* If it did turn out to be true, and there was a body here, it was way worse than it *not* being true, even if the Twitter troll was at the heart of some sort of campaign of intimidation.

But she was getting ahead of herself. Catastrophising wasn't going to help Conor. He was the clear and present issue here – wasn't that the phrase they used in the movies?

Now, sitting in her kitchen with Aidan, two mugs of strong coffee in front of them, Tess took a deep breath and tried to focus. He'd sat her down the minute they'd got inside and had put on her all-singing-all-dancing machine, the smell of grinding beans a comfort in the madness of the day.

Perhaps keeping busy was his way to stay calm, too.

From working in Dubai to now, Tess had organised all sorts of things, some of which had subsequently gone wrong. Her events team had been responsible for all of the prince's entertaining, from diplomats to foreign heads of state, and everything from a political faux pas to a food allergy had happened at some stage. Whenever anything went pear-shaped, they'd held their nerve and afterwards, when they could breathe again, the phrase 'nobody died' was meant with sincerity.

Right now, the irony wasn't lost on her. This time she had everything she owned tied up in Kilfenora, and it would be touch-and-go for Conor for more than the next few days. Tess had thought she'd had all the bad luck that could ever manifest in her life land on her the summer after her finals, but clearly she'd been wrong.

'We have to keep going, you know. We can't cancel.' Leaning back in his chair, Aidan ran his hand over his buzz cut, grimacing as he said it. 'Liam knows all the lines, and he's the right age – he can play Faustus.'

Looking at her phone, only half listening, Tess took a shaky breath. She'd missed several calls from Lynch, as well as his non-stop texts. She tried to focus on what Aidan was saying about continuing, clearing her throat before she answered.

'We'll need to get the all-clear from the insurance assessor – he's coming out tomorrow. Do you think they'll want to keep going? The rest of the cast, I mean.'

'Absolutely. I'll talk to them.'

She nodded slowly. Could she ask them to go on after this? It would definitely come better from Aidan. They had a sell-out month ahead of them, with two shows a week, and a press reception organised for Friday night. Cancellation would be a logistical nightmare, to say nothing of the cost. Sliding her chair back, Tess stood up.

'I'm sorry, I missed a call earlier. I'll just be two minutes.'

Aidan picked up his coffee, sending her a sympathetic smile. He was so calm, had been since she'd arrived in the ballroom.

At least one of them was.

Tess looked at Lynch's latest text. This had to be the fourth this afternoon. And there was still nothing from the local Garda inspector, so the only way she was going to find out what was happening was to ask more questions.

He picked up after one ring.

'This is Tess Morgan. Sorry I missed your call.' Tess bit her lip. *Why was she apologising?*

'Thanks for getting back to me.' Lynch sounded as if he was inside now, somewhere a lot quieter than he had been the last time she'd spoken to him.

'Can you tell me about this tip-off? Why haven't the guards been in touch with me?'

'The information's come from a reliable source inside Mountjoy jail.' Lynch paused. Tess almost rolled her eyes at the irony of his statement. She was sure everyone in Mountjoy was super reliable. *Characters without blemish.*

'Go on.'

'I'm working with a TV crew on a new programme called *Unsolved*. We're bringing in a forensic psychologist and a geographical profiler – all sorts of experts, actually – to see if they can find new evidence in a series of unsolved and cold cases.'

'And you're working with the Gardai?' In the back of her mind, Tess remembered reading something about a new cold case unit being formed in Dublin. Clarissa had mentioned it, but she was much more interested in that sort of thing than Tess.

'We're alerting the Gardai to our findings, yes.'

Tess frowned. That sounded like a heavily disguised 'no' on the 'working with' part of her question.

'And what does this tipster say, exactly?'

'He believes several bodies have been buried on the edge of the Kilfenora estate where it borders the national park.'

'Several?' Tess felt her knees go a little weak. *This just kept on getting better.* 'The guards didn't seem to know anything about it when I spoke to them.'

'We've alerted the team dealing with the Radio Snatcher disappearances, but they need more evidence before they can commit resources. Which is why I need to talk to you. We want to bring cadaver dogs and a film crew up and see what's in the area that's been highlighted.'

What was she supposed to say to that – sorry, I'm a bit busy at the moment, or yes please, roll on in and make my land a crime scene? There was no good answer. She could see the headlines tomorrow: 'Landowner refuses access to possible murder site.'

'I'm going to need to think about this. And see a map. Can you email me the details please? Precisely what sort of access you require, all your insurance information, who these experts are.'

'No problem. We are hoping to get down on Thursday.'

'As I say, I'll have to think about it. We've a major event happening next weekend. I have to consider the safety of the public if there are people digging holes all over the place. I'm not sure the timing would be ideal.'

The safety of the public? She wasn't even sure where that one had come from, but it sounded plausible.

'Obviously the sooner we can get access, the sooner we can see if the information is correct.'

Tess closed her eyes for a moment. She felt like saying that if there *was* anyone buried there, they'd been dead for at least eight years so they weren't likely to be going anywhere fast, but it really didn't feel like the right time. Then her PR brain kicked in.

'I presume you want to keep this out of the public eye until you have a broadcast date, and have done your editing? And you don't want Eoin Doyle leaving the state as soon as he gets wind of something happening?'

'God no, we need to keep everything under wraps.'

Tess cut in, 'So it might be best to wait until later next week when there are fewer people here? The place is going to be packed over the weekend.' She paused. 'Email me all the details and we can go from there.' Her tone was much more confident than she felt.

Hanging up, Tess looked at her phone. Eoin Doyle *had* been a suspect in the Radio Snatcher case. That much she knew was true, but the rest? According to local gossip, quite a few people had met sticky ends over the years on this estate, but this was the first she'd heard of a connection with the Radio Snatcher.

But what was really worrying Tess, was whether all this was linked somehow to the Twitter troll. Could *he* be the Radio

Snatcher? The abuse had begun when she'd started tweeting about the house restoration and her plans for the estate. Was he trying to frighten her off the land that he knew hid evidence that could lead directly to him?

Chapter 8

'WHERE ON EARTH are you going?'

Megan looked up sharply at her middle sister as Ally burst through her bedroom door and stopped abruptly, her face aghast. Ally had changed when they got home, into a scruffy pair of jogging pants and a sweatshirt. 'Comfort clothing,' Ally called it. 'Fit for the bin' in Megan's opinion. She'd said it often enough: they might both be uni students but there was no need to let standards slip. Laetitia was hippie enough for everyone. Megan looked critically at Ally's faded top. Honestly, she might be bright, but she had no style. They lived in the *biggest* house in the village – apart from Kilfenora, obviously, their father was the *doctor*; people looked to them for direction.

'Any chance you could knock? I mean, privacy?' Megan scowled at her. Ally was an absolute mess, her face streaked with tears, her long dark hair pulled haphazardly off her face.

As if she could feel she was being judged Ally came properly into Megan's room, pushing the oak door closed behind her, and sat down heavily on the edge of the unmade double bed.

'You can't be going out, *tonight*? I mean, after everything . . .' Ally looked at her incredulously. Swivelling around, she threw her phone on the bed beside her and picked up some of Megan's jewel-coloured velvet scatter cushions, pulling them into a pile on her knee so she could lean on them.

Megan looked at her and sighed inwardly. It was as if she was using the cushions to build a wall between herself and the real world. But that was Ally all over: she kept everyone at arm's length, happier with her books than with real people. Megan had no idea how she was going to manage when she graduated and got to the law library, but perhaps she'd be one of those researcher types who did all the background stuff on cases and never actually represented anyone in court. She really was the absolute opposite of Laetitia – she might be the youngest of the three of them, but she was a total people person, saw the good in everyone.

But Megan had other things, apart from her irritating sisters, to think about this evening.

'What time is it now?'

Ally let out a sharp sigh and leaned over to check her phone.

'Almost nine. And Laetitia still hasn't replied to my text about the rehearsal tomorrow, or the one about going into town on Monday.'

Megan looked at her sister. 'She's probably turned her phone off. I *cannot* believe she had a thing with Aidan and you never said.'

Ally sighed. 'You know Laetitia, she leaves broken hearts behind her all over the place.'

Turning to the mirror, Megan looked at Ally in the glass. She was checking her phone to see if she'd missed a message. *But –* Megan's mind worked quickly – *if Laetitia wasn't answering her texts, it was a sign she didn't want to see or talk to anyone tonight.* So that was one less thing Megan had to worry about in her grand plan to seduce Aidan Gaunt, although Megan's opportunity to call over and bring him an update from the hospital, hot off the press, was diminishing with every hour that passed. She still had no news yet on Conor Kelly. She'd persuaded their father to ring Conor's mother, and the hospital, to see if he could find out what was happening. But, annoyingly, there was no news. Conor was just about alive and in ICU, and that was all they'd had to say.

Megan looked critically at her reflection in the huge mirror on the Victorian wardrobe door. Given the lack of information available, she hadn't decided if she *was* going to go out yet. But taking a stroll down the main street to see if she could maybe bump into Aidan might not be a bad idea. He'd be terribly upset after the drama today, and *might* need someone to talk to. And if Aidan's heart was broken, there could be even more reason for him needing comfort with someone sensible. That was assuming this Laetitia thing wasn't ongoing, but there was every chance she'd already moved on.

Megan pulled the elasticated shoulders of her lacy white blouse down so that it was more Bardot style. It was still baking outside, so she could get away with slightly more revealing clothing, and her shoulders were one of her best assets. She flicked her hair back and twisted around to look at her side view in the mirror.

Despite not having any breaking news, Megan was sure that if Aidan bumped into someone who had been right there in the ballroom when it had all happened, *and* who had been the person who called 999 and stayed on the line while the ambulance people relayed instructions – who had been *very* involved in the whole thing – then sitting down for a chat about it all would be the most natural thing in the world. Perhaps he'd even like to go for a drink in the pub. The Cross Keys wasn't exactly blessed with cosy nooks, but it was an improvement on the chipper.

Behind her, Ally sighed loudly. 'God only knows how this could have happened, I mean, so close to opening night. It's such a huge disaster. Tis could barely speak afterwards, she was just so shocked. I mean, what if he *dies*?'

Megan adjusted the lacing at the front of her blouse. This was her third change and she still wasn't sure if she'd got the post-disaster-shoulder-to-cry-on look quite right. She needed casual enough to look as if she was just popping into the Spar or going for an evening stroll to walk off the trauma of the day, but sexy enough to tantalise if she got the opportunity.

Because there was no point in wasting an opportunity.

She'd been working her way closer and closer to Aidan Gaunt since the start of the summer break, and was finally feeling as if she might be getting somewhere. Helping Laetitia in wardrobe made her indispensable, and casually chatting to him about the history of Kilfenora House, she'd felt as if she was making some real headway. He'd been really interested. Her Leaving Cert history project was finally coming in useful, to say nothing of her English degree course. She'd read a *lot* of plays. She was absolutely sure that if anything had happened with Laetitia, it had to be a fling. An intelligent man like Aidan Gaunt needed a woman with brains in his life, not some dippy hippy who lived in a van.

She suddenly tuned in to what Ally had said.

'He's hardly going to die, is he? I mean, the paramedics said Aidan was amazing, that he'd probably saved Conor's life.'

'But you saw him, Meg, and there was just so much blood, I don't know how I'm going to sleep tonight. I just keep seeing him lying there. What if he *does* die?'

Chapter 9

TESS'S EYES JERKED open, the sound of a thump making her whole body stiffen. In her head, it was the sickening echo of a car colliding with a body. But somehow it sounded as if it was in the room.

Lying rigid in her bed, Tess listened hard, every nerve tingling. Now wide awake, she held her breath, faking sleep. How could someone have got into the room without her hearing a noise downstairs?

Lynch's voice spiralled in her head – his talk of Eoin Doyle and her living alone, a fact that the Twitter troll had been obsessed with, too . . . *Bitches like you should make sure they lock their doors at night.*

At the time, she hadn't even wanted to think about what he was implying.

What do you think you're doing in that big old house? Auditioning to be the next Miss Havisham?

Was he back now, and actually here in the house?

The online abuse had gone on and on until she'd decided her mental health was worth more than social media shares, and she'd taken all the apps off her phone. Gen had told her that her silence had made him even more angry for a bit, and then he'd gone quiet. With the grand opening so close, had it started again and no one had told her?

Had the troll finally made good on all those threats and stepped things up?

Tess held her breath again, listening hard. Something had woken her – she had definitely heard a noise. And she was sure that she'd felt a sense of movement, one that wasn't her own.

Lying as still as she could, Tess scanned her bedroom, straining to see into every corner. If there was someone here, she didn't want them to know she'd heard them. But as she tried to listen for movement in the room, her heart was thumping so loud in her ears, it was drowning out any sound.

Had the noise come from the landing? Her bedroom door was ajar, exactly as she'd left it, the landing even darker than her own room with its gauzy curtains.

Tess felt sweat breaking out across her body, pinpricks of fear, red-hot. Her featherweight curtains lifted gently in what little breeze was coming in through the open window, but it was too dark to be able to see clearly.

Surely she *must* have been dreaming? The images in her head were all mixed up but so vivid: Lynch's voice on the phone; Eoin Doyle; snatches of a country pub; her boyfriend Kieran lying on the ground, melding into Conor Kelly lying on the stage. Blood. So much blood. *Adam O'Donnell's name written through it*. Had she dreamed the noise, too?

Sadness welled up inside her as memories of Kieran and the pub surfaced: a fire burning even though they didn't really need it in September, Olly Murs on the radio, 'My Heart Skips a Beat'. Everything was so clear, as if it had happened yesterday, not almost ten years ago. Glimpses of that night – weaving through the crowd from the bar to their table, putting Kieran's lager down, the light catching the golden liquid, bubbles gathered on the side of the glass. Her purple top reflected against her gin and tonic, the ice cracking in the warmth of the crowded room.

It had been the perfect night. And then walking home down the dark winding lane, damp leaves brushing at her as they tried to keep in off the road. Laughing and messing on the verge.

'*Hold my hand.*'

Tess didn't let herself go further. Her life had changed then. The master's degree that she'd been about to start had soured in her mind like milk. She hadn't wanted to return to Trinity. She hadn't even wanted to be in Dublin.

And then the job in Dubai had come up, and before she knew it she was on a plane to a country where it never rained, and where there were no country pubs with open fires or blind twisty lanes.

Fighting back the memories, focusing on the room, Tess pulled her light summer duvet up to her chin, gripping the edge, trying to calm her beating heart.

The bitter taste of fear was in her mouth now. The sound she'd heard could have been a car door closing on the lane outside. But who would be here at this time of night?

She replayed it in her head, sure again that it had come from inside the room. She closed her eyes, but it did nothing to shut off her mind.

Tess felt as if she was underwater, her chest tightening as it suddenly became hard to breathe. She couldn't have a panic attack now, but thoughts stung at her like angry wasps. Being here was supposed to be wonderful, fun, a new lease of life for herself and for Kilfenora. *Why had she ever thought she could take this place on?*

As she'd stood in the huge stone-flagged hallway with Genevieve and Clarissa, raising a toast to signing the deeds, Gen had joked about the Kilfenora Curse, about how it was said that the women who lived here died tragically. Clarissa had told her not to be stupid.

'That curse is nonsense – it was just a convenient way for men to justify not paying for doctors when they were needed.' Clarissa had raised her glass. 'Now's your chance to change history. You are probably the first ever woman who's had outright control of this place since it was built. You're the new mistress of Kilfenora. Nothing can stop you building it into the great house it once was.'

Lying in the darkness, the summer heat cloying, Tess felt a tear slip from the corner of her eye. Clarissa and Genevieve had such faith in her. The whole village had taken on the project, seduced by her enthusiasm and energy. But could she do it? Could she pull it off? *Right now, she really wasn't sure.*

A sudden movement to her left made Tess physically jump, her heart thumping against the inside of her chest so hard that it hurt.

It took her a moment to focus on the shape at the window – more accurately, sitting on the window sill – but as it became clear, she breathed a sigh of relief, tension flowing from her like lava. Framed by the sash, Clarissa's cat Merlin looked at her, regarding her stoically, his green eyes mirror-like in the gloom.

'Did you have to do that? I mean, this isn't even your house.'

By way of an answer, the huge cat began washing his front paw, apparently unconcerned that he'd frightened her awake.

He must have woken her jumping off the bed – he was so heavy he'd hit the floor with a mighty dull thump, a sound not dissimilar to one that she'd tried so hard to push from her mind: the impact of steel on flesh. *Would she ever be able to forget that night and move on?*

Relaxing on her pillow, Tess pushed her hair out of her face with her hand, running her fingers into the roots. She'd thought Dubai had helped, that she was ready to come home, but with its constant bright lights and endless sunshine, it had never been dark. She'd never had to face the shadows.

Kilfenora was supposed to have been a new start – a house that needed rebuilding, just like her life – but then the troll had targeted her. She'd been so frightened that he might turn up in person . . . and now there was Lynch with his news of bodies, and Conor's accident. It had opened up everything she thought she'd hidden away – all the hurt, all the pain, all the darkness. Would she be able to cope?

Turning over, Tess curled up with her knees to her chest. How was she going to get through tomorrow with broken sleep? How was she going to get through the next few days at all, knowing that Conor Kelly was in the hospital?

Chapter 10

ANNOYINGLY WIDE AWAKE, Gen shifted on to her side and reached for her phone. Four a.m. One of these nights she'd manage to get through the whole night without waking.

Tapping the Facebook icon, she opened the group to see what had been happening during the course of the day. And what people were saying about it. She scrolled down the posts as she read.

Lou Lou O'Neill
Any news on Conor Kelly?

> **Carrie O'Connor**
> **Lou Lou O'Neill** Still in intensive care, collection in the Spar 4 flowers.

> **Tracker Maguire**
> You'd think Tess Morgan would have made sure the lighting rig was safe before anyone went on the stage

> **Carrie O'Connor**
> **Tracker Maguire** Heard she hammered the sparks who put it up down on price. Didn't use locals either.

> **Tracker Maguire**
> sounds like shes cutting corners. hope she's got good insurance.

TrackerMaguire
that house is a historic monument, it's a disgrace having everyone tramping all over it. SHe's a blow-in with no idea of the history. she'll come to grief mark my words.

Trixie Bell
Tony Lock from Lock Developments was up looking at the site the other day. My brother saw his car in the village.

> **Carrie O'Connor**
> **Trixie Bell** Bet he wishes he never sold it.

> **Trixie Bell**
> My Joe said he was in the pub asking questions about the opening.

> **LakeviewBandB**
> **Trixie Bell** He sold Kilfenora because his planning application for a load of apartments and massive housing estate on the land was turned down. Maybe he thinks he can buy it back and develop it now McGill's on the council

> **Trixie Bell**
> Tess Morgan better watch out, I heard he can be ruthless. Didn't he burn out that halting site? Maybe he had something to do with the fire.

> **Carrie O'Connor**
> **Trixie Bell** Thought it was a chimney that went up?

> **Trixie Bell**
> **Carrie O'Connor** Supposedly but there was nobody living there. Who lit it? House was empty for years. Everyone said it was the curse.

> **Carrie O'Connor**
> **Trixie Bell** nobody died in the fire, the curse is all to do with the owners dying in horrible accidents.

> **Trixie Bell**
> **Carrie O'Connor** Only the women!

LakeviewBandB
Insurance job. He lost everything in the crash, owed the banks millions. Only reason he's still going is a load of developments in Spain that Irish gov couldn't touch.

Carrie O'Connor
People like that always bounce back.

Trixie Bell
Carrie O'Connor Tess better watch out.

Ally O'Riordan
Single Air pod found beside the monument. Contact the surgery if it's yours!

Gen shifted on her pillow, pursing her lips. It was just as well Tess didn't use this group any more; she didn't need to be reading posts about curses and horrible accidents, she had quite enough on her plate. Hitting *reply*, Gen typed rapidly:

FortuneFinds
Rumour and conjecture. Tony Lock was in with me buying a clock. He went into the pub for his lunch. The fire was years before he bought the house. There's no curse.

TrackerMaguire
FortuneFinds that's what he wants you to think

Honestly, Tracker Maguire was such a grumpy old trouble maker. There was always one who was never happy, whatever you did. There were times when Gen thought he must sit in his front room overlooking the main street with his birdwatching binoculars out, just watching who was going where. She looked down at the next post.

FinnMacCool
Late Tidy Towns update, looking for help on Friday for the bed on the corner of Rockfield Road and Ballymount Lane. Will be

removing all the weeds and planting insect friendly plants. Bring gloves, nettles are thick!

Gen's finger hovered over *reply*, about to congratulate the Tidy Towns team on getting organised for the influx of tourists they'd have next weekend, but she knew she'd get pulled into helping if she wasn't careful, and she had enough to do. Turning over, she closed the app and put the phone beside her digital clock, the illuminated numbers taunting her. Sighing, she rubbed her eyes. She just hoped Tess was sleeping better than she was.

FRIDAY

One Week To Go

Chapter 11

TESS COULD FEEL the heat of the sun on her face even this early in the morning as she sat in the garden of Clarissa Westmacott's cottage, the sound of water splashing into the lake behind the hedge a reminder that life continued around them unabated. She always found this corner of the estate, the original Gardener's Cottage, and Clarissa, an oasis of calm. Perhaps it was her life experience – between her long acting career and being widowed three times, she had plenty of that. This morning, as Tess had got dressed ready to face the day, she'd felt a half hour of calm was precisely what she needed.

Tess wrapped her hands around her mug as if it was a lifebuoy, the warmth therapeutic as it travelled through her palms. The tiny diamond on her right hand caught the light, flashing at her from its delicate gold mount, the shank of the ring so fine she often worried it might break. She still felt groggy from her interrupted night and, judging from the way Clarissa had looked at her when she arrived, was several shades too pale.

Clarissa leaned across the mosaic tiled table and rubbed Tess's arm again, her touch firm, reassuring. She was wearing one of her trademark Liberty shirts and, despite the heat, a moss-green cardigan that was almost the same colour as the foliage behind her. The sound of cartoon canned laughter spilled out of the back door – Gen was in the shop today, and Malachi, worn out from a morning session on Clarissa's treadmill, was lying on the sofa watching the TV.

Clarissa's voice cut softly through Tess's thoughts.

'Tell me what happened *then*.'

Tess took a steadying breath and lined the handle of her mug up with the edge of a tile the colour of sunshine. The design on the table had been created with shards of pottery Clarissa had dug up in the garden, a connection to the generations who had occupied this estate before them. Whenever Tess thought about Irish history, it was laden with emotion, people doggedly surviving through years of anguish and tears. She could only imagine the stories that were locked into these pieces of delft.

'He's in a coma but they said we'd got his heart restarted. Honestly, they've no idea if he'll recover fully. And the next few days will be touch-and-go.' The words tumbled over themselves. Tess took a breath, trying to slow down her racing mind, as she relived the scene.

Clarissa sighed. 'His poor parents. He's so young.'

'I spoke to his mum.'

Tess bit her lip. She was starting to feel as if this was all her fault. If she hadn't had this mad idea about restoring the house, about opening to the public with a gala weekend, Conor Kelly would be up a ladder fixing a satellite dish, making sure the women of Kilfenora got a good look at his buff physique.

How on earth had she arrived at the idea of a play being the centre of the opening weekend events?

She hadn't even known Aidan Gaunt this time last year, and then his chance conversation with Genevieve in the antique shop had led to a meeting, and this was where they were. She'd agreed with him that a production would showcase the ballroom's potential perfectly, but it hadn't been this sort of potential she'd been thinking of. Part of her knew that the play had been the distraction she'd needed to help keep her so busy she didn't get time to think, but now everything was closing in on her, and it felt too late to stop it.

It had been like an episode of *Casualty* yesterday morning.

Tess realised she'd stopped speaking mid-sentence. Trying to refocus, she went on.

'Conor's mum's so lovely, though. She said he'd always wanted to act, that he was so excited to be playing the lead.' *Could this be any more terrible?* 'That just made me feel like jumping off the roof, to be honest.'

Tess put her hands to her face, fighting the tears, the exhaustion of the last few weeks coupled with . . . well, everything, threatening to overwhelm her in a suffocating wave. And her stomach had felt even worse after Aidan had left yesterday; perhaps it was coffee that was upsetting it? Could you suddenly get allergic to something? Tess sighed inwardly. She'd drunk so much of it recently she'd probably given herself coffee poisoning.

Interrupting her thoughts, Clarissa squeezed her arm.

'This is *not* your fault. You've brought so many incredible things to this house, to the village. You gave people work in the middle of a pandemic, you've breathed life into the rafters. Remember that. This was an accident. Sometimes things happen just that are outside our control. No amount of planning could anticipate a weakened piece of steel.'

Tess took a ragged breath. 'Assuming that's what it was. The insurance assessor is coming out after lunch today to examine it. I think we're going to have to take the whole lighting track down – and I don't have the budget to rebuild it, if the insurance people won't cover it. Aidan just keeps saying that the show must go on. I don't know what's best, to be honest, but Liam knows all the lines, he'll be able to step in.'

'He's a lovely lad, he'll do a good job. How are the others taking it?'

Tess focused on a blackbird that had settled on the neat lawn in front of them. It took her a moment to answer.

'Laetitia was hysterical – I mean, everyone was in shock, but she was the worst. Megan called 999, but she fell apart a bit afterwards. Ally seems to be the only one in that family who's properly grounded.' Tess smiled weakly. 'I can see why they were so upset, it was quite shocking.'

'It was probably not as bad as it looked – scalps bleed a lot, you know.'

Tess looked at Clarissa, half amused by her practical attempt to comfort her.

'I really hope you're right. It was supposed to be a big opening, but not like that . . .'

'"Till swollen with cunning, of a self-conceit / His waxen wings did mount above his reach / And, melting, heavens conspir'd his overthrow."' Clarissa pursed her lips.

Tess sighed. 'That's exactly it. Thank goodness Aidan knew what to do – according to Meg, he reacted incredibly fast.'

'He's a useful man to have around.'

Tess sighed. 'I think he must have been in the military at some stage, his life runs like clockwork. And he obviously learned CPR somewhere.' She glanced at Clarissa. 'I just feel so sick. That Twitter troll kept saying horrible things would happen if we went ahead with the opening . . .'

Clarissa reached forwards to grasp her arm again, the egg-sized sapphire in her ring catching the light as she moved her hand.

'Stop. You know that was all nonsense. Some crazy from the other side of the world, probably.' Tess could feel the strength in Clarissa's steel-blue eyes as she looked intently at her. 'After this much work, I think you need to keep going. Conor would have wanted it. He loved the adulation, he's been all over social media apparently with the show, has quite a fan club. He really is centre stage now.' She said it without a trace of irony. 'He's getting his fifteen minutes, just not in the way he expected.'

Chapter 12

THE SHOP BELL tinkled and Genevieve groaned quietly to herself. She was on her knees behind the counter, and while she'd like to think that it was a customer, so far this morning all she'd had was a steady trickle of people popping in en route to the post office or the Spar, looking for updates on Conor Kelly's situation.

Gen had absolutely no idea how or why everyone thought she would have the latest news from the hospital, but it seemed linked to her being admin of the forum. That made less sense still, but then the local gossips didn't always take logic as the first path.

She'd even had someone call in to complain about a loose dog down beside the pub. She had no idea why that should be her problem.

Perhaps she should put up a sign charging for citizens' advice.

Crawling backwards from her inspection of the deep drawer under the counter where she held lay-away items for anyone who needed to spread payments – a totally ridiculous idea in Clarissa's book – Genevieve looked out over the top of the counter.

'Good morning, Katie-Lou, what brings you in on a Friday? Have you got a few hours free to help me out?'

Pulling the skirts of her flowing dress up around her so she didn't step on them as she stood up, Gen struggled to her feet in a jangle of jewellery. As she appeared over the top of the counter, Katie-Lou jumped sideways as if she'd been caught with her hand in the sweet jar.

What on earth?

Standing in the middle of the shop with her baby pink handbag looped over her elbow and her phone in her hand, Katie-Lou had turned a delicate shade of pink herself. Obviously up to something, she swished her long, white-blonde hair over her shoulder and laughed in that slightly insane, giddy way she had that drove Clarissa nuts.

'No, I was just . . .' She raised her heavily darkened eyebrows innocently and pointed at the chessboard laid out on the mahogany dining table that dominated the central section of the shop. 'Did you notice someone's moved these pieces?'

'Don't touch them.' Gen's reaction was a little too explosive. 'Sorry, that's Clarissa's pet project.'

Katie-Lou looked at her, frowning hard. 'Oh. I see. I'd noticed they've moved a bit before. I, er . . . Sometimes I moved them, too. Is that bad?'

Gen faked a smile. 'It's fine, Clarissa seems to keep track. Just perhaps don't touch it?'

How many times had she said not to go near the board?

Gen resisted the temptation to roll her eyes, and instead took in Katie-Lou's freshly applied fake tan, emphasised by a white gypsy top and skin-tight jeans, shell-pink toenails peeping from her high-heeled mules, matching her long fingernails.

Katie-Lou took a step backwards, both hands raised in the air in mock terror.

'I know you said don't touch it before. I was just dusting, like.'

Not very well. Genevieve could hear Clarissa's voice in her ear.

'It's fine, there's always plenty to dust. You can leave the chessboard to Clarissa. How can I help?'

Katie-Lou's eyes opened wide as if she'd just remembered why she came in and was shocked all over again.

'Did you hear about Conor?'

Keeping her face deliberately blank, Gen looked at her for a moment longer than was normal, biting back her retort. It wasn't Katie-Lou's fault that she was at the end of her tether with questions about Conor. Despite Gen's frequent critical thoughts on Katie-Lou's skill set, Gen had taken her on because she was just so genuine, even if sometimes she was a little testing. You got what you saw with Katie-Lou, sometimes hilariously so, and despite everything, Gen wholeheartedly appreciated that about her. She was the most guileless girl Gen had ever met. Taking a breath, she said calmly, 'I did – terrible accident.'

'It was. Awful.'

Katie-Lou looked as if she was going to ask more, but finally seemed to read Genevieve's expression and paused for a moment as if she was mentally changing tack.

'So I was just on my way to the Spar and I wondered if you knew anyone who would want to share a stall at the craft market at opening weekend. I've booked and paid for it. I'm going to be doing cakes and jam and Mam's eggs, but I don't think I've got enough to fill a stall. Mam's going to her sister's this weekend, so she's going to see if she's got any of the flower baskets she makes, but I heard Mark said he'd put it into some sort of ghost hunters' forum and there are loads of people coming.'

Ghost hunters' forum? It took a moment for Genevieve to process. She looked at Katie-Lou quizzically. How on earth would she, Genevieve Fortune, have any idea about who was taking stalls in the craft market?

'Tess has a waiting list, as far as I know. I'm sure if you drop her an email through the website she can find you someone who wants to share.'

'I thought of that.' Katie-Lou said it proudly, as if doing her own thinking was something to put up in lights. 'But I thought Tess might be too busy, what with Conor and everything.'

Gen leaned on the counter. She had a point. 'You could be right. Have you put it onto the forum? There's bound to be someone.'

'Well, that's what I wanted to check, to see if it was OK to do that.'

'Let's do it now and then it's done.' Genevieve nodded, reaching for her phone.

And I can get on with my tidying. She didn't say that part.

Gen opened the forum, quickly scanning the posts so far today. It might be a closed group, but she'd still discovered that she had to moderate it a bit. Some people didn't have the common sense they were born with when it came to appropriate questions and comments. She scrolled down and found the post from Mark Mulligan about ghosts.

Mark Mulligan
Opening weekend will be crazy busy. I put a post into **Ghostly Houses Ireland** about the Kilfenora Curse and it got hundreds of likes and replies.

> **LakeviewBandB**
> **Mark Mulligan** I saw a woman there when I was a child, she walked right through the front door!!! Scared me half to death. Lots of people have seen the children

> **TrackerMaguire**
> **Mark Mulligan** are they putting up decent signage for carparking? place will be jammed

Gen deftly answered. Tess did *not* need the whole village up in arms about signage today. She knew the AA signs were going up next Thursday, and that Tess was getting marshals in place to organise the parking on O'Loughlin's field.

'Right, pop in a note about the stall.' Gen paused. 'I saw your post about Laetitia O'Riordan's number – did you get her OK? A tarot party sounds fun.'

Taking Gen's phone instead of using her own, Katie-Lou blushed.

'All sorted, thanks.' She said it in a chirpy sing-song that made it sound as if it was an outright lie.

'Oh, OK.'

Gen didn't quite know how to follow up that one. It was pretty clear Katie-Lou wanted to get her own cards done, although why that might be a secret, Gen couldn't imagine.

Gen's phone in her hand, Katie-Lou suddenly stopped.

'Actually, I could ask Laetitia to share the stall. I never thought of that. She makes things with flowers, you know, and does the cards, obviously.'

'Flowers?'

Gen wasn't sure she really needed to know the answer, but part of her was fascinated by Laetitia and her hippy lifestyle. She'd been living in her camper van in the staff car park in Kilfenora for months now.

Katie-Lou nodded vigorously. 'Lotions and potions, all sorts. Gorgeous hand cream. She's got this really ancient herb book and she told me almost all of them grow in Kilfenora.'

'Really?'

Gen almost squinted at her, trying to sort out everything she knew about Laetitia O'Riordan in her head. Was Katie-Lou telling her that Laetitia had moved into the car park in her camper van so that she could collect wild flowers and herbs from the Kilfenora grounds – to sell? Gen wasn't so sure Tess would be impressed with that. Although perhaps if the products were any good, she could sell them in the tourist shop she was planning. Before she could finish forming the thought, Katie-Lou had rushed on enthusiastically.

'Yes, there's a poison garden and everything. She doesn't use real poison, obviously, but they've incredible herb beds. She sent me a photo.'

Poison? Gen sighed. She couldn't remember Tess mentioning a Poison Garden, but she made a mental note to ask when everything calmed down next week. Gen was sure the gardeners knew and would have any noxious plants removed from the public spaces.

Katie-Lou realised she was still holding Gen's phone and handed it back with a grin.

'Let me say it to Laetitia tonight and then I might not need to put up a post at all.' As she spoke, Gen's phone pipped with a text. 'You better check that. I'll be in Tuesday, leave me a list. Tatty bye.'

Katie-Lou gave Gen a big smile and turned around, swooshing her hair over her shoulder again as if she'd been practising in front of the mirror.

Tatty bye? The saints preserve us.

Gen watched her sashay out of the shop, the bell tinkling like an alarm as she pulled the door open.

Chapter 13

THE NIGGLING FEELING of dread in Tess's stomach was growing as she waited for the insurance assessor outside the front door of the main house. He'd already texted to say he was in the village. By her calculations he'd be here any minute.

'Boy, it's hot.' Beside her, Aidan Gaunt rubbed the back of his neck, his pristine white T-shirt almost blinding in the sunlight.

'He shouldn't be long.' As she spoke, Tess caught the glint of metal in the distance between the gates. She shaded her eyes to peer through the heat haze shimmering across the avenue. 'This must be him.'

She glanced anxiously at Aidan. He didn't look worried. But then he didn't know about the troll, or her fears that this could have been some sort of sabotage – fears she needed to park firmly during this visit. This was an accident. A terrible, horrible accident, one that she prayed wouldn't push up her premiums too high.

A sleek silver Mercedes sports car pulled into view, rounding the fountain and stopping beside them, the driver's door swinging open. Getting out, the driver looked at her over the roof.

'Tess Morgan?'

Tess stepped forward. 'That's me. Thanks for coming out so quickly, I'm sure you're busy.'

'Garry. Two r's. No problem. Delighted to get out of the city, in all honesty.'

He ducked into the car and reappeared with an iPad and a phone in his hand. His tie loose, shirtsleeves rolled up, he looked about the same age as Tess, and was remarkably jovial given the circumstances. But then high premiums meant high commission, which was probably how he could afford to drive such a fancy car.

Closing the door, the sidelights flashed as he hit the central locking and looked up at the house, his hair slicked back with far too much gel.

'Nice spot you've got here.'

'Thank you. Bit of a labour of love. This is Aidan Gaunt, the director and producer of the play. The ballroom's this way.'

Tess turned to push open the huge oak front door.

Climbing the wide stone stairs that swept up to the first floor and the mezzanine overlooking the hall, Tess ran her hand along the polished brass handrail, its uprights supporting swathes of brass ivy that furled and tangled as the stairs rose. It felt solid. And right now she needed solid.

She'd always loved this staircase. It was one of the things that had totally wowed her when she'd first seen the house. Each tread was shallow, lipped, the polished granite marble-like in the light slanting through the upper windows. Normally she was in a hurry, skipping up and down, always on the move. Now, as Garry commented on the giant elk horns over the fireplace in the hallway and made small talk with Aidan behind her, she savoured the coolness of the hallway, drawing on the calm of the building.

She thought she'd had all the disasters possible as she'd restored the house, but there had been nothing to compare to this. Ireland was a massively litigious society; insurance premiums were high without accidents. And now they'd had an accident.

She glanced behind her as she reached the top of the stairs.

'It's this way.'

Halfway along the broad corridor that ran parallel to the front of the house, bisecting the main reception rooms, the doors to the ballroom stood open. Aidan had already brought a stepladder onto the stage so Garry with two r's could get a proper look at the lighting track, although he looked like the last person in the country to be an expert on electrical engineering.

'Mind if I have a quick look?'

Tess was halfway down the corridor when she realised Garry had ducked into the first of the reception rooms that overlooked the drive. Her eyes met Aidan's as she doubled back and followed him inside.

The rooms along the front felt vast: dark wood floorboards swept clean, the only furniture two white marble semicircular occasional tables pushed against the walls between the huge floor-to-ceiling windows, their legs flourishes of gold ormolu acanthus leaves.

She'd known from the start that she'd never be able to furnish the house as it had been, but Clarissa had had the rather brilliant idea of using these rooms as a sales floor for Fortune Finds – these tables were the first pieces to arrive. The rest was being delivered later in the week – sofas and dining tables and, Tess hoped, some of the porcelain from the shop that would make it feel more like a home and less like a showroom.

These rooms overlooking the avenue – this drawing room, the central salon, and what would become the 'dining room' – were connected with huge folding doors. Filling them with antiques would bring one surprise after another as guests were shown around. It was the part of the restoration, of bringing life back to Kilfenora, that Tess was most looking forward to.

Garry stood in the middle of the room, looking up at the plaster ceiling, obviously impressed.

'Very nice. Don't envy you the heating bills. Is the ballroom a similar size?'

'A bit wider, and there are no connecting doors. It's on the other side of the corridor overlooking the gardens.'

Tess held her arm out, inviting him into the corridor. She didn't think her nerves could cope with this visit lasting all day. Now he was here, she wanted to get him out as fast as possible. Taking the hint, he followed her.

Garry hesitated in the doorway as they entered the ballroom, looking around.

'Impressive. You can do a lot with this.'

'That's the idea.'

Tess hung back as Aidan led him to the stage, showing him the lighting unit that remained where it had fallen, in the middle of the black-painted boards. Garry bobbed down for a closer look, taking photographs of the clamps at the rear of the lighting unit where it bolted on to the track.

After a few minutes, he looked up, and over to the stepladder.

'Let's just see what's up there, will we?'

Aidan steadied the ladder as Garry climbed up, his leather brogues and suit trousers hardly suitable for clambering around scaffolding.

Standing in the middle of the ballroom, her clipboard clasped to her chest, Tess could feel her heart beating hard. She felt as if the house was holding its breath with her, as if it was waiting for something to happen. Would they have to take the whole lighting track down?

Watching Garry inspecting it from below, Tess felt a headache building. She glanced across at the double doors they'd come in through. As she'd led him down the corridor she'd suddenly realised that the doors weren't locked. Ever. And while the main door to the house was kept locked at the moment, the side doors were open, allowing contractors to come in and out.

Had someone slipped into the ballroom and tampered with the light fitting? Aidan had been sure that the electricians had got distracted and not screwed the clamps up properly, but what if it had been someone else? Someone who had been intent on trying to destroy her online and who, with a week to go before opening, had come here in person?

Tess took a deep breath. She could feel her heart pounding as the idea circled in her head like a vulture over carrion. Could all this really be coincidence?

Aidan glanced across at her as Garry reached the top of the ladder, humming and hawing and tutting a lot, taking more photos with his phone.

'This should all have been checked when the lighting technicians put it up.'

At the bottom of the ladder, Aidan rolled his eyes. 'You can see the one that fell is right in the middle of the track, so maybe it was time for lunch or the guy's phone rang and he thought he'd come back to finish it.'

'Maybe.' Garry pulled a Maglite out of his trouser pocket and played it along the scaffold track. 'It looks like the other brackets are secure. The track itself is in good shape, but there seems to be only one clamp in place on the unit that fell, rather than the three that are needed. The weight of the unit must have sheared the threading on the bolt.'

Aidan shifted slightly at the bottom of the ladder.

'I think the contractors have got some explaining to do.'

Garry played his torch along the track, the beam dancing on the stage and the ceiling as he did so. Tess couldn't see his upper body properly behind the scaffolding, but she guessed he was double-checking the steel bars that supported the rest of the lights. A moment later she realised he was speaking.

'I called them this morning. They reckoned everything was perfect when they left.'

Aidan looked at her from the stage and raised his eyebrows.

'They're going to say that, aren't they? I mean, unless they took a picture of each light in situ, we're not going to know quite what happened, are we? What we do know is that it fell, and it wasn't the fairies. If the safety cable had been attached properly, it wouldn't have mattered if the bolts sheared.'

Tess almost sighed in relief at Aidan's brusque tone. He was voicing her thoughts exactly, but personally she needed to keep Garry with two r's sweet. There was no question Conor's family would look for a settlement, but she couldn't afford for her premiums to skyrocket; she needed every favour she could get from Ravenhill Insurance to make sure Kilfenora stayed in business. Without public liability insurance she couldn't open, let alone run the events she planned. Even the house tours were set to be a major revenue stream once they opened properly. And every cent was accounted for.

Chapter 14

LEANING ON THE open side door of the orange camper van in the far corner of Kilfenora's under-used staff car park, Megan O'Riordan looked in at her sister Laetitia despairingly.

'Would you shut up, Tis, crying never helped anyone.'

Sitting opposite Laetitia at the fold-down table, cups of coffee and a half-eaten packet of chocolate digestives in the middle, Ally looked up from her phone and scowled across at Megan.

'Don't be horrible, we're all upset. You know she's more sensitive.'

'Oh, give me strength, Ally. It'll be her artistic temperament next – you're worse than Dad with the "more sensitive".' Megan made rabbit ears with her forefingers and twisted around to lean her back on the hot side of the van.

Their father's acceptance of Laetitia's every whim had been like a stone in Megan's shoe since . . . well, forever. It was anxiety, apparently, with an eating disorder thrown in that they weren't allowed to talk about. Tis was the youngest of them, and had their parents wrapped around her finger. Even her nickname was ridiculous, having come about because she had had so much difficulty saying Laetitia when she was small. But then Megan had spent her life with people wondering why she had sisters with exotic names. Alecto was even worse.

Megan turned to look inside the van, leaning her shoulder on the open door. Finally joining the conversation properly, Ally put her phone down with a scowl as she answered.

'I am *not* worse than Dad, I'm just being practical. Let her bawl a bit and then she'll be over it.'

'We were all there, Ally, but we've not all turned on the waterworks. Tis, you should be on the bloody stage.'

Laetitia sniffed loudly and tucked a stray curl behind her ear. Her raven hair was pulled into a clip. Like her sisters', it was thick and glossy, hanging in coils down her back.

'How can you two be so cold? It was awful, I could see everything.' Laetitia gulped back more sobs. 'Aidan's face . . . I just . . .'

Ally rolled her eyes and picked up her phone again.

'You might have to come out of wardrobe and take a part if Liam steps into the lead. I don't know who'll be able to do stage manager, though.'

'Aidan should do that, he knows all the lines and who comes on when, and all the lighting positions. He's the professional here.'

Megan folded her arms and began to scuff the loose gravel with the toe of her ballet pumps, the rose-gold leather reflecting her cream linen cut-off trousers. She might have overdressed a bit for the day, but there was always a chance she'd bump into Aidan if she was up at the big house. Last night had been a disaster; she'd been up and down the main street about four times and there had been no sign of him anywhere. Today she was aiming for casual elegance, although the cream silk pussy-bow blouse, even with its short puffed sleeves, hadn't been a good plan in this heat.

Laetitia sniffed again loudly. 'You're just jealous he didn't ask you to be stage manager straight away, Meg.'

'Don't be ridiculous. I just told him I know the play. I wrote my bloody undergrad thesis on it.'

'But not his version, his re-imagining.' Ally put on a plummy English accent, mimicking Aidan's, and pulled a face.

He wasn't that bad, but it made Megan smile. She was still a tiny bit annoyed that he hadn't taken her seriously when she'd offered to help. Apparently, he wanted to run the show like a proper production, and she might know the play but she didn't know how a theatre worked – unlike Liam, who had done a whole module on stage as part of his sound course. Conor's smirk in the background had made her want to kill him. But then Laetitia had volunteered for set design and costume, and couldn't possibly do them both on her own, and there wasn't anything else to do in Kilfenora during the summer unless she wanted to sell ice cream or stack shelves in the Spar, so Megan had given in graciously and had ended up backstage.

In truth, as well as the play having definite advantages in bringing her into constant contact with Aidan Gaunt, she had her sights set on helping Tess run the place as a venue next year when she'd finished her master's, so she needed to be involved somehow. And if she was on site, she could step in wherever she was needed and make herself doubly indispensable. As their mother was always saying, English might be interesting, but an arts degree wasn't exactly vocational.

Ally continued, her practical voice back in place.

'Aidan's got heaps of acting experience, apparently, he should take the lead role and let Liam stay running the staging end of things. It's brilliant for him with that sound technician course he's doing.'

Megan sighed. Ally was probably right. And if she wasn't, she knew how to present her evidence and make it sound so convincing you ended up thinking you were wrong to begin with. She'd been a natural lawyer since she could speak.

'Honestly, I think Liam's course is more to do with music and that band he's in than it is to do with stage. He's got a bigger following on Insta than Conor had.'

'*Has. Has*, Meg. He's not dead *yet*.'

Across the table, Laetitia burst into noisy sobs again. They both looked at her, Ally shaking her head. Megan could see that she was getting a bit fed up with the waterworks as well. Laetitia might be the arty one and forgiven every hysterical moment at home, but it was her and Ally who had to constantly sort out her dramas. And there was no question that they were expected to get proper jobs, but it was fine for Laetitia to travel around festivals in the van selling her potions, vintage remade clothing and paintings, and reading people's cards.

The fact that she even had a van had taken them both a while to get over. Neither of them had been given cars for their eighteenth birthdays.

Ally turned to Megan. 'Aidan keeps saying he wants *us* to shine, to use the experience—'

'He doesn't want to be photographed on stage with a bunch of amateurs, more like. He's got a profile to think about. Conor's brilliant at installing satellite dishes, but I'm not so sure he'd cut it on a real stage.'

Laetitia blew her nose again. 'That's mean, Meg, why are you being so horrible today? And how can you talk about Conor like that?'

The way she stuttered on Conor's name made them both look at her. Megan pursed her lips and glanced over at Ally. Despite their differences, one thing about being close in age – so-called 'Irish twins', with less than a year between them – was that they fairly regularly had the same thought at the same time. They even looked alike, and were often taken for each other, with their manes of mahogany hair. In Ally's first year doing law in Trinity she'd been ambushed by Megan's English tutor and swept into a lecture on *Hamlet* before she'd had a chance to protest.

Looking across at her, Megan knew Ally was thinking exactly the same thing as she was. Ally said it first, a note of incredulity in her voice.

'You really do fancy him, don't you? Conor Kelly? God, he's such a prat, Tis.'

Laetitia was about to protest, but Megan cut in before she could say anything.

'So was it him you've been going on these late night "walks" with?'

Ally raised her eyebrows as Laetitia scowled by way of an answer, grabbing another tissue from the box.

'I keep telling you I wasn't meeting anyone. I couldn't sleep, that's all. It's roasting in here at night, even with the windows open. And it's a good time to collect herbs.'

'Hang on a minute, what have I missed here?' Ally looked between her and Tis, frowning hard.

Megan shrugged. 'Not a lot. Tis has been "wandering"' – Megan did the rabbit ears thing again with her fingers – 'around the gardens at all times of night, and she managed to lose my watch in the process.'

Ally put her hand to her forehead and rubbed her eyes.

'I can't keep up. Conor Kelly? I thought you had a thing with Aidan Gaunt.'

'I *still* can't believe that.' Megan looked at Laetitia, her eyebrows raised.

At least she had the decency to blush.

SATURDAY

Chapter 15

CLARISSA MANOEUVRED HERSELF past an antique hatstand on her way to the shop door and flipped the sign to 'welcome'. It was still early – Kilfenora village wouldn't be moving for another hour or so – but she liked to open on the dot of 9.30 when she was looking after the shop on a Saturday.

Clarissa glanced over her shoulder. 'So what happened *exactly*? Tess was so upset when she came over, I didn't want to probe.'

Behind her, Genevieve leaned back on the glass counter, her arms folded, and sighed deeply before she answered.

'Poor Conor's parents. There's no way of knowing what the prognosis is with a head injury.'

Peering out of the door and glancing out of the windows on either side of it, Clarissa had a quick look up and down the main street before she replied.

'He's young and fit, so he's got the best chance of everything being fine. If it had fallen on me it might have been a different matter.'

'You didn't want to *be* on that stage, Mum. You're right, it's not really your thing. This is basically amateur dramatics with a couple of retired luvvies who are helping Aidan out.' Gen shook her head. 'And when did you ever do *Faustus*?'

'I played Helen of Troy at the Old Vic, young lady, I know that play backwards. As you well know, your father was one of the best-known directors in London.'

'Before he ran off with the Trollop?'

Clarissa raised her eyebrows. 'He did a couple of plays afterwards, too. He'd gained a certain notoriety. He was never out of *Private Eye*.'

Gen didn't look as if she was listening. The problem with only having one daughter was that Gen had heard all of Clarissa's rants about the Trollop before.

But she still needed reminding of her heritage.

Of course, if Richard hadn't run off with the Trollop right before Gen's second birthday, he'd have never had a heart attack and Genevieve might actually remember him.

It was Clarissa's turn to sigh. The men in her life had spectacularly underperformed. When she'd despatched Husband No. 3, some snide journalist in the gutter press had called her the Black Widow.

Nasty.

And her grieving.

She fingered the faceted black Tahitian pearl set in gold filigree that she wore on a long chain around her neck. It had been Dominic's last gift to her. The only good thing about him was that he'd been very well insured, which, as well as his personal wealth, had left her very comfortable.

'So tell me, daughter, what did Tess say about what happened with Conor? She really doesn't deserve this.'

Gen grimaced. 'When I spoke to her last night, she said the insurance assessor had been and had a look. When it happened, she was advised not to go near the lighting track until he arrived.'

'That makes perfect sense.'

'But she said he's cleared the track itself, so it doesn't need rebuilding. It was just that light that was the problem.'

'And the weight of it did the damage?'

Clarissa put her hands into the pockets of her lilac cashmere cardigan, turning it all over in her mind and looking speculatively around the shop, the broad mirror above the sideboard crowded with fine china and glass catching the prisms of light cast from the huge Waterford chandelier.

'Have you dusted this week? There are spiderwebs in here you could knit with. You really do need a better girl, one who doesn't need glasses.'

'I've got a girl, Mum. Katie-Lou comes in when I have to go to auctions, you know that. She gave the whole place a good going-over on Tuesday. And she can see perfectly well, as far as I know.'

Clarissa raised her eyebrows again. 'Are you sure? I think she needs a new duster in that case. I'll order one, shall I, and leave her a note?'

'Mum, I think I can manage the cleaning. And please don't rearrange everything again this week. I can't find anything when you've been having one of your sprees.'

'It's not rearranging, it's display. It is *so* important people can imagine these pieces in their homes. You need to be a bit more artistic.'

Clarissa picked up a pretty chintz cup and saucer and checked the maker's marks on the bottom of each one. Genevieve wasn't charging nearly enough for the set. Clarissa made a mental note to change the price as soon as Gen left to pick up Malachi.

'So what's the upshot? Are the insurance people letting rehearsals continue?'

Genevieve reached for her handbag – a large brown leather sack that, it seemed to Clarissa, she almost lived out of.

'Yes, they're bringing in a completely new team today, to check every nut and bolt that the other crowd put up. So it's back to normal tomorrow. Aidan's asked everyone over to the pub for a rehearsed reading this afternoon. Mark's letting them use the room upstairs.' Genevieve rooted in her bag, no doubt looking for her car keys, 'It's nice of him. They really can't afford to lose a day with opening night on Friday and all the parts changing.'

'I do hope they don't need any more props. We don't want anything broken by falling scenery.'

'Oh, Mum, stop. I'm helping out with the props and that's it, they can have whatever they need.' As if Clarissa's comment reminded her, Gen checked her phone. 'I texted Laetitia this morning to see if she needed help moving any of the costumes or the set to the pub, but she's not come back to me yet. Maybe they can manage with chairs or something. Look, I've put the float in the till. I'm going to take Malachi into Blessington after I pick him up, he needs shoes for school.'

'That's not for another month – will they still fit? I'd wait if I were you. Take a day off for once and enjoy this sunshine. It's not often we get a run of weather like this.'

Genevieve appeared to sag. 'I might, actually. The thought of dragging a sleep-deprived eight-year-old around the shops in this heat isn't exactly filling me with joy. He's always a nightmare after a sleepover.'

'Go and see Tess. Malachi can play while you two have a cup of tea. She's working far too hard.'

'Yes, Mum, I'll do that. Will you be OK?'

'Of course, why wouldn't I? Aren't I here every Saturday? I think I may have missed my vocation in fine art.'

Genevieve raised her eyebrows. 'See if you can shift that jardinière. I'm sick of looking at it.'

They both turned to look at a giant turquoise majolica piece in the shape of a dolphin, its open mouth gaping. Clarissa nodded.

'I've no idea why you bought it, it's singularly the most ugly thing I've ever seen.'

'Thank you, I know. Right, where are my keys?' Genevieve began rooting in her bag again.

With her daughter distracted, Clarissa glanced surreptitiously at the chess set laid out in the middle of the shop. The pieces were large, carved from white alabaster and black onyx that glistened in the light from the chandelier.

It was her move next.

Chess was a game of skill, of planning, something she enjoyed very much. One of the things she loved most about Saturdays was checking on the progress of the game.

'Here they are.' Genevieve held the keys up triumphantly. Clarissa pursed her lips. 'Give my love to Tess. And Gen . . .' She hesitated. 'It seems strange to me that three clamps *and* a safety cable could have failed all at the same time. Tess is *quite* sure that it *was* an accident, isn't she?'

Chapter 16

*I*T WOULD ALL *be fine.*

Tess could hear Genevieve's voice in her head as she clicked off her phone and got up from the kitchen table to pour more beans into the coffee machine. Maps and diagrams were spread all over the pine kitchen table, each one marked up with sets of notes as the opening weekend had taken shape.

But right now she was looking at them for a different reason.

Lynch had emailed her the co-ordinates of the area his TV people wanted to examine, and she'd spent the last half an hour trying to work out exactly where he meant. Finding Fury Hill itself wasn't difficult, but every time she looked for the exact spot she was distracted by the notes she'd made on the maps.

Perhaps part of her didn't actually want to find it.

There was so much to remember, and now her head was hopping with things to do as well as worrying about things she'd forgotten, about Conor's accident and the play, whether the Twitter troll was back, as well as this buried body business. Once again she'd barely slept, would need all the caffeine to get through today.

She really needed to put off the body hunters until next week.

There was no question in her mind that the families of these women needed closure, but if she let Lynch on to the property and they found something, Kilfenora would forever be known as the house with the serial killer. If she said yes and they didn't find anything, word was bound to leak out and there would be reporters all over the place. If she said no, she'd look like an absolute bitch. She'd thought about it long and hard since his call, and really couldn't find a good solution.

Tess took a deep breath and decided to run through her lists before she went back to the map – at least she'd have a clear head then.

The trestle tables and tents for the craft fair and farmers' market weren't coming until Thursday, but today she needed to walk the entire route, from arrival at the main gate to the car park and up to the field where the market would be laid out, to make sure she had all the signage in place and the flow worked. She knew from experience that you only spotted the holes when you walked through everything as if you were a visitor.

Over on the kitchen counter, the coffee machine gurgled reassuringly and Tess checked her phone again. Nothing new from Lynch, thank God, and Gen had texted to say she'd be up around lunchtime. She was bringing sandwiches and cake, and she was expecting Tess to stop everything for an hour while they sat in the sunshine and took a moment to appreciate what she'd done so far.

Tess smiled. Genevieve hadn't changed one jot since they'd been in school together; she was just as supportive and positive as she had been then.

Clarissa was married to her second husband, Gen's stepfather, when they'd moved into the huge mausoleum of a house a few doors down from Tess's parents, beside the sea in leafy Glenageary. She'd been almost forty when Gen had been born, and had taken a break from the stage, occasionally taking character TV and film parts while Gen was small, but nothing that required her to be away from home for very long.

Both only children, Tess and Gen had hung out together all that summer, had walked up the hill to their new senior school together, sitting next to each other in most classes. But while Genevieve had studied history, Tess had focused on business and languages. They'd both got in to Trinity College, and just finished their degrees when everything had gone wrong, and Tess had gone off to Dubai while Gen had married an English banker with the opportune name of Fortune.

Tess sighed, thinking about it. She'd only just arrived in Dubai when she'd had to turn around to come home for her mother's funeral. It had been totally unexpected – Sheila Morgan, taken in her sleep only two years after her husband had succumbed to cancer. Tess wasn't sure she'd ever really come to terms with it. Sudden death seemed to haunt her.

Only a few months later she'd been back again for Gen's wedding, a huge affair in a castle in Kildare, a coach and horses to the door. A few years older than Gen, Richard Fortune had swept her right off her feet and got her pregnant. He worked in international finance and spent so much time in New York, things had gone downhill from there. It hadn't ended well. Gen had kept the name and a significant payout, but she'd almost lost her sanity in the process.

Moving to Kilfenora, nestled high in the Wicklow mountains, had taken her away from the gossip and scrutiny of south County Dublin and given her a whole new life.

Now she was the proud owner of Fortune Finds, and after the loss of her third husband, Clarissa had moved to Kilfenora, too, to be closer to her daughter, minding Malachi after school and in the holidays, and running the shop on Saturdays so Gen could take a day off.

In the end, despite the tears and heartache along the way, it had all worked out.

Tess still smiled at the thought of Genevieve sharing the auctioneer's Instagram post about Kilfenora with her. Gen knew her so well – their closeness growing up hadn't diminished, despite the distance and the changes in their lives.

Even Genevieve hadn't expected Tess to call the auctioneer and fly home the next weekend to take them both with her to view the property. Clarissa had loved the Gardener's Cottage – and the Butler's Lodge, even with its Laura Ashley nightmare decor, was perfect for Tess. In just a few months, Tess had raised the finance and signed the papers.

How mad had she been?

Tess sighed as she thought back. Taking ownership had been a wonderful moment. She'd thought she was putting the past behind her once and for all.

Now she wasn't so sure.

A sharp rap on the front door made her start. Tess realised her coffee cup was still full and checked the time again. It was only 10.30. Too early for Gen.

Opening the door, it took a moment for Tess to realise that the man standing on her doorstep was Mark Mulligan from the pub. He had his back to her, his headphones on as he looked across to the stable yard gate where Merlin was slinking out of the entrance like a shadow, flopping dramatically on the gravel in a patch of shade.

Mark obviously hadn't heard the door open behind him and continued to watch the cat as Tess hovered, unsure if she should tap him on the shoulder.

His hair was longer than that of most of the men she knew, curled over the collar of a white T-shirt that strained across his shoulders. He had his hands slotted into the back pockets of his jeans. Even from behind, she could see that he worked out. She was wondering how she could let him know she'd opened the door when he suddenly turned around and they both jumped.

Smiling, he took off his headphones. 'Sorry, last chapter of the Agatha Christie I've been listening to. I should have waited for it to finish before I knocked, but I wasn't sure if you were in.'

Momentarily surprised that he was listening to a book, Tess smiled.

'You just caught me. I'm about to walk the route, make sure we've got enough signage for the weekend, check that I haven't forgotten anything.'

'From what I've heard, this opening sounds like it's being run like the Normandy invasion. I'm sure you *have* thought of everything.'

Tess sighed. 'Well, I hope so, but less military expertise, more experience and a good dose of luck. Although that looks like it might be running out after what happened to Conor.'

Mark frowned. 'Poor lad. You just never know what's around the corner, do you? You have to live every minute.'

'You sound like Clarissa. I think she must embroider that on her handkerchiefs.'

He laughed. 'Does she use handkerchiefs?'

Tess shrugged, smiling. 'Not sure, but she's got loads of embroidery thread and knitting wool in her living room.'

'Like Madame Defarge?'

Not following, Tess screwed up her nose.

'*A Tale of Two Cities* – she put the names of the worst aristocrats in her knitting.'

'Oh, I see.'

His smile showed that he could see that she didn't.

'It was a list for the guillotine.'

'Oh, I *see*. Goodness, I hope Clarissa's not putting anyone local in her designs.'

He laughed, shaking his head. 'She's quite a character.'

'She is. So, how can I help you?'

'Oh, sorry, I came about the ghosts.'

Chapter 17

IT WAS MID-MORNING, and Clarissa was again contemplating the chessboard in the middle of the shop when the door opened with its characteristic tinkle. She looked up, even more irritated at the interruption when she saw that it was Aidan Gaunt, as opposed to a high-worth customer who might get her day off to a flying start.

'Morning. I was wondering if Genevieve was about?'

Clarissa forced a smile. 'Just me this morning. I do Saturdays.' She almost added 'as you know', and could have also added 'and I'm rather busy', but then she'd have to explain about the chess game and why standing with her arms folded in the middle of the shop could be described as busy.

'I was wondering if we could borrow the dolphin vase. You heard about . . .' He let the sentence trail.

'Poor Conor, I did indeed.'

'Liam's got all the lines off pat except one about the book and candle. I thought if we could tape a prompt to the back of a prop, he'd feel a bit more secure. That big dolphin vase would be perfect. It should fit in with the period feel of the set very well.'

'"Bell, book and candle, candle, book and bell / Forward and backward, to curse Faustus to hell!"?'

Aidan looked surprised. 'Yes, he keeps mixing up the bells and then it throws him off. It's one of the lines I've kept from the original. You know the play?'

Clarissa smiled enigmatically. 'I do indeed. I'm sure Genevieve will be absolutely thrilled for you to take this glorious thing. We may get someone falling in love with it.'

'It's very handsome.'

Handsome wasn't the word Clarissa would have used. Grotesque was closer to the mark, but some people had no taste. She did love early Minton, but much of the majolica left her cold, its garish colours unsettling. A bit like Aidan Gaunt, really. She couldn't see why half the village had gone doolally over him at all. He had classical proportions and a chiselled jaw, looked not unlike a young Gregory Peck, and there was something vaguely familiar about him, but perhaps that was because she'd seen him on the TV. According to the IMDb website he'd had several very minor parts in shows she may or may not have seen, enough to make him into a bit of a sensation in a country village.

There were times when Clarissa cursed her failing memory. It was one of the reasons she had become obsessed with keeping super-fit. If one bit of her wasn't working well, she wanted to make damn sure the rest of her was in great shape. And she'd hit two minutes on her plank last weekend, so she wasn't completely falling apart yet.

Clarissa smiled, going for vaguely uninterested in her tone.

'Are you pleased with the performance so far?'

'Everyone's amazing. So dedicated.'

'Don't you find it a huge change from London? Provincial am-dram is a bit different from what you mentioned you've done before.'

Aidan looked as if he was thinking hard. 'Yes, sometimes. I miss the city, but you know, it's fabulous to have your own play performed. You create something new whenever you go on stage, but it's different when you write the words and can direct.'

'I'm sure. And what brought you to Kilfenora originally?' Clarissa was about to add 'of all places', but thought better of it.

'Space. I wanted to write. I was taking some time out when I wrote the play originally, then life intervened – I wanted to get back in touch with my creative side. I found that very hard in London. I saw somewhere to rent and here I am.'

'Do you still have family in Dublin?' Clarissa picked up the white rook, suddenly realising she sounded as if she was giving him the third degree. The piece was large, delightfully heavy in her hand.

Aidan shook his head. 'Not to speak of. Lot of history there. You know families.'

Cradling the weight of the piece, Clarissa nodded sagely. 'I certainly do.'

As if he was getting comfortable chatting, Aidan stuck his hands in the front pockets of his jeans. Designer, no doubt. At least his polo shirt was, the navy Ralph Lauren logo clear against the burgundy waffle fabric. He just didn't quite carry quality off; Clarissa wasn't sure why. Perhaps it was his jewellery. He was wearing a chunky silver ring on his right hand, a coiled serpent. She'd noticed it before and always wondered what its significance was. She suddenly realised he'd started speaking again.

'Genevieve mentioned you'd appeared in *Blithe Spirit*. One of my favourite plays.'

Clarissa put the chess piece down on the table. She needed to wait for him to leave before she moved it. Chess was a game of skill, of planning, something she enjoyed very much, and she didn't like to be rushed.

'Mine, too. I was Elvira in my last performance.'

Aidan nodded, his face showing he was impressed.

'The wife – great part. You really can't beat Noël Coward, can you? So, the vase?'

Clarissa didn't react immediately to his comment; instead she gave him a long look and then smiled benignly.

'Of course, you must need to get on and here I am wittering. Can you carry it?'

Chapter 18

TESS SMILED AT the babble of voices and clank of china as she glanced in through the stable yard arch at the tea rooms on her way to meet Genevieve.

Soon they would operate all week, not just at the weekends, serving light lunches to the bus tours who were already booking. Stripped back to the stone, the stables themselves had been knocked through to create one of Tess's favourite parts of the estate. The tea rooms had such a warm, welcoming feeling. Perhaps Mark Mulligan was right about good and bad spirits and overlapping worlds, but she was sure if there was anyone still wandering around the stables and yard, that they were happy spooks.

She wished they could have talked for longer. When Mark had left earlier, she'd started to think about some of the places in the house where she'd felt a bit weird. And there were quite a few. But anything that had happened or she'd heard, she'd always sought a rational reason for. It had never occurred to her that the house or grounds could be haunted, whatever the locals said about sightings.

Mark's phone had rung as they'd been talking – one of his staff calling about a disaster in the pub kitchen he'd had to go and sort out – so they hadn't had time to get into much detail, but she was looking forward to finding out more.

In fact, she was quite looking forward to working a bit more closely with Mark Mulligan full stop. It was a shame he'd had to get back so quickly, but she'd looked at the time and realised that she needed to go, too, and she still hadn't had a proper look at the co-ordinates Lynch had given her. It was starting to feel like doing her taxes; she knew it was urgent, but she kept putting it off. While she was avoiding finding the spot on the map, it didn't feel quite so horrifyingly real.

Leaving the tea rooms and stable yard behind her, Tess headed towards the gardens, taking a short cut through the Rose Walk and down beside the wishing well. Gen had suggested the adventure playground was the best place for an al fresco lunch, which had sounded perfect. Malachi would probably find some of his friends from school to play with while they chatted, far enough away from everyone not to be overheard.

Gen was waiting for her when Tess got there, jewel-bright picnic plates and cups spread out on a table in the shade beside the giant spiderweb climbing frame on the edge of the playground. Malachi was already scrambling to the top, pursued by two other boys of a similar size.

Gen waved when she saw Tess, a flask of coffee and a picnic basket beside her. Dressed in her usual multicoloured tent dress, her hair held back by a bright red scarf, Gen's huge turquoise drop earrings made her look like an exotic bird of paradise against the backdrop of the woods.

Feeling decidedly dull in her jeans and navy T-shirt, reaching the bench, Tess swung her leg in and sat down with a bump opposite her.

'This was a *very* good idea.'

'You said it. All Clarissa's, though, I can't take credit. You need to take more breaks. Especially this week. You want to look gorgeous on opening night, like the lady of the manor, not like an overworked hired help.'

'Thanks for that.' Tess smiled ruefully. Genevieve had always said exactly what she thought ever since Tess had known her. 'But this is all your fault, you know.'

'What? You working 24/7 is my fault? I think that's an issue you have with your work–life balance, T. And paying off this investor you won't tell me about.' Gen arched her eyebrows, meaningfully. They'd never had secrets growing up, and Tess knew Gen couldn't understand why they did now.

'You're right, I stand corrected.'

Tess held up her hands as if she was stopping traffic. She didn't want to get into the finance conversation again – not today, when she was finally taking a moment to relax.

She sighed. None of them had realised how the house restoration would grow, the project getting bigger and bigger by the day. Without Gen and Clarissa as her backroom team, Tess didn't know if she'd have managed everything without completely losing her mind.

Raising the extra capital she'd needed to buy the estate hadn't been as difficult as she'd thought. She had a sound business plan, had got backing from Wicklow County Council and the Arts Council, and with the money from her parents' house added into the pot, had been halfway there. Then she'd been offered a chunk of money by a private investor, and it had suddenly all become possible. She was sworn to secrecy as to their identity, much to Gen's disgust, but she was indebted to them for their intervention. It had all looked a bit shaky until they'd come on board.

Tess really hadn't anticipated half the work that needed doing, or the bloody pandemic, but she'd started a skills project with the local enterprise board that had been a godsend. That had been another one of Clarissa's good ideas. For a woman in her seventies, Clarissa was remarkably switched on, and their re-found friendship had been one of the best things that had come out of this whole crazy scheme.

'So what news? Is everything coming together?' Gen picked up the silver bullet flask and unscrewed the lid, her bracelets jingling as she reached for two bright yellow mugs. 'I got the girls to fill this with latte on the way past the tea rooms, so you're spared my usual instant. *And* I've brought elderflower pressé – don't say I don't look after you.'

They both laughed, any tension dissipating immediately.

'My favourite. You're a star, Gen.' Tess picked up her coffee. 'Any update on the mysterious chess game?'

Gen lifted a plastic box of sandwiches out of the basket and took the lid off, tapping it to indicate Tess should help herself. She shook her head.

'Nothing. I've given up asking, in all honesty. I reckon it's someone in London, texting her the moves. I mean, there's no way it could be anyone here, I'd have noticed them coming into the shop.'

Tess took a sip of her coffee, weighing up Gen's theory as to who Clarissa's secret chess partner might be. She wasn't so sure. Gen interrupted her thoughts.

'Oh, I promised to ask – Malachi was wondering about the Sugar Canister Tower.'

Tess reached for a sandwich. 'I don't think it's going to be ready for opening. It's so far over on the other side of the gardens it

97

hasn't been a priority. I don't think anyone will notice that it's still fenced off.'

'Shame, it's so pretty. But you're quite right. There's going to be tons for people to do.'

'I can take Malachi up again if you like, before school starts. Those spiral stairs are a bit of a killer, though.'

'He's got young legs. He'd love that.' Gen glanced over at the climbing frame. 'He's like a goat, he loves heights.'

Tess grinned. 'You can see for miles from the top of the tower, but I don't want to open it to the public yet, it's an accident waiting to happen. The window slits are so big and come right down to the floor, and there's no handrail on those stairs, it would be so easy to fall.'

'I don't think it was designed with actual use in mind. Just to look like a fairytale tower for anyone taking a stroll around that side of the lake. It's not even as old as it looks, I don't think.' Gen looked into her basket as she spoke and pulled out a Tupperware box of fruit. 'You should get some film location people up here, it's perfect for Disney.'

'*That* is a brilliant idea – it would certainly solve my cash flow issues.'

Tess took a bite of her sandwich. Gen had missed her vocation with the antique shop; Tess had always thought she should be in catering.

'So is everything else on track?'

Tess looked at Gen for a moment, wondering what she should say. Where did she start? She sighed, reaching for her mug.

'Well, apart from the whole Conor thing . . .' Tess hesitated, unsure if she should tell Gen her suspicions about the troll tinkering with the lighting to sabotage the play. Here in the sunshine with the sounds of children playing behind them, it sounded completely mad, even in her head. Deciding against it, Tess cleared her throat. 'The very good news is that Mark Mulligan's volunteered to do ghost tours of the main house. The Cross Keys hasn't been open that long, with the pandemic and everything, but he wants something legit to get him out from behind that bar. He really doesn't love it.'

Gen nodded. 'That was Clarissa's idea, too. I don't know how she found out, but he's got a PhD in parapsychology or something.'

'He said he did research for his PhD into the historical context of hauntings and their relationship to out-of-body experiences, dreaming, and the impact of psychic ability.' Tess pulled a face. She really hadn't been sure what he was talking about, but it had sounded very impressive.

Gen took a sip of her own coffee. 'I heard he did it online when he first came back from Australia. I don't think he was very happy that his dad left him the pub. There was talk of him selling it for a while so he could go back. It might still be on the market, actually.'

Tess glanced over at Malachi. 'That does seem a strange combination, but obviously he's multi-talented.'

Gen cupped her mug in her hands, her face troubled.

'He had a big business in Australia, I think. Tours around Ayers Rock. But his wife committed suicide – at least they didn't realise it was suicide for ages'. She frowned. 'Apparently he was investigated for her murder.'

Chapter 19

LOOKING ACROSS AT Gen, Tess felt her eyes widen in surprise. *What was it about Kilfenora?* She'd been here two and a half years and suddenly she was finding out all this stuff about people being murdered all over the place.

One thing she'd learned on her travels around the world was that some locations seemed to attract broken people, like some sort of bizarre magnet, but she'd thought the occasional eccentricities she'd seen in Kilfenora were just caused by living in a village in the middle of the mountains. Perhaps she was wrong.

'You're not serious? How am I only hearing about this now?'

'I had to dig into the local papers in Australia to find it. I don't think anybody knows here – once he went to boarding school he was barely in the village. And obviously his parents wouldn't have wanted it broadcast.' Gen ran one of her pendants along its chain. 'It's not the sort of thing you bring up in conversation really, is it?'

'How did she die?'

'Hanged herself, from what I can find online. Not that I was looking *that* much, obviously, but he is single and rather gorgeous—'

Tess interrupted her. 'Due diligence. Always important.'

Gen grinned. 'I've no idea how they thought he'd staged it. The case was thrown out after a week of evidence. It's really not my business so I'm not going to ask him about it, but the local papers suggested he'd upset someone in local law enforcement and it was some sort of revenge thing.'

'How could you do that?' Tess frowned, processing what she'd heard.

Mark Mulligan didn't strike her as the sort to get mixed up in anything that nasty. She hoped not, anyway. With all he knew about the Kilfenora ghosts, he'd be invaluable. It had been on her list to find a guide for the main house – several, in fact – but all the tour parties who had booked so far had wanted Tess to give them the tour herself. She'd been quite looking forward to showing the groups around, but basic history was about her limit, to say nothing of the time involved. As he'd so rightly pointed out, ghost tours would be a huge draw.

Tess took another sip of her coffee. It really was good. And a break away from her desk was exactly what she needed. Tess suddenly realised that Gen hadn't heard her, had her eyes fixed over her shoulder. She turned around to see where she was looking. Malachi was standing at the highest point of the climbing frame, his arms raised in triumph.

'Careful, Mal, don't you slide down that pole, you know what happened last time.' Gen had her mother's lungs and diction – her voice carried clearly.

'He doesn't look like he's going to slide . . .'

Gen grimaced. 'It's what comes next in the game. He twisted his ankle the last time and we spent five hours in A and E.'

'You never said that happened here.' Tess's mouth dropped open.

Malachi's injuries were legendary in Kilfenora; Gen had the ambulance on speed dial. Her attention back on Tess, Genevieve shrugged.

'Some things you don't need to know, you've enough on your plate.'

Tess rolled her eyes, taking another sip of coffee. What other surprises did Gen have for her? She cleared her throat.

'Tell me, how well do you know Eoin Doyle?'

'The electrician?'

Tess nodded.

Gen grimaced. 'Barely. I try to avoid him, to be honest, he sort of gives me the creeps.'

Tess nodded slowly, her eyes on her coffee. 'What's the gossip in the village about him?'

'About the murders, do you mean? Well, assuming they were murders and four perfectly healthy women with good jobs didn't all decide to up and walk out of their front doors in some sort of alien-induced trance.'

'Do people think he was involved?'

Gen did an elaborate double take that made her earrings swing.

'Er . . . yes. Although he has numerous reasons why he wasn't, obviously. But he knew them all somehow – had worked in their houses, or met them on his travels.'

'Seems a bit of a coincidence.'

'I'd say so. He has all sorts of alibis apparently. I can't remember the details, but the windows of opportunity are small from what I gathered, and he tried to use that as his principal defence.'

Tess screwed up her nose. 'You don't need much time to disable and kidnap someone if you've had a bit of practice. Especially if they know and trust you to start with.'

'And you've a van handy to hop them into. That seems to be the consensus of opinion. The fact is that they all just vanished and he's one of the few common denominators between them.' Gen continued sarcastically, 'The others being that they all lived alone, they were all women and all in their thirties.' She glanced up to check on Malachi again and lowered her voice. 'Because he'd been in all of the houses, his fingerprints were present, but you can't date a fingerprint, can you? So they could have been left on the day the women disappeared, or six months earlier.'

'And the Gardai haven't any other ideas?'

Gen shook her head. 'I mean, you don't walk out and leave the radio on, and all the doors open and half a cup of coffee on the table, do you? Something happened to them. All of them. Why do you ask?'

Tess bit her lip. 'A reporter was on to me, saying Doyle had worked here on the house. And . . .' She trusted Gen absolutely, but saying it made it seem more real. 'Don't say anything to Clarissa yet, but this guy's with the *Daily News*. He's working with one of those true crime programmes and they've had a tip-off that one of the women might be buried here.' She didn't dare say 'all' of them; that was too much to think about.

Gen's eyes opened wide as she spluttered her coffee.

'Like here?'

'No – not exactly here, but on the estate where it borders the national park.'

'Christ.'

'I know, he rang just before Conor Kelly's accident. They want to bring a film crew and dogs out to search one of the fields.'

Gen looked at her, her mouth open. 'Not this week?'

'Yes, this week. As if there isn't enough happening already.' Tess grimaced.

'What do the guards say?'

'They don't seem to know anything about it. I've been calling the station here and in Rockfield, but as soon as I mentioned this reporter Jerry Lynch's name, they weren't exactly complimentary. He's informed them but they don't seem to think his "information" is reliable.'

Gen frowned. 'Perhaps it isn't. I mean, this all happened years ago. Why should it come up now?'

'*That* is a very good question.'

Chapter 20

MEGAN CHECKED THE time on her phone again and looked over her shoulder. There was still no sign of Laetitia and the costumes. The door to the function room was firmly closed, the sound of the Saturday crowd in the main bar in The Cross Keys filtering through the worn floorboards from below. Today was supposed to be a rehearsed reading, but now they needed to all try on the costumes after the dress rehearsal had been so dramatically interrupted. If anything needed altering, they needed time to do it.

When everyone had arrived earlier, they'd arranged the function chairs in a semicircle around the tiny stage normally occupied by a band. Now Megan sat near the front beside Ally, watching the action unfold, waiting, like them all, for the costumes to arrive. The rest of the cast who were needed today were sitting on the other side of the stage, and becoming increasingly agitated. With the change in schedule caused by Conor's drama, instead of the reading, this was now going to be the first full technical 'stagger-through' of the play – Megan had smiled at Aidan's description – with lights, *costumes* and sound, after the other one got interrupted.

Megan glanced over at her sister, who was still on her phone, scanning Reddit by the looks of things. Ally hated doing nothing, and without the costumes, it was a waste of time them both being here. Well, a waste of time for Ally anyway. Aidan's rich voice interrupted Megan's thoughts and she sat up a little straighter in the chair.

'So you're coming in like *this*. I know it's hard on this stage, but remember it's late at night. He's the only person in the room. The Devil has just left. Let's try it.'

Megan watched as Aidan jumped off the low stage, leaving it to Faustus and the actor playing Mephostophilis. Megan couldn't remember his name; he was older, late middle-aged, and what her mother described as 'willowy'. He stooped slightly, as if he'd never got used to his height. He'd been pretty distant and aloof when they'd first been introduced and Megan had taken an immediate dislike to him.

The 'professional' actors – Ally had done the rabbit ears thing with her fingers as she'd described them to their parents over dinner at the start of the summer – were all acquaintances of Aidan's, apparently. So far, they had only shown up at the weekends and the odd evening to rehearse because they were getting paid and Tess didn't have the budget for more. It made the whole thing a bit disjointed, but Megan supposed it was better than nothing. She and Ally and Laetitia had stood in on rotation when they were needed, which at least meant they could understudy if the situation demanded it.

'"Now, Faustus, what wouldst thou have me do?"' The actor swept onto the stage. He'd improvised his lack of costume with a tablecloth, and swirled it around him as he spoke.

Liam turned to him, pensive, his face troubled. He really played a very good Faustus. Megan had been impressed, particularly given the fact that he was doing music production, because she'd heard his Leaving Cert results had been pretty terrible. She'd always thought you had to be quite bright to act, but perhaps he'd missed his vocation. Liam's voice carried clearly across the vaulted room.

'"I charge thee wait upon me whilst I live, / To do whatever Faustus shall command, / Be it to make the moon drop from her sphere, / Or the ocean overwhelm the world."'

The lines echoed through Megan's head. She had to admit that Aidan's version was pretty impressive. He'd kept a lot of the original, but tweaked sections to make it resonate with a modern audience. It reminded her of one of those videos where classical music was blended with rap to create a completely different piece of music.

There were many things about Aidan Gaunt that were pretty impressive. Megan watched him out of the corner of her eye as he concentrated on the stage, the tattered pages of his script in one hand.

Megan looked quickly at her phone again. Where the hell *was* Laetitia? She was just so bloody unreliable. She could see Aidan was getting annoyed. He'd decided to keep going despite not having the costumes, but the whole point of the rehearsals was to check everything fitted and people could change and move about without any issues.

As if there hadn't been enough to throw them off track already.

'Just try that again, Liam – this time, look at Mephostophilis.'

Aidan's voice interrupted her thoughts and Megan gave Ally a nudge.

'Ouch, *elbows*.' Ally glared at her.

'Anything from Tis yet?'

Ally shook her head and went back to scrolling through her phone.

Megan let out a sharp sigh. She'd bet Laetitia thought she could swan in with the costumes when it suited her because she was having a thing with Aidan. Megan felt resentment rise like a hot wave. There was no question that her littlest sister was beautiful, but she was an absolute train wreck on every other level. Between her tarot and her art and her weird friends, she was so unlike either Megan or Ally; there were times when Megan had been convinced she was a foundling.

Megan looked at Aidan again. He'd stuck the script in the pocket of his jeans, was wearing a thin T-shirt that showed off the muscles in his back. What had Laetitia said? She'd bumped into him in the gardens one evening and they'd 'sort of started chatting'. Megan would bet they had. How long had it taken Tis to get him to the van and get his clothes off?

It was typical, really. Tis had guessed Megan liked him from the minute he'd appeared in Kilfenora and she'd bumped into him in the Spar. Well, not *exactly* bumped into him, but he'd been in there looking for a pestle and mortar, of all things. Megan had been sent over by her father to get milk for the surgery, had been in a hurry until she'd decided to grab a packet of digestives and seen him beside the eggs, discussing baking with Katie-Lou. She'd looped back and hovered beside the cocoa, listening in, trying to find out who the beautiful stranger with the English accent was. Then, of course, her father had texted to hurry her up. It had been a few days later that she'd realised Aidan had actually moved into the village and wasn't just passing through. Which, at the time, she'd thought was very good news.

And now bloody Laetitia had a thing with him. It was easy for her, with that van. Living at home was the absolute pits sometimes. Theirs might be the biggest house in the village, and their father's GP practice the hub of local gossip, but privacy was practically non-existent. That said, if she and Ally had been living in Dublin, they wouldn't have got involved in the play, to say nothing of being totally broke with the price of rent in the city.

If Megan wanted to seduce him, she'd have to find a way to get invited to the tiny apartment he rented above Sheil's Solicitors, and no doubt someone would see her going in.

Megan uncrossed her legs and put her arm over the seat beside her, conscious that if Aidan did turn around, she should be looking her best. She flicked her hair over her shoulder.

'Here, watch it, Rapunzel. Nobody's looking at you,' Ally muttered, glaring at her. 'Christ, this is such a waste of time. Where the hell is Tis?'

'I've tried her phone about twenty times.' Megan kept her voice as low as she could. 'I'm not walking over there to find her in this heat.'

Ally let out a sharp breath. 'Let me see if Tom's working today. He can nip up and see if she's in the van. She's probably slept it out.'

Megan watched as Ally deftly changed screen and texted one of the Kilfenora gardeners. They'd dated briefly last summer, discovered that they were polar opposites, and decided to stay friends. Ally seemed to stay friends with everyone, Megan didn't know how she did it.

Tom responded immediately. Ally read out his response. '"Pruning. Will go over now."'

'Well, that's something. Let's see if he can wake her up.'

A single round of applause made Megan start. Aidan was clapping, the script folded in his hand. A few other members of the cast joined in.

'That's excellent. Well done, everyone. Right, Scene Four next, who do we have?'

The cast members on the stage jumped off and those who were needed next stood up, getting ready to get into the 'wings' beside the tiny stage.

'Any news on those costumes, ladies?' Aidan turned to look at Megan and Ally, and Megan found herself blushing hard.

Thank God Ally's phone pipped with a text.

'I just got one of the gardeners to check the van. She's not there but it's open, and the radio's been left on, so presumably she's up and about and getting ready to come over. She runs the van on a caravan battery, but she wouldn't leave anything on for long.'

Chapter 21

A S TESS WALKED up to the house from the playground, she left the sound of the river and the excited cries of the children behind her. The woods ran down to a wide stream, the water level low now, crystal clear where it played around the moss-covered boulders and rocks. One day she'd go down there early in the morning and go for a paddle. One day when everything was up and running and there were no disasters looming.

Weaving past the wishing well and cutting through the Rose Walk, she headed to the house. The sun was almost overhead, the heat caught between the high walls, the air filled with a riot of scents.

She'd switched on her phone when they'd finished lunch and now, as she walked into a receptive patch, it pinged. Several times. She'd missed about four calls and two texts from Garry the insurance assessor. He'd confirmed that he'd organised a team to check all the staging this afternoon, and while they were at it, to make sure that the smoke detectors were all working and the fire notices were all in place.

You can't be too careful

Thanks, Garry.

His last text said that the contractors were on their way.

Passing her own front door, Tess strode into the stable yard, and one of the waitresses waved her down.

'There was a young lad looking for you. He's in the ballroom. He's here to fix the lighting track, I think. We sent him up, hope that was OK.'

Tess smiled her thanks. 'All good here? Make sure you take your breaks, won't you. If you need cover, call me.'

The young girl nodded and bent to clear the table she was standing beside.

At least the insurance company had got these people organised fast; they must have a panel of tradesman on their books for emergencies. She hadn't asked who they'd send, had just hoped they'd be quick. Despite his sliminess, Garry had seen the predicament that they were in. This week was supposed to be the full technical run-through of the play, which was something they couldn't do in the pub.

Pulling open the door to the back stairs, Tess immediately felt the temperature drop. The stone staircase rose above her, only wide enough for one person. She had a sudden flashback to Laetitia's purple cape dragging up ahead of her. At least there would be no nasty surprises this time.

In the ballroom, an extending steel ladder with scaffolding supports had been set up two thirds of the way across the stage, steadied at the bottom by a young lad with tattooed forearms and a very professional tool belt hanging from his hips. From this side of the room she could only see the lower half of the man at the top of it, his upper body concealed by the pelmet hiding the lighting rig.

She called across the room. 'Hello, I'm Tess Morgan. How are you getting on?'

The lad holding the ladder looked around it and grinned.

'We're almost done. We've checked everything, we've just this last spotlight to go. Everything seems to be in order. Fire alarms are all grand.' He had a strong Eastern European accent with a dash of inner-city Dublin, and had obviously been here long enough to pick up some Irishisms.

Tess nodded to him and opened her mouth to speak just as her phone rang, the old-fashioned telephone bell loud in the huge room. She checked the screen. It was Aidan Gaunt.

'Do you mind if I just take this?'

Turning her back to the stage, Tess walked to the far corner of the ballroom, the phone to her ear. Aidan didn't bother with pleasantries – he sounded cross.

'Have you seen Laetitia O'Riordan around today? She was supposed to collect the costumes and bring them over in that van of hers, but Ally got one of your gardeners to check and they said the van's still in the car park, unlocked.'

'That's a bit odd. Perhaps Laetitia has nipped out and forgot to lock it. I can check to see if the costumes are still here, maybe she's on the way. If not, I can bring everything to you if you're stuck.'

'That would be amazing, thanks.'

He hung up before Tess had a chance to reply.

Turning around, Tess stuck her phone in her jeans pocket and walked towards the stage. The young guy at the bottom of the ladder steadied it as the man at the top began to come down, ducking under the pelmet.

'That all looks grand now.'

Tess took a step backwards. It was Eoin Doyle. It took her a moment to find the words, the press photos of the women who had gone missing flashing through her memory – Fidelma Hoey, the most recent, the clearest. Tess fought to sound as if she was in control.

'That's great. Thank you.'

'You might need to get someone to look at the security lighting in the stable yard. The main light over the archway's not working. You don't want to be going into the winter and find you've no light over there.' He paused. 'Do you want us to take a look at that while we're here? We can check those strings of lights that run across the yard, too. The last thing you want is a fire after all the work you've put in.'

She looked at him, confused. How did he know the yard light was gone? It was a photosensitive light; it only came on when it was dark. And even though the sun set at 9.30, it didn't get properly dark until after ten at the moment, the sun coming up at 5.30 a.m.

Had he been wandering around the property at night?

Chapter 22

TESS DROVE AROUND to the stable yard gate while Eoin Doyle finished up, very grateful that Aidan had called and given her something to do that meant she needed to get on. Less keen that Doyle had heard her volunteering to bring the costumes to the pub and had offered to help bring them to the car.

She had no idea what the truth was about Doyle, but he was one of those men who had a creepy presence, and like Gen, she felt very uncomfortable around him.

In his forties, he was good-looking, with piercing blue eyes, but with his shaven head, tattoos up both arms and one on his neck, there was something aggressive about him that made her instinctively want to steer clear.

Dumping his armful of garments into her open boot, Doyle stood back and looked up at the lantern hanging over the middle of the gateway.

'We'll get those lights checked for you. My old mam loves what you've done here. She's always saying it.'

Tess smiled weakly, not entirely sure that she was delighted at being discussed in the Doyle household. She didn't want him around for any longer than absolutely necessary, but with everything else going wrong this week, faulty wiring was the last thing she could cope with.

Dumping her own armful of costumes in the boot, Tess turned to speak to him, and started. He was standing a tiny bit too close to her and seemed to be studying her. The blush hit her at the same time as her heart started to pound.

'Thank you, that would be great. I'll just take these over to the pub. If you need anything, the girls in the tea rooms can help. They have access to the fuse board in the stables.' Tess pushed the boot closed and pulled her car keys from her jeans pocket. 'The girls will get you coffee, too. Right, better be off.' She hurried around to the driver's door.

Her red Golf was baking inside, the leather seats scalding hot, but she didn't want to hang about to let the heat out. Slipping inside, she got the key into the ignition and pulled off as fast as she could without looking as if she was hurrying, raising her hand to wave her thanks. Despite the temptation to accelerate, she kept to the stately twenty kilometres an hour limit, glancing in the rear-view mirror as she turned right around the front of the house.

Now she owed him one. The thought gave her a sick feeling. How that debt might manifest filled her with a nagging fear.

Perhaps she could give his mother a voucher for a cream tea and they'd be square?

As she pulled into the pub car park, Tess was still trying to work out how Doyle knew that the stable yard gate light wasn't working. She was sure it had been earlier in the week. Perhaps there wasn't a problem with it at all? She should probably have waited until this evening to check it before agreeing to get it fixed, but the benefit of avoiding a big call-out fee right now couldn't be ignored.

The cast was in the middle of a scene when she got up the stairs at The Cross Keys with the first armful of garments. The three semi-professional actors Aidan had brought in were in the centre of the stage, young Liam coming on as she shouldered open the door. For a moment she stood and watched him.

The stage was relatively small, but they seemed to be managing with it, had pushed the round tables normally scattered across the polished wooden boards to the side of the room. The chairs had been spaced out in rows in front of the stage. Above them, lights and microphones hung from beams that supported the vaulted roof.

Watching for a few minutes, Tess was impressed. Liam was very good, clearly enjoying the role, the lines flowing naturally. Beside her, she spotted a bar stool that had been pushed up against the wall, and put her armful of costumes down as quietly as she could. She was about to slip out of the door to go back to the car when Megan O'Riordan glanced over her shoulder. Tess nodded, smiling. The air was so filled with concentration she didn't want to interrupt, but she could see that Megan was frowning. Perhaps she was concentrating on the show, or from what Aidan had said, worried about whatever Laetitia was getting up to today.

She really didn't understand the O'Riordan girls; they seemed to be as thick as thieves one minute and bitterly opposed the next. The middle sister, Ally, had always seemed to be the most focused to Tess, although there was no question that Megan was just as clever as her sister. Both of them were very results-orientated. When Mark Mulligan had arrived to talk to her about the ghost tours, he'd mentioned something about Megan wanting to get more involved with things at Kilfenora House beyond the play, which could work out to be very useful. Help moving forward was going to be vital. And if the someone she recruited was someone she could train into the position, all the better.

It seemed so odd that Laetitia was such an absolute flake compared to her sisters. But then perhaps she was just very different, and didn't look for happiness in success. Which was just as well – from the tone of Aidan's voice on the phone, Laetitia might not be involved in the play for much longer unless she could come up with a very good reason for her absence and total silence today. The whole cast were under pressure with Conor's accident; it was the worst possible time for her to go walkabout. What on earth could she be doing?

SUNDAY

Chapter 23

A SUDDEN POUNDING ON the front door made Tess start awake. Lying stunned for a moment, she glanced at the clock beside the bed. It was seven o'clock. Her alarm was about to go off.

The pounding began again. Who on earth was on the doorstep at this time in the morning?

Throwing aside her light summer duvet, Tess reached for her dressing gown and thrust her feet into her slippers beside the bed. Whoever was downstairs wasn't giving up. Tess ruffled her hair, letting her curls bounce back from where they'd been flattened by her pillow. Starting for the bedroom door, she realised she hadn't got her phone and turned back to pick it up from the bedside table, flipping it open to check her messages as she went out onto the landing. Merlin was loafing at the top of the stairs as if he was guarding them, all four paws tucked beneath him and his tail tidied into a neat curl. He looked at her suspiciously as she stepped over him and skipped down the stairs.

The banging was going in bursts now. In the hall, Tess hesitated for a moment. *Who could it be?*

What was she worrying about? It was broad daylight. It was probably one of the gardeners having a moment about the Apollo fountain getting bunged up with algae again.

Tess turned the key on the mortise lock and pulled the latch, opening the door to come face to face with Ally O'Riordan.

'Whatever's the matter? What's happened?'

Ally looked as if she hadn't slept; her mahogany hair was pulled back in an untidy ponytail and she was wearing a T-shirt and jeans. The whole look was decidedly haphazard.

'It's Laetitia. She's disappeared and nobody can get hold of her. She wasn't at rehearsals yesterday, but we've just realised that nobody's heard from her since Friday.'

Tess looked at her blankly. Today was Sunday. Laetitia could hardly be missing in twenty-four hours, surely?

'And how can I help?'

'Well, she must be here, mustn't she? She could be lying injured somewhere. I mean, her van's here and you can't get out of Kilfenora at the weekend, there are no buses.'

Still muggy with sleep, Tess held her hand up.

'Come in and we'll work it out. She could have got a lift into Dublin last night with a friend?'

'She doesn't have any friends. No, I mean she's got lots, but they're all in a band and the band is in Spain. She was supposed to go but she wanted to get involved in the play.'

Tess took a moment to work out how this was something that they needed to get excited about at seven o'clock in the morning.

'So what makes you think she hasn't left the estate?'

'I just know she hasn't. If she was going into Dublin she would have texted. I've got a dress that needs to go back to Penneys, she said she'd take it with her next time she's there.' Ally closed her eyes as if she was trying to still her mind. 'Her van was unlocked when Tom checked it yesterday. It was like she'd just gone for a walk and intended to get back.'

Tess still wasn't seeing why there were grounds for panic, but she supposed Ally knew her sister the best.

'OK, OK. Look, I need to get dressed. Will you go into the kitchen and make some coffee and I'll be as quick as I can. Let's go and look at her van and we can have a think.' Tess took a step backwards. 'Kitchen's through there. I'll be five minutes tops.'

Ally headed through the kitchen door, her trainers silent on the wooden floor. Turning around, Tess ran up the stairs, meeting the steely gaze of Merlin on the landing. She had no idea how he came in and out of the house, but he seemed to think he lived here as much as he did at Clarissa's.

Tess went straight into the bathroom. She was still sticky from the hot night and she couldn't think without a shower.

When she got downstairs, Ally was leaning on the kitchen counter, gripping a mug as if her life depended on it, her knuckles white. She inclined her head at a full cup sitting on the kitchen table.

'Thanks. So just tell me everything you know and let's see if we can work out where to look.'

Ally looked at her, aghast. 'We need to go now, we haven't time.'

'She's been off the radar for a day and a half, and this estate is the best part of a hundred acres. I need a bit more information. Who spoke to her last?'

Ally took a slug of her coffee. 'Me and Meg, we were over at the van on Friday afternoon. Tis was supposed to bring the costumes on Saturday.'

Tess nodded. 'So when the van was checked on Saturday, did anyone see her phone? I mean, did it look like it had been broken into or anything?'

'No, but Tom said there were cups in the sink. They must have been the ones we'd used on Friday. I should have twigged then, but it was only when I woke up this morning that I realised. She's such a neat freak, there's no way she would have left them. Something has happened to her, I know.'

Tess put her coffee down. 'Right, let's start with the van.'

Chapter 24

LAETITIA'S VAN WAS exactly as Ally had described it. The elderly VW Camper with its dull orange paint looked abandoned in the corner of the gravelled car park, the windows dusty.

Opening off a service entrance on the far side of the house, nestled in beside the west wing, the car park had a view across the main gardens and access to the area that Tess hadn't opened to the public yet. Apart from the Sugar Canister Tower, which was a hazard in itself, there was another ancient well up here that only had a rusting grating over it, presenting all sorts of danger to visitors until it was replaced. Laetitia had been thrilled with it, insisting she could use the water so she would be totally self-sufficient.

She'd caught Tess at a weak moment when she'd asked if she could stay for a few weeks while she sorted out her accommodation issues. That had been in May, and there was no sign of her moving on, but Tess had quite liked the idea that there was someone else on the property. Clarissa's cottage was on the very far side of the lake, in the corner closest to the adventure playground, south of the Sugar Canister Tower – in fact, you could see her roof from the top – but that was a good ten-minute walk from the tower and the tower was almost fifteen minutes from Tess's house.

By the time they had reached the van they were both hot and flushed. Ally had almost run over, Tess had barely kept up.

Grabbing hold of the stainless-steel handle on the sliding door behind the passenger door, Ally hauled it open. The sound of the early morning radio show filled the car park.

Her face drained of colour, Ally glanced at Tess.

'She never listens to the radio, she uses Spotify on her phone.' Ally looked back into the van. 'Even if she'd just popped out for a minute, she'd have locked it. All her stuff's in here.'

Jumping in, Ally beckoned for Tess to follow her. Glancing inside, Tess wasn't sure where she'd fit; there wasn't a lot of space.

'Come on in and sit down. See – this table turns into a bed, but this is exactly how we left it on Friday. There are still rings from our coffee cups. If she'd slept here, wouldn't they have rubbed off?'

As Tess climbed inside, Ally leaned in between the front seats and flipped the radio off. If silence could ever be called golden, it was now. The sound had set Tess's teeth on edge. Slipping into the bench seat beside the table, she looked around.

The inside of the van was tiny but incredibly well designed. Behind the front passenger seat there was a sink area with a tiny two-ring gas stove beside it. Every crevice looked as if it was a cupboard or a drawer, concealed handles folded flat so all the surfaces were smooth. It reminded Tess of some of the yachts she'd been on in Dubai, just much smaller. Beside her was a window ledge with a pile of books on it, a well-worn pack of tarot cards on the top and what looked like a heart-shaped fabric pin cushion hanging from the curtain rail above it. Tess caught the scent of lavender when she leaned forward to look at the books.

'If she hasn't slept here, do you think she went out after you saw her on Friday?'

Ally pushed her hair out of her face, anxiously tucking it behind her ear. She was keyed up, as tight as a spring.

'She must have done. She was really upset about the accident, she's got the hots for Conor. Actually, she's got the hots for Aidan, too, she said they'd had a fling or something.' Tess felt her eyebrows shoot up, but fought hard to keep the rest of her face still as Ally went on. 'Meg's at home calling everyone she knows and seeing if she can work out where her phone was last used . . .'

'Let's take this one step at a time. Phone first. If she left it here, that could be why she didn't answer.'

'This thing has so many places to look.' Turning around, Ally indicated a socket in the wall. 'There's the charger though, still switched on.' Ally shook her head. 'She never goes anywhere without her phone. It's like she just got up and walked out.'

Tess suddenly felt her mouth go dry. That was the exact phrase the press had used when they talked about the Radio Snatcher's victims. The realisation came crashing into her head as Ally began to rifle through drawers. Tess suddenly felt very sick.

Ally slid the first drawer closed and went to look through the one below it.

It took a moment for Tess to find her voice.

'Have you thought about calling the guards?'

'Yes, last night. They said she's an adult and there's no sign of foul play, so she's probably gone to a party and is stoned out of her head somewhere. Well, they didn't say exactly that, but something along those lines. Basically, she's over eighteen so she can choose to leave.'

Tess almost added 'And she's only been gone a day', but held it back. She didn't know Laetitia well, but she knew that she was very close to her sisters and she'd have mentioned if she was going out somewhere.

'You've tried all her friends?'

'Obviously. I told you that.' Ally still had her back to her, was now on the next drawer.

'Is there anything under this seat?' Tess slipped out from where she was sitting. All the boats she'd been on had masses of storage in the benches.

'Clothes mainly. You can flip up the bottom cushion.'

Tess spotted a pull handle halfway along and wriggled the cushion she'd been sitting on, up. Below it a smooth wooden base lifted easily to reveal Laetitia's clothes meticulously folded in the space below. Ally was right about her being tidy. Somehow, from Laetitia's boho appearance, Tess hadn't quite believed her. She checked between the folded clothes to see if the phone had slipped in by mistake. Nothing.

Behind Tess, Ally had moved on to what looked like a cupboard of cooking utensils.

'Here's her laptop.'

Ally pulled a slim silver case from the side of the cupboard where it had been slipped in upright. It was a very strange place to keep a laptop, but then this wasn't a normal home.

'Do you know her password?'

Ally turned around and sat down heavily at the table, opening the lid.

'I think I can guess it.'

Tess pushed the seat closed again and sat down opposite Ally.

'Bingo.'

'You've got in, already?' Tess couldn't keep the surprise out of her voice.

'My sisters are very predictable. Our cat's name is her passcode for lots of things.' Ally frowned hard, her eyes on the screen as her fingers flew over the keyboard. 'She hasn't checked her email since lunchtime Friday. And there's a discount voucher here for Fabio's.'

'The chip shop?'

Ally nodded in reply, not taking her eyes off the screen. 'Tis loves their spice bags. If she'd seen that, she would have opened it.'

Tess's forehead wrinkled. 'What is a spice bag?'

'You've never had a spice bag?' Ally looked at her in disbelief. 'Chips and spices, mainly, chicken strips, onions. Delicious.'

'Can you see if she's searched for hotels or flights or something, or maybe a concert? She really might just be in Dublin?'

'Stoned out of her head.' Ally finished the sentence for her. 'Not Tis, she doesn't even drink.' There was a pause while she opened the browser. 'I'm looking at her search history. The last search is for acrylic fabric paint. And there's one for historic buttons. Before that it's for purple flowers.'

'Like for sending a bouquet?'

Ally shook her head. 'Looks like she was trying to identify something.' She clicked again. 'Wolfsbane, flowers June and July, tall purple flowers. It has lots of other names, too – monkshood and aconite.'

Tess glanced at the books beside her. Moving the pack of cards, she lifted the top one, a novel. Under it was a book on Irish wild flowers. There was a tarot card poking out of the top. Tess flicked the book open to a photo of purple flowers that looked familiar.

'Perhaps she wanted to make a natural dye?'

Ally put her head in her hands, pushing her thick fringe out of her face.

'Something's happened to her, I know it. I can feel it.'

Tess was starting to feel it, too.

Chapter 25

TESS FROWNED AND looked across the camper van at Ally. She was scrolling through the laptop again, trying to see if there was any indication of where Laetitia might be.

If this was a normal situation, Tess knew she would be telling Ally not to worry and that Laetitia had probably just hooked up with some guy and had headed off for a night out.

Perhaps she'd been too distracted to lock the van; perhaps her phone had rung just as she'd pulled the door.

Tess knew she'd done that a good few times herself. One night she'd even managed to leave her keys dangling from the front door lock, had spent hours combing the house looking for them before she'd decided to go out and check the car. She'd had her hands full of plumbing supplies for the tea rooms, had knocked the door closed with her hip, and only noticed the keys were missing the next morning.

Which, given what Jerry Lynch and Gen had told her in the last few days about Eoin Doyle, coupled with his knowledge of her security lighting, made her feel physically sick. She'd been so busy over the past few years, the news that he was a person of interest in the disappearances had barely registered before.

One of the biggest factors in not apprehending whoever was involved in the Radio Snatcher cases, Tess was quite sure, was the slowness of the Gardai to react. Granted, they couldn't go chasing after every woman who went off for the day – or night – who didn't think it relevant to explain her movements to her immediate circle. Any one of the women could have been minding her own business, or sneaking off for an illicit rendezvous; people did it all the time. Perhaps that's what Laetitia was up to.

But equally, perhaps she wasn't.

Would Tess say anything? She could just imagine Ally's reaction to Tess thinking that elements of Laetitia's disappearance were consistent with cases attributed to the Radio Snatcher. She was definitely the calmest and most sensible of the three sisters, but even so . . .

Ally had mentioned that Laetitia liked to walk in the grounds at night, though. Had she had an accident – slipped somewhere in one of the isolated parts of the garden and dropped her phone? Or perhaps her phone was out of battery. Tess had gone through phases with her last phone when its charge only seemed to last a few hours. Was that what had happened here?

There had been no new cases linked to the Radio Snatcher for the past eight years, but the more Tess thought about it, the more her thoughts circled. The one thing she did know for sure was that if something had befallen Laetitia – whether she'd slipped and broken her leg in the woods, or if something more sinister had happened – Tess would never forgive herself for not trying to find her.

She'd failed to save a life once, and it wasn't going to happen again. Ever.

'You are absolutely sure no one has heard from her since Friday evening?'

'That's what I keep telling you. It's so unlike Tis, I mean, she phones me or Meg at least two or three times a day. We've always been really close. She'd never go off without saying something. She really wouldn't.'

Tess bit her lip. 'OK, the first thing we need to do is search the grounds. Once we can establish she's not here, we can start looking further afield. Putting something on social media seems to be the quickest way to spread a message these days. And we can use the community Facebook group.'

Tess thought quickly, working out how many people it might take and how long to organise a physical search of the estate.

'If I get the gardeners to check the upper fields, can you get some people from the village to come down? We can get everyone in *Faustus* up here early, and if we spread out we can cover most of the river, the adventure playground and the formal gardens. The cast should be able to get back for the rehearsal in the ballroom by lunchtime.'

Ally looked at her, the relief clear on her face – the relief at being believed. Tess understood that feeling all too well. She reached across and patted her hand reassuringly.

'I don't think a few hours out of people's weekends is going to hurt, and if something has happened to her, the sooner we find her the better.'

133

Chapter 26

'GO, QUICKLY, WE'LL be absolutely fine.' Shaking her head, Clarissa shooed Genevieve towards the open front door of the cottage.

'Are you sure you don't mind? I can take him with me.'

Genevieve hovered in the hallway. Malachi had already run straight down the passage, to the kitchen and out into the garden, holding a Lego rocket over his head, his blond curls bobbing as its trajectory pointed to Mars. He adored Clarissa's garden, made up endless games in the hidden passages between the trees.

'Don't be ridiculous. Tess needs you to help her organise a search party, not a children's tea party. How are you going to do that and keep your rocket boy amused?'

Gen took a deep breath. 'You're right. Thanks, Mum.'

'Go now, so I can spoil him without feeling guilty.'

'Do you ever feel guilty about spoiling him?'

'Never, but if you're watching it inhibits my ability to break the rules.' Clarissa made another shooing motion with both hands. 'I won't say it again.'

Gen seemed to be about to say something, but changed her mind and instead headed out to her car. Clarissa leaned on the front door watching her go. As soon as she had turned on the patch of loose gravel in front of the cottage, and her red tail-lights had vanished around the corner of the lane, Clarissa closed the front door firmly.

Leaning against it, she drew in a breath and frowned, worry nipping at the corners of her mind. Gen hadn't had time to tell her the whole story. In fact, she hardly had any of the story – only that Ally had arrived in a panic on Tess's doorstep this morning and it looked as if Laetitia had disappeared.

That was the bit that Clarissa really didn't like. She kept a close eye on the news, and ever since Gen had moved up here to Kilfenora after her divorce, Clarissa had been aware that Eoin Doyle lived here.

Clarissa had always been very interested in people and their motivations – it helped her on stage enormously to really get inside a character – and the one thing that her Saturdays in the shop gave her was a wonderful view on the village and what was happening. Between her own observations and those of her chess partner, she had a very good measure of who was who and what was what in the village.

People could be very indiscreet when they thought they were alone, and just because the main street was empty, it didn't mean that no one was watching. It also helped considerably that the only decent bit of mobile reception was right outside the shop window, and sound really did travel, especially when you were dusting all those little trinkets that were so handily positioned in the corners. Gen had several times suggested that the windows should be double-glazed to keep out the draughts, but Clarissa had told her to get another cardigan. An oil heater behind the counter had solved the problem.

Clarissa walked slowly through to the kitchen, running her faceted black pearl up and down its gold chain. The moment that

Tess had mentioned that Laetitia's van had been left unlocked, alarm bells had gone off in Clarissa's head. She had no idea why the local Gardai weren't taking this more seriously. Obviously Laetitia was an adult, but really . . .

Reaching the kitchen, Clarissa glanced out of the back door. Merlin had returned and was lying across the closely cropped grass in a patch of sunlight, his thick black coat almost brown in the rays. Clarissa liked that he spent most of his time up with Tess; he was like her familiar, even if she didn't know it, protecting her from whatever might be lurking around the house. Rumours of a curse were pure conjecture, she was sure – servants trying to find logic in the dreadful things that happened in times gone by – but knowing Tess had Merlin for company made Clarissa feel better.

She glanced out of the door again to see that Malachi was collecting flowerpots, building a Martian landscape in the rockery. He'd be engaged in interplanetary travel for quite a bit longer, giving Clarissa a few minutes to check some things out. Her iPad was on the coffee table in the living room, beside her embroidery basket. She'd saved all the news reports about the Radio Snatcher and Eoin Doyle's connections with the women who had disappeared. Now would be a good time to go through them and see if there were any parallels with the situation here, any tiny detail that might give them a clue to what had happened.

Putting the iPad down on the scrubbed pine table, Clarissa flicked on the kettle to make herself a cup of tea, opening the cover while she waited for it to boil.

She'd engaged Eoin Doyle in conversation several times, and in fact had deliberately called him to wire up the Waterford chandelier in the shop. She'd wanted to get his measure.

He was definitely a little odd. He talked far too much, about everyone – from his neighbours to his clients – his tattoos were just appalling, and he lived with his mother. But that wasn't at all unusual in this country, for a now unmarried son.

Did it make him a murderer? Clarissa wasn't sure. She'd always felt that the cases she'd read about had to have someone clever at their core. Someone who was a planner. Perhaps that was Doyle.

He certainly seemed to know everyone's business, and she'd been able to fill in quite a few gaps in her own observations from his incessant chatter.

He'd been very open that he didn't talk to his wife any more – she had a barring order against him. She'd never got on with his mother, and that's where the friction had come from, apparently. He wasn't a violent man but the police had taken her side. Clarissa had looked up the details of the case after he'd left and eventually found the court papers.

They'd both been drunk. She'd whacked him with a frying pan and he'd grabbed it from her and slapped her back. And knocked her out.

The kettle boiled behind her and Clarissa popped a camomile teabag into a mug, taking it to the table and sitting down. She really wanted to go through all the press reports. She woke up the iPad and opened Chrome. It was still showing the last page she'd been looking at – a search on Aidan Gaunt. She was quite fascinated by his background.

She typed in Eoin Doyle's name and began to trawl again.

Chapter 27

IN THE CAR park beside the west wing of Kilfenora House, Tess had set up mission control beside Laetitia's van. She'd never organised anything like this before, but she'd watched enough true crime on TV to have an idea how it should be done.

The guards had been utterly useless when she'd called this morning – doubling up on Ally's conversation, Tess knew, but thinking that with some persuasion and the news about the radio being left on, they might actually do something. Instead she'd got a lecture about Tis being an adult and how some people just needed space and that leaving a radio on wasn't an offence. Which hadn't been her point at all.

Basically they'd repeated exactly what they'd said to Ally, with a healthy dose of 'mind your own business' thrown in.

Now, leaning into Gen's hatchback, maps spread all over the rear compartment, she marked off another square on the patchwork of fields, gardens and woodlands that made up the estate, double-checking the WhatThreeWords co-ordinates from the text on her phone. Behind her she heard another car pull into the almost full car park, and the crunch of feet on gravel.

'I brought you coffee.' She turned around at the familiar voice as Aidan materialised behind her, a takeaway cup in his hand. 'Thought you might need it. Latte, two sugars, right?'

Straightening up, Tess smiled gratefully. She didn't think she'd ever needed a coffee more.

'Thanks so much – how did you know?'

Aidan grinned and tapped his nose, nodding a greeting to Gen as she hurried to the car, her phone in her hand. The reception was patchy here and she had been walking about the now full car park, trying to pick up the incoming messages from the searchers.

'Sorry, Genevieve, didn't realise you were up here, too, or I'd have got you one as well. I can run back?'

Bending to mark off the square just confirmed by text, Gen waved her pencil in the general direction of the rear seat.

'I brought a flask, you're fine, but thanks.'

Aidan took a sip of his own coffee. 'How's it going? Expecting a long haul?'

Tess grimaced. 'It's going to take the day to search the grounds. I've got your people doing the woods and the adventure playground. They should be finished in time for your rehearsal, but we've no news yet.'

'Honestly, where could she be, assuming she's still on the estate at all?'

Cradling the warm coffee cup in her hands, Tess looked out across the gardens and heaved a big sigh. She really didn't know where Laetitia could be, but if she was here and had lost her phone and hurt herself, they needed to find her.

Her mind snapped to Jerry Lynch and his body hunters, but she really couldn't bear to think that something like that had happened to Laetitia.

Below the car park, the gardens fell away towards the woods, Apollo in his lake in the centre, reached from here via a terrace that ran the full width of the house, broad elegant steps carrying you down, sweeping around to embrace the view of the mountain peak in the distance. On this western side of the house, winding paths led through specimen trees, past the lake, down to Clarissa's cottage and the adventure playground. On the eastern side, the Rose Walk with its chain of flower beds and ponds began by the glasshouses and led down to the wishing well and yew maze. There was just so much ground to search, but starting at the bottom of the formal gardens seemed sensible, working up towards the house and stable yard. Tess had divided the surrounding fields between the gardeners, who had taken quad bikes to try and cover them before dark.

The thought that Lynch's tracker dogs could be useful in all of this was nipping at the corner of Tess's mind, but she wasn't about to tell a tabloid journalist that a woman was missing from a location that Eoin Doyle had access to – again. The guards definitely needed to be told long before him if the searchers found anything – or, more to the point, if they didn't.

'Where do you want me?'

Aidan's voice interrupted Tess's thoughts and she realised she'd drifted off. She looked around for Genevieve, but she'd gone off again to the other side of the camper van, waving her phone in the air trying to get a signal, her dress, blues and greens today, flashing like a peacock's tail in the sunlight.

Tess paused for a moment. What was the best thing Aidan could do? Start searching closer to the house? Megan's words about him and Laetitia having a fling were nagging at her.

How well did he know Laetitia? Could he shed any light on any of this? Was it even her place to ask? He looked worried, but not distraught. But then people had one-night stands all the time – well, they had when Tess had been in college. She just wasn't the sort of person who could understand how that worked. And in her experience, there was usually one party who was hoping it would be more than one night.

Maybe it hadn't been a fling at all, but had all been in Laetitia's head? Tess was quite sure Aidan Gaunt's dark good looks featured in quite a few of the locals' imaginations, although there was something about his face that didn't appeal to her at all. He was too pretty for her taste.

'Ally said Laetitia was having problems sleeping, that she sometimes wandered around the grounds at night.'

Tess wasn't even sure where she was going with that statement, but she watched his reaction carefully. Had he met her here, perhaps?

Aidan frowned and took another sip of his coffee. 'That's a bit worrying. The estate is very peaceful, but . . . Well, it's not like it's super-secure. It's so big, anyone could be wandering around.'

'I know, that's half the problem with launching a search.' Tess took a sip of her own coffee. 'I'm just really getting worried about her mental health – the argument with her parents that landed her living in the van in the first place. She's what Clarissa describes as highly strung.'

'I think you're right – it seems to come with being an artist, doesn't it? I mean . . .' He turned to nod at the van. 'She seemed very happy living here, but I know she got quite depressed sometimes. Do you think Conor's accident could have pushed her over the edge?'

141

Chapter 28

'BUT WE CAN'T stop, she has to be here somewhere.' Looking pale and exhausted, her hair falling loose from her ponytail, Ally leaned on the side of Gen's car and ran her hand into her fringe. As she spoke her phone pipped with a text. She glanced at it. 'Meg's on her way back up. She's been right down to the river.'

It was almost seven and Tess had had to let the staff go, the last few stragglers from the village heading to the pub around six, where Mark Mulligan had organised sandwiches for the searchers. She'd been a little overwhelmed when he'd texted her to let her know. He'd sent his bar staff to help out, too, had been manning the bar himself for the afternoon.

'We've covered everywhere up to the line of the house. The tea rooms have been open all day, and she's not there, someone would have seen her.' Tess pulled her map out of the back of the car and spread it across the windows at the side so Ally could see. 'Now we've just got this strip around the terrace and the greenhouses, and over around the Sugar Canister, then the house itself to search, but everyone's exhausted. I can't keep them any longer.'

'But . . .'

Tess raised her hands. 'I know. Let's take a break and grab something to eat and we can come back this evening. It won't be dark until almost ten, so we've got a bit more daylight. I'd rather search the house in the morning, to be absolutely honest, but we can finish here and at least we'll know the grounds are done.'

Ally began to protest again but Tess cut her off. 'You and Meg need to take a break. Go home and I'll meet you here at eight. Clarissa's got dinner on for us, so we won't be far away. Can you check in with your mum and dad and Laetitia's friends again?'

'My parents think we're both overreacting and that she's wandered off with some guy.' Ally sighed and ran her hand over her eyes. 'They think she's a total flake. She's gone off on holiday and not told them before, but she always tells us.'

'Look, we'll all be fresher after a bit of a break. We really need to find her phone – it has to be somewhere. If we can find it, we can see who she was talking to most recently. They might know if she was planning to go away.'

'Meg tracked it on Google. This is the last place it pinged. She wouldn't have it with her and have left it switched off for this long.'

'Unless the battery had died.' Tess grimaced. 'But I know – then she would have come back to charge it.'

'Meg's going to try the guards again, see if they can get her phone records or something. She didn't have her phone or her WhatsApp linked to her laptop, so we can't look there, but we'll go through Facebook and Instagram again. She used them a lot.'

Tess leaned over to give her a hug.

'We'll find her, really we will.'

Tess could smell the barbecue in Clarissa's garden as she got out of the car and followed Gen inside, her stomach queasy with

143

what she hoped was hunger. She hadn't stopped all day and she had no time to be ill now.

Clarissa had left the front door open, and as they went inside the single-storey cottage, they could hear the sounds of a video game in the front room. Gen stuck her head in to check on Malachi as Tess made her way straight through into the kitchen and out of the door that connected it with the sun trap of a garden.

Standing in front of a very professional-looking gas barbecue, Clarissa was wearing her bright red apron and had a long fork in one hand and a glass of wine in the other, her green reading glasses balanced on the end of her nose.

'Malachi wanted burgers. I thought as I had the barbeque on we'd take advantage of it. Wine's on the kitchen counter.'

Tess backed up and, seeing an open bottle of white, poured herself and Gen a glass each. Gen preferred a spritzer and would add ice and water when she was ready. The bottle was just out of the fridge and deliciously cool. Popping it back inside, Tess picked up her glass and went outside to join Clarissa, who was manoeuvring the steaks on the griddle.

She glanced up as Tess approached. 'How did you get on?'

'We actually got much more ground covered than I thought we would. But nothing yet. It's just so weird – it's like she popped out for a minute and never came back.'

Clarissa grimaced. 'I do hope she's OK. I always found her lovely.' Sliding the last steak on to the heat, she took a sip of her wine. 'Malachi's very happy to stay with me tonight if Gen wants to keep looking with you. No need for her to come back here.'

Tess sighed. 'I told Ally we'd meet her and Meg at eight by Laetitia's van. I'm exhausted, we all are, being out in this heat all day is draining, but we need to keep looking. At least then they will know we did our best.'

Clarissa flipped over the steaks on the barbecue.

'I don't know how Laetitia could park in that car park and stay there all night on her own. I wouldn't walk around the grounds at night in all honesty, and I don't even believe in ghosts.' Clarissa looked over her glasses at Tess. 'Gen updated me on your most interesting conversation with Mark.'

Tess took a sip of her wine. 'I did wonder if Laetitia had seen or heard something strange. She never mentioned anything, but then I didn't know she was walking around at night.'

Gen emerged through the patio doors as Tess spoke, ice clinking in her glass.

'Mal's had a fabulous day, Mum, you *have* been spoiling him.'

'I didn't want him running around in the woods or the adventure playground, so we've been baking and sorting out the flower beds. Merlin has been assisting ably as chief watcher of workers.'

Tess looked around at the borders. She could see where they'd cut back the overhanging foliage.

'I thought I could smell lavender.'

Clarissa shook her head. 'We did the ivy. Mal likes chopping things.'

Gen laughed. 'That's for sure. And he's wiped out now.'

Clarissa smiled benignly; she'd obviously enjoyed her day a lot more than they had.

'It's the heat, I think, we were outside all day. Will you keep going tomorrow?'

Tess swished the wine around her glass. 'Yes, until we've checked everywhere. We've had brilliant help from the village.

Everyone was out at some point, so we've got most of the gardens covered. I didn't want to interrupt rehearsals any more, but we had the full cast, too, until after lunch.'

'Was Aidan helping as well?'

'Yes, the only people I think we were missing, apart from the Gardai obviously, were Mark because he had to keep the pub open, and Dr O'Riordan – he was on weekend cover. His wife was manning the phone at home in case Laetitia called.' She stopped speaking for a moment. 'I can't believe he went back to work, in all honesty, but he's very old-school. Perhaps his work and patients are more important than his family.' She took a sip of her wine. 'Ally thinks they aren't taking any of this seriously. They seem sure Laetitia's utterly unreliable and has gone off with a friend and not told anyone. They seem more upset at the fuss than the fact that she's actually missing.'

Gen snorted. 'That sounds about right. Dr O'Riordan hates anything that's not running precisely to plan. Whenever I need to call out of hours, I'm always relieved to get his locum.'

Clarissa opened her eyes wide. 'I'm hoping Malachi might be inclined to do medicine, given his extensive experience of the profession. Definitely better than the stage.'

Despite her exhaustion and the constant worry of the day, Tess couldn't resist a grin. Clarissa had a way of delivering lines that were testimony to her acting successes.

'You loved it really. All actors do. Aidan's the same – you both love controlling an audience.'

Clarissa raised her eyebrows and took a sip of her wine.

'How do you like your steak, Tess?'

'Rare, like my men. Although chance would be a fine thing.'

Gen looked at her sideways. 'Aidan seems very interested in you.'

'Is he?' Tess did a double take. 'I never got that impression.'

'Definitely. I told you that when he first moved into the village he was full of questions about you and the house, and look at him popping up with coffee today . . .'

Tess frowned. 'He's always arriving with coffee. God, I hope I'm not missing something. He's really not my type. Goodness only knows how he landed up in Kilfenora with his background.'

Clarissa picked up a plate from the wing of the barbecue and lifted off the first steak.

'Knives and forks are on the table, salads in the bowls.' She poked the next steak to see how well it was done. 'I'm not sure about his background. He seems to have done some bits of TV and local theatre, but like many of us, there are gaps in his résumé.'

Moving over to the garden table, Tess put her glass down and pulled the cling film off the bowls of salad and coleslaw Clarissa had prepared.

'That seems to be par for the course for actors, though, doesn't it? More time waiting tables than for the curtains to open?'

'For some, indeed.' Clarissa lifted off another steak. 'This one's ready, too. You should have time to relax for five minutes before you go back up.'

Tess pulled out a chair to sit down at the mosaic table.

'There really aren't very many places left to look, except the house, of course. But I'm in and out all day, I really don't think she could be there.'

Clarissa looked thoughtful. 'But all those rooms, and there's the attic and the cellar to check. The servants' passages are an absolute warren. She could have slipped and fallen down the back stairs.'

147

Bringing her plate to the table, Gen pulled out another chair.

'You're in and out of the ballroom, but there are rooms in the wings that nobody's been in for years except the builders.'

'True. I'm sure there are passages I haven't even found yet.'

Tess was about to say more when she stopped dead. A distant sound like a wail had suddenly filled the air, growing in intensity as it repeated.

'Is that a fox?' Gen opened her eyes wide in alarm.

'I really don't think so.' Tess hesitated for a second and then pushed her chair back. The sound was a scream – she was sure of it. 'I'm so sorry, Clar, I think we need to go. Can you put this in the fridge?'

Chapter 29

THE ONLY CAR left in the car park when Tess and Gen arrived was Ally and Megan's dad's sleek Audi, parked where it had been all day. As Gen pulled on her handbrake, Tess looked across at her and let out a sharp breath. They'd had the windows open on the way up from Clarissa's, taking the narrow service road that ran between the gardens and the fields on the western side of the estate. It had only taken a few minutes at the speed Gen had been driving.

The sound of screaming had stopped halfway.

Tess wasn't sure if that was a good thing or not.

As Tess swung the car door open, she saw Ally running towards them down the narrow yew walk that led to the Sugar Canister Tower. Tess wasn't sure if she was running towards them or her father's car, but as she burst out of the trees, she spotted them.

'Get my dad, quickly, we've found her. I think it's too late.'

Gen started the engine again as Tess slammed the door closed behind her, reversing at speed to throw the car into a three-point turn.

Ally's face was taut; even her blue eyes looked pale. She was incredibly calm, but there was a sense of urgency about her, of energy about to be released. Tess could feel her own heart rate increase as she ran to her, and Ally grabbed her by the upper arms as if she was trying to steady herself.

'I've got through to call an ambulance but it'll be ages. She's cold, Tess, so cold. I need you to help me get her down.'

Questions tumbling around her head, Tess registered the word 'down' and felt a dark hole open in her stomach, but Ally had already turned and was running down the yew walk, her trainers throwing up clouds of dust from the tinder-dry path.

Tess followed her, the trees opening up to reveal the gravelled areas looping around the tower. The builders had erected huge steel frame fences on the inside of the path to keep people out, but a section of the hoarding had been pulled free and, ahead of her, Ally squeezed through it.

This was the one place that they hadn't looked yet. Tess could feel her heart thumping as if it was trying to break out of her chest.

Tess pushed through to the path on the inside. A castellated stone platform had been built into the hill to support the building. The fairytale tower, that looked more like a rook from a chess set than a sugar shaker, rose from its centre, the walls constructed from rough granite stones. It appeared to be medieval, slit windows on each side giving the impression that archers were drawing their bows.

The ornate wrought-iron gate was wide open at the bottom of the tower.

Swinging down the narrow steps to the gate, Ally glanced over her shoulder to see if Tess was following and then slipped inside and ran up the stairs. Tess could hear footsteps echoing on the spiral stone treads as Ally ran up.

Checking the gate as she passed through it, Tess followed, her legs burning as she skipped up the steps. From the main room at the top of these stairs, a smaller flight of stone steps brought you to a walkway that ran around the very top of the castellated tower. Tess had only been up here a few times, but the view of the estate was spectacular.

As Tess emerged at the top of the stairs, she saw Ally get in beside Megan under something that was hanging from the rafters. As Ally took the weight, Megan literally fell to her knees, her face alabaster, streaked with tears.

It only took Tess a moment to work out what had happened.

Looking up, she could see that a rope had been slung over one of the rafters, and Laetitia, wearing a long black dress, was hanging from it. Her body swung as Ally adjusted her position, her shoulder under Laetitia's feet. One of Laetitia's bright red ballerina shoes had fallen off, was lying uselessly to one side. Tess felt as if time had suddenly slowed and everything was happening in some sort of jerky freeze-frame horror video.

Ally's eyes met Tess's as Megan curled up sobbing on the floor, her arms wrapped around her knees, her cries like a wounded animal. Tess pulled her phone out from her jeans pocket and looked for reception. There wasn't any – Tess took a step sideways, checking to see if she could pick up a signal. They needed to know where that ambulance was. How long did they have?

Holding Laetitia's legs steady, Tess could see Ally was trying to hold herself together, her voice hoarse.

'Meg came up to see if she could get a view across the gardens.' Her voice cracked as she spoke. 'I heard her screaming . . . I just don't understand, this doesn't make any sense.'

Above them, the load-bearing rafter creaked like a tree in a high wind. Tess glanced up nervously. The roof was well over a hundred years old, the beams dried out from the constant breeze that channelled between the slit windows. Another creak and

Tess felt her stomach flip. Could the whole roof come down on top of them?

Her eyes fixed on the screen of her phone, Tess skirted the small circular room, keeping as close to the wall as she could, her feet ringing hollow on the dusty wooden floor.

Checking back anxiously, Tess dared to look up. Laetitia's head was hanging uselessly to one side, her lips black, the rope tight. How on earth had she got up there? There was no stepladder or stool in the tiny room. Had she somehow scaled the wall and jumped from one of the window sills? A line from the play suddenly leaped into Tess's head: "*Cut is the branch that might have grown full straight.*"

Tess glanced at her screen, biting her lip. Ally was right that it was too late. How long had she been here? Had this happened on Friday evening and no one had realised?

Chapter 30

LEANING BACK IN her desk chair, Tess could just see out across the low garden wall and the lane to the coach house entrance, the moon creating shadows on the cobbled stable yard inside.

Today felt as if it had been the longest day of her life. And now, on top of feeling exhausted, she was feeling distinctly queasy. Hardly surprising, really, given what had happened, but part of her wondered if she'd had too much coffee. Or perhaps it was just . . . well, everything – the events of the day coupled with the intense heat.

She still couldn't believe it. The ambulance had come eventually, along with a patrol car from Rockfield. Tess didn't think she'd ever forget the expression on Ally's face, the hardening of her jaw as the officer had asked her about Laetitia.

'So she lives in a camper van in the car park here?' His tone had been a mixture of incredulous and disbelieving. 'She's a bit of a hippy, then?'

'She's not a hippy. She just needed a bit of space. That happens, you know.' Ally's tone had been cold; his assumptions about Laetitia were clear on his face. 'And before you ask, she didn't take drugs, she didn't even drink. This is absolutely out of character.'

'And does she have a boyfriend? Could she have had a row with someone?'

Ally had glared at him 'She wasn't in a long-term relationship, no, and no, she hadn't had a row that I know of. Look, we were with her on Friday and she was upset about Conor Kelly's accident, but she wasn't *suicidal*.'

The guard had nodded and chewed the end of his pen for a few moments before he flipped his notebook closed and slipped it into the top pocket of his shirt.

And that had been that.

Tess tore her eyes away from the paned window and sighed loudly. Ally and Megan would be home by now, but she didn't imagine anyone in that house would get much sleep tonight. It was just such a shock. Laetitia had been a bit alternative, but to Tess she'd always seemed to be so grounded, said she loved living here, being so close to nature.

Tess tried to clear her mind, but the images from this evening kept scrolling through her head like some bizarre TikTok reel. Gen had decided to go to Clarissa's rather than stay overnight – to be close to Mal, Tess was sure. It was one of those nights when you needed to be close to those you loved. Tess twisted the thin gold ring on her finger. It was at times like this she missed Kieran more than ever.

She was shattered. Perhaps that was why she felt so unwell. She ran her hand over her face. She'd opened her spreadsheets to try and distract herself, but her figures still weren't working and her head was too full to focus on projected profit and . . . 'loss'.

She didn't even want to think the word, especially not tonight, let alone say it. There definitely wasn't room at Kilfenora for loss. This whole venture just *had* to work.

Putting her hands into her curls on the top of her head, massaging her scalp, Tess closed her eyes. She'd thought Friday had been bad, with Jerry Lynch and then poor Conor. But today it had all got worse.

Tess felt awful even thinking about it all like that, under these circumstances, but the whole village needed Kilfenora to be a success, and the TV crew who had been following the restoration needed a happy ending to the Kilfenora story.

They'd filmed all the dramatic bits – or so they'd thought: the storms ripping tiles off the roof; the sewage system backing up the day the first couple came to look at it as a possible wedding venue. Now it was time to show the world how hard work paid off, how buildings like Kilfenora could be turned from crumbling ruins into community hubs. And to show the Twitter troll that he'd failed to intimidate her, that she was stronger than him and his vicious nonsense.

There was still a part of her frightened that he had reappeared in her world, but the more she thought about it, the less likely it seemed he might physically appear. Maybe he *had* tipped off Jerry Lynch, but bullies like that rarely came out from behind their screens. They were cowards at the end of the day. Tess was sure it was her success that had made her a focus, and that was something people like that would never have.

One thing she knew for sure, though: when they returned to film the finale of the series, the *Country House Restoration* team really wouldn't want Lynch's TV crew on site filming the place being dug up by the guards in search of human remains. That wasn't part of the Kilfenora narrative at all.

When she'd first arrived, between the damp and the remnants of a chimney fire, the house had been a wreck, room after room in the east wing blackened with smoke. *Teams* of people had worked on the house over the past few years. She'd managed to restore the main part of the house, uncovering ornate plaster and hand-printed wallpapers in the process. There was still a lot to do, but she'd felt from the first day that the house was happy to have her here, that it loved being occupied, being used again, that somehow it had been lonely without a family living here. Now she was Kilfenora's family, and she had a responsibility to the house – as well as to the village – to bring it back to life.

She deliberately looked away from the screen and yet again became aware of the 1980s Laura Ashley wallpaper that someone, at some point in the year of bad taste, had chosen for the study. China blue with a tiny white floral repeat.

She'd always particularly hated this mid-not-quite-blue, and the size of the flowers on the print drove her insane; it was irritatingly small. Whoever had decorated this cottage must have had shares in Laura Ashley or loved flowers. There wasn't a room without them. At least they'd gone for big blowsy roses in the bedroom.

Perhaps it was the office that was making her feel ill now. Perhaps she needed someone to look at the feng shui and the colours in here, to make it more conducive to success. If, when she'd moved in, she'd known how much time she was going to spend in here, she'd have painted it all white. But there hadn't been time.

Tess sighed. A headache was forming behind her eyes. She needed to finish up here. She knew the figures would *sort of* balance eventually, but she didn't dare total the columns yet. The week after next, when they were over the opening weekend festivities, the tours had started, and there was money coming in, then she'd take a look. That was assuming she could put off this other TV crowd and Jerry bloody Lynch from the *Daily News* long enough to get the place open without a scandal.

Would people want to bring their families to a house where awful things seemed to be occurring with alarming regularity and a serial killer had buried the remains of his victims? She really didn't think so.

MONDAY

Chapter 31

THERE WERE MANY ways that Tess had thought she would be spending the Monday morning of opening week, but none of them involved the Gardai and grieving relatives, or Mark Mulligan sitting at her kitchen table talking about ghosts.

Although by the time he appeared on her doorstep, he was a very welcome distraction.

Between the phone ringing and the doorbell, Tess was starting to feel as if her cottage was becoming some sort of branch of lost and found, or the Samaritans. There was a collective shock about the events of yesterday, deepened, Tess was sure, by the whole village being involved in the search for Laetitia. And this morning everyone seemed to need to talk.

She'd just put the phone down to Gen when the local guard, the keen young one with the acne – Tess had forgotten his name already, but she'd seen him occasionally patrolling the village in a squad car – had dropped in to say that they'd finished with the Sugar Canister Tower. As he'd lingered on the doorstep, his colleague waiting in the patrol car outside her gate, he'd mentioned that his mum was in a book club with the doctor's wife when the girls were small, and nobody could believe the news.

Tess was with him on that one.

The patrol car had just pulled away when Aidan appeared, again the bearer of coffee. As she opened the front door, Merlin materialised beside her, hissing as he stalked past Aidan on the doorstep and vanishing into the flower bed. Tess almost rolled her eyes. He really was the most contrary cat. He had an opinion on everything and seemed to come and go like some sort of spirit.

The scent of summer flowers wafted in from her tiny front garden as she stepped back, holding the front door open wide for Aidan.

'I'm sorry, ignore him, he doesn't even live here. You heard the news?'

Aidan sighed, pausing on the doorstep to pass her one of the takeaway coffee cups he was holding, his face grim.

'I did. I thought you might need this.'

She followed him into the kitchen as he pulled out a chair and sat down. It didn't take him long to get to the point.

'I really think we need to keep going with the play. Laetitia put so much work into the set and the costumes, they are really a legacy to her. I hope her parents and sisters will be proud.'

Tess sat down heavily at the head of the table and sipped the coffee he'd brought her. She'd been feeling distinctly off since yesterday, and lack of sleep was catching up with her.

'I think you're right. Meg and Ally are distraught, obviously, but they both said she'd have wanted the show to go on.' Tess shook her head, leaning her elbow on the table to run her hand over her eyes. 'They really can't understand how she could suddenly do something this drastic. None of us can.'

Aidan nodded slowly. Dark stubble added to the impression that he hadn't slept very well either.

'I don't understand it, in all honesty. I . . .' He faltered for a moment. 'We . . . er . . . had a sort of a thing. Very casual, but the last time I saw her she was fine. I mean she's always a bit . . . well, "alternative", but she seemed to be in great form.' He shook his head. 'I don't know, it doesn't make sense, but I suppose these things rarely do.'

'When did you see her last?' Suddenly more alert, Tess warmed her hands on the takeaway cup, trying to fight the shivers that were running up her spine.

'Friday. I wanted to check she was OK after Conor, I mean it was such a shock.'

'And was she?'

Tess screwed up her nose. Had Laetitia told Aidan that she'd also had a bit of a thing for Conor? Tess rather doubted it, but it could have been a factor and made her reaction more extreme.

'Shaken. But she didn't say anything that would make me think . . . I mean . . .' He raised his hands helplessly. He seemed to have run out of words.

'I know. I've been thinking a lot about it – perhaps she really was suffering and we just didn't know it.'

Aidan shook his head. 'I blame myself. I should have seen it.'

Tess leaned across the table and patted his arm, exactly as Clarissa had done with her.

'It's not your fault, it's nobody's fault. Sometimes the demons and feelings of despair just get too much and people take radical action, do unexpected things.'

Tess drew in a breath. She'd been that person once. She'd been young and emotional, and then the unimaginable had happened, and it had been devastating for everyone involved.

Kieran's death had brought her close to the edge. The one thing she'd learned was that you had to move forward in life; you couldn't carry regrets with you or they dragged you down.

A knock at the door brought them both out of a deepening silence. Tess brushed away a tear. Laetitia had been so full of creative energy, constantly inquisitive, very in touch with what Clarissa called her intuitive side. It was a terrible loss.

Taking the interruption as his cue, Aidan stood up.

'I'd better go. If you're happy for us to go on, we'll get everyone focusing on the play. It'll help us all get through this. We'll dedicate opening night to Laetitia and to Conor's recovery.'

Tess slid her chair back, her smile weak.

'That's a lovely idea.'

Opening the door to let Aidan out, Tess was surprised to see Mark on the doorstep. He stepped aside to let Aidan down the path, clapping him on the shoulder with an understanding grimace as he passed.

As Tess opened the door wider to let Mark in, Merlin appeared from the undergrowth and shot inside with him, winding around his legs.

'He likes you.'

Mark turned towards the kitchen, trying to get through the hall without tripping over the cat.

'I seem to have an affinity with animals.'

Mark bent down and scooped Merlin up. Tess hesitated, wincing slightly, waiting for Merlin to lash out, but instead he started to rub his head on Mark's chin.

'Goodness, you really do. He spends half his life here and he won't let me pick him up.'

Mark walked through into the kitchen and spotted the takeaway coffee cup on the table.

'I'm sorry to interrupt . . .'

Tess shook her head. 'I think Aidan wanted someone to talk to. Can I get you a coffee? I need intravenous caffeine today.'

Chapter 32

PEERING OUT DOWN the main street, Genevieve flipped the sign hanging inside the salvaged art deco shop door to 'open'. She'd come in for nine to get ready for the day, but really hadn't felt like opening, and from the preoccupied faces of anyone passing, she didn't think, today of all days, that she was going to be overwhelmed with locals dropping in either. Calling Tess to check in and see if she was all right hadn't made things any better.

It was almost eleven now, though, and she was here, so it seemed silly not to unlock the door. Whatever about the village being quiet, Fortune Finds had become a bit of a destination after the TV show focusing on the restoration of Kilfenora; people came from all over the country looking for specialist pieces, in person and online. Although realistically she made most of her money at the auctions, buying and selling, the handful of high-end interior designers from around the world who retained her services were not in the slightest bit worried about price tags. Which was something of a blessing. Selling the odd vintage china plate to an American tourist wasn't going to put food on the table, to say nothing of keeping the considerable number of lights on in the shop itself.

As Genevieve turned to look up the street towards the pub, she saw Clarissa walking purposefully towards her, one hand raised in a wave, her wicker shopping basket over her other arm. Smiling, Gen pulled the door open, the heat of the sun reflecting off the pavement and tarmac hitting her. Even in this weather, Clarissa had one of her many cardigans slung around her shoulders, today cornflower blue, picking up the forget-me-not print on her short-sleeved Liberty shirt and the sparkling ring on her finger. Clarissa had done very well for jewellery from all three of her husbands. There were times when Gen wondered if she had intentionally picked men who were likely to have heart attacks as partners. But then trying to keep up with Clarissa would give anyone a heart attack.

Gen shielded the sun from her eyes with her hand as Clarissa reached her.

'What have you done with Mal?'

'Play date, just for the morning. The solicitor's son, I can never remember his name. I've just dropped him off. He heard me on the phone mentioning the tower and wants to go back up it with Tess. I needed to distract him.'

Gen sighed. 'Good plan. If he thought you weren't going to take him, he'd probably escape and go by himself.' She stood against the door. 'Come in out of the heat. Are the guards still up there?'

Clarissa came inside and headed for the counter to put her basket down.

'No idea, but I'd imagine they need to take photographs or something. At least the tower isn't in the main part of the gardens.'

Gen sighed and, letting the door fall closed, the bell tinkling, she followed Clarissa to the counter, slipping around her onto her stool. Putting her elbows on the counter, she rubbed her face with her hands.

'They seemed quite satisfied that it was suicide yesterday, though God only knows how she managed it. That ceiling beam is so high, she must have been determined to climb up.'

Clarissa pursed her lips. 'I wondered about that, too.'

'I suppose there will have to be a post mortem. God, it's just so awful for her family. I mean . . . Laetitia?'

Clarissa leaned her hip on the counter and pulled the basket towards her, lifting the red and white check cloth covering the contents.

'The least likely person in the whole village to have mental health issues? I thought that, too. I know not everyone wants to live in a camper van, but whenever I met her walking in the gardens, she was just so relaxed and happy and in tune with the place.' She took a pile of table napkins out of the basket and put them on the counter. 'I suppose sometimes we just never know what's happening below the surface. The most happy-go-lucky people can slip into deep dark places. They work so hard at being bright and outwardly OK that it drains them even more.' Clarissa grimaced at the thought. 'I bought you lunch for later, just sandwiches and the end of the chocolate bread.'

'There's some left?' Gen raised her eyebrows in surprise. Malachi's love of chocolate was legendary.

'It's *very* rich.' Clarissa lifted a plastic box out of the basket. 'Why don't you take tomorrow off? Do you have to go to that auction? I thought we could all go to the waterfall or something. I'm thinking of taking Mal to Glendalough this afternoon.' She sighed. 'When something like this happens it makes you think about quality of life and time spent.'

'That's for sure. And you're right. I'd love to, I just need to confirm Katie-Lou is good to come in tomorrow.'

'Why wouldn't she be?'

Gen frowned. 'I texted her again on Sunday about the sugar box from that Minton cabaret set you couldn't find on Saturday, and she still hasn't replied.' Gen paused. 'I think she said her mother was away for a few days, but I don't think she went with her.'

Clarissa raised her eyebrows, voicing Gen's thoughts.

'If they were both away she'd ask Mal to feed the chickens. Did you try her again today? Not everyone's attached at the hip to their phone, you know.'

'You might not be, Mum, but Katie-Lou definitely is. I've never seen it out of her hand.'

'Perhaps she's sick?' Clarissa opened the lid of the Tupperware box.

Gen bit her lip, worry swirling inside her.

'Something must be wrong. I've never known her to take this long to reply.'

Chapter 33

As Tess brought the freshly made coffee to the kitchen table, a yawn slipped out.

'Oh God, I'm sorry. I didn't sleep very well.'

Mark smiled at her. 'I'm not surprised. There's been a lot happening.'

Tess rolled her eyes. 'That's for sure. And now I really need to talk about something different. I'm not sure it's ghosts, but try me.'

Mark hesitated for a moment, as if he wanted to ask her something, but then picked up his own coffee.

'I had a good look at the legends and stories surrounding this place. I'm guessing you want as much publicity as possible for the opening, so I've put posts in a few forums about the house opening to the public. A lot of people came back and asked about ghost tours.'

'Anything that gets people here is wonderful, but have we got any *actual* ghosts?'

There were all sorts of stories in the village of ghostly women and children playing on the lawns. But she'd lived here for two and a half years, and she'd had a few strange feelings walking around the place, particularly in the winter when it got dark early, but she'd never seen anything herself. She'd heard doors slamming occasionally when she'd been in the house on her own, but she'd put that down to the wind getting in under the eaves.

Mark smiled at her over the rim of his mug, his eyes a warm blue.

'There have been a lot of sightings over the years. Auditory and visual, smells . . . the whole lot, really. It's the ley lines – lines of energy. They cross here. I think that's why Laetitia O'Riordan loved living in the grounds. She was a very psychic person. Not in an actual predicting the future sense, but very connected.'

Tess's surprise must have shown on her face. Mark's eyes filled with sadness.

'She had quite a reputation within the community. She was one of the most respected tarot readers in the country, quite sought after at festivals. I don't think anyone here realised how good she was.'

'Really?' Tess couldn't keep the surprise out of her voice. She certainly had had no idea, and she would bet Gen didn't either. But perhaps it wasn't something Laetitia needed to broadcast locally; it didn't strike Tess as something Laetitia's parents would understand. 'But isn't tarot about predicting the future?'

It came out before she had a chance to stop it, the words hovering between them, magnifying the unanswered questions about Laetitia and how her future had been so abruptly curtailed.

His face grim, Mark shook his head. 'Not exactly. Tarot tells us stories about our lives and ways we could live them better. Have you never had your cards done?'

Tess shrugged. After Kieran's accident, she'd been tempted, but then she'd spotted the job in Dubai. She'd felt she didn't need to know more about the future at that stage – she just needed to get on with it. She frowned as she considered what he'd said.

'Do you think we're OK running ghost tours when we've had a recent death on the property? I mean . . .'

'It's not in very good taste?' Mark finished the sentence for her. 'I was thinking about that. A lot, actually. I think we need to be very respectful. They would be framed as part of the history of the house.' He shifted in his seat. 'But I know what you mean. I heard you found her . . .'

The reminder made Tess's stomach lurch. The scene in the tower was imprinted on her mind, like when you looked at a bright light and closed your eyes and it was still there. She realised she'd finished her coffee and stood up, turning to the coffee machine, focusing on it while she gathered herself.

'You know that phrase, "some things you can't unsee"? Well, that.' Tess took a deep breath and leaned on the counter. 'Ally warned me, but I really hadn't expected . . . Her lips were black.'

Tess turned around abruptly, trying to get the impression of Laetitia's face out of her mind. Mark was staring out of the kitchen window, his face pale and taut, Merlin, now on the kitchen chair, nudging his hand. He seemed to be in another place entirely. It took Tess a moment to realise why.

Tess's hand shot to her mouth. 'My God, I'm so sorry . . . Your wife.'

It was as if her voice had broken a spell, and he turned to look at her, his blue eyes full of pain.

'Robin Williams said it, didn't he? "All it takes is a beautiful fake smile to hide an injured soul and they will never notice how broken you really are."' He sighed. 'Then something snaps and all the feelings they've been wrestling with suddenly overtake them, and there only seems to be one way out.' He realised Merlin was nudging him and stroked the back of the cat's head gently.

'Sometimes, in that moment, people can make a wrong decision – I mean, we all do it all the time, make wrong decisions, it's just normally not so absolute.'

Tess blinked, searching for suitable words and failing. He didn't realise how right he was. Mark cleared his throat, as if he needed to change the subject.

'You're doing an incredible job, you know, bringing life back to this place.'

'Thanks. Really. Sometimes I wonder if I'm totally mad. It's just been one thing after another since I moved in. I haven't done anything except work here 24/7. I've barely even been to the pub.' She smiled, her eyes meeting his for a moment.

'I noticed. Sit down now and take half an hour off. Everyone needs a bit of headspace. Especially after last night.' He picked up his mug and stood up, gesturing for her to sit. 'I'll make the coffee.'

He was right – she did need to switch off, even more so now; her head felt very full. She did as she was told.

'So tell me about yourself, Mark. How does a man with a PhD end up running a pub?'

Standing beside the machine as it started whooshing and grinding, he grimaced in reply.

'Fate, I suppose you could say. I have a good business in Australia, good partners who run it.' The machine finished and he passed her mug over. 'You heard about Sally, my wife. Around the same time, my parents got sick . . . The Cross Keys has been a family pub for generations. It felt like the right time to come home. I needed the space, but I was only here a month and my dad had a huge heart attack, and then my mum went within a week of him. It was like he was waiting for me or something.'

He sighed. 'Then the bloody pandemic arrived on top of us and I had to close the pub. And I couldn't go back to Oz because the borders were closed, so I decided to do my PhD.'

He said it as if it was the most normal thing in the world. But she'd lost both her parents quite close together, and it unmoored you somehow. And he'd lost his wife as well. She could see why he'd plunged himself into studying.

Catching her look of concern, he sighed. 'I think I'm like you, I'm not very good at doing nothing. Gives you too much time to think.' He hesitated. 'When you lose someone, you start to look at every area of your life. What's that phrase, "You only regret the things you didn't try"?' Well, that's me. I took a year out after my master's to go to Australia and ended up staying there and starting a business, but there was always more I wanted to study – still is.'

Tess sighed inwardly. 'You're right about losing someone. That's how I ended up in Dubai.'

'I'm sorry.' His look of understanding was genuine. 'Someone close?'

Tess hesitated. 'Very. We'd just finished our undergrad finals, we were on the way home from the pub and . . .' She faltered. 'It was a hit-and-run . . .'

'Christ. Did the cops catch him?'

Tess nodded, not quite focusing on the mug in her hand as the images resurfaced. Headlights dazzling, the bramble thorns as she'd fallen into the bushes. Then needles of rain on the back of her neck; trying to do CPR in the dark.

'There was a speed camera further along. It got a clear shot.'

'Reliving that at a trial is doubly traumatising.'

Tess turned her cup, the tiny diamond in her ring catching the light.

'I gave evidence by video link. I'd got the job in Dubai by then, I needed to get out of Dublin.'

'What did he get?'

'Four years. It's pathetic, really. He was drunk. Plastered. I don't know much about him except he worked for some city bank. He was a trader or something, only a couple of years into his career but already a high-flyer.'

'Who thought the law didn't apply to him.' Mark finished the sentence for her.

She nodded. She couldn't bear to even think about him – the driver, the man who she had been full sure had ruined her entire life.

'To this day I haven't ever seen a proper photograph of him – only the one of him going into court with his head down and his hood pulled over. I'm glad – there's no room in my head to obsess about him. I see the car too often in my nightmares to add him into the mix.'

'What brought you back here?'

'I think I was ready. I did . . . what, just over six years in Dubai? It was great but it's not the real world. You can get your car filled up with petrol in the drive at two in the morning, and you never have to lift a finger in the house, but it's an empty place. Everyone is just marking time, making big money while they can, then moving on.'

'But why Kilfenora? You're not originally from around here.'

'No, not at all. I only found this place because Gen had moved up here.' Tess smiled. 'I needed a challenge, something to keep me busy. Everyone I knew in Ireland had moved on, too, or got married. Gen was the only one I was still in touch with properly.'

He grinned. 'You're not afraid of hard work, that's for sure. What's the game plan when it's up and running?'

Tess grimaced. 'That's always the problem with me – I dream up these big projects, get all excited, and forget about the exit strategy.'

'I wouldn't worry about that yet. Get everything ticking over and you can bring in a manager to do the day-to-day stuff while you dream up the next idea. I know Megan O'Riordan would love to get involved. A bit of me thinks she's incredibly jealous of your achievements, but she wants to be part of it, that's for sure.'

'Maybe that's what I need. Someone hungry for success.'

'You're not short of people like that around here. Is this play still happening after everything?'

There was something in his tone that made Tess glance up. She nodded.

'That's what Aidan was here about earlier. He felt Laetitia would have wanted it to go on. A bit of me is worried that the press will twist it to turn me into a money-hungry landlord who's so callous they want to the show to go on despite the accidents, but . . .'

Before Mark could answer, Tess's phone started to ring at the same moment as the house phone, the sound accompanied by a banging on the front door. She looked across at Mark, startled.

'What on earth?'

Chapter 34

CLARISSA LOOKED AT the clock on her kitchen wall. It was almost twelve, the second hand clicking past the bold 1940s style numbers on its ivory face. She was due to pick Malachi up at one, had a little while longer to herself before she headed back to the village.

Exploring Glendalough would keep him busy this afternoon; he'd love roaming around the monastic ruins and the walk to the upper lake. There was something utterly magical about the location – you could sense it as you wandered the twisting narrow paths between the ruins and lurching gravestones.

Part of her felt that she should stay on hand in case Tess needed her for anything, but with Gen in the shop, there were limitations on what she could usefully do with Malachi in tow. Despite spending the morning with his friend, he'd be bouncing about again when she collected him. Clarissa had been exactly the same as a child, and if truth were told, was still like that.

And as she grew older, it was even more important than it had ever been to find joy in everything she did. Life was short.

"*The stars move still, time runs, the clock will strike.*" The line from *Doctor Faustus* came to her as she reached into the fridge for the orange juice. Time was definitely ticking this week. In a few short days Kilfenora would be open to the public, and all Tess's plans would come together.

Clarissa couldn't have been prouder of her, but anxiety nipped at her – worry about everything running smoothly, but also about how Tess was coping. She was hiding it, but Clarissa had the distinct impression that she hadn't been feeling at all well recently.

And if Laetitia was anything to go by, some people were able to conceal how they were feeling quite incredibly. She needed to keep a close eye on Tess.

Clarissa still couldn't fathom Laetitia's death, or the way she'd chosen to go. It just seemed too violent for such a serene person. Clarissa bit her lip. Something must have really tipped her, something they couldn't see. She was sure the guards would look into everything, but the Twitter troll who had plagued Tess was nagging at the back of Clarissa's mind. Gen had said that the abusive messages had started again – the student running the accounts just ignored and blocked them, but what if the troll had targeted Laetitia as well? Clarissa knew she'd been posting pictures of the set and costumes on her accounts, tagging Kilfenora. Had she become a victim, too? Tess was strong but she'd been frightened by some of the messages, felt they were personal, almost as if someone was watching her. Had the same happened to Laetitia?

Filling her glass with ice from the dispenser on the fridge, Clarissa looked up sharply – had she heard a yell on the other side of her hedge? The back door was wide open, but it was hard to tell over the sound of ice cubes cascading into her glass.

Perhaps it was the gardeners. They were putting in huge work to make sure everything was beautiful for the weekend, had been charging around the lake on the ride-on lawnmower for days. The noise had driven her mad. She just hoped they'd finished – while Malachi was out, she was going to have a quiet moment in the garden and work out what she could do for dinner. Having a child around seemed to mean constantly having to think of something new for the next meal.

She took a sip of her juice, glancing at the clock again. She had a strange feeling today, as if something was shifting. Perhaps the pressure of worrying about Tess and the opening was getting too intense.

Outside, she pulled out a chair from the mosaic table. She could half hear the gardeners calling to one another, but there were no lawnmowers today, thank goodness, just the dapple of water from the fountain in the gardens, the gentle buzz of bees, and the sound of a breeze playing through the trees. It felt so idyllic, yet as she sat down, Clarissa could feel the tragedy of Laetitia's death preying on her again, gathering in the quiet moment like a storm cloud. She'd experienced death so many times before, but when it was someone so young and beautiful and so talented, it hit home even harder.

Sighing, Clarissa closed her eyes, the sun on her face, the scent of lavender wafting over from the border. Over the hedge she could hear snatches of conversation, the tone increasingly urgent, but her mind was already full.

Sudden death was always shocking – however it came. As Genevieve had put it when Tess's boyfriend Kieran had been killed, it was like someone ramming a knife through your heart.

In Clarissa's opinion, the main problem was that, as a species, we thought we were somehow immortal – always planning, looking to the next thing, and not living in the moment. Opening her eyes, she took another sip, savouring the sweetness of the juice. It was delicious, but with thoughts of Laetitia bobbing to the surface like the ice in her glass, Clarissa was starting to feel as if she needed something stronger – some of her gin juice, as Malachi called it.

This was the first time since it had happened that she'd allowed herself to stop and think about Laetitia's death, and the loss ran deep. Perhaps that's what she was feeling in the air – the resettling of the universe as it adjusted its plans for them all.

She couldn't imagine how Laetitia's family were coping. The doctor and his daughters had always struck Clarissa as rather dysfunctional, living in their grand Georgian manor on the edge of the village, the mother some sort of recluse now, who rarely ventured out and suffered with her nerves apparently. Clarissa had no idea how they would weather Laetitia's death.

Tess was devastated, too, but she was one of those people who calmly got on with the job, even in a crisis, her focus on what needed to be done blanking out the emotion that clouded judgement until she had space to deal with whatever the issue was. When the opening was over next week, it would hit her, and the storm clouds would open.

Toying with her glass, Clarissa was about to take a sip when she became aware of more voices on the other side of her hedge. A proper commotion. Then from the direction of the lake, she caught what they were saying more clearly.

'The guards are on the way. Did you get hold of Tess?'

Then another voice in reply: 'Tom's gone for her. Holy fecking God, can you believe it?'

Chapter 35

THE DARK SHAPE bobbing in the middle of the Apollo Lake was unmistakably a body. Blue and white crime scene tape had been strung across the whole garden, and now a wheeled gurney was waiting on the path on the opposite edge of the lake. Beside it a black body bag lay on the gravel. The guards had brought a bright orange inflatable dingy with them, and had it moored close by, sunlight bouncing off the surface of the water around it, shimmering as if it was scattered with diamonds.

Tess took a step back from the side of the bridge overlooking the water and turned around to lean on the stone balustrade. She closed her eyes, but the images of men in white forensic suits and ink-blue Garda uniforms was imprinted on her mind. She felt distinctly unwell, a combination of shock and revulsion spiralling dangerously in her stomach. She leaned more heavily against the side of the bridge, her legs suddenly weak.

At least the guards had come quickly this time.

Beside her, Mark was leaning forward, his forearms resting on the stone capping on the side of the bridge, his eyes fixed on the corpse. He hadn't said much since they'd arrived. It seemed as if he was taking everything in. She suddenly realised that she was leaning against him. But he felt warm and solid, and she needed warm and solid right now. Even when she shut her eyes, everything felt as if it was swimming a bit.

There was a flurry of activity in front of her and Tess heard feet on the steps leading down from the house. She opened her eyes to see Aidan heading down towards her.

'Christ, what's happened now?'

Tess let out a breath, unable to form the words. Beside her, Mark turned to look over his shoulder at Aidan, thankfully staying where he was. If he moved, Tess had a feeling she might sway.

Mark sighed before replying. 'It's a woman's body. We'll know more when they are able to get her out. They had to seal everything off first.'

'But how did she get there? I mean . . .'

Mark shrugged and Tess realised he was starting to move. She reached for the balustrade to steady herself as he turned around and folded his arms.

'Hopefully the pathologist will be able to shed some light on that, although whether they'll give us any of the details remains to be seen.' He glanced over his shoulder at the activity on the opposite bank. 'The water flows into the lake from a stream that comes out in the boathouse under here.' He nodded towards the steps, hidden in thick foliage, that ran down the side of the bridge. 'Looks like the current washed her over to that side. Although goodness only knows where she went in.'

Despite there being a boathouse, nobody had taken a boat out on the lake, as far as Tess knew, for years. Tess had been enchanted when she'd ventured down the hidden steps for the first time. With stone statues on either side and the thick planting, it was like the entrance to Fairyland. Or somewhere more sinister.

As Mark continued, a dragonfly flew up to them, hovering for a moment beside Aidan, its body iridescent in the sunlight.

'Perhaps she slipped and fell in, and the current eventually carried her into the middle.'

Perhaps.

Mark glanced over his shoulder again. 'The weed's so thick around where the trees overhang, and under here around the boathouse, it's a wonder she was discovered at all. She could have got stuck anywhere.'

Trying to relax, Tess stuffed her hands into the front pockets of her jeans. The sun was high in the sky now, hot on her face and her bare shoulders, adding to the feeling that if she moved an inch she might throw up. She could almost feel Apollo's eyes boring into her back, staring at them accusingly.

Now she was getting delirious.

'It's definitely a woman?' Aidan shook his head in disbelief. 'Do we know who?'

Mark's voice was grim. 'They can't say for sure until there's been a formal identification. Which could be tricky if the body's been submerged for a while. There's no telling how long it's been there.'

'You seem to know a lot about procedure.'

Tess looked at Aidan in surprise. His comment felt barbed. But perhaps Laetitia's death had affected him more than he had let on. They were all on edge.

As if he hadn't noticed that the air had suddenly become charged with tension, Mark's jaw tightened.

'I do. Too much. I'd rather be pig-ignorant, without question.'

Aidan frowned and was about to retort when Tess cut across him, her voice more confident than she felt.

'Hopefully they can tell us soon.'

'Do they think she jumped in? Maybe it's a friend of Laetitia's. I mean, what are the chances?'

Frowning, Aidan looked past her, across the lake. She really didn't want to turn around to see what they were doing.

Following Aidan's look, Mark turned to watch the activity on the far bank. Tess barely caught his muttered words.

'What are the chances indeed?'

Chapter 36

AS TESS HEADED up to her cottage, Mark striding purposefully beside her, his words echoed in her head. What *were* the chances of all these things happening, and here, of all places?

And Mark didn't even know about Jerry Lynch. Or the Twitter troll.

Thoughts of the Kilfenora Curse rattled through her mind like a freight train, but she didn't let it stop. There was no way she was going there. This was bad enough without superstitions and gossip.

She'd been full sure earlier when she'd answered her mobile and the local Garda sergeant had introduced himself, that he was ringing to say they had evidence supporting Lynch's claim.

She *really* hadn't expected him to be ringing to tell her there was a body in the lake.

'*We're sending in a team. We've called the pathologist, please ensure no members of the public are given access to the area.*'

Moments later, Mark had opened the door to one of the gardeners. The sergeant's words had bounced around her head like ping-pong balls as he'd blurted out what they'd found.

Tess put her keys in the front door and turned to Mark.

'How long will they need to keep the lake and the formal gardens taped off, do you think?'

She pushed it open as she spoke and Merlin shot out, winding himself around both their legs in a figure of eight. Mark scooped him up.

'Depends when they can clear the scene. They need to be satisfied they have all the forensic stuff first.'

They walked through the hall into the kitchen, where their coffee cups sat abandoned on the table, the contents now cold. Again. Tess sighed, and rubbed her face with her hand.

'By Friday, do you think?' She hardly dared say it. But she could see from his face that he understood she wasn't being callous.

'Let's hope so. I think you need to talk to the local guys and see what they say.'

Tess paused for a moment, her head battling with everything that had happened, trying to sort it out into a logical sequence.

But there was nothing logical about sudden death.

'Even if the gardens aren't fully open, can we still have the opening night and run the weekend as planned, do you think? The adventure playground and the Rose Walk are far enough away from the formal gardens. They could open once there was some proper fencing up to keep people away from the lake?'

What was she even talking about? How could she open with dead bodies turning up all over the place?

Mark nodded, absent-mindedly putting Merlin down on the chair and picking up their cups, taking them to the sink. He had the water running and was looking for washing-up liquid before Tess fully realised what he was doing.

'I don't usually expect my guests to wash up.'

He looked up, surprised. 'Oh God, I'm sorry, I wasn't thinking.'

'You're fine, don't let me stop you. I'm very happy to resign responsibility for all domestic chores.'

He smiled at her. 'Get that fancy coffee machine warmed up and we'll see if we can finish it this time. I think we both need double espressos after that.'

Tess reached up to open the cupboard and lift out two more mugs as, behind her, Mark rinsed the crockery they'd used earlier.

'You know . . .?' His back to her, his hands in the sink, Mark shifted from one foot to the other as if he was having difficulty finding his words. Then he glanced over his shoulder, meeting her eye. 'With Conor's accident, and now this, it's really starting to feel like someone doesn't want you to open.'

Tess stopped, one of the mugs in mid-air.

If someone else thought it, too, did that make her suspicions less mad?

She opened her mouth, about to speak, and then closed it again. She needed to approach this whole thing carefully. She had no idea what was going on, or who had been trolling her on Twitter, but with the timing of Jerry Lynch's call and everything else, it really *did* feel as if someone was trying to sabotage the grand opening. She couldn't see how Laetitia could be connected, but the other stuff . . . and now there was another death. On her property.

Tess put the mugs on the counter carefully.

'This must have been an accident, surely? It could be some tourist who was here one weekend, who drank too much or something?'

Mark put the mug he was washing on the drainer and looked around for a tea towel to dry his hands. Leaning on the counter, he frowned for moment, deep in thought.

'It's infinitely possible that this person went into the water months ago and got caught in the weeds. And then, for some reason, the body became dislodged and floated into the middle today.' He grimaced. 'But with everything else happening? If you put a bet on it, the odds would be ridiculous.'

He pulled his phone out of his back pocket.

'I have a feeling . . .' His thumbs flying over the screen, he stopped speaking to read whatever page he'd brought up. 'Here we are. Bodies usually float to the surface if they aren't anchored down in some way, after about three days. It's the gut bacteria – they keep working and producing gases after the person has passed. That makes the body buoyant. I'm sure the heat must speed things up, too.'

Tess looked at him as what he was saying clicked into place in her head.

'So if today's Monday, this person could have gone into the lake on Friday, and have been submerged until now?'

'Or perhaps early Saturday, while everyone was focused on looking for Laetitia. I mean, she could have been one of the searchers who slipped and fell in. Maybe.' Mark didn't sound convinced.

'But if it's someone from the village, surely it would have been noticed that they were missing? I mean, it's the land of the squinting windows in Kilfenora – that Facebook forum is like *Private Eye* sometimes.'

'Maybe, but if it's someone who lived alone, or on the outskirts, or everyone thought was away for the weekend, perhaps nobody realised. Did you keep a list of who was in the search parties?'

Tess shook her head. 'God, no, should I have done? I can't even remember who was there, we were just focused on covering the ground.'

'Don't worry, I'd guess we'll know soon enough who it is.'

As he said it, Tess's phone rang, the bell loud and demanding. Pulling it out of her back pocket, she looked at the screen and her heart sank. Jerry Lynch again. She was going to have to talk to him, at least to see if she could put him off a bit longer.

She glanced at Mark as she answered, mouthing the word 'sorry' and pointing at the phone.

'Hello, Tess Morgan.' She could barely hear Lynch; the signal was patchy. Then she realised what he was talking about. 'What do you mean, you're outside?'

Chapter 37

'WHAT'S UP?'

Tess heard Mark from across the kitchen as she finished the call and slipped the phone onto the counter, but her head was swimming. She put her hands down flat on either side of it, trying to steady herself. Letting out a deep breath, she looked up at him.

'Oh God.' Tess closed her eyes. 'Oh God. I don't think I can deal with this now.' She paused, conscious he was waiting, the look on his face showing his confusion. 'I know this sounds mad, but there's a reporter outside. He's working with a forensics TV show, one of those cold case ones.' She faltered. *Where did she start?*

'He's outside, at the door? What does he want?'

Tess took a deep breath. 'He thinks there's a body, maybe more than one, on Fury Hill.'

Mark raised one eyebrow, 'OK.' He drew the word out, obviously weighing up what she'd said. 'I think maybe you need to bring him in before he realises half the county's Gardai are hanging out in the gardens.' He looked serious. 'Whatever about this reporter's theories, I think it would be a plan to keep the body in the lake quiet until you know more. The last thing you need is it splashed all over the tabloids four days before opening.'

'You're right. Give me two minutes. Would you mind staying? I really don't trust this guy. I can explain properly when he's gone. There's been quite a lot happening here.'

'Of course not. Will I get the door?'

'Would you? I don't want him to think I live on my own.'

Tess cringed inside as she realised what she'd said. Thoughts of the Radio Snatcher were affecting her more than she thought. She hadn't meant to ask Mark to pretend that they were living together, but that was exactly what it sounded like. Fortunately he seemed to understand what she meant. Putting the tea towel down, he gave Merlin a stroke as he headed for the hall.

Tess needed to sit down. Her legs had gone weak and shaky again, as if she'd had a sugar crash and needed food fast. But she didn't feel like food. Not one little bit.

'She's just through here. Can I get you something? We were about to have a cup of coffee?'

Mark showed a balding man in his thirties into the kitchen, his stomach hanging over his jeans like a status symbol. Pulling out the carver at the head of the kitchen table, Mark invited Lynch to sit with a wave of his hand.

Red-faced, his lime-green polo shirt already showing broad swathes of sweat, Lynch looked surprised at the welcome. Tess sat down gratefully while Mark got the coffee underway. He turned to Lynch as he waited for the machine to do its thing.

'Tess has given me some details. Why don't you start from the top?'

Tess felt a surge of relief. Mark made it sound like the most natural thing in the world that Lynch should explain everything. Perhaps if he ran through it again, she'd be able to get a better grasp of how he'd been led to Kilfenora. And if the Twitter troll might have been involved.

Sitting down, Lynch ran his hand over his chin. Jowly and still perspiring, Tess thought he was possibly the most unattractive man she had ever laid eyes on, although being in the same room as Mark would put anyone at a disadvantage. She glanced back at him as he opened the fridge, looking for milk as if he knew exactly where it was.

Lynch leaned forward on the table.

'I'm working on a new TV show, we've got some top people in looking at cold cases. We want to gather enough evidence to get some of them opened up again.'

Mark came around behind Tess's chair and slipped a full mug of coffee in front of Lynch.

'What sort of people have you got?'

'A geographical profiler from Norway, Dr Carla Steele, the facial reconstruction expert from Garda Headquarters, and Dr Grace Franciosi is presenting the TV show. It's part docudrama, part true crime. She's a forensic psychologist and a real force.'

They were names Tess recognised from the press. *Oh God. This show sounded like it was going to be big.*

'And what exactly makes you think there's something buried here?' Mark paused, perhaps realising how that sounded. 'Someone.'

'We've had a tip-off from inside Mountjoy. Cell talk. It's hearsay – the cops are being very slow to react, but we've looked in detail at who said it, their connections to our informant and the timeline, and it looks very strong. The message was that at least one of the Radio Snatcher's victims is buried on the land along your border. We want to bring some specialist dogs, see if they can find anything. We've X-ray equipment that can show us what's below the surface. Then we use endoscopes to have a good look before there's any digging. If we can get enough evidence, we turn it all over to the guards so they can do the excavation. We don't want to interfere in the chain of evidence.'

'That all sounds very complicated.' Tess ran her hand over her face.

Lynch looked at her intently. 'The thing is, we don't need to bring any cameras in until we've found something. Filming is expensive and we can recreate the scene if there's something there. There's no point in bringing down a whole crew to film a doggo finding a rabbit hole.'

He had a point there. Tess was about to speak as there was a knock on the front door, the sharp rap from the polished brass knocker ringing around the house. Tess felt herself jump.

What now?

She really was going to have to get a doorbell, one that played something calming when it rang.

'I'll get it.'

Mark patted her on the shoulder as he passed her chair and went back into the hall. Tess heard the door open and the tone of a male voice. She just hoped to God it wasn't the guards, or Jerry Lynch would think all his Christmases had come together. She turned to him, keen to distract him from the interruption.

'So no cameras at first. You can be discreet?'

'Yes, of course. We don't want it leaking out what's in the show any more than you want local gossip, so we'll be very careful. I saw you're opening to the public this weekend. We'd love to get in before the people start arriving.'

'Yes, opening this weekend was the plan.' *At least, it had been.* 'How many of these experts do you need to bring down?'

As Lynch explained the number of vehicles and personnel involved, and the course of action if remains were found, Tess wished Mark would hurry up. She wanted him to hear this, too. The way she was feeling right now – as if she'd stepped into some alternative reality where the mist was so thick she couldn't even see her hand – she didn't know how much of it she was taking in. She needed someone to discuss it all with who was less emotionally involved, who had heard the details.

Normally she had no problem making decisions – that was one of the things she loved about running her own show; she could be responsive and change plans as required – but right now there was so much happening that she was beginning to lose sight of her goals. And the thought that this could all link back to the Twitter troll was still in her head, flashing like a red light. Mark was right – it was *really* looking as if someone didn't want her to open.

Tess heard the front door close and Mark came into the kitchen, a large box in his hand.

'That was a guy called Rick, he's an electrical wholesaler. He said Eoin Doyle had been telling him about our lighting situation and he just got in this new movement-sensitive security light.' He held up the box. 'It looks like a coach light. It's new, state-of-the-art or something. Anyhow, he said Doyle can probably add it to the insurance company's bill and put it up on the house here so there'll be lights on both sides of the lane.' Mark put the box on the table. 'He was coming up to the village to drop some parts in to Doyle – he thought he was working up here today.'

Tess looked at him sideways. 'Eoin Doyle is worried about my personal safety?' She looked from Mark to Jerry Lynch. 'Is that something *I* should be worried about?'

Mark crossed over to the coffee machine. 'He looked pretty surprised to see me, although he could have recognised me from the pub. I think when he tracks Doyle down, the village gossip machine is going to have more to worry about.'

Chapter 38

'LADIES AND GENTLEMEN of the company – this is your Act One beginners' call. Act One beginners, please.'

As Tess let the main doors to the ballroom fall gently closed behind her, Aidan was sitting on an old wooden chair in the middle of the ballroom, facing the stage, a stopwatch in one hand and a pencil in the other, the tip hovering over the heavily marked prompt script. He glanced up and nodded before turning back to the stage. The curtains weren't up yet, or the scenery in place, but Gen's jardinière and a few key props, chairs and a table, were in situ. Aidan was going through everything as if it was the first night.

Perhaps she was putting it off again, but she'd needed to see that everything was running OK up here before she followed Jerry Lynch over to Fury Hill. Mark had said he'd come with her, and had nipped to the pub first to check his staff were managing the lunch trade.

'Ladies and gentlemen, at this point on the night we will be awaiting front of house clearance. Please stand by.' Aidan's voice filled the empty room, bouncing off the boards and the raw brick walls.

Tess hung back, leaning against the door frame, her phone balancing on her clipboard, a scribbled checklist on the top of her notes for today. She'd turned her phone off when Lynch had arrived, not wanting to be interrupted, and realised now that she still hadn't turned it on. But it could stay off for the moment; she could do with a few minutes' more headspace today.

'LX, please stand by. House lights to half and house lights, out.'

Aidan's voice broke into her thoughts as he spoke in what sounded like code.

'LXQs one to three and visual follow-on. Sound, please stand by. Sound Qs one to four. Flies, please stand by. House tabs out. Thank you.' He glanced across at her again before looking back at the stage. 'Ladies and gentlemen, we now have front of house clearance. Stand by, please, cast, stage management and technical crew.'

From the moment he'd pulled the cast together, Tess had been impressed with how professionally he'd approached the whole production. Now he was in his element.

'House lights to half, *go*. House lights out, Q one, *go*.' She didn't understand a word of it, but evidently those behind the scenes did. 'Ladies and gentlemen, the curtain is now *up* on Act One.'

His rich voice sounded almost Shakespearean, in complete control. He was like a conductor commanding an orchestra.

Tess imagined the curtains swishing open to reveal the set – what would be the influencer's bedroom, a peculiar mix of antique and modern. The extremely ugly jardinière was at the front of the stage – Clarissa had been right about that.

Thank God for Aidan.

This was the one area of the whole proceedings where she didn't have to worry. He was professional to the core, and one of those people who seemed to cope with issues. Watching the opening scene unfold, familiar now with the lines, Tess felt a surge of relief. She'd thought Aidan's idea of a play for opening weekend had sounded a bit mad that first night they'd discussed it. But he'd put his case well: it *would* show off the capabilities of the space; it gave the press a hook and lots of photo opportunities; and it would bring people in to see the ballroom. Tess knew that the real money would be in hosting weddings and corporate events on top of the coach tours and day visitors, and the more people who could see the ballroom in action, full of people, the faster word would spread.

When Gen had introduced Aidan that night in the pub, he'd told them about the play he'd been working on, an original production that dovetailed so well historically with the original building of Kilfenora House, it was almost as if it had all been pre-planned. Any qualms she'd had about not knowing anything about theatre had been swept aside by Gen, who had reminded her that Clarissa had spent a lifetime in the West End and would be able to step in if needed. She would always be there if there was anything Tess needed clarifying.

Aidan glanced at her and then at the action on the stage. Focusing on the actors gathered in the centre, he walked backwards, facing the stage all the time, to stand beside her.

'You OK?'

She glanced at him. His eyes hadn't left the performance.

'As OK as can be expected.'

'Any news on who it was?'

'Not yet. Female is all they've let me know. I really don't know who it can be. Or how they ended up in the lake. It's not like there aren't a load of loughs up here in the mountains.'

He nodded slowly, hesitating, as on stage, Liam faltered over his lines, taking a glance at the jardinière before continuing. Tess felt Aidan let out a breath.

He turned to her, his voice low.

'I just keep thinking, whoever it is must be connected to Laetitia somehow. I mean, the timing.'

Tess closed her eyes and ran her hand over her face.

'I know. But who could it be? And when did it happen?'

'The pathologist will be able to work out time of death. I mean, something could easily have kicked off on Friday night. Perhaps they had an argument. Or it could have been some sort of pact.' He frowned. 'It feels like a row that went really wrong to me, and then Laetitia couldn't deal with what had happened, so . . . You just never know what the real story is in people's lives.'

That was for sure.

Aidan didn't know how close to the truth he was.

He grimaced. 'We may never truly know. I mean, with them both gone.'

Tess was about to answer when Liam's voice rose from centre stage.

'"What art thou, Faustus, but a man condemn'd to die? / Thy fatal time draws to a final end; / Despair doth drive distrust into my thoughts."'

It was as if he was voicing what she was so desperately trying to quash. With every new drama, she was starting to question the whole plan. But she couldn't give up now, or even think about it. They'd all worked so hard. She just prayed everything would come together without anything else happening . . .

Chapter 39

THE AFTERNOON SUN was hot on Tess's neck as she got out of Mark's car. The battered Volvo hatchback looked as if it broke every environmental rule there was, but he'd had a new engine fitted when he'd inherited it from his dad, Gen had told her, which seemed bonkers to Tess. But apparently he loved it. And he'd offered to drive.

'You sure you want to do this?' Mark's voice broke into her wandering thoughts and she realised her mind was again deliberately avoiding dealing with the issue at hand. She'd sort of switched off on the way over. He must have guessed from her silence. Closing the passenger door, Tess glanced over at him.

'Are you sure *you* do? You're the one giving up your time.'

Mark shrugged in answer. 'Good cause. If I ever get out of that pub, I'm going to need a new job.' A smile crept on to his face. 'I've a vested interest in making sure you get up and running. I feel a whole new career beckoning.'

Glancing up the hill, he came around the front of the car to join her.

Tess looked back at him and smiled despite herself.

'Giving ghost tours? Is that what doctors of supernatural stuff do these days?'

His face twitched. 'I was thinking of true crime specials – this place is turning into murder central.'

Tess gave him a shove. 'We don't know anyone's been murdered, Lynch's information could be all wrong. And we don't know about whoever was in the lake, but surely that can't have been murder. I mean, up here in the wilds? It wouldn't make any sense.'

They'd stopped at the end of the track that led up to Fury Hill. Lynch and his people were already there: a small white Ford van was parked beside a Range Rover, a red sports car on the far side. Further up the field they could see a woman with a shock of bright red hair in a pale outfit standing away from two men who were being tugged along by a pair of German shepherd dogs. As Tess watched, the redhead moved, revealing the unmistakable form of Jerry Lynch on her far side, his overhanging belly silhouetted against the sky.

'We'd better go up.' She started walking, speaking half to herself. 'I've no idea why whoever she is chose the lake, though, I mean, it's not even deep.'

Tess realised Mark had stopped beside her. 'That's the whole point, isn't it? Think about it.'

Holding her hand up to shield her eyes from the sun, Tess looked at him.

'Think about what?'

'Er . . . the depth. I know it's called the Apollo Lake, but that's a bit of a misnomer – it's not exactly glacial.'

He was right, but Tess still wasn't quite getting what he was saying. Seeing her confusion, he shook his head.

'It's not the sort of depth you'd drown yourself in, is it? Not that I've tried personally, but it looks like you could walk across it fairly easily.'

Tess suddenly felt incredibly stupid. He was completely right about the name. By definition it wasn't a lake at all. Perhaps it was her brain's coping mechanism kicking in, but part of her hadn't really questioned how whoever it was had got into the water. She certainly hadn't considered that it could be anything more than an accident or suicide. Granted, two suicides in close proximity to each other, both in geography and time, was a bit odd, but now he'd said it, the Apollo Lake was the last place you'd try and drown yourself in.

'So, do you mean . . .? Do you think . . .?' Tess faltered, unable to find the words.

Mark frowned. 'I mean – and I'm guessing – but it seems unlikely that she went in unaided. Unless she was incredibly drunk, fell in and knocked herself out.' His voice was rich with scepticism. Tess screwed up her nose and let out a sharp breath. Was that what she had thought had happened? Maybe it was. He glanced at her, 'I don't imagine they'll share it, but the pathologist's report will give a clearer picture.'

'But she couldn't have been murdered, *here*, really?'

Tess's mind was suddenly in overdrive. Part of her had been sure the Twitter troll was somehow at the root of all this bad luck, but they couldn't possibly have killed someone. That was just ridiculous. The whole psychology of abuse on social media was rooted in the perpetrator being behind a screen, distanced from the victim.

There was just no way.

Mark looked at her, his blue eyes full of concern.

'I need to talk to you about that. About the "here" element of all of this. Let's see what's happening up there first.'

Chapter 40

JERRY LYNCH TURNED as Tess and Mark headed up the hill, ambling down to meet them. There was absolutely nothing endearing about the man and Tess felt a wave of irritation surge as he got closer. She deliberately tried to quash it. She needed time to think about what Mark had just said, but getting snappy and annoying Lynch wasn't the way to get this over and done with as swiftly as possible. She just prayed it was a dead end. Police investigations hit hundreds of dead ends.

But what if they found something?

Tess curled up inwardly at the thought. There were just so many ways that this alone could be a total disaster, without everything else, and she hated herself for even thinking it. They had to investigate if this was a genuine lead.

They *had* to find out what had happened to these women, but part of her just kept thinking that an extra few weeks wouldn't make any difference to the bigger picture.

There she went again.

Torn didn't even begin to describe how she felt about all of this. And she didn't like what Mark had just said about the lake one little bit, but thank God he was here to help her navigate everything. As Gen was always saying, he was the one really dependable person in Kilfenora, never had an agenda, just got on with his own thing and didn't care what people thought about him. If someone got messy in the pub, he threw them out, whoever they were; there was no worrying about who was related to who, or what people might say.

Before she had time to think more, Lynch reached them.

'Thanks so much for enabling this. We're going to be as quick as we can. Come and meet Grace.'

Sweat was showing through Lynch's T-shirt under his arms, and as he turned to indicate the searchers, Tess saw he was soaked down his back, too.

He was puffing as he walked up the hill. Tess and Mark followed. Standing statuesque against the bright blue sky, the woman with the red hair was carelessly carrying off a stylish cream linen trouser suit as if she was wearing jeans, the narrow legs tucked into brand new dark green Hunter wellingtons.

Perhaps she had been expecting mud – she didn't look the sort who did fields. More as if she was doing a country shoot for *Vogue*.

'Grace, this is Tess Morgan. Tess, Dr Grace Franciosi.'

The woman turned, her smile warm, and Tess immediately recognised her from the TV. She was one of those super-intelligent experts who was always called in to comment on crime, and Ireland had its fair share of that. Tess had seen her hold her own in several debates about violence against women.

'Thank you for letting us do this. If there are any remains here, closure is absolutely the most important thing for the families involved.' She held out her hand to shake Tess's, her grip confident and firm. This woman could do elegant *and* compassionate; she was the real deal. Grace frowned. 'Not knowing what happened to your loved one is soul-destroying.'

Tess managed a smile. Thoughts about how her livelihood being devastated by a TV crew would be pretty soul-destroying scudded through her head, making her feel rotten again. This week seemed to be testing her at every turn.

'Do you think it'll take long?'

Grace shook her head. 'The dogs are very efficient. We're not sure of the exact location, but they search quite quickly. We'll cause the minimum of disruption.'

Tess nodded again. At least if the investigators were up here away from the village, there would be a delay in the gossip hitting the ground, but she imagined everyone would be enthralled when word did leak.

Tess crossed her arms, watching the two German shepherds snuffling along the border between her land and the national park. It was more of a notional border – a line on a map rather than a full chain-link fence. Which was one of the reasons why this whole story rang true. Not very many people came up here. How many even knew that there wasn't a physical barrier? Tess, like Gen and Clarissa, had assumed there was some sort of sheep fence at the very least, rather than the national park just rolling on to Kilfenora. Huge patches of gorse, known as furze locally, straddled the hillside and made it even harder to know where the line between the two ran.

Tess watched as the dogs and their two handlers worked through the undergrowth, and suddenly the reality of the situation hit her all the more strongly.

Why had she come up to see what they were doing? This was suddenly the last place on earth she wanted to be.

'I can see that you're busy. Can you text me an update if . . . if anything happens?' Tess stuck her hands into the pockets of her jeans and tried to keep her voice strong.

Beside her, Lynch shifted his weight from one foot to the other. 'You'll be the first to hear.'

Tearing her eyes away from the dogs, Tess turned to Mark. 'We should probably push on.'

He was standing with his arms crossed, surveying the hillside. Tess followed his gaze. There was a slight change in the landscape on the national park side of the border, where outcrops of rock littered the hill, overgrown with bracken and huge patches of dark green gorse, the spikes angry against the gentle blue of the sky. Tess's land had been used for grazing sheep, the fields cleared of random boulders, the grass much richer around where the gorse had sprung up. The bushes were heavy with yellow flowers, the scent of coconut strong. If you listened carefully you could hear the seed pods popping, spreading on the wind.

'We really will be as quick as we can. We don't want anyone knowing we're up here any more than you do. This really is a magnificent place you have. Jerry was telling me you haven't been here that long.'

Mark appeared to tune in to what Grace had said and turned towards them as Tess answered.

'Yes, I needed a project to keep me busy, something to bring me back to Ireland, and here I am.'

Grace nodded slowly. 'Brave. That's impressive. I caught bits of the restoration programme during lockdown, for some reason I thought it was a family property. You've had some big choices to make.'

Tess sighed. Grace didn't know how true that was. Her whole life felt as if it had been about choices, good ones and bad ones, since she'd been in university. She bit her lip. Her life had always felt as if it had been in two halves. Before the accident and after.

The time in between was hazy and filled with pain, blue-black like the night. There had been moments when she'd thought she wouldn't survive it, but she'd tried to stay focused, and coming here had helped her to move on. But in doing so she'd invested so much of herself in the project, the house, that having her plans derailed would be utterly devastating. She'd always been adaptable in her approach to life – Gen laughed at her motto that there was always a Plan B – but if this all went wrong, Tess wasn't sure there was a Plan B. The only B she could think of right now was bankruptcy.

Chapter 41

AS THEY DROVE across the estate towards the cottage, farmland opened up on either side of the narrow lane, only a low dry-stone wall stopping the sheep from wandering into the path of the traffic. Her eyes on the road ahead, the hills rolling as far as she could see, Tess felt grateful to live here. Despite everything.

What did they say about Irish people and the land? After 800 years of occupation and oppression, owning your own land held incredible significance.

Mark changed gear and slowed for a bend in the road, glancing over at her. He hadn't spoken since they'd left Fury Hill, seemed to be preoccupied with something. Hardly surprising, given the circumstances.

As they turned to swing down into the woods that ran down from the formal gardens to the river, the shade felt like a relief. The trees were cool and dark after the glare of the sun, the trunks dense, ivy twisting from the branches.

Her elbow resting on the open window, Tess ran her hand over her forehead, smoothing back her curls; even they lost their bounce in this heat. She could feel the prickle on her shoulders where she'd caught the sun from standing on the hillside.

Had someone really taken a woman up there and murdered her? Tess felt sick thinking about it. It was always those last few minutes that haunted her whenever she thought about anything like that – those last few minutes when the victim knew they were going to die, the intense fear. Tess felt her stomach turn over. She'd been feeling even more nauseous since this morning. If there had been anyone in her life since she'd returned to Ireland, she'd be worried that it was some sort of all-day morning sickness, but at least that was one thing she could discount.

It had to be stress. She had plenty of that.

Pulling out of the woods, following the service road around the Rose Walk, the high walls on their right casting long shadows, Mark was almost at the cottage when Tess saw Gen's car was parked outside. She must have seen them at the same time. Her door swung open as Mark pulled up in front of her. Tess had her own door open before he'd quite stopped.

Gen had been crying. Her eyes were puffy and red and she was clutching a tissue. Tess ran to her but, unable to speak, she raised her hands and waved them helplessly in the air, her bangles cascading down her arm.

Tess put her arms around Gen, glancing back to see Mark was half out of the driver's door, his face creased in concern. Their eyes met and she could see he was signalling that he'd slip way. She threw him a weak grin, a 'thank you for earlier' and a 'thank you for now' all rolled into one. As if he could read her mind, he nodded once and got back into the car, starting the engine and swinging around Gen's car to head around to the front of the house.

'What on earth's happened, Gen? Tell me – has something happened to Mal or Clarissa?'

Chapter 42

GEN CLUNG TO Tess, sobbing, unable to form a coherent sentence. Several times she tried, but she couldn't catch her breath. Tess tried to steer Gen towards the house. Merlin was waiting for them on the doorstep, his tail lashing from side to side. Sometimes Tess felt that cats were far wiser than humans gave them credit for.

'Come inside. Then you can tell me what's wrong.'

Fear nipped at Tess's subconscious. Had something happened to Mal – something terrible? Was Clarissa with him now? Or perhaps both of them had had an accident. The roads around here could be lethal in the summer, with tourists who didn't understand the speed limits, and Clarissa was worse; she drove like a thing possessed. Although she was usually better when Mal was in the car with her.

Pushing open the gate, Tess eased Gen up the path, and pulled out her keys to open the door.

It was already open.

Hesitating, Tess faltered for a moment, but Gen had her full weight on her. Merlin hung back as Tess pushed the door open wider and helped Gen over the threshold to the worn honey-coloured boards inside.

Had she left the door open when she'd gone out with Mark? She'd been preoccupied enough.

'Hello!' Tess called out, about to close the door but thinking better of it. Perhaps she should leave it open just in case there was someone here and she and Gen needed to make a quick exit.

In the moment she was thinking it, Aidan Gaunt stuck his head out of the kitchen door.

'Hello, you're back. I see you've heard the news.'

'What news?'

He anticipated the question almost before she said it.

'I came up to tell you myself, I didn't think the phone was appropriate, but the front door was open.' He glanced at Gen anxiously, as if he didn't want to say anything in front of her. 'I didn't want to leave it in case . . . Well, with everything right now, and I wasn't sure if you'd only slipped out for a second and didn't have your keys, so I didn't want to close it and lock you out.'

He was trying to tell her something with his eyes, so he didn't have to say it in front of Gen, but Tess wasn't getting it. He shifted from one foot to another awkwardly.

'I waited outside for a while, but then I thought it might be better to come in. To make sure there wasn't anyone here who . . . er . . . perhaps shouldn't have been. With all the workers you've had up here.' He ran his hand through his hair. 'I'm sorry, it feels like such an imposition now. I was overthinking.'

Tess shook her head, suddenly sure he was talking about Eoin Doyle. She took a deep breath. She was jumping to conclusions. He was right, though. What if Doyle or someone like him had seen the door open and wandered in? That didn't bear thinking about. She opened her eyes wide, trying to show Aidan that she knew what he meant.

'No, no, it's fine, really. I appreciate the thought. It was just a surprise, that's all. Could you help me with Gen?'

'Oh God, yes, sorry, yes, yes, of course. Will I make some coffee or find something stronger? She looks like she needs it.'

Aidan stood aside to let them in through the kitchen door and then slid back one of the solid wood carvers. Still gripping Tess's arm, Gen slipped into it, like a puppet whose strings had been cut, her face wet with now silent tears.

Gen's hand was tight on Tess's wrist, and it didn't feel as if she was ready to let go yet. Tess glanced at Aidan, glad he was here.

'There's brandy in the living room – would you mind?'

Tess slid into the chair beside Gen and reached for the hand clasping her arm.

'Gen, Gen, you need to tell me what's happened. I can't help you fix it if I don't know.'

In the living room, Tess could hear Aidan checking bottles in the wine cabinet, their glass bottoms ringing as he put them onto its glazed top.

Gen closed her eyes and finally pulled herself together enough to speak. Her eyes red-rimmed, she looked straight at Tess.

'It's Katie-Lou. It was Katie-Lou in the lake. They couldn't say till they'd told her mum.' Gen closed her eyes and stopped speaking, holding her breath as if she was trying to hold the emotion in. 'Something happened to her. It wasn't suicide. They said she had bruises.'

Tess's free hand shot to her mouth. 'My God, what sort of bruises?'

Behind her, Aidan appeared with two glasses of brandy. Sitting down opposite Tess, he slid one towards her.

'Thought you might need one, too. It's such terrible news, everyone in the village is devastated.'

212

Tess opened her mouth, glancing quickly between them, struggling to form words.

'What . . .? I mean, how . . .?'

Aidan frowned and shook his head, pursing his lips as if he was fighting with his emotions, too. He wiped his eye.

'They don't know yet. But there's going to be a post mortem. The cops think that she didn't go in unaided, shall we say. And Meg was saying that she didn't think that it's very deep – the lake, I mean.'

Reaching for her brandy, Tess shook her head.

That's what Mark had said.

Tess took a sip. The liquid burned the back of her throat.

'What sort of bruises?' It came out as a whisper.

Glancing anxiously at Genevieve, Aidan shook his head and wiped his eye again.

'I don't know the full details. It's hard to tell what's conjecture and what could be fact, but there were some on her shoulders, apparently.'

Tess looked at him as the pieces of information began to fall into place. Her mind seemed to be working in slow motion, as if it was too full and her processing power was reduced. She put the brandy down.

'Like maybe she was held down?'

Beside Tess, Gen let out another gulping sob. Tess reached over and gripped Gen's hand where she was still holding firmly on to Tess's arm.

'Have some brandy, Gen, it'll make you feel better. You're in shock, too.'

Gen nodded helplessly and reached for the glass, her bangles clacking on the table. She picked it up and knocked it back in

213

one. Out of the corner of her eye, Tess could see Aidan hastily hiding his look of surprise. Before either of them could speak, Gen heaved a deep, ragged breath.

'Her mum . . . Her mum called me. They needed to do a formal identification and she couldn't do it, so I had to go.' Gen gripped Tess's arm, making it go white, but Tess barely noticed as Gen continued. 'Oh God, Tess, she was so pale, even with that silly tan, and her hair was all tangled. She looked like a mermaid lying there.'

'Why didn't you call me?'

'I tried, but I didn't have much time and there was no signal wherever you were. I kept getting the voicemail. I was going to leave a message, but I couldn't. You couldn't hear something like that on the phone.'

Gen stared hard at the table as if she was reliving every moment of the last few hours.

'I had to drive into town, to the morgue. It was . . .' Tears started pouring down Gen's face. 'She was so young, Tess, and so terribly silly. They thought maybe she'd arranged to meet someone and it went wrong.'

Tess felt her eyes opening wide in surprise. 'But here? Why here? Why didn't she meet them in the pub?'

Gen shook her head, her earrings jangling. 'The guards wondered if it was someone married. That it was a secret meeting. There are no cameras or anything up here. Nobody comes here at night.'

Tess almost said 'You'd think not', but somehow Eoin Doyle knew her security light wasn't working. Had he been up here at night? And Laetitia. Meg had said something about her wandering around the gardens at night.

She needed to get cameras.

There was an angry mew and Tess jumped. Merlin was sitting in the kitchen doorway, regarding them all with suspicion. Honestly, he was the most difficult cat sometimes.

A thought hit Tess. 'Who else knows? Surely the guards need to keep the details quiet?'

She suddenly had a mental image of news camera vans again. As if one body wasn't enough. Except there wasn't just one – now it looked as if there could be three: the woman who might be in the field; Laetitia; and now Katie-Lou.

Could this get any worse?

Tess rubbed her eyes with her spare hand and looked from Aidan to Gen. She was actually glad he was here; he was a sort of steadying influence. She'd felt it when he'd worked on Conor, he'd seemed so calm. And calm was what they all needed now. She didn't know what was going on but it felt as if it was escalating. And she had no idea what might happen next.

Chapter 43

AS TESS SAW him out, Aidan hovered for a moment on the doorstep of the Butler's Lodge, as if he wasn't sure how to say goodbye. It was still bright, the heat sitting heavily in the air. Inside, Gen was crying again, a soft keening.

Hesitating, Aidan looked off into the distance, but he didn't seem to be focusing.

'The guards are going to want to interview everyone. I'm sure they've been trying to call you, too.' He turned back to her, his face grim.

'I'm sure they will. Do you think what happened to Laetitia is connected somehow?'

He shrugged. 'Timing seems very coincidental if there *isn't* some connection. I didn't know they were friends, though.'

Tess sighed and crossed her arms, feeling chill despite the heat.

'I've no idea who their friends were, but Meg and Ally will know. I mean, they were about the same age, lived in the same village . . . I don't think they went to the same school, I'm sure Clarissa said the O'Riordans were home-schooled. But they knew each other, that's for sure.' Tess tried to find her words. 'I think we may need to cancel the opening weekend events now.'

She'd been avoiding saying it all evening.

Saying it made it feel real.

Aidan grimaced. He was feeling this as much as she was, she could tell. He cleared his throat.

'I know, it's a terrible mess. But we don't need to make any sudden decisions. It's possible that it was an accident, that the bruises were old. I don't know. I just feel for Laetitia and Conor – we planned to go on and we should think about them. Katie-Lou was really popular, she had a heart of gold, but she wasn't as involved as they were. I sort of feel we owe it to them.' He sighed. 'It's such a waste when you see a young life go like that. Like Laetitia. I don't know, perhaps they were best friends and something happened between them.'

It took Tess a moment to grasp what he was saying, then she felt her eyes open wide as the realisation dawned.

'You mean, you think Laetitia could have done something to her?'

Aidan shrugged. 'We've really no idea, have we, but young girls can be . . . I don't know. I'm not qualified to judge.'

Tess shook her head slowly, looking down at the worn wooden sill and granite slab of a step but barely seeing it, thoughts of an argument going horribly wrong swirling in her head.

'I don't think any of us are.'

He nodded as if in agreement. 'I just think that we need to be open-minded about this. Who's to know what was happening in either of their lives that we couldn't see? People often have secrets, you know, secrets they hide until something happens, and then the fear of it coming out can be greater than life itself. You used to see it a lot with theatrical types. I'm sure Clarissa has seen it, too.'

Tess crossed her arms tightly. There was just so much going around inside her head, she couldn't sort it out. Had Gen ever mentioned Laetitia and Katie-Lou knowing each other? She'd have to ask. Could something have happened that was so bad that Laetitia had pushed Katie-Lou into the lake and held her down, and then gone to the tower to kill herself? How would they ever know?

Aidan interrupted her thoughts.

'Anyway, it's your call, but I'll keep the guys rehearsing. It'll help take their mind off things.' He paused. 'I mean, not in a bad way, but you know what this place is like for speculation. We don't want everyone coming up with a mad theory and being tricked into talking to the press. We need to remember Katie-Lou's mum and friends. Everyone will be devastated.'

'And Gen. Katie-Lou's worked for her since she opened the shop, and she looked after Mal for ages before Clarissa sold her house.'

Tess let out a sigh and glanced inside the house. The sound seemed to have petered out, but she didn't want to leave Gen for long on her own.

Aidan cleared his throat. 'I didn't know her at all, really.'

She smiled sadly. 'Gen's always saying that she could get the wrong end of the stick about anything, but she was so genuine, she wasn't bright enough for guile. She just told it how it was.' She sighed. 'Her mum will miss her so much.'

'I think everyone will, it sounds as if she was very popular.' He paused. 'Oh, I almost forgot, did you leave a book in the ballroom? I found it on the stage when I got there this morning. Old copy of *Great Expectations*. It had a bookmark in it. I've checked with everyone else. I meant to ask you earlier.'

Thankfully he was looking out towards the stable yard and didn't see her blanch. Tess shook her head. It took all her effort to keep her voice level. 'Not mine. Drop it in if you think of it – it could belong to one of the other staff.'

What do you think you're doing in that big old house? Auditioning to be the next Miss Havisham?

The Twitter troll had been obsessed with Miss Havisham. Jilted on her wedding day.

Still looking away from her, Aidan nodded as if to himself.

'I'd better go.' He turned back to her. 'Watch you lock that door, won't you? I don't know . . . but with everything, you need to be careful.'

Tess couldn't get the front door closed fast enough.

TUESDAY

Chapter 44

AIDAN'S WORDS ABOUT keeping the front door locked were ringing in Tess's ears as she made breakfast the next morning.

Great Expectations.

She'd had great expectations for the opening weekend before all this had started. And she'd lost her fiancé on the day they got engaged. It had to be the troll.

It had been the Miss Havisham references that had finally made her delete all her social media apps.

The troll had been here – had been on her property, in the house. What the hell was going on?

Tess closed her eyes. She hadn't been at all impressed to hear that Eoin Doyle had been talking about her. Did all this route back to him somehow?

Oh God, she didn't know.

There was so just much; it felt woven together like a giant spiderweb, but the intersecting threads were invisible.

And who was the spider in the middle?

Calling a security company to get cameras installed had suddenly shot to the top of every one of her lists. It didn't matter how much it cost.

At least she hadn't been on her own last night.

She'd messaged Clarissa to say Gen would stay over – Mal didn't need to see his mother in this state and Gen needed some space to grieve. People experienced death all the time, but sudden death, Tess knew from experience, was a whole new level of pain. Tess had given Gen some of her sleeping tablets in the hope that they'd help, and led her up to the spare room, barely able to function. Shock manifested in so many different ways, but this was one Tess recognised.

Barely sleeping herself, she'd gone across the landing to check on Gen in the early hours. The spare room door was open and Merlin had stretched out beside her as if he was protecting her. From the gentle sound of her breathing, Tess was sure she was soundly asleep. Merlin had opened one eye and regarded her stoically, and Tess had crept back to her own bed.

The coffee machine gurgled and spluttered as Tess watched her cup fill. It had all been going so well; everything she'd dreamed of for Kilfenora had been coming together, like the blend of coffee beans it had taken her so long to get absolutely right. It was all starting to flow towards the opening event she'd dreamed of.

And now this.

Great Expectations.

Lost in her thoughts, Tess didn't hear Gen come into the kitchen behind her until one of the chairs scraped on the tiles. She jumped, her movement startling Merlin, who had evidently arrived at the same time looking for his breakfast. He hissed loudly and jumped onto the kitchen table. Tess turned around, giving him a grimace in return for the hiss.

'How did you sleep?'

Gen had pulled her hair into a messy topknot and was wearing her turquoise earrings, picking up the blue in her patchwork dress, creased from being thrown over the chair last night.

Sitting down at the end of the table, she rubbed her face with her hands as she answered, braving a grateful smile.

'Much better than I expected. Those tablets are amazing.'

Tess grinned, relieved.

That was something, at least.

'They need to be, to knock me out. Now tea, hot chocolate or my special coffee? I've croissants about to go into the oven.'

'Chocolate would be amazing, and so would a croissant. I realised when I woke up I didn't have dinner yesterday. My system isn't used to that level of deprivation. I need sugar.'

Tess crossed the kitchen to the oven to pop the tray of croissants in. She'd invested in a convection oven when she'd moved into the Butler's Lodge, installed beside the huge green Aga. In this heat, an Aga was the last thing they needed running.

Gen hardly seemed to notice Tess move, even though she crossed her field of vision on the way to the oven, and then to the microwave. She was staring out of the kitchen window into the back garden, twirling one of the strands of hair that had escaped from her bun, her face blank.

Was she remembering the last time she spoke to Katie-Lou?

More than likely.

Tess knew what it was like to lose someone close suddenly.

She shivered as an image of Kieran's smile broke into her subconscious. She could still hear his laughter, right before it had been taken away.

The worst of it was that the driver of the car that had hit him had been in the same pub as them that night. Apparently he'd

225

had a row with his girlfriend and they'd broken up, and that had fuelled his speed. Tess could even remember the car in the car park as they'd tumbled out of the door, laughing. Kieran had made some crack about how ridiculous it was to have a white car in the countryside.

But she couldn't go there now.

Tess cleared her throat. 'Almost ready.' Waiting for the milk to heat in the microwave beside her, Tess reached for the sugar bowl and put it on the table. 'Tell me, did Laetitia and Katie-Lou know each other?'

Coming out of her trance, Gen turned to her, surprised.

'Yes, although I don't think they were actually friends. Different sides of the tracks.'

Tess pursed her lips, thinking, as the microwave pinged. Turning to open a drawer, she pulled out a couple of teaspoons, and slipped the solid earthenware mug of hot chocolate down in front of Gen.

Reaching for the sugar, Gen frowned. 'It's funny you should ask. Katie-Lou said she was going to see Laetitia the other day. You know Laetitia did tarot cards? Katie-Lou wanted her to do a reading.' Gen sighed. 'She was going to ask Laetitia to take the other half of her stall at the craft market. She said she'd emailed you – she didn't think she'd be able to fill the space she'd booked.'

Tess looked at her, confused.

'Laetitia was going to read cards on the end of Katie-Lou's cake stall?'

'No, silly. Laetitia was big into natural remedies, she made all sorts of creams and things from herbs, apparently.' Gen suddenly looked unsure. 'I meant to tell you the other day, actually. Katie-Lou said that Laetitia was getting herbs from the gardens for her lotions and potions.' She grimaced. 'Sorry, I forgot to mention it. It's a bit cheeky, but I'm sure she didn't take much.'

Tess picked up her mug and leaned on the counter.

'It really doesn't matter now, but it might have been nice if she'd said something. I didn't know she was selling stuff.'

'I think it was a personal thing – made to order for people. Presumably there would be all sorts of health and safety issues about selling that sort of thing properly. Katie-Lou wouldn't have thought of that.'

Tess took a sip of her coffee. 'I found a wild flower book in her van when I went with Meg. She was researching something, by the looks of things.' She frowned, trying to remember what Meg had called the plant Laetitia had been searching for. 'Something tall with lots of purple flowers.'

'Aconite?' Gen raised her eyebrows in question.

Tess looked back at her in disbelief. 'Yes! How did you work it out from that stunning description?'

Gen took a sip of her coffee. 'Clarissa loves it. It's a gorgeous colour. She has it in her garden. But it's massively poisonous, Mal's been warned off going anywhere near it.'

'Why would Laetitia have been looking it up? Surely she wasn't making creams with a poisonous plant?'

'Maybe she'd found an old cure for something and wanted to test it out.'

Gen sighed. 'Clarissa says it can also induce a heart attack, and that it's untraceable. Perhaps Laetitia picked it by accident and needed to identify it.'

Tess frowned, thinking. How was Clarissa an expert on poisonous plants? She really was a woman for surprises. But was that why Laetitia was looking this aconite plant up? She made a mental note to ask the gardeners if there was any growing within reach of the public – she could do without someone's child ingesting it.

'Did Katie-Lou say when she was going to see Laetitia?'

Gen put her head on one side and screwed up her face, thinking.

'She popped into the shop the other day and I got the impression that she was going to meet her that evening – that would have been Friday.' Gen turned slowly, her eyes wide as she looked at Tess. 'Oh. That would have been . . . You don't think . . .?'

Before Gen could finish her sentence, Tess's phone rang, the jangling telephone bell sound making them both jump. It was lying on the kitchen counter beside her, and as well as ringing, vibrated on the granite surface. Even Merlin turned to see what the buzzing was. It sounded as if someone was tormenting an angry insect.

Putting down her coffee hastily, Tess snatched the phone up, her mind still reeling from Gen's realisation that Katie-Lou could have visited Laetitia on the night she'd died.

Tess looked at the screen in disbelief. It was Jerry Lynch.

Now?

Chapter 45

'KNIGHT TO C6.'

Clarissa looked across the garden table at Mark and pursed her lips as he moved the white knight. She was not going to let him win again. It was still early, the lawn damp with dew, but the moment Gen had called yesterday about Katie-Louise, Clarissa had popped Malachi into the car and gone down to the shop to put up a sign that said they were closed on compassionate grounds. And collected the chessboard at the same time.

Clarissa didn't imagine that they'd open for a week at least, and this game was nearing its end. One thing she had discovered in life was that when events felt as if they were spiralling, holding on to something solid helped you keep your perspective. Clarissa didn't know what was going on at Kilfenora – and something definitely was – but chess helped her think. And thinking helped her worry less, because just now she was getting very worried about Tess. It was starting to feel as if whatever it was that was spiralling was getting tighter. And Tess was trapped at the centre, like a fly caught in a web.

Mark picked up his ginger tea and, nursing the mug in his hand, looked speculatively at the board. Would she be able to beat him this time? Clarissa wasn't sure, but she was going to try. It was rare that she was bettered by any man, and being at a disadvantage brought out her killer instinct, even with someone as pleasant as Mark Mulligan.

It was also rare that they got to face each other across the board. Normally Mark popped into the shop early on a Tuesday, his day off, ostensibly to say hello to Katie-Lou, or look at a small piece that might make its way into the pub bar, but in fact to make his next move. If Katie-Lou was dusting with her headphones on, dancing around the shop, sometimes she didn't hear him at all. He slid in like a shadow, made his move, and slipped out, leaving the shop bell jangling, heading to the Spar for the paper and a freshly baked croissant.

On Saturday, the first thing Clarissa did when she arrived for the day was to check the board to see what her next move would be. This was a game of strategy, and in taking their time they were now playing at competition standard. He dropped in on a Saturday morning to say hello, if he could get away from the pub, but they had never really had a chance to sit and play properly.

In this game, Clarissa had sussed that Mark had tried using a grandmaster's move, recorded in detail on the internet. Seeing her countermoves, he'd realised he'd been rumbled, and had gone back to his own plan.

They'd started texting each move once it was made, just to be sure the full game was recorded. A few odd changes to the positions caused by Katie-Lou's dusting had mixed things around a little too much. And there was always the possibly that some stupid customer would tip the board. Texting meant they could recreate any game if required.

But there was something wonderful about the expectation of seeing the pieces on the board, of seeing what each move looked like and how it might play out across the game. Every single one was strategic, part of a bigger plan.

'They have to be connected, you know.' Mark sat back in his chair and folded his arms, his faded navy-blue T-shirt untucked over denim shorts. He was wearing battered brown leather sailing shoes today, clearly not risking the comments his Crocs normally elicited from her. Clarissa glanced up at him as he took a sip of his tea.

Her eyes on the board, Clarissa nodded.

'I know. That is what is worrying me rather. And the vast majority of people are killed by someone they know. It feels rather unlikely that a total stranger has decided to bump off the young people of Kilfenora in a variety of bizarre and disparate ways.'

Behind Mark, Merlin slid out of the bushes and stalked across the lawn, rubbing his face on the cast-iron table leg as he arrived beside them. Absent-mindedly, Mark reached down to tickle him.

'Which means, either someone in the village is very unhappy with several of their neighbours and has a list they are working through, or something more sinister is unfolding.'

'A murderer with a list isn't sinister?' Clarissa looked at him over the top of her glasses.

He shifted in his seat. 'Well, yes, obviously it's not great, but how many serial killers are there in the world who go to the trouble of finding a different way to kill each time? I mean, isn't part of the pleasure reliving the experience? Ritual comes into that somehow, doesn't it?'

Clarissa tapped a manicured fingernail on the mosaic tabletop, half her mind on the game and half on the situation he was referring to. He had a point.

231

'I have to say my experience of serial killers is limited, but I do agree that changing the method of killing suggests either a disorganised individual, which most serial killers aren't, an individual who has planned these "accidents" in detail, or someone who isn't planning at all, but reacting. But to what, I'm not quite sure.' She paused. 'Or we have more than one culprit. Also a possibility.'

'Christ, what are the chances of that?'

Clarissa smiled. He sounded so much like Crocodile Dundee sometimes, and he had that same impatience for stupidity portrayed by the character. Clarissa had watched all the films with Malachi when he was in his animal phase. He hadn't been impressed with the kissing, but he had taken to wearing a huge hat and saying 'g'day' to everyone.

Clarissa looked pensive. 'What really concerns me is that all these incidents have happened at Kilfenora House. I mean, if you want to bump someone off, a hit-and-run up here in the mountains would surely be easier.'

He grimaced and shook his head. 'Not so sure about that. Hard not to damage the car, and then you're looking at all sorts of forensics.' He took another sip of tea.

Clarissa's hand hovered over the board. 'Did Tess tell you about her Twitter problem?'

Mark arched an eyebrow. 'No – what was that?'

'A troll – an extremely abusive troll who seemed to know an awful lot about her. And who threatened her more than once.' Mark's eyebrows shot up as Clarissa continued. 'It started when she first bought the house, a few days after the first article was published about her, in fact.'

'Nasty. So it was linked to the house somehow?'

Clarissa put her hand back on the table. 'Very possibly.'

'And could be linked to what's happening now?'

'Also very possible.'

Mark nodded slowly. 'I think it's the location that's worrying me the most in all of this.'

'It does feel like someone is trying to stop her opening. But I'm worried it's more personal, to be perfectly frank.'

He frowned thoughtfully. 'Maybe it's someone with a history with the house, and they are targeting her because they don't want people tramping through it?' He tapped his hand on the side of his mug. 'Although, honestly, all of this is a rum way to go about preventing an opening.'

'It would be easier to set it on fire.' Clarissa opened her eyes wide for emphasis and picked up her Earl Grey in its fluted bone china teacup.

Mark nodded slowly. 'Agreed, but then the house would be lost. So perhaps it's someone who wants to create such bad feeling about the place that Tess puts it on the market and they are able to get it for a knockdown price. With its history, I'm just waiting for a story about the Kilfenora Curse to emerge.'

'I thought that was an old wives' tale.'

'It seems the events it relates to are real enough, but I can't find any reference to it in contemporary documents. But you know what villages are like.'

'I do indeed. Every pimple is commented on. Not a bit like the city, where you can do just about anything and no one takes a blind bit of notice.'

'I don't think you can get away with murder anywhere.'

Clarissa raised her eyebrows and took a careful sip of her tea.

'The thing about murder, as Agatha Christie has so brilliantly shown, is that if it doesn't look like murder, it can be very hard to detect. I mean, before yesterday, we – and I'm sure the Gardai – were looking at Conor's accident and Laetitia's suicide as entirely separate incidents, but what if you are right and they are part of a bigger . . .' She took a moment to find her word. Looking back at the board, it came to her. '. . . game.'

'That's what's been worrying me, to be perfectly honest, especially if there's some social media nutter in the mix. I think I need to have a chat with Tess.'

Chapter 46

TESS LOOKED ACROSS the kitchen at Gen, anxiety swirling in her stomach. *How could Jerry Lynch be calling right now?*

'I need to take this, I won't be a second.'

Gen waved away Tess's apologies. The room had filled with the smell of baking croissants and Gen got up to check on them as Tess clicked through to answer the call. She hardly had her mouth open when Jerry Lynch spoke.

'We've found something. Well, one of the dogs has. Quite a way from where we were looking, too.'

Glancing at Gen again, Tess's hand went to her forehead. She turned around, leaning her elbows on the counter. Her knees felt decidedly shaky.

'What sort of a something? Where? When?'

Lynch sounded as if he was up on the hill. Tess could hear shouts in the background, but the words were too muffled to make them out.

'We came up here early this morning, wanted to beat the heat and the crowds.'

'Crowds?' Tess could hear the note of panic in her own voice.

'Sorry, I was joking.'

Joking? She almost yelled it at him, a trail of profanities crossing through her head but fortunately not exiting her mouth. She took a deep breath, trying to keep calm. She could feel her heart thumping in her chest, the tension in the back of her neck making her shoulders ache. It was a struggle to keep her voice level.

'Can you tell me what you've found?'

Obviously unaware of her reaction, she could hear the excitement rising in Lynch's voice.

'OK, so we packed up at about seven last night, and got back here at six. The dogs were a bit wired this morning, so the lads let them have a run around the place before we got started. One of the shepherds is called Casper, he's always disappearing. Anyhow, we got ready to get started and Casper's handler called him back. But he didn't come, we could just hear this distant barking.'

Still leaning on the counter, Tess closed her eyes, seeing the hillside in her mind's eye, the rich green grass of the field against the brilliant blue of the sky.

'Go on.'

'So we went to find him. He'd gone what felt like miles, way up on to the mountain. And he'd found something.' Tess wanted to yell at him to hurry up, but he was evidently enjoying keeping her in suspense. Eventually he carried on. 'He was pawing at the ground under this huge gorse bush. We cut a load of it back as much as we could, and we could see that the ground had been disturbed underneath it. I mean, not recently, it was all grown over, with the gorse on the top, but the ground wasn't even, if you know what I mean.'

Behind her, Tess heard Gen open the oven door and pull the tray out, the smell of baking intensifying.

'I do.' It came out as a croak. Tess reached for her coffee but the smell of it turned her stomach.

Lynch was warming to his subject. 'Remember we said we had those endoscopes for looking deep into the soil? Well, we used those and there's definitely something down there. We found what looked like blue plastic and a bit further over, what could be a piece of tarp.'

Tess tried to process what he was saying. How could they think that was a body?

'Could it just be rubbish that's been dumped?'

'I doubt it. Casper's trained to find human remains. He was going mental, only delighted with himself, and his pal, Lara, she was fairly going mad, too.' He paused. 'The thing is that the most recent suspected victim, Fidelma Hoey, wore a blue belt. And it's thought she was wearing jeans when she disappeared, they weren't found anywhere in her house.'

Oh, holy God. This was all she needed.

'So what happens now?' Tess hardly dared ask.

She moved over to the table. She needed to sit down. Across the kitchen, Gen had put the croissants on the plate Tess had taken out earlier. Catching her eye, she brought them to the table and sat down opposite her mouthing, 'What's wrong?'

Tess took a ragged breath and leaned on the table, shaking her head to Gen as Lynch continued.

'We need to bring the guards in to excavate. It's not your land, you'll be pleased to hear. We will need to check further along the border where we were yesterday, where we were told to look originally. It's possible that there really is more than one body up here, in all honesty. I mean, there are four disappearances linked to the Radio Snatcher and this place is so isolated and lonely, it's not even on any of the walkers' maps as a track.'

Lynch was loving all of this. His voice was speeding up as he spoke. She supposed it would make great TV. Tess's stomach turned over at the thought.

The only good thing in everything he'd said was that it wasn't on her land. Maybe she was reaching for a lifeline, but a trickle of relief began to build as she processed it.

Thank God, just thank God.

'Do I need to do anything?'

'No, sit tight. Leave it to us and I'll give you an update as soon as I know anything.'

'Thanks. That would be great.'

Lynch ended the call and Tess looked at the phone in her hand in disbelief.

Gen's voice brought her back to the kitchen. 'What's happened? Tell me, Tess, you've gone as white as a sheet.'

Tess touched her cheek. 'Have I?'

It took a moment for her brain to catch up. A moment in which Merlin stalked across the table and, balancing on his hind legs, butted her chin with his nose. Tess put her hand out to stroke his sleek back and he did it again, making a growling sound that could have been a purr.

'That was that reporter guy I told you about. The one from the *Daily News* that's making a documentary about cold cases.'

Gen looked at her across the table, then screwed up her face, wincing in anticipation of what Tess would say.

'What's happened?'

'He thinks they've found a body. One of the Radio Snatcher's victims. He's calling in the guards.'

Chapter 47

MEGAN O'RIORDAN picked up a bag of doughnuts and added it to the wire supermarket basket swinging from her arm. She and Ally needed sugar if they weren't going to murder both their parents before the end of the day. Dithering for a moment, she picked up another bag, just to be on the safe side. The way she was feeling today, she'd eat five on her own.

Trying to organise their sister's funeral when they didn't have a body, when their father refused to discuss anything related to the arrangements and their mother kept talking about a terrible accident, was driving them mental. After breakfast, Ally had gone up to her room and immersed herself in her law books, and Megan had gone up to her room and stared out of the window at the wizened apple tree in the garden. At least her room overlooked the back garden and she didn't have to watch the trail of sick people wandering down the drive to the surgery built into the side of the house. It had a separate entrance and the Georgian house was huge, but still, Megan had always been conscious that certain areas needed to be avoided unless she wanted to catch something awful. Too many people who should have stayed in bed and called the locum came brazenly into the surgery, sniffing and coughing all over the place.

Megan glanced at her basket, taking in the chocolate bars, fun pack of Maltesers and the doughnuts. She'd forgotten what she'd come into the Spar for now. Milk, probably. It was always milk. She had no idea how her father and his nurse and the receptionist got through so much. Or why her mother couldn't get it with the weekly shop she did in Blessington. Frankly, she thought it was ridiculous, the surgery being open at a time like this, but then her father had always buried himself in work whenever there was any sort of a crisis in the family.

Turning around abruptly, Megan came face to face with Aidan Gaunt, balancing a tray of coffees. At least, he had been. Now they were all over the floor and down the front of his jeans, the cardboard holder that they must have been sitting in redundant in one hand.

'Oh, my God, I'm so sorry. I was miles away. Are you OK?'

Looking down at the pool on the floor and his splashed jeans, Aidan took a moment to recover and then looked up at her, his blue eyes full of concern. A bit of Megan melted inside.

Christ, he was gorgeous.

'I'm fine, really, just a bit of coffee. How are you doing is more important. Have you heard anything?'

Megan realised she was watching his mouth move but not actually registering what he was saying. He had a really beautiful mouth. Trying to focus, she pushed her hair over her shoulder, wishing she'd washed it this morning. At least she was wearing a clingy T-shirt with her jeans – a slightly transparent one in lemon yellow, that emphasised her blue eyes. Her father had looked at it disapprovingly this morning, which had to be a good thing. Did she still have lipstick on?

'Sorry – heard?'

'About Laetitia? I presume there needs to be some sort of an investigation?'

Megan raised her eyebrows. Why was he asking about Tis? She was gone. Out of the equation. Leaving room for her, perhaps. Maybe.

But the coffee.

Megan cleared her throat, her mind flying. She needed to look sad – distraught would be better – and burdened by the whole situation at the same time. Perhaps he'd feel the need to comfort her. She sniffed, just for good measure, and touched her finger to the corner of her eye.

'No, I don't think so.' She look a long breath, as if gathering herself. 'They won't release her body yet. Something to do with Katie-Lou, I've no idea what. Ally and I have been trying to sort out the arrangements, but . . .' Megan sighed and trailed off, looking down sadly as she did so.

There was coffee all over the floor and all over him.

Christ, how had she done that?

She suddenly became aware of the scent of his aftershave over the smell of the coffee.

Oh, holy crap.

Reaching over for a napkin that was protruding from a container beside the coffee dock, Aidan started to pat it down his jeans.

'Here, let me help.' Megan reached for another one just as he turned, managing to bump into him again.

Could this get any worse?

'I'm fine, really, it's nothing. I can get more. Have they done a post mortem? That makes everything take longer, it's so awful for you.'

Taking her cue from his tone, full of concern, Megan let out another big sigh and touched her eye again as if she was brushing away another tear.

What should she say?

Ally was dealing with everything, although she wasn't going to tell Aidan that – it made Megan look useless. Ally always did all the legal stuff, and honestly Megan really didn't want to know. Laetitia had annoyed her enough in life and now, even in death, she seemed to be making life difficult for all of them. The funeral was going to be a nightmare, and here she was again, popping up between Aidan and any chance Megan had of getting closer to him.

As Megan was about to reply she heard a siren blaring behind her. Surprised, she turned to look out of the shop window and saw the Rockfield patrol car weave around a tractor and disappear in the direction of Kilfenora House.

'Oh, goodness, whatever's happening now?'

Conscious that it might be a bit obvious if she went to the door to look out, Megan craned her head to see if she could see further along the street, but there was a sun cream display stand between her and the glass doors that was blocking her view.

'Blimey, I hope nothing's happened to Tess.' Suddenly Aidan's voice was right in her ear and she realised her shoulder was touching his chest. Megan put her hand to her forehead.

'Oh, goodness.'

Leaning back slightly as if in a faint, she felt his arm suddenly supporting her waist, the air around her filled with aftershave.

CK One. It came to her as she leaned into him.

Delicious.

Chapter 48

THE PATROL CAR got to the site where Jerry Lynch had gathered his team just ahead of Tess. She pulled up beside it – the doors had been left wide open, strobes still flashing.

Inwardly she cringed. They hardly needed the lights and sirens at eleven o'clock on a Tuesday morning in Kilfenora, but then they didn't get much excitement up at Rockfield station – a call like this would make their year.

The whole village would be wondering what could possibly have happened up here now.

Ahead of her, further up the field, she could see the young guard who often did foot patrol in the village deep in conversation with Jerry Lynch. Her dark shiny hair was pulled into a blunt ponytail, her hat under her arm. She had evidently decided the stab risk from an eight-year-old body was low, and had abandoned her protective vest; she was wearing her short-sleeved uniform shirt and thick navy trousers with impossibly hot-looking heavy black boots. Despite the shirt, she had to be baking.

Sticking her hands into the pockets of her jeans, Tess walked slowly up towards them, a path worn in the thick grass in just the few days they'd been there. She heard one of the dogs barking and looked up, expecting to see it, but it must have been over the rise behind the gorse bushes. Was that where the body was? Tess's stomach was really churning now. And her head hurt.

And she was way too hot.

She pulled at the navy-blue silk neckerchief she'd found this morning in the bottom of her drawer. With her hair cut this length, the back of her neck was exposed. When she was getting dressed this morning, it had suddenly occurred to her that perhaps she was feeling so off because she'd had too much sun. She could feel it now, the rays penetrating the thin fabric of her loose white T-shirt. She was basically ginger, after all, and spending a lot of time outdoors at the moment. Perhaps vest tops and factor 50 weren't enough to beat the effects of this heat.

Tess caught her breath, trying to centre herself. She looked around, as if she was inspecting the landscape. She felt rotten, but she couldn't let anyone know that she was flagging at this stage. It was her energy that was holding this whole project together.

There was a fabulous view from up here, the mountains thick with heather, a carpet of purple and yellow, the colours strong against the clear blue of the sky. The hills rolled away to lake-filled valleys. Bees were buzzing around the brilliant yellow gorse flowers, the scent of coconut strong at this time of the day. When everything was up and running and she was feeling better, she really needed to take some time out and enjoy this place.

She knew she was putting off the inevitable – a proper conversation with Lynch – but she really wasn't in a hurry to find out what was happening here. The thought of a woman lying lost in the cold ground made her stomach churn again.

Over the last few days she'd thought not feeling well was down to the sun and working too hard, combined with the shock of everything. It probably was too much sun, but now she was beginning to wonder if it was actually a bug. Her legs hadn't felt too steady the other day and they felt weak again now. Although perhaps she was just horribly unfit and the trek up this hill was the problem. Perhaps she needed to talk to Clarissa about an exercise programme.

Before she had a chance to think about it more, Lynch spotted her and, calling a greeting, waved her up.

'You know Garda Edwards?'

The guard nodded by way of hello.

'The team working on the lake should be finished this morning, and then they're coming straight up here. It was quicker than calling a new team out from Dublin. I'll be securing the scene.'

The guard's face was serious but she was almost glowing. Tess could understand it. She was quite sure Garda Edwards hadn't joined the force to spend her career looking for lost sheep and solving boundary disputes. Cracking one of the country's most infamous cases and catching the Radio Snatcher could be the biggest investigation she'd ever deal with. This presumed that Katie-Lou's death was an accident, of course, but Tess was beginning to get the creeping feeling that perhaps there was some link between her and Laetitia that none of them knew about. Something that could involve the Twitter troll and *Great Expectations*.

And that made the picture rather different.

Garda Edwards didn't seem to notice that Tess hadn't answered.

'We'll be as discreet as possible. We'll be keeping this all very quiet. If the suspect is in the area, we don't want to spook him. The fewer people who know there's been a find, the better.'

Tess nodded.

That made sense to her.

The sound of barking drew her attention. She still couldn't see the dogs, but they sounded excited. She turned back to Garda Edwards.

'We'll have to think of a reason why you came up here with the lights on.'

'Just tell people I needed to check something urgently. They all know about Katie-Louise O'Neill, and how dodgy the mobile reception is around here.'

Tess wasn't sure that sounded very convincing. Higher up the field, the dog handlers appeared, both dogs trotting obediently on their leads, tails wagging.

'If things can be kept discreet, that would be amazing. You know we've the opening scheduled for this weekend? Are we OK to go ahead?'

'I'll have to check with my superiors, but the area of interest is a long way from the house. We'll keep the public out of this area and you should be fine.'

Well, that was one thing.

'Thank you. I'd better get on. Can you keep me posted?' Tess addressed both of them.

Lynch nodded in response. His nose was red and peeling, but he was looking quite delighted with himself – although perhaps she wasn't being fair. If this was the body of one of the Radio Snatcher's alleged victims, then it could offer a real lead to his identity, and Lynch was the one who'd got the information – his team had made the discovery.

And it wasn't on her land, quite.

So that was something to be thankful for.

As Tess turned to return to her car, Garda Edwards fell in beside her.

'I'll walk down with you. I need to get the kit out of the car.' Tess could feel the guard looking sideways at her. 'Are you OK? You look a bit pale.'

'I'm not feeling amazing, it's been a busy few weeks.'

Garda Edwards grimaced. 'I can't share the details, but the post mortem's been completed on Katie-Louise. It's been confirmed that cause of death was drowning.'

'I heard a rumour that there were bruises on her shoulders?'

The guard nodded. 'I can't say much, but there are indications she tried to fight back. She broke a fingernail. They are checking to see if there's any recoverable DNA under the remaining nails.'

Tess's eyebrows shot up. Seeing her expression, the guard continued.

'DNA isn't quite the magic they make out on the TV. We need a match before we can make any arrests, and to get a match we need to have a sample to compare it to, but it's very useful.'

'I'm surprised after being in the water there was anything left under her nails.'

'It's a long shot all right. My sergeant said the same thing. He reckons the killer might have thought that, too, and that's perhaps why she ended up in the lake in the first place.'

'Are your people going to need to section off the gardens for much longer, do you think?'

Garda Edwards shook her head. 'A diver went down yesterday. I know it's not that deep, but it saved us having to dredge it. He found a mobile phone – well, a few of them actually.'

'Do you know who they belong to? They could have been dropped by tourists.'

Garda Edwards glanced at her from under her lashes as if she was measuring Tess up.

'One of them is the same make and model as Laetitia O'Riordans actually, but we won't know anything until the technical guys take a look. Obviously all of that's confidential. Like here . . .' She gestured with her head back up the hill. 'We need to keep everything quiet. It's possible what happened over the past few days is somehow connected to this discovery.'

Tess looked at her, part of her dying inside.

Chapter 49

TESS WAS ONLY half concentrating when she heard a knock at the front door of the Butler's Lodge. Her headache and nausea had been improved by a possibly dangerous level of seasickness tablets she'd found at the back of the bathroom cabinet, and she'd had a few minutes sitting down in the cool of the living room, but she still didn't feel great.

And sitting in her office looking at her laptop screen blankly really wasn't helping. Right now, any interruption that got her up from her desk was very welcome.

She almost laughed when she opened the door. It was Aidan. With coffee.

'You do know I've got a state-of-the-art coffee machine here, don't you?'

Standing on the doorstep with two takeaway cups in his hands, he smiled sheepishly.

'Sometimes it's nice to have one done for you. I'm early for rehearsal, so I thought I'd drop in to see how you're doing.'

She opened the door wide. 'Let's sit in the garden, there should be a bit of shade.'

He followed her through to the living room. She quickly found the key to the patio doors, hidden in an Indian mother-of-pearl inlaid box on the coffee table, and opened them.

Merlin was waiting for her on the patio as if he knew she was on her way. She mentally shook her head. It was as if he could read her mind.

It was considerably warmer outside than in the house, but Tess felt as if she needed some air. When she'd originally moved in she'd ordered the garden table and four chairs, thinking she might have barbecues and people over for dinner, but between the pandemic and getting sucked into the restoration project, she hadn't got out here nearly often enough.

And the furniture was already starting to look the worse for wear. She could relate to that.

She sat down, pulling her hair off her face while Aidan worked out whose coffee was whose. It only took him a second, and he sat down opposite her with a sigh.

'I don't know how you're keeping going with, well, everything . . .'

Tess rolled her eyes. 'I'm starting to wonder that myself.'

She reached for her coffee. Could she talk to him? She felt the need to spill it all out. He wasn't local, and from the limited time she'd known him, he wasn't a gossip. And he'd been brilliant since Conor's accident. She looked at the coffee cup in her hand. It was so thoughtful, and it was the little things that made a difference when you were under pressure.

Not noticing her hesitation, he went on. 'At least one thing you don't have to worry about is the play. Rehearsals have been going really smoothly. Whatever happens, even if the opening night gets delayed, we'll be ready.'

'That's good to hear.' Tess lifted the lid off her coffee and was about to take a sip, when she stopped. 'How are Meg and Ally? I need to call them.'

'They're fine, absorbed in making arrangements. There's some sort of hold-up with Laetitia's body being released, or something, so it looks like the funeral won't be for a while.'

Tess rubbed her face with her free hand. 'Having the funeral this week would have been a bit of a distraction. That feels very selfish of me, even thinking it, never mind saying it.'

'I said to Meg that people will want time to grieve. Everyone knows the doctor, obviously. The funeral will be huge, and keeping it clear of this weekend makes sense. She seemed very receptive.'

'Thanks. Thanks for thinking of that.' Tess really meant it. 'I need to call Conor's mum and see how he's doing, too.'

'I saw her yesterday in the village. He's still in a coma and it's all a bit unknown, but his friends are going into the hospital and playing his favourite music and talking to him.' Aidan smiled. 'He's got quite a few female fans, so it's like O'Connell Street in there, apparently. She seemed hugely comforted to know he had so much support.' Aidan stared into the garden and shook his head. 'It was such a freak accident. I suppose we're lucky it was only him on stage.'

'Very true. We have to look on the bright side.'

'Have you heard anything about what happened to Katie-Louise? I saw the Kilfenora Garda car heading this way this morning – they looked like they were in a terrible hurry.'

Tess hesitated and rubbed her face again, trying to massage away the drama of the last few days. The urge to share the load was strong, and she knew she wouldn't be able to talk to Gen; she was far too upset about Katie-Lou. Garda Edwards had said it was all confidential, but Aidan was part of the team. Tess cleared her throat.

'I think we may have actually just swerved another potential disaster this morning.'

Aidan arched one eyebrow in question.

'Another one?'

Tess nodded. She was sure she could trust him.

'This can't go any further at the moment, but you know those women that went missing years ago, the ones linked to the Radio Snatcher – Fidelma Hoey was the last one?' Her name had become etched on Tess's mind. Young, attractive, an accountant in Dublin. Like the others, she'd had absolutely no reason to walk out of her house and disappear, leaving the front door wide open and the radio on. 'Well, this is a bit of a long story, but a journalist got a tip-off that one of them might be buried on Kilfenora land.'

'You're not serious?' Aidan looked at her, aghast. 'I can see why it's confidential.' He winced. 'The fallout from that going public would be meteoric. You'd have crowds up here looking at the site and causing chaos. To say nothing of the press. That wouldn't be good for business at all. Even if it's only a rumour, these things stick.'

Tess smiled weakly; she really didn't need reminding.

'Well, the good thing is – if there is a good thing in it all – that the guards think they have found something – a body, but it's not on Kilfenora land. It's higher up the mountain, on the national park side.'

'They've *found* a body?' Aidan looked at her incredulously.

'I know. They brought dogs up. They were having a run about and they found a piece of ground that had been disturbed. They said the tip-off was pretty vague, so it was very lucky. They hadn't intended to look on the park side at all, it's so huge.'

Aidan shook his head in disbelief. 'My God, it's one thing after another.'

Tess nodded slowly and went to pick up her coffee just as Merlin jumped onto the table. The whole structure rocked slightly and he jumped off again, sending her cup flying, the entire contents pouring into Aidan's lap.

'Merlin! What are you playing at? My God, I'm so sorry. Is it hot?'

'You won't believe it, but this is the second time this has happened to me today. Does he always jump on the table?' He said it in that way non-cat people can only just keep the disgust out of their voices at the thought of paws on tables.

'Let me get a cloth.'

Jumping up, a moment later Tess returned with a pile of tea towels. Aidan mopped at the stain on his jeans. Tess sat down and wiped the table with the damp cloth she'd brought from the kitchen. Merlin sat on the edge of the lawn and coolly looked back at her.

'He's so bold, and he doesn't even live here. He's Clarissa's cat.'

'Clarissa Westmacott?' Aidan sounded surprised

'Yes, she lives in the Gardener's Cottage on the other side of the estate. I think he thinks he owns the whole demesne.'

As they both looked at him, Merlin turned around and stalked into the house through the open patio door, his tail held high like a flagpole.

Chapter 50

TESS WAS AT her desk, staring blankly out of her office window, when Mark pulled up in front of her cottage. It was already six o'clock. She really didn't know where today had gone. She'd been on the phone all afternoon, checking deliveries and confirming what was coming when. It really was starting to feel like a military operation. And she was well ready for a break.

'I wondered if you'd like some company.'

Mark shifted uncomfortably on the doorstep and rattled his keys in the pocket of his denim shorts.

'Your timing is perfect. Come in. Don't you have to make sure there are enough barrels on for the evening crowd or anything?'

Mark wrinkled his face thoughtfully before answering, as if he was considering his options.

'As tempting as it is to make sure the pub isn't covered in puke, or the toilets blocked before the evening shift begins, no, thank God. I've a duty manager minding the place. I needed to go into the National Library, so I took the day off, and I'm aiming to make the most of it.'

Despite everything that had happened today, Tess found herself smiling.

'It's not really that bad, is it, being a landlord?'

'Sometimes it's worse. As you can tell, I love every minute of it. I'm completely cut out for the service industry.'

As Mark followed her into the kitchen, Tess looked at him quizzically.

'But I thought you ran a tour company back in Australia. That's service, isn't it?'

'Not the same sort. Everyone was sober, for one thing. High-end tourists can be extremely demanding but . . . Let's just say it's a whole different game. And I was CEO back then. I had staff who dealt with the clients face-on.'

She leaned on the counter as he pulled out one of the kitchen chairs.

'Clients?'

'Exactly – clients, not customers. Very different.'

As he was speaking, Merlin appeared at his feet, weaving around his leg and the chair leg.

'Careful with him, he's in disgrace today.'

'How could a beautiful animal like this possibly be in disgrace?'

As if pandering to his fan club, Merlin stood on his hind legs and rubbed his chin on Mark's knee. Tess laughed.

'He certainly likes you. Beer or a G and T? Then let's go outside, I need some fresh air.'

'G and T for sure.' He grinned. 'I've not gone full Aussie yet.'

The patio doors were open and outside the evening was balmy, foliage that had been planted for its scent truly coming into its own as the day faded. Daphne blended with white lilac, the fragrance trapped by the high granite walls that surrounded the garden, barely visible behind the dense shrubs and trees. Tess loved the feeling of privacy the walls gave. She could truly get away from everything when she came out here, often thinking about the conversations the walls had heard over all the years since they'd been built. She was sure the Butler's Lodge had been the centre of staff gossip for generations.

Tess put their glasses down on the garden table, one leg now supported by a folded piece of newspaper to level it up. She leaned forward to light the citronella candle that sat in a terracotta dish in the middle. It took a moment to catch, and then she sat down heavily, now noticing that the cracks between the paving stones were filling with weeds and the small lawn was a carpet of dandelions. Why hadn't she seen that earlier? Perhaps she'd just had too much on her mind.

Tess didn't know why she felt embarrassed, but Mark had obviously noticed the state of the garden, too. She smiled, raising her eyebrows.

'I'm going for the country garden look. Wild spaces are good for bees.'

He smiled, reaching for his glass, holding it up in a toast.

'That's very true. Here's to getting to the end of the week without anything else . . . er . . . unexpected.'

'God, I'll drink to that.' Tess lifted her glass and took a sip of her gin. She needed it more than she thought.

After a few moments and another sip, she turned to him.

'I'm a bit worried that you're right about the lake.'

Mark put his glass down and turned it carefully, the bubbles reflecting the light from the candle.

'I'm a bit worried I might be right about that, too.' He cleared his throat. 'There are a few other things that . . .' He screwed up his face. 'Have been bothering me as well.'

Tess felt her stomach sink. She'd had a feeling he was going to say something like that ever since he'd been so preoccupied up at Fury Hill. It felt like a lifetime ago, but she hadn't forgotten how quiet he'd been on the way back. She'd been quiet, too, emotionally drained, her head too full to find anything idle to chat about, but she'd sensed he was thinking. And it had been a niggle in the back of her mind ever since.

'Hit me with it. After the last few days I think I'm beyond shock.'

He cleared his throat and, looking across at her, rubbed the shadow of stubble on his chin with his hand.

'Come on, it can't be that bad . . .' Tess hesitated. 'Can it?'

'I'm really not sure.' Mark took a breath and turned to face her, his face creased in a frown. Tess smoothed her curls away from her forehead and rubbed the back of her neck as he continued. 'It's just there seemed to be some parallels between what's happening now and the tragedies that occurred here in the past.'

Tess took another sip of her gin and squinted at him.

'I'm not getting you.'

He looked across at her, frowning, as if he was mapping something out in his head.

'OK, so let's start with Conor's accident.'

Tess nodded slowly. The longer he took to get to the point, the tighter the knot in her stomach became. What on earth did he mean?

'The insurance people are sure it was an accident. Well, from what Garry with two r's has said, they are.'

'It's not so much whether it was an accident or not – it's more the type of accident that's worrying me.' He paused. 'And what has followed it.'

Chapter 51

SITTING IN THE calm of her garden, the ice cracking in their glasses as it melted, Mark pursed his lips for a moment as if he was thinking. Behind him, Tess caught a glimpse of something moving in the undergrowth – Merlin, probably, heading to Clarissa's for his second dinner. The evening was still bright, the heat making the air feel thick.

Mark picked up his glass and swirled it around.

'When I was doing my PhD I did a lot of research on the house – it was on the doorstep and steeped in history, it seemed logical. Obviously I couldn't get in to the archives to check the records during the pandemic, but there are a lot of sources available online, and in old books if you dig a bit. I've ended up with quite a few. Anyway, that was why I went to the National Library, to check up on a few things.' He looked at her. 'How much of the history of the house do you know?'

Tess blushed. 'Not nearly as much as I should. I've got a broad outline from Wikipedia and the internet, and everyone keeps telling me about this damned curse, but I've been intending to get a proper history written. It's on my list.'

He smiled sympathetically. 'With a lot of other things.' Tess rolled her eyes by way of an answer as he continued. 'You know that in the 1830s Lady Kilfenora was killed in an accident?'

'Yes, I heard it was a falling flowerpot or something, but I can't imagine that's true, really. That's not something that would have been on a window sill back then, surely?'

Mark half smiled. 'Window boxes came into fashion in the Victorian period. Lady K had planters full of lavender put on the bedroom window sills so the scent came in. Apparently she'd got Lord Reginald to spend a fortune on decorative stuff like that, and on the statues around the lake – she was the one who had the Apollo fountain put in.' He took a sip of his G and T. 'Which is interesting, given that Apollo was the god of truth and prophecy – the god of divine justice, who made mortals aware of their own guilt and purified them.' He swished the ice around his glass. 'You'll understand the significance of that in a moment. Apparently Lord Reginald didn't want to spend more money on having cast-iron cages made for these planters, as they were only in use in the summer, so it was just sitting on the window ledge. So you're right, it wasn't quite a flowerpot.'

Tess looked at him for a moment, an echo of a memory nagging at her.

'Full of lavender? Are you sure?'

'So contemporary records say. Is that significant?'

Tess pursed her lips for a moment. She didn't know; she'd need time to think about that one.

'How did it fall? It must have been an accident.'

'Nobody's very sure about that. I've been over the contemporary reports to double-check.' He sipped his gin. 'The window sills on this house, as you know, are about a foot deep on the upper levels. It would have needed a real shove for it to have fallen, given the weight of it. Records show that there had been some wind – you know, summer storms.'

'But you don't sound like you think it could have been moved by the wind?'

Mark leaned back in his chair and toyed with his glass, frowning.

'Stop me if this is boring, but it was 1839. In January that year there had been a huge storm – they call it the Night of the Big Wind, *Oíche na Gaoithe Móire*. It caused significant damage and several hundred deaths. About a quarter of the houses in north Dublin were damaged or destroyed, and forty-two ships were wrecked. Lady K was killed the same year. So with the memories of the Big Wind fresh, it's possible that people believed the story and local myth grew up around it.'

'But lavender's in flower in the summer. And surely summer storms wouldn't have been strong enough to move a planter.'

'Indeed – she was killed in late May, according to the records I can find, but those are mainly anecdotal. The fire in the Public Records Office in 1922 destroyed so much that it can be tricky to piece information together.'

Tess nodded. Fire was the enemy of history. The fire that had destroyed much of the main part of Kilfenora House in the early 1990's had taken with it most, if not all of the remaining family papers. What had been saved had apparently been entrusted to the National Archives of Ireland by the then owners. She'd wanted to have a look at them when she'd first moved in, but then she'd got caught up in the restoration.

'So if it didn't fall by accident, it must have been deliberate – is that what you're saying? But who could have pushed it? Who was here then?'

'This is where we get into conjecture, but it's said that only the governess and Lord Reginald were at home. I think it was the staff's half-day, and by all accounts only the butler's wife was on the property – here, in fact. She heard the crash and went rushing to the front of the house.'

Tess rolled her hands, indicating that she needed more of the story.

'She found Lady K badly injured on the drive, and the planter shattered beside her.'

'I'm not seeing the link with Conor. The play?'

Mark shook his head. 'It was more the falling object that I was thinking of. Which could have been an unfortunate coincidence on its own—'

Tess looked across at him, cutting in. 'But it's not in isolation?'

'Well . . .' He drew the word out. 'Not exactly. Some other things have happened here that also seem to have rather significant parallels.'

Tess let out a sharp breath. 'Tell me. I thought the stories about the accidents here were all village gossip, tied up with the rumours of the place being haunted. Someone mentioned there are stories of ghostly children but—'

'There's also the governess. I mean, as well as the children.'

'Oh?' Tess looked surprised; she didn't know about that one.

Mark frowned. 'In the research I've done, the most consistent story is that the governess was having an affair with Lord Reginald, which is what makes me think that there was significance in Lady K's choice of Apollo for the fountain – him being the god of truth and prophecy. It feels to me like she could have been making a point about her husband's infidelity.' He cleared his throat. 'It's rumoured that one of them, either Lord Reginald or the governess, deliberately pushed the planter in order to finish off Lady K. It could hardly have been one of the twins, they were only nine, but who's to say that they didn't see what happened?'

The knot in Tess's stomach was growing. She looked at her glass but she didn't really feel like drinking. The gin was sour on her tongue.

'So what happened to the governess?'

Mark looked directly at her. 'She hanged herself in the Sugar Canister Tower.'

Tess's hand shot to her mouth. 'No! Why?'

'Who knows? It's possible that she did indeed kill Lady K, but when it came to it, Lord Reginald wasn't that enamoured with continuing their relationship. Perhaps he did it, but had other ideas about who the next Lady Kilfenora would be.'

'But that's awful. And Laetitia . . .'

'Exactly.' He looked across the table at her, his face serious. 'Which could have been another coincidence, but while the household was in a flap about the mistress and then the governess meeting tragic endings, no one was watching the twins properly.'

'Christ, what happened to them?'

'It was young Lady Anastasia who was first. They think she took a boat out onto the lake. She was trying to catch fish or something, but the boat turned over. One of the gardeners spotted her body floating in the reeds.'

Tess looked at him, the knot in her stomach starting to roll. She was suddenly feeling as if she actually needed something a lot stronger than a gin and tonic.

'Then what happened?' It came out as a whisper.

'This is the bit that's really worrying me.'

Like the rest wasn't. She almost said it out loud.

Mark put his hand flat on the table and spread out his fingers as if connecting with the wood was somehow grounding him, then he continued.

'It seems the other twin, Lady Catherine, had been left to her own devices and was playing in the garden. Nobody's sure quite what happened, but she died quite quickly after her sister. It's thought she had made tea from something poisonous.'

'Do they have any idea what?'

'According to the reports I found, there were stems and flowers from a plant called aconite found near the well. It has very pretty purple flowers, so perhaps she thought it would . . .' He shook his head. 'Who knows what she was thinking, honestly. Perhaps it was a game the twins played with mint or lemon balm or something, and she just picked the wrong thing.'

'So you're telling me that the only thing that hasn't happened yet is a poisoning? With aconite?'

Chapter 52

CLARISSA LEANED INTENTLY across her kitchen table, keeping her voice low. Malachi had gone hunting for Merlin in the garden, but she didn't want him catching any of their conversation through the open back door.

'I know it sounds wild, but I think Mark might have a point.'

Clarissa waited while Gen absorbed what she'd said. It hadn't taken her long this morning to grasp the implications of Mark's theory, and she'd been rolling it around her head ever since. He'd wanted to check up on a few things before he spoke to Tess, but had run the idea past her first.

It did sound mad, but the parallels were undeniable.

Her face creased, Genevieve fiddled with the knife on her cheese plate, lining it up with the gold pattern around the edge. They'd had an early supper with Malachi, but Clarissa had had to cajole Gen into eating anything. Now she could tell from the look on Genevieve's face that she was having a hard time with Mark's discovery.

'But really? I mean, Conor was an accident.' Gen shook her head. 'I'm not seeing it at all.'

'Everyone is assuming that the light falling was an accident, but three bolts and a safety cable had to fail for that to happen. I did mention it at the time.'

'I know you did. But the rest?'

'The rest follows the pattern of tragedies a bit too closely to the historic events, if you ask me. If Katie-Lou hadn't wound up in the lake, as Mark said himself this morning, he may never had made the connection.'

'And the other child died from some sort of poisoning?'

'Precisely.'

Gen bit her lip. 'I'm still not seeing how these things can be mirroring past events. I mean, if we assume Katie-Lou went up to Laetitia's van to get her cards read that Friday evening, you're suggesting that something Katie-Lou said must have upset Laetitia so much that she attacked Katie-Lou, and then went and took her own life . . . I mean, what on earth could that have been? It's Katie-Lou we're talking here, not . . . I don't know, Meg O'Riordan. Katie-Lou was as innocent as they come.'

Gen ran her finger under her eye, catching a tear. Clarissa didn't want to upset her, but she needed to reason this through with someone; it had been boiling in her mind since Mark had explained it all to her.

'That does sound rather unlikely, but you are assuming that there was no one *else* there.' Clarissa hesitated, unsure how to put her next idea forward. 'Hypothetically speaking, what if, for instance, Meg was with Laetitia that evening, too?' Clarissa paused. 'I'm not saying I think she did anything, but looking at the bigger picture, perhaps she instigated an argument or something. I've sensed a resentment between those sisters for a long time. Jealousy, even.' Gen was still frowning as Clarissa tapped the arm of her reading glasses on the table as she made her point. 'And Meg's fingerprints would be all over that van. You don't need a degree in forensics to work out that tying her to all of this would be extremely difficult. Particularly as both witnesses are deceased.'

Genevieve was silent for a moment. Clarissa could almost see the cogs in her mind going around as she wound a strand of her hair around her finger.

'Meg told Tess that she and Ally had spent Friday afternoon with Laetitia.'

'Exactly. What if she went back later, and found Laetitia doing Katie-Lou's cards? Or perhaps she went back and was arguing with Laetitia when Katie-Lou arrived. Bless her, you know how dopy Katie-Lou was. Maybe she saw something or heard something, and Meg felt she had no choice but to push her into the lake?'

'But why? Why would she do that? You're always talking about understanding a character's motivation when you're on stage. What could Meg's possibly be?'

Clarissa laid her glasses down carefully. 'What are the usual motivations for murder? Greed, lust, jealousy? It could be any one of them. We don't know what their relationship was really like, but I've always found Meg a bit . . . I'm not sure . . . disingenuous? Her sole priority in life is herself. She tries to hide it but it's in everything she does and says.' Clarissa pursed her lips. 'One possibility, and this may not be it, but if everything went wrong for Tess, it would be logical to assume she'd have to sell up, that she wouldn't be able to keep Kilfenora afloat.'

Gen frowned. Clarissa could see that she wasn't following.

'If Tess decided to sell, I'd imagine she'd have to take a drop in the price, given the state of the market. And a property like Kilfenora could take years to sell – look how long it was on the market before Tess bought it. The only people around here who might be able to raise the capital are the O'Riordans, and, again following the logic of this, it would be right to assume that Tess might be more inclined to take a local offer than one from some nouveau riche beef baron, even if it was lower than she wanted. Particularly if it was fast.'

'I've heard Meg say that she wanted to work on the estate when it's all open. Do you think she meant she wants to run it, like Tess does?'

Clarissa shrugged. 'It's a possibility. I think Meg gets obsessed with things, and honestly, all this is so complex it feels like it could be part of a play.'

'She got really mad when she couldn't run *Faustus*, you know.' Gen frowned. 'But murdering her sister? That's literally something out of a Greek tragedy or Shakespeare.'

Clarissa nodded, restraining herself from saying 'My point exactly.' Instead, she waved her glasses in the air as if she was hypothesising.

'Perhaps the sisters were working together originally to sabotage the opening, as part of a plan to get control of Kilfenora. Laetitia was involved with the play. She could have gone to the ballroom early to do something with the set design and, in fact, loosened those brackets on the lighting track. Perhaps they never intended for Conor to get so badly hurt at all. But perhaps Katie-Lou got to the van early on Friday and heard them talking about it.'

Gen fingered her earring. 'Do you really think so?'

'I'm only hypothesising, but if Meg's behind this, perhaps she got rid of Katie-Lou on an impulse, and Laetitia felt it had all got out of hand and threatened to go to the police? In order to save herself, Meg had to murder her sister?'

Gen sighed. 'Well, I don't know how Meg could have faked Laetitia's suicide, but she *was* the one who found her. And very dramatically.' Gen sighed. 'It's a puzzle, all right. I don't think we've got all the pieces, but when you line them up, what Mark said looks more and more plausible, doesn't it?'

Clarissa turned her ring to straighten the sapphire.

'Precisely.'

'And . . .' Gen took a deep breath. 'Tess said Laetitia was looking up aconite – that she had a book of wild flowers in her van and she had the page marked.'

'Oh.' Clarissa's eyebrows shot up. 'Really?'

She knew a lot about the properties of aconite.

'Perhaps Laetitia was planning to poison someone as well? Perhaps she had *already* poisoned someone and we just don't know about it yet, and the someone else she was working with needed to get her out of the way because she knew too much, or had outlived her usefulness.' Gen looked at her across the table, her eyes full of fear. 'Laetitia was a bit odd, let's face it. Maybe you're right, and she really was working with someone to bring down Kilfenora.'

'That is what is worrying me. It all feels planned and her "suicide"' – Clarissa made rabbit ears with her forefingers – 'was another piece of the puzzle.'

Gen pulled at her dangly earring. 'Should we tell the guards?'

Clarissa glanced at the aconite stems in the vase on her kitchen table and thought for a moment.

'We don't want to interfere. This is their job, after all. But I do think we need to keep a very close eye on the O'Riordans for the moment. There is one thing that they haven't taken into account of in the bigger picture.'

'What's that?'

Clarissa paused, but in light of recent events, it was time she told Genevieve.

'As you know, when Dominic departed this life so suddenly, I inherited his significant estate. What I didn't tell you at the time is that he was also really rather well insured. So I was left *very* well-off. I'm Tess's angel investor. I own a third of Kilfenora and there is no way, whatever happens, that Tess will ever have to sell.'

Chapter 53

Tess needed a walk. It was getting dusky, but she had to get out of the house and have a think. Ever since Mark had left she'd been thinking about everything, and now she felt as if the walls were closing in on her.

As she pulled the front door behind her, making quite sure it was locked, Tess could feel that the air was heavy, as if a storm was coming. If she was lucky she'd get out and back before it rained. As if he'd been waiting for her, Merlin suddenly appeared on the end of the garden wall, padding delicately along the top to meet her.

She smiled. She'd hesitated at the thought of walking around the grounds on her own in the evening, and then, furious that she'd even had to think it, had made sure her phone was fully charged and decided she'd do a quick circuit of the main gardens. *Great Expectations* or not, there was no way someone was going to frighten her into being a hostage in her own house.

Now, seeing Merlin, she felt somehow comforted and safer. Which was ridiculous, given that he was a cat, but the last few days had been utterly ridiculous. The way things were going, if he spoke to her, Tess didn't think she'd be surprised.

Tomorrow the antique furniture was being delivered, all carefully chosen to fill the main rooms in the house, and on

Thursday the trestle tables and tents for the craft market. Thank goodness that was all being set up in the pasture on either side of the avenue, at the front of the house. The guards hadn't released the formal gardens yet, and would probably be there for a while, but they could be closed off. She just needed to focus attention on the main house and the tea rooms. Visitors could come back another day to see Apollo and his lake.

But this evening, the play was her biggest concern. She very quickly needed to make a decision about whether that should go ahead. It was Tuesday today; it already felt too late to cancel it. Knowing how much work had gone into it, how many hours Aidan had spent on it, part of her felt that it should go ahead, that the main performance should happen as planned on Friday, but then perhaps they should give it a break for a week before doing the month of twice-weekly performances, as originally planned.

She'd seen Aidan's reluctance to shelve it – but they could hardly run the full celebratory opening weekend under these circumstances.

Pulling the garden gate behind her, Tess bent to give Merlin a tickle and set off to her right down towards the Rose Walk. He ran in front of her, criss-crossing her path as if he was leading the way, playing with the evening shadows. Above her, bats dipped in and out of the trees, flashes of movement in her peripheral vision.

Reaching the fork in the lane where it split – one branch taking her to the rear entrance to the gardens, the other running on beside the walls of the Rose Walk and down to the woods – she followed Merlin to the five-bar gate that kept the public from wandering into the gardens. When the house was fully open, there would be a charge to see them, and access would be through the main doors. Over the years that she'd been restoring the house, she'd allowed visitors in for free, with a voluntary contribution, but after this weekend there would be a charge towards the upkeep of the place.

Tess pushed the gate closed behind her and glanced into the huge Victorian glasshouses that had been built up against the red-brick wall at the rear of the stables. They were packed full of summer bedding plants that would give the front of the house a splash of colour.

The greenhouses behind her, Tess cut across the lawn to the towering wrought-iron gate that marked the start of the Rose Walk, the evening sun catching the elaborate gold rondels and flower heads picked out in the ornate design, the thick navy-blue paint still shiny. Her Converse crunched on the gravel. Ahead, the chain of circular rose beds and contrasting square ponds awaited her, jewel-like, the water mirrored. This area had been designed for stillness and contemplation, the borders crammed with fragrant plants.

Merlin waited for her as she walked slowly along the edge of the first pond, peering into the crystal-clear water, looking for life. Water boatmen scudded across the surface and a puff of silt suggested a newt had swished its tail.

Past a bed crammed with pink roses, in the second pond, a huge water lily floated on thick rubbery leaves, one huge flower, the petals virgin white, beginning to close as the sun dipped. She loved this walk; the deep borders were a heady blend of colour and scent, extending in points between the ponds and the rose beds as if they were holding each one in a colourful embrace. Perhaps it was the fragrance of the flowers, heavy in the warmth of the dusk, that made it feel so incredibly calming. Whenever Tess came this way, she felt as if time had stopped here, a stillness caught between the walls; that she might meet the previous residents of Kilfenora walking towards her as they headed back to the house.

Walking on ahead of her, Merlin had stopped beside a bench positioned opposite the herb bed. Waiting for her to catch up, he took a moment to wash the base of his tail.

In this part of the Rose Walk, the Mediterranean scent of rosemary was strong, other herbs Tess couldn't identify vying for attention. And in the middle of the bed opposite the bench, delicate bell-like purple flowers rose on tall stems.

The aconite that Clarissa had mentioned.

The plant that Tess had seen marked in Laetitia's book.

Had Laetitia come here to pick it? Tess had checked with the gardeners and this was the only place in the gardens that they knew it grew, in the middle of the poison garden. Lines from Blake's poem 'A Poison Tree' circled around her head.

> *I was angry with my friend;*
> *I told my wrath, my wrath did end.*
> *I was angry with my foe;*
> *I told it not, my wrath did grow.*

"*My wrath did grow*". Had opening Kilfenora House to the public somehow brought out the Radio Snatcher? She hated the nickname the press had used; it glorified the perpetrator somehow, gave him a celebrity status that was sickening.

But whatever the press said, there had been four disappearances over a two-year period, and then, eight years ago, they'd stopped. The speculation was that perhaps the Radio Snatcher was in prison, or had left the country for work. Had he been sharing a cell with Lynch's informant? Was he out now, and around here somewhere? Or was he actually Eoin Doyle?

Looking anxiously up and down the Rose Walk, despite the cloying heat, Tess shivered at the thought. Did he feel threatened by the house opening to the public, of the land being used again, and for obvious reasons really didn't want people tramping all over the estate? Was there more hidden here to find – more bodies?

She sincerely hoped not.

Tess's stomach lurched at the thought. When she'd bought Kilfenora, it had been empty for years; the gardens had gone wild, ivy stems as thick as her arm covering every statue.

Anything could have been buried here.

Eoin Doyle's face flashed into Tess's mind, alongside the pictures of the Radio Snatcher's four alleged victims. Doyle lived in the village; there was every chance he was familiar with the stories about the Kilfenora family and the house. Was he trying to draw everyone's attention away from the hills, away from what else might be hidden in the gardens, by focusing these terrible things on the house itself? Perhaps he was buying time by delaying the opening so that he could move the bodies.

He'd get some shock when he discovered that Lynch and the local Gardai were one step ahead of him.

Tess suddenly realised Merlin was circling around her ankles, pressing his warm body into her leg. She bent down to stroke him. He was a very solid cat, like a small but strong-willed panther.

Tess ran her hand along his back and up his tail, taking strength from his silent presence.

If this Radio Snatcher character thought he could intimidate her and mess up everything they'd all worked on for so long, he could just feck off.

Restoring Kilfenora and bringing it back to life was much more than just a crazy project. Tess knew that with every brick repointed, with every floorboard replaced, she was rebuilding her own life, too, bringing it back from the devastation of Kieran's death.

She needed this house as much as it needed her.

Kilfenora *would* open as planned, and Tess would say something in her speech at the opening of the play about Laetitia and Katie-Lou, and Conor, obviously. It would be a tribute to them, and to the Kilfenora family, to everyone who had come into contact with the house over the years. And to everyone who had died here.

Glancing up at the sky, dark clouds gathering, Tess turned to head to her cottage. She was going to keep going. The play would go on. She owed it to everyone to bring life back to Kilfenora.

WEDNESDAY

Chapter 54

TESS PUT HER phone and keys down on the edge of the copper planter beside the front door of Kilfenora House and glanced up at the furniture van that was pulling around the fountain. The storm she had felt coming last night hadn't materialised, only a light spattering of rain falling to settle the dust.

Beside her, Genevieve was dressed in her usual bright colours, pink dominating today, but she was distinctly subdued, her face pale.

'Are you OK, Gen? You don't have to do this, you know.'

Before Gen could answer, the dull pip of the van's reversing warning cut through the early morning stillness. It slowly rolled backwards, the driver lining up the tail lift with the double front doors thrown open behind them.

It wasn't even eight yet, but Tess had always loved early mornings. There was something optimistic about the start of a new day, the promise of things to come. And today felt fresh; mist was hanging in pockets across the fields in front of them, the sun just warming up. When she'd woken this morning, she'd felt as if everything might actually come together. Maybe.

The way things were going this week, she didn't want to hope too hard, but if they could get Friday evening over and done with without any further incidents or accidents, she'd consider it a major success.

Then she could think about what Mark had said about the history of the house, and the implications for the business if the press picked up on it. It was all really rather horrible; it gave Tess a hideous creeping feeling, as if she was being watched. And that was before she even started thinking about who might have left that copy of *Great Expectations* in the ballroom. She still didn't feel well, and the next three days were likely to be the busiest of her life.

Mark had dropped into the Garda station the previous evening, on his way to the pub, to let them know his thoughts, but he hadn't exactly been received with open arms. They said they'd look into it.

When Tess had got his text she'd felt her stress levels peak. But she couldn't do the guards' job for them – she had enough to do here. And the guards were the experts, so perhaps they *were* imagining the parallels and were all overreacting. Mark had acknowledged how mad it all sounded as he'd told her.

But whatever about the guards' scepticism, if anyone else made the same connections that Mark had, she could see the press going nuts for a proper country house mystery that would give Miss Marple a run for her money. She knew Mark would keep it quiet. He said he'd discussed it with Clarissa, if only to make sure that he wasn't joining the dots wrongly and sending Tess into a tailspin for no reason. But she knew he wouldn't discuss it with anyone else.

Beside her, Gen let out a loud breath.

'I'm good. I need to pull myself together, that's all. I've been looking forward to this stuff arriving for weeks, it's going to look amazing. It'll be the perfect location for magazine shoots once I get it all styled, and it'll look fabulous on Instagram.'

As the van driver's mate jumped out from the passenger side, Tess's phone began to ring. The loud jangle of her old-fashioned ringtone was straight out of a 1940s movie.

She froze for a second.

Who was ringing at this time in the morning?

Part of her didn't want to answer it. At all.

Gen glanced behind them at the planter where Tess had balanced the phone, her face expectant and then puzzled as Tess ignored the call. At the front of the van, the driver jumped down and walked around to them.

'Good morning, ladies. We've got another two vans like this one on the way. We'll be in and out in no time, though. The gaffer showed us where everything needs to go.'

'Everything's labelled.' Gen smiled at him gratefully. 'And the rooms are all colour-coded so everything ends up in the right place. Once you can get it all in, we'll make it look pretty.'

Leaning against the van, he pushed his flat cap back slightly, the sweat already starting to show on his head.

'Excellent, very organised.'

Tess's phone began to ring again.

The driver looked at her. 'Sounds like you need to get that. Somebody wants you.'

Tess took a deep breath. Her heart rate had increased at the sound of the first ring and it was now thumping inside her chest. She really couldn't take any more bad news right now.

'Will you be OK for a minute?'

Turning to pick up her phone out of the planter, Tess reluctantly looked at the screen.

Part of her had known it was him.

She looked at the van driver. 'Won't be a sec. Can you get started? There's no lift, I'm afraid, but your boss said you'd be OK.'

'Don't you worry, miss, we do old buildings all the time. It's our speciality.'

Tess smiled appreciatively. The phone pipped – it had gone to voicemail. As she turned, walking away from the furniture men, Tess could feel Gen's eyes on her back. She didn't try and pick up Lynch's message, instead hit his number as she headed across the gravel at the front of the house and around the side. Out of earshot.

'Jerry, good morning.' She tried to sound cheerful, but the words stuck in her throat.

'I've got the film crew here. The guards are exhuming the body this morning and then we'll film a recreation.' Obviously excited, he spoke too quickly for Tess and it took her a moment to catch up.

'It's definitely a body?'

'No question. The forensics team started at first light and they've excavated the whole area.'

Tess closed her eyes, a feeling of despair welling up inside her. Despair for the victim, for her family, and for herself and the house.

'Do they think it's the Radio Snatcher?'

'They'll have to do a proper ID, dental records, I'd imagine, but it's looking a lot like Fidelma Hoey. There's fabric wrapped around the body that corresponds with the clothes she was last seen wearing.'

Tess felt her legs weaken again, like they had when she'd gone down to the lake. But she didn't have Mark to support her now. She leaned against the stone wall of the house, the rough granite cutting into her shoulder, reminding her that the wall was there, holding her up.

'Can they tell how—' She whispered it, but Lynch cut in and finished the sentence for her.

'The body's badly decomposed . . .' He drew breath and Tess prayed he didn't go into more detail; there was only so much she could take. 'But it's been bound with heavy-duty electrical wire.'

Chapter 55

CLARISSA KNOCKED SHARPLY on the white PVC front door, and a second later spotted the bell hidden behind a dangling wind chime that was attached to the front wall of the cottage.

It was ridiculously early to be calling on anyone, but yesterday when she'd called, Katie-Lou's mother had explained that she got up early to feed the hens, that nine o'clock was almost mid-morning for her. Clarissa would have been more than happy to go home and have coffee after dropping Malachi to his play date, but Marie Therese O'Neill would have none of it, insisting that she call over while she was in the village.

And now here she was, with an armful of roses still damp with dew from her garden and an apple pie she'd made with Malachi yesterday.

There was a clicking sound on the other side of the door, as if it was being unlocked, and thoughts of fire safety shot through Clarissa's head. But the house was a bungalow; she was sure the back door was easy enough to open without keys. Clarissa mentally chided herself; she really needed to focus on her own business and control her enquiring mind.

Fortunately, before she could think any more on it, the door opened and there was Katie-Lou's mother, a tiny bird-like woman who had always reminded Clarissa of a sparrow. She had the same bright eyes and quick movements, although today, Clarissa could see her weak smile didn't quite reach her eyes, dulled with grief.

She stepped aside to let Clarissa through to the tiny living room.

'Come in, come in. It's so good of you to call.' She indicated the flowers. 'How did you know? Pink's our favourite colour, Katie loves roses.'

Following Marie Therese into her overstuffed living room, a palette of pastel pinks and purple that carried from the very many scatter cushions and hearth rug to the figurines above the electric fire, Clarissa could smell lavender.

'Do sit down. I've got the tea drawing. I'll just put these in some water.'

Clarissa handed her the apple pie. 'Something from Malachi for your coffee later.'

'That's very thoughtful. I won't be a minute, make yourself at home.'

Marie Therese indicated the sofa, and disappeared back into the hall. A moment later Clarissa could hear the kitchen tap running.

As Clarissa moved to the sofa and put her handbag down, she spotted a small occasional table pushed around the end of the couch nearest the armchair, a chessboard on top, a game obviously in progress.

Looking over the arm of the chair, Clarissa started. The pieces were in the same positions as her own had been until a few days ago.

Surprised, she looked around the room properly and her heart broke all over again.

Photos of two little blonde girls crowded every surface; Irish dancing medals were displayed proudly in a glass case behind the armchair that faced the front window.

Hearing Marie Therese's step in the hall, Clarissa picked up her handbag, searching for a tissue. This visit was going to be even tougher than she'd anticipated. Marie Therese came in carrying the roses in a pale pink cut-glass vase and put them down on the central coffee table.

'Those are only lovely, you're very good.'

Clarissa smiled. Roses seemed such a meagre offering.

'Your photographs are wonderful.'

'Dancers, both my girls. Eileen's in America now. They could have been professional you know, but Katie hated all the razzmatazz. She loved dancing with her sister, but . . . Well, it's tough on that circuit and Katie's a sweetheart, always has been, has no competitive spirit at all. She'd be more worried about her opponent if they picked up an injury, sprained an ankle or something, than she would about winning.'

Clarissa realised that Marie Therese was still speaking in the present tense.

Clarissa pulled a cushion behind her as Katie-Lou's mother hovered over the roses for a moment, straightening the stems, as if she wasn't ready to sit down yet.

'I need to get over and see Genevieve. She said such lovely things on the phone. Katie loved that shop, you know. She was mad about that chessboard, even got a book from the library on how to play it so she could work out some moves.' Marie Therese nodded towards the chessboard at the end of the sofa. 'She must have watched *The Queen's Gambit* about six times.'

For a moment, Clarissa didn't know what to say. She'd been so sure that Katie-Lou wasn't the brightest button. Well, there was no question about it, she hadn't acted as if she was ready for *Mastermind*, but perhaps there was a whole side to her they didn't know about.

Fancy Katie-Lou being interested in chess.

'She loved that board in the shop.' Marie Therese turned to the mantelpiece and picked up a phone. She smiled sadly as she punched in her passcode.

'Look.' Marie Therese came to sit on the end of the sofa beside Clarissa. 'She used to take pictures of it every time she was in and send them to me. She was desperate to know who was playing, and Gen always said she didn't know.'

Clarissa half smiled. Gen didn't know Mark was her chess partner; there had seemed to be no reason to mention it. Looking at the phone screen as Marie Therese scrolled through a few photos, Clarissa recognised their board.

'See, she took a picture of every move and sent them to me, and I had to move the pieces we have here. We used to see if we could work out what the next move would be. She said it was like solving a mystery.'

Marie Therese passed Clarissa the phone and, leaning in to her, swiped to show her photo after photo of the board from different angles, each move recorded.

'She loved a puzzle, did Katie – she was mad into mysteries, you know.' Marie Therese blushed. 'She always said you reminded her of a cross between Poirot and Marple.'

It was Clarissa's turn to smile. She looked back at the phone and swiped on, remembering the moves as the game unfolded.

But the next photo wasn't of the chessboard.

It was of a mass of purple flowers. Flowers that Clarissa recognised.

'Aren't they pretty? I think poor Laetitia sent her that, and she sent it to me. She knows how much I love that colour.'

Clarissa felt her heart rate increase as she looked closely at the picture. She thought fast.

'Oh, *so* lovely. Do you know, that's the exact shade I'm looking for, for a new blouse? Would you be able to send it on to me? Fancy that, I've been all over the internet trying to find just the right colour.'

'Of course.' Marie Therese took the phone and clicked to forward the photo just as it started to ring. Marie Therese froze, looking at the number. 'That's the guards.' She put out her hand and clutched Clarissa's arm. 'I don't think I can answer it.'

Chapter 56

TESS DUSTED THE muck off her jeans and looked over to where Gen had collapsed into a mustard-coloured velvet high-backed sofa. The back and arms formed three sides of a luxurious box, finials on the corners holding the sides up, bound with purple silken rope, tassels hanging down the back.

'I daren't sit down, I'm filthy. I hadn't realised it was so dusty up here.'

'Sit on the window sill.'

Coming into the room, Mark handed them both ice-cold cans of Coke that he'd liberated from the fridge in the tea rooms. They were closed today, but the girls were in, getting everything ready for the weekend rush. He sat down himself.

'You could have warned me.' He looked at his watch. 'It's not even coffee time and I'm knackered. I hope you're insured if I've wrecked my back.'

'You *volunteered*.' Tess opened the can with a hiss.

Mark wrinkled up his face as if he was going to disagree, then said, 'Maybe, but that's not the point. I was only coming over for a chat, I wasn't expecting manual labour.'

Gen leaned back, her face flushed from moving the furniture around. She put the back of her hand on her forehead in an exaggerated pose.

'You know Clarissa is going to want to come in here and move everything around again.'

Tess snorted into her Coke. 'I've been expecting her all morning – where's she gone?'

'Malachi's over at a friend's for a play date. She wanted to drop in to Katie-Lou's mum and see how she is.'

Tess sighed. 'That's lovely of her.'

Gen grimaced. 'It must have been such an incredible shock for her to get back from her sister's on Sunday night and find that Katie-Lou wasn't at home. The chickens were starting to peck at each other, they were so hungry, apparently. I think when she saw they hadn't been fed, that's when she knew something was really wrong, but she kept thinking Katie-Lou would just walk back in. I mean, nobody expects something like this, do they?' Gen struggled further upright and took a sip of her Coke. 'You know, Mark, this theory of yours has to be a coincidence. I mean, really, very few people know as much about the history of this place as you do. Even Tess didn't – did you?'

Leaning against the imitation panelling that came to shoulder height in this room, looking out of the tall window over the drive, Tess shook her head slowly. She'd written a leaflet with an outline of who had lived here and when, but when she'd researched it, she'd found very little detail about the Kilfenora family whose title had come from the demesne. It was as if history had lost interest in them. Definitely nothing about how the children had died. She'd sort of assumed it had been TB or something.

Sitting down beside him on the window sill, she looked at Mark.

'If what you're saying is right about the mirroring of events, then are we going to discover that this body Lynch has found was poisoned?'

Mark sighed sharply. 'Given that Lynch's looking for a victim from . . . what . . . eight years ago, I doubt it somehow. I can't make any sense of how his information fits into the picture, either, but I'm thinking, if someone else does know Lynch has been in touch, or that the information had been passed on that one of the Radio Snatcher's victims could be buried here, then one way to make it look like that victim *wasn't* connected with the other women who went missing, might be to create a smokescreen.'

Tess looked at him incredulously.

'Killing someone else seems a bit of a dramatic way to cover up a murder.'

'It could be several murders, if they are connected, and the indications are that these women's disappearances are linked somehow.' He glanced at her. 'Maybe it is just complete coincidence. The pattern of events mirroring the historical tragedies sounds cracked to me, too, but killing people to start with isn't exactly normal behaviour. I don't think we're dealing with someone rational here.'

Tess shook her head emphatically. 'They can't be connected, I mean, really. Why now and why here? If this person wanted to deflect attention from Lynch and his film crew, surely they'd want to draw the hunt away from here?'

Mark took a large gulp of his Coke. 'True. Very true. But murder isn't always logical. And Lynch *has* found something.' He shifted uncomfortably on the window sill. 'The *other* thing is . . .' He paused. 'The bit that's really worrying me, if I'm right about the connections with the past, is that everything that's happened here is very particular to Kilfenora, which makes me think that the house, and perhaps you, are the target. It's a complicated way to stop the opening, if that's what the plan is, but if the press find out about the links, no one is going to want to hold a wedding or an important corporate event where there's a history of people mysteriously dying. You'd be tainted for years.'

Tess looked at him, the surge of fear she felt, she was sure, showing on her face.

'You mean someone's not only trying to stop the opening, they're actually trying to ruin me, too?'

'It's one possibility. I mean . . .' He faltered. 'The thing I was thinking when we were up at the field, was that we don't know *when* Lynch got his information. Maybe it's taken him a while to react. Maybe someone thought that the whole crime scene, bodies on the property, thing would be enough to prevent you opening. But whoever gave him the info doesn't know how TV works – that scoops need to be kept under wraps.'

Tess nodded slowly. That did make sense. But who on earth would want to prevent Kilfenora opening? Who could hate her that much?

Chapter 57

SITTING IN Marie Therese's pastel living room, seeing the fear on her face as she recognised the incoming number, Clarissa's heart broke all over again. Having experienced three close deaths herself, Clarissa knew what it was like when the guards rang unexpectedly – how frightening it could be that they'd have more bad news.

Clarissa held Katie-Lou's mother's hand tightly as she answered the call, Marie Therese's face turning a shade of alabaster not dissimilar to the chess pieces they'd been talking about, her eyes locked on the photographs of her girls on the mantelpiece.

Clarissa could hear the caller clearly in the stillness of the room: an older-sounding man, his voice echoing slightly as if he had the phone on speaker at his end. Was anyone else listening? Clarissa dearly hoped not. She knew it was vital to build a picture of Katie-Lou's life, but this type of questioning felt so intrusive. Taking a ragged breath, Marie Therese's voice began to crack as the guard – Clarissa assumed he must be a detective from his tone – continued. Clarissa rubbed her hand as Marie Therese answered him.

'But I've been through all this. She wasn't dating anyone. She went up to talk to Laetitia to get her cards read because her old boyfriend had messaged her on Facebook, but she was interested in someone else.' Marie Therese shook her head as the caller stopped her. 'Yes, I've given you all his details. You've been to talk to him. Honestly, I couldn't keep up with her love life sometimes, but I really don't think there was anyone else on the scene.'

But the caller's next question made Clarissa hold her breath. It was preceded with the words 'partial profile' and 'DNA'.

'Can you tell us if she knew a man called Adam O'Donnell?'

Clarissa sat stock-still, fighting the shock that almost made her cry out.

'No, I'm sorry, I don't know that name at all, never heard of him. Maybe he's a customer at Fortune Finds? Genevieve might know?' Marie Therese glanced at Clarissa, shrugging.

Clarissa smiled encouragingly, nodding. She didn't want to say it now, but Genevieve *would* recognise that name, and so did she.

Adam O'Donnell.

Good *God*.

It had taken all Clarissa's willpower to stay with Marie Therese for a reasonable time after the call had ended. She'd asked about the chickens and they'd talked about the craft fair and then, politely, she'd refused another cup of tea, saying she had to get back to Malachi, assuring Katie-Lou's mum that she'd call in again.

Waving as she'd climbed into her little Mercedes, Clarissa had headed straight for Rockfield Garda station to find the detective handling Katie-Louise's case.

Now, sitting opposite her in a small airless room, a flimsy wood-effect table between them, the walls painted a dismal cream, the detective looked just as confused as Clarissa felt.

'Are you quite sure?' In his fifties, his navy tie secured with a Garda pin, he was flushed despite the light cotton of his jauntily striped short-sleeved shirt.

Clarissa sighed, thankful that he was taking her seriously.

'I'm afraid so, without question. I'm hardly going to forget, now, am I?'

'But for him to be here, in Kilfenora . . . Surely someone would have seen him, recognised him?'

Clarissa shrugged. She'd have thought so, too, but people changed over the years, and Adam O'Donnell's circumstances had changed significantly since she'd last seen him.

'Why would anyone recognise him except the people involved? And it was what, ten years ago. In another county. He could look completely different now. He must do, or I would have recognised him.'

The detective nodded, his collar tight, face florid in the heat. There were patches of sweat forming under his arms.

'We'll check for a photo on the system, show it around. Check vehicle movements on Friday evening.'

Clarissa leaned forward, trying not to appear as anxious as she felt.

'There are traffic cameras in the village?'

'Yes, and CCTV on the drink link and at Fabio's chipper.'

'Drink link?' Clarissa had looked at him, one eyebrow raised. It was as if he was speaking a foreign language.

'The ATM.'

'Oh, right.'

Drink link.

She must remember that and ask Mark if he was familiar with the term. There were times when Clarissa felt she'd lived in

London for far too long, and had lost so many Irishisms. She still called the airing cupboard the hot press, much to the confusion of all her husbands, but *drink link* was a new one for sure.

'And we'll look again at Katie-Louise's phone records. He must have arranged to meet her at Kilfenora House. Unless he just wandered in.'

'That is my point, though. It is highly unlikely that he *did* just wander in. This man has an historic connection to Tess Morgan, and looking at the evidence you have, it's possible that he's killed at least one person in the last week. I really feel we should warn her. Tess, I mean.'

The detective sat back in his chair, toying with the biro he'd been using to write in his notebook. He tapped the pen on the table, sliding it end to end through his damp fingers.

'He's definitely a person of interest, but we don't know that he's killed anyone. I mean, the DNA is a link, of course, but there's no guarantee his skin got under Katie-Louise's nails when she died. It could turn out that they'd been having a roll in the hay that afternoon and he was nowhere near her when she went into that lake.'

Clarissa pursed her lips and tried to hold back her irritation.

'It could indeed. He would need a very good reason for being in Kilfenora in the first place, though, don't you think?'

He conceded her that, at least.

Clarissa glanced at her kitchen clock as her laptop sprang into life. Gen would be busy moving furniture with Tess all morning, and she had a bit more time before she needed to pick Malachi up. She'd come straight home, leaving the detective to do some more checks, reluctantly agreeing not to alert Tess and frighten the living daylights out of her until he had more information.

Rerunning the conversation through her head, Clarissa's fingers raced over the keys, pieces of information steadily falling into place as they did so. There was still a lot she didn't understand, but some things were definitely clearer.

Pausing for a moment, Clarissa picked up her phone to look again at the photograph Marie Therese had sent her. Aconite was certainly a beautiful colour, although the picture looked as if it had been taken with a flash, draining the flowers slightly. Clicking on it, she emailed it to herself.

There had to be a way to see exactly when it had been taken. Clarissa hadn't thought to check the date that Katie-Louise had sent it to her mother, but it seemed likely that it was recent. And Gen had said something about Laetitia picking herbs in the poison garden to make lotions from. Was this one of them?

Clarissa's email pinged with the incoming message and she opened the attachment, clicking again to look at the technical data hidden in the photograph itself. She pursed her lips. There was a string of code, but it wasn't shedding any light on what she needed to know. Perhaps the guards would be able to make something of it. She'd mentioned it when she'd called into the station but they hadn't seen the significance at all. Nobody had been poisoned yet – *as far as they knew.*

Enlarging the photo, Clarissa pushed her reading glasses up the bridge of her nose. She moved her mouse over the image. In the corner, she could just see a flash of something shiny.

Clarissa peered at the picture again. It was blurred, as if the camera hadn't been properly focused, or it had been taken too quickly. The stems were held in a gloved hand, but in the foreground there was something else; silver, textured. Something she knew she'd seen before.

Chapter 58

IT WAS LATE afternoon by the time Tess had finished helping Gen sort out the furniture delivery and got up to Jerry Lynch and his team. The guards had sectioned off an area of the heathland, and even from this distance she could see blue and white crime scene tape fluttering in what little wind there was.

Lynch was in his black Seat, parked at the bottom of the path. With so much traffic, the grass was completely flattened around his car, a turning circle clearly visible. As Tess pulled up beside him, she prayed that this would be the last time she'd ever see Jerry Lynch.

His eyes on his phone, thumbs rapid on the keyboard, he turned in the driver's seat and put one foot out of the door as if to acknowledge her arrival. Sighing, Tess heaved open her car door. She must have done too much this morning; she was feeling utterly wiped out again. Walking around the front of her car, she leaned on the bonnet, her arms folded, waiting for him.

The moment he finished, he beamed at her. Today he was wearing a thin red polo shirt that set off his sunburn beautifully. Lumbering out of his car, he closed the door and leaned on it. Tess didn't think she'd ever seen anyone look so much like Lewis Carroll's Cheshire Cat.

'I think we've got him.' Lynch said it with such excitement and pride that Tess could almost feel his energy. She felt as if he might bounce off across the field at any moment.

Tess looked at him, one eyebrow raised. Finally realising that she was missing some key parts of the story, he shoved his phone in the back pocket of his jeans.

'The forensics lads are pretty sure it's Fidelma Hoey. Post mortem should be tomorrow, but they have her dental records so identification will be fairly fast.'

'You said something about wire?'

He nodded slowly, his eyes wide. 'Industrial copper wire. The sort used by electricians. Eoin Doyle's being brought in tonight. He's got a lot of explaining to do.'

Despite the heat, Tess shivered, the memory of Doyle standing too close to her and his eyes boring into her, still fresh.

How had he known that light wasn't working?

She tried to push it from her mind, but it kept popping back up like a message in a bottle on a stormy sea.

'Where are you with the filming for your documentary? Do you need to do more?'

'We've got everything in the can. Fantastic footage. I mean, this is just exactly what we need for this show to really hit the networks. The Americans are mad for true crime and it doesn't come much truer than this. We'll need to shoot reconstructions, and the linking pieces with Grace and the experts back at base. We've got an incident room set built over at the Virgin Media studios in Ballymount. Still a lot to do, but honestly, it's TV gold.'

Something inside Tess curled up and tried to hide when he mentioned the Americans and networks. There was a whole trade in murder tourism, guided tours and God knows what. She closed one eye and tried not to think about Kilfenora becoming a stop on a ghoulish coach tour. At the rate they were going, it was starting to feel as if the only thing people would be coming to Kilfenora for would be its body count.

'So what happens next? Will you be able to keep me posted on the case? And the more notice I have of the broadcast date, the better.'

Lynch nodded. 'What I really want to do is try and find the other victims. One of our experts is a geographical profiler. There are all sorts of theories about the areas killers work in, and where they dump bodies in relation to the kill site.' Tess winced inside, but Lynch didn't notice; he was warming to his theme. 'Obviously it would be closure for the families, just to know what had happened to their loved ones. But if we could get a conviction after all this time, that would be incredible.'

Well, he was right there.

'How did you get the original tip-off? It seems such a long time since the last disappearance.'

Lynch looked smug. 'It was rather random, actually. Guy got in touch with me who was in Mountjoy for a few years. He shared a cell with someone who had shared a cell with another lad who had boasted about knowing the Radio Snatcher. The information that the bodies had been buried beside Kilfenora filtered through. He'd seen my byline in the paper, told me the information had been on his mind, he just had to tell someone, and he didn't trust the police, for obvious reasons.' Lynch stuck his hand in his pocket. 'It was always a bit of a long shot, but once we traced who had been sharing cells with who, it looked like it could hold water. That was when I realised it would work for the TV show. The production company had already been on to me, but it takes ages to get the ball rolling on these things. Just shows you, once more than one person knows a secret, it's not a secret any more.'

'So will the guards be questioning the guy who provided the information? They are going to have to open up the whole investigation?'

Lynch looked non-committal. 'I can't reveal my sources – that's one of the reasons he came to me, I'd guess, but it was all hearsay. Yer man told me about it over two years ago, and he'd been in the Joy years before that, around the time the Radio Snatcher was first active. I doubt he could add any more to what he told me.'

Tess did the sums in her head. The first woman had gone missing ten years ago, while she'd still been in Trinity, the fourth just as she'd been heading off to Dubai. She vaguely remembered the story in the press. And just over two years ago was when she'd bought Kilfenora.

Mark's words came back to her. Had someone found out that she'd bought Kilfenora and hoped to ruin her plans by revealing the information, but it had taken longer than they'd thought to be followed up?

She looked at Lynch and liked him even less. How could you sit on information as important as this in order to land a TV show? What sort of person was he?

The Radio Snatcher was still out there. What if he'd struck again in those two years? What if another woman had been abducted? For a moment when Tess had arrived at Laetitia's van the other morning, she'd thought that she could have been a new victim, and that thought had made her feel utterly wretched. Jerry Lynch was as much a monster as the perpetrator.

Tess closed her eyes, trying to focus, emotion swirling around her stomach, making her feel ill again. She couldn't talk to Lynch for a moment longer.

'I'll be at home if you need me.'

He nodded, grinning. 'I'll call as soon as we get an update.'

Chapter 59

MERLIN WAS WAITING for Tess on the doorstep when she got home, the hairs on his back standing up as if he'd seen a dog.

'Whatever happened to you?'

She thought about picking him up but decided not to; he was prickly on a good day, and if he was having a cross moment, she didn't want to be the one he lashed out at. He had very sharp claws.

She reached down carefully to tickle his head instead. That was usually safe enough. He made a strange half-purring, half-mewing sound and stood up to circle her legs.

Tess had the key in the door and was about to push it open when she spotted the bottle of red wine leaning up against the doorstep. She'd been concentrating so hard on Merlin's teeth and keeping all her fingers she hadn't noticed it.

Who had left that?

There was a large white parcel tag tied around its neck with 'Put your feet up tonight' written on it in blue biro. The handwriting looked familiar – sort of angular, as if a spider had run across the page.

She picked the bottle up; it was lovely of whoever had left it. But how did they know this Chateau was her favourite? It was so thoughtful, and right now a drink was exactly what she needed.

Tomorrow was going to be full-on.

She wasn't the slightest bit in the mood for more work after her encounter with Lynch, but as Merlin followed her into the kitchen she decided she'd spend half an hour in the office making sure tomorrow's lists were up to date, and taking a final look over the technical running order for Friday.

She dithered for a second beside the kitchen table, wondering if she'd take a glass of wine into the office with her, but decided against it. She put the bottle on the counter. Once she'd checked everything, she could relax properly and enjoy the wine.

She looked at Merlin, who had jumped onto the kitchen counter expectantly.

'I'm going to be two minutes and then I'll find you a treat, OK?'

He looked mournfully back at her.

Grinning, she doubled back on herself and walked across the hall to the study. Her clipboard was on the desk with tomorrow's notes on it. Opening her master file, she clicked on the technical running order for Friday.

One of the first things she'd learned when she'd got to Dubai was that every event, no matter how small, needed a sheet like this. Contractors and staff telephone numbers at the top, and then a minute-by-minute breakdown of the events of the day.

It was the only way, as you ran through everything in your head, that you realised what was missing.

One of her first jobs in Dubai had been a house party, a baby shower for one of the prince's Western friends. She'd arrived to organise the caterers to discover there was no toilet roll anywhere in the house beyond a single roll in the downstairs bathroom, and no time to get any delivered. She'd been forced to scour cupboards in every room, and in the end had found three more buried in a distant en suite bathroom.

It was the fine detail that made an event a success, and she had every intention that the first day Kilfenora was open to the public would run like clockwork.

She'd dithered over which day of the week they should open, but decided the Saturday after the play was perfect. Tomorrow – Thursday – the trestles and tents were being delivered for the craft market, along with the chairs for the ballroom. She'd asked everyone who could to set up their stalls during the day on Friday. The vintage cars would arrive then, too, so they could be parked to their best advantage.

On Friday evening at seven, the gate would be opened to everyone who had booked first night tickets, and to their invited guests – press, mainly. The curtains would rise at 8 p.m. There would be a champagne reception in the ballroom before the performance started, for everyone to mingle and for her to introduce Aidan to the press.

The main gates would be thrown open to the public at ten o'clock on Saturday. The TV crew who had been filming the restoration were coming in to set up their cameras on Friday for the performance. They would be back at six to get set up to capture the first moments of opening, from Tess ceremonially pulling the gates open, with Clarissa as the resident famous face beside her, to the first members of the public arriving.

Running her eye over her lists, Tess made a note to double-check that she had enough ice buckets for the drinks station in the ballroom. She'd hired a long table and cloths from the company who were delivering the trestles for the craft market tomorrow, pleased that she'd been able to get everything in one place. Their staff would cable-tie the ballroom chair legs together to ensure that if there was an emergency evacuation, the chairs themselves didn't become a trip hazard. She'd groaned over the risk assessment that she'd had to do for the insurance company, but she was glad of it now.

All the emergency signage was in place, and she'd made sure that the cast used the back stairs to the stable yard while the guests used the main staircase. There were two flights of narrow servants' stairs that ran from the downstairs kitchens to the drawing room at one end of the row of rooms overlooking the front of the house, and what was now the dining room at the other, but only she and Clarissa knew about them. In fact, Tess had never even been down the far one in what Gen was calling the dining room. She'd opened the door once and it had been covered in spider webs, enough to give her the creeps that one might fall down the back of her neck if she even ventured in. But she'd had one of the gardeners tackle the webs on the drawing room stairs, which came out closest to the stable yard. They had proved very handy when she was in a hurry and there were cast members arriving for rehearsal. They did seem to dither so.

Tess had entrusted Clarissa with the spare keys to all the doors in the main house, and the Butler's Lodge, ready for the inevitable moment when she locked herself out. It hadn't happened yet, thankfully, and she was sure Clarissa had forgotten all about the back stairs, but as the place became busy with tourists, Tess needed to remember to keep those doors locked.

Satisfied that she had everything covered, Tess printed off Friday's and Saturday's running orders. She could add any other notes by hand.

She smiled as the pages appeared out of the printer. This was it – this was the culmination of all her activities over the past two years.

Now she was going to enjoy that wine.

Chapter 60

CLARISSA LOOKED UP from her laptop screen to see Merlin stalking in through the back door. Malachi and Genevieve had gone home a few hours ago, and much as she loved Malachi, she was enjoying having the place to herself.

She had a lot to think about.

Taking off her reading glasses, she laid them on the kitchen table and picked up her lemon tea, sitting back as she took a sip.

Merlin sat down and regarded her speculatively, like a judge watching the jury file into court. His thick tail was wrapped perfectly around his paws, curled at the end as if he was posing for a photograph. Clarissa looked at him as she sorted everything out in her head.

She wasn't sure where Merlin had come from originally, but shortly after she'd moved into the Gardener's Cottage he'd appeared on the kitchen windowsill waiting to be let in. Sometimes she wondered if he'd lived all his previous lives on the estate – had been the kitchen cat perhaps at some time in the past, although he was far too elegant to be a kitchen cat. Shortly after he'd moved in, she'd called over to Tess to discover him curled up on one of her chairs. He'd twitched an ear when he'd heard her voice, but not shown a moment of remorse about having two homes. It seemed true, as Clarissa had heard, that you never owned a cat. They owned you.

Putting down her tea, Clarissa reached for her phone.

'Mark, good evening, I hope you don't mind me calling at this hour. The bar must be busy?'

'Always happy to talk to you. I'm glad you rang, actually, I'm a bit worried about Tess.'

Clarissa leaned forward and picked up her glasses, waggling the arm up and down. In the background she heard the sounds of the bar receding as Mark moved into a quieter space.

'Me, too. She's been looking very pale for the last few days.'

She heard him open a door and close it behind him.

'I know there's been a lot happening. I mean, Laetitia and Katie-Lou have hit everyone hard, and it's worse for her because it's on her land.'

Clarissa smiled to herself as she answered, 'I can hear a "but" coming here . . .'

'You know her much better than I do, but from everything I know of her and our conversations recently, I know she's a strong person. I'd go as far to say that she's irrationally positive sometimes. She's got everything set up this week to run like clockwork, but she really hasn't been feeling at all well.'

He was right.

'I know, I wondered if it was a stomach bug. She's not going to listen if we tell her to slow down, so I think we just have to be as supportive as possible and take the weight where we can.'

'Could you get her to see Doc O'Riordan next week? It will sound weird coming from me. It could be a bug, or something stress-related, but if she drives herself into the ground, it will take a long time for her to recover and I can see Christmas at Kilfenora is going to be a big deal. That's going to be on top of us before we know it.'

Clarissa smiled at the concern in his voice.

'Couldn't agree more, which brings me to why I'm calling. I was thinking about Friday night. I think we should do something for the cast after everything that's happened. There's always a bit of a feeling of anticlimax after opening night unless there's a really good after-show party.'

She heard him chuckle. 'I've seen the society papers from back in the day, Clarissa. If you weren't at a party in London, it wasn't happening. You were on everyone's guest list, one very popular leading lady. What were you thinking?'

Clarissa glowed for a moment. He was right – she'd been pivotal on the London scene when she'd been in the West End. They had been such good times, but she wouldn't have changed anything; she'd gone out on such a high, receiving the Trewin Award for her Ophelia in the National Theatre production. She'd retired to give her full attention to Gen, and then, as she'd grown older and more independent, Clarissa had returned to acting and taken on the film roles that had proved a lot more profitable than the stage.

Selling her big empty house, and moving back to Ireland permanently to help with Malachi after Gen's divorce, had been exactly what she'd needed. And helping Tess with Kilfenora had been energising. She'd kept on her apartment in London, renting it out; she adored her cottage and her cantankerous cat.

Clarissa focused back on Mark, and the reason for her call.

'Well, how about we open up the tea rooms and whizz everyone down there for a surprise gathering after the show? Could you look after the booze? It doesn't have to be fancy, just red and white, and perhaps a barrel of Guinness.'

'No problem, I'll sort it out with the girls in the tea rooms. And we'll need food. I'll look after that, too. I'll have a word with Fabio's and see if they can do cocktail sausages and chips and deliver it up. Everyone will be up to ninety, we'll need a bit of soakage or the hangovers will be mighty.'

'So very true. The tea rooms have stacks of small baskets they are going to use once they're open full-time – they will be perfect for serving up. No need to hire in plates then.'

'Sounds like a plan – I've boxes and boxes of spare glasses here. Leave it with me and I'll organise everything. I'm guessing you don't want to involve Tess?'

'She's enough on her plate, I think. Let's keep it as a surprise for everyone. I'll tell them as soon as we close on Friday evening and hoosh them down. The house is packed full of antiques now, so we'll want to clear everyone out and lock up as soon as we can.'

'Good point. I'll look after that. Are you going to tell Aidan, or surprise him, too?'

'I think I'll surprise him. After everything he's done, he deserves it.'

THURSDAY

Chapter 61

'*HOLD MY HAND.*'

Tess could hear Kieran's voice, insistent, his laughter swirling around her through the darkness. How much had she had to drink? She could barely move, her chest tightening. The inside of the pub came back to her: the firelight dancing on her glass, the bubbles rising in his lager. Surely she wasn't that drunk?

He'd had the ring in a box, dark blue leather, hidden deep in the pocket of his waxed jacket, had been fiddling with it all evening. Then when she'd got to the table with their second round, she'd been so busy talking that it had taken her a while to realise he wasn't listening. He'd sat there silently, staring at the table. For a moment she'd thought something was really wrong.

Then he'd pulled out the small box, opening it to reveal a slim gold band with a tiny chip of diamond, and looked at her like a puppy dog.

The music went around her head in snatches, all mixed up with the babble of voices in the bar and Kieran's voice.

'I know this is ridiculous and we're too young, and we've no money, and I've got another year to do of my master's, but will you marry me? I don't want to be with anyone else. Ever. Will you, Tess? I love you so much, I don't think I can live without you.'

315

He'd said it in such a rush, in one breath, that it had taken her a moment to put all the pieces together. But then she'd burst into tears of total joy and taken the ring out of the box, and slipped it on her finger and kissed him. It had been the most perfect moment of her life.

She could hear him as she slipped in and out of the dream.

'*You're tipsy, missus, I don't think I want a sop for a wife. I think we'll have to call it all off.*'

Outside the pub she'd laughed out loud and kissed him, and could feel his arms around her, and they'd laughed again, thrilled by the moment, and set off to walk to his parents' farm, joshing and messing. He'd tried to tickle her and she'd got him back . . .

Christ, she felt so terrible. Her face felt numb and she could barely lift her arms.

Then the flash of the headlights came again, like an electric shock, as she'd pushed him away from her. And she felt the rain, needle-like, making her fingers tingle.

She was going to be sick.

Confusion swirled in her mind. She felt something damp against her face, then a scratch. She was so nauseous, as if she was going to vomit any second, but she couldn't move. Had the car hit her, too?

Tess tried to open her eyes. Somewhere in the distance she could hear a plaintive mew, then a thump. Then she realised it wasn't dark; there was light coming from somewhere, but the part of her mind that processed information seemed to have shut down. She felt so, so ill.

She closed her eyes and started to drift.

Chapter 62

HER PHONE TO her ear, Clarissa tapped her glasses impatiently on the kitchen counter as she listened to her call ring out, and glanced through the open back door at Malachi. He had his breakfast bowl in one hand and was searching for Merlin, combing the bushes with a magnifying glass in the other, a pair of antique opera glasses slung around his neck. Clarissa knew she should be worried about the glasses, but she had other things on her mind, and keeping him busy for a few minutes was essential.

Suddenly the call was answered.

'Mark, have you heard from Tess today?'

He immediately responded to the urgency in her voice.

'No, nothing at all. I texted to say I'd be up this morning early, but she hasn't responded. I assumed she'd be busy.'

'I've just had a call from the girl in the tea rooms. The hire company have arrived with the trestles and the chairs for the ballroom and there's no sign of her. They need to know where to unload.'

'No sign of her?' Clarissa could tell by his tone that he was thinking exactly the same thing as she was. Something was wrong. 'You've tried her phone?'

'Yes, and Martina from the tea rooms tried the cottage, there's no one answering. She thought Tess might be in the gardens or have run into the village for something.'

'I doubt it this morning, not with all the stuff to set up. Can you sort out the deliveries and I'll go straight to the cottage? I can be there in ten minutes. She may have had a fall or something.'

He clicked off the phone before Clarissa could respond, and as she turned to call Malachi in, a streak of black hurtled across the garden, shot through the door and landed on the counter in front of her with the most blood-curdling yowl she'd ever heard.

Merlin. His green eyes were wild.

Clarissa ran her hand down his back, the fur standing up in spikes, and called Malachi at the top of her voice.

Mark's car was already outside Tess's cottage when Clarissa pulled up. She had no idea how he'd got there so fast, and really didn't want to know.

'Malachi, be a love and pop over to Martina in the tea rooms. Tell her I sent you and can she give you some ice cream. I just have to pop into Tess's house.'

'No problem.'

He was already clambering out before she had her own door open. She reached for Tess's house keys on the passenger seat and, jumping out of the car, hurried across the lane. Mark was waiting for her on the doorstep.

'I've been right around and looked in all the windows. She's not downstairs.'

'Perhaps she's still in bed.' Passing him the keys, she could see the fear in his eyes, and suddenly got a flash of what might be going through his head: his wife. She put her hand on his arm as he put the key in the lock. 'Do you want me to do this?'

He grimaced. 'I'll be fine. You double-check the downstairs rooms, I couldn't see right in from the windows. She could be lying on the floor somewhere.'

A moment later they were inside. The hall stank of vomit. Mark glanced at her and went straight up the stairs two at a time.

Clarissa steadied herself against the door frame for a moment. What had happened to Tess? There was no way she would disappear today, just no way, not without telling one of them.

A second later, Mark's voice boomed down the stairs.

'I've got her. Call an ambulance.'

'How bad is she? You might be quicker taking her.'

Gen's experience with Malachi's frequent accidents had proven that going to the hospital yourself was much quicker than waiting for an ambulance to get all the way up here first.

'Bad. Call them anyway, we're going to need the chopper if it's available. And call Doc O'Riordan.'

Clarissa was already dialling as she climbed the steep stairs, pausing on the half-landing as the call connected.

'Yes, I need an ambulance, at Kilfenora House, the Butler's Lodge. Yes, I'll hold.'

In Tess's bedroom, Clarissa could hear Mark opening the window. Crossing the landing, the phone still to her ear, she hesitated in the doorway. Tess was still in bed, a grey Snoopy T-shirt barely covering her thighs. Mark had thrown vomit-soaked pillows off the bed and put her in the recovery position. The room stank.

Clarissa could see the fear in Mark's face as he turned to her.

'Her pulse is really weak.'

The call connected before Clarissa could reply.

'Hello, yes, we need an ambulance very quickly. Is the air ambulance available? Thank you, there's really no time to delay.'

Mark held out his hand to take the phone.

'Hello, yes. It's a thirty-year-old female, looks like she's ingested a toxin of some sort, she's barely conscious, pulse weak and she's been vomiting. I've got her in the recovery position but . . . Yes, yes, I can do that. Thank you. I'll meet them at the gate.' He paused. 'Not this number – I'll give you mine.'

He reeled off his phone number and ended the call.

'There's been a crash on the M50, they said it would be quicker for me to bring her in. A patrol car can meet us at the gate and give us an escort across to Vincent's.'

'Tallaght Hospital's closer.'

'That's where all the traffic accident casualties are going – they're hammered. There's foam bed rolls and a sleeping bag in the back of my car. It's unlocked, can you roll them out? I don't think she'll be safe in the front seat.'

Turning, Mark scooped Tess up in his arms as if she was a doll.

'Yes, it's this way, let me open up for you.' Clarissa pulled out her set of spare keys and unlocked the huge double front doors of Kilfenora House. 'Martina's legs are younger than mine, she'll show you the route to the ballroom. I'm so sorry to hold you up. Medical emergency.'

The delivery driver nodded sharply as Martina from the tea rooms glanced at Clarissa anxiously and led him inside. Clarissa turned to look at the lorry. It was huge, but then she supposed two hundred banqueting chairs, along with a market's worth of trestle tables and tents, took up a lot of space. At least he'd be tied up for a while unloading, and that would give her time to catch up with Mark. Thank God he'd had a Garda escort to the hospital; he'd texted when he arrived, had definitely got there faster than an ambulance would have taken to drive all the way up here.

Now Clarissa needed to get into Tess's office to see what else was on the list for today and set up Operation Opening Emergency Headquarters.

Chapter 63

A S CLARISSA PUSHED open Tess's front door, a text came through. She reached for her phone in her cardigan pocket and looked at the screen.

Any news???

It was from Gen.

Not yet, waiting to hear. Will be in touch soonest.

Clarissa tapped her nails on the door frame. If she was right about the cause of all of this – and Clarissa was absolutely sure she was right – they needed the guards down here to seal off the house. Persuading them that Tess's collapse was more than a case of overwork and food poisoning could be a challenge, though. Clarissa pursed her lips. She was getting very impatient with the speed that law enforcement moved in this village. 'Waiting to see' wasn't something she was good at, at all.

Leaving the front door open to try and air the place out a bit, Clarissa went into Tess's kitchen. It was as tidy as it always was; Tess was a fanatical organiser in every element of her life. Clarissa glanced around, scanning the Aga, running her eye over the sink and coffee machine. Everything was spick and span.

Surely there had to be some evidence that would prove her right about how Tess had become so drastically ill, so suddenly.

Then Clarissa spotted it. The red light on the dishwasher was on.

Walking over, Clarissa bent to open it. Its cycle was long finished, but it still felt warm, and there was only a wineglass left in it.

Clarissa raised her eyebrows. There was absolutely no way that Tess would have left the dishwasher to run overnight. She was utterly paranoid about appliances catching fire, and in an old building like this – tinder-dry, especially in this weather – there only needed to be a spark and the whole place would go up.

And why would she have unloaded everything except one glass? That didn't make sense at all. Even if she'd been interrupted, something like that would keep Tess from her sleep. She'd have come back down and put it away.

And she definitely wouldn't have run the dishwasher with only one glass in it. Which meant that someone else had – someone who wanted to clean that glass thoroughly.

And who had, no doubt, wiped the dishwasher door and knobs down afterwards.

Clarissa looked at the cycle that the machine was set to. Seventy degrees. Well, that would fairly clean off traces of just about anything – from fingerprints to traces of a toxin.

Because Clarissa was absolutely sure of what had happened here, and as Mark had glanced at her before leaping into the driver's seat, she'd said it.

'Get them to test for aconite poisoning.'

He'd nodded sharply and a moment of understanding had passed between them.

Clarissa's phone pipped again and she scrambled for it. It was Mark.

Stabilised. All good. You were right.

Clarissa felt a surge of rage building inside her. Not only did she know exactly what was going on – she knew precisely what she was going to do about it.

Chapter 64

'RIGHT, EVERYONE, can we have a bit of calm, please? I know you've heard that Tess has been taken ill, but Clarissa Westmacott is taking over tomorrow to do the honours and introductions. Everything will run as planned.'

Aidan Gaunt stood on the edge of the stage, the full cast seated in front of him on the chairs that had just been delivered.

The place looked super-impressive. Megan had been amazed when she walked in to see the delivery team lining everything up, Clarissa with a sheaf of papers in one hand, and a tape measure in the other ensuring, apparently, that the aisles were all the correct width for the fire regulations.

Megan turned to look at Aidan as he continued.

'I'm sure Tess will be absolutely fine. We all know how hard she's been working, but it's really down to us to pull it out of the hat tomorrow night. The press will be here, we've got the film crew from the restoration show coming, too – it'll be full-on. But it'll be huge fun. I've never worked with a cast more able or more ready. Give yourselves all a round of applause.'

Aidan began clapping, his script folded under one arm. Megan cringed a bit – he sounded as if he was at some corporate team-building event – but it seemed to do the trick. Even the three luvvies he'd brought in from theatreland, although she doubted very much they had appeared in anything more than local rep recently, seemed to be buoyed up.

Grinning, Aidan continued. 'Right, this is our last rehearsal apart from your line runs tomorrow. Let's do this, people.'

'All good here?'

Megan looked up at the sound of Aidan's voice to see him leaning with one elbow on the end of one of the rails of costumes she was sandwiched between. The lighting wasn't fantastic backstage, and she was trying to find the right side of a grey twill overshirt that doubled as a suit of armour. It had got tangled when it was last taken off, the arms left inside out. She smiled coquettishly.

'All fine, I *think* . . .'

'You're very good to stick with this. You don't have to, you know, particularly given the circumstances.'

Looking at him in his white Ralph Lauren polo shirt, the collar turned up, and neat fitting jeans, Megan melted a little inside.

''Tis worked on all of this so hard, someone needs to keep it going. And I had to get out of the house. There are even more delays, apparently, and everyone is upset. Dad went straight back to work and Mum's furious with him and Ally's buried herself in her books. I can't stare out the window any longer, I'm the type of person who needs to be busy.'

'But still . . .' He reached over and touched the top of her arm, his eyes locked with hers. *Oh God, he was so gorgeous.* 'I'm sorry to hear things are so rough at home. What's the delay with the funeral?'

Megan sighed, looking suitably downcast as she basked in his full attention.

'Another post mortem or something. I mean, as if it isn't obvious what happened. It's horrible to think about her being there all cold and people cutting her up.'

Megan shivered, sighing deeply and putting her hand to her forehead. She wasn't sure if she could get away with another swoon, although the last one had gone so well, with him taking her for a coffee in the pub to raise her sugar levels.

He could do that all on his own, that was for sure.

'I think it's something to do with Katie-Lou and that spiking thing on the news – you know, in the nightclubs where people are getting drugged. Well, I'm putting two and two together and I could be making five, of course. Perhaps they were talking about Katie-Louise and not Tis at all. I heard Dad on the phone talking to the inspector in Rockfield. Apparently there's been a rash of spikings in Blessington. They were talking about the post mortem, and then he was asking Dad about the sorts of drugs that are used. They think Katie-Lou and Tis died the same night or something.' Megan realised she was still holding the twill overshirt, and gave it a shake to make it look as if she was focused on what she was doing, rather than completely on Aidan. 'Honestly, you'd think there was only one duty doctor the amount of calls he gets, but they play golf together – Dad and the inspector, I mean – so perhaps that's why he's on speed dial.'

'Died the same night? That's strange.' Aidan looked surprised. 'It's awful not knowing about the funeral. Will you keep me posted?'

Megan felt a surge of emotion. 'Of course, you'll be the first to know.' She managed to imbue it with just the right amount of dignity, compassion and confiding. 'It's great news about Conor, though. Did you hear?'

'That he's come around? I did indeed.' Aidan glanced at the folded pages in his hand as he answered.

'My dad said they're saying he's going to make a full recovery. I'm so glad. I half wondered if he'd make it tomorrow, but I don't think he's that much better.'

Aidan looked up at her, his eyebrows raised. 'I think that would be a lot to expect, don't you?'

Megan froze for a second; he'd said it as if she was a complete idiot. That wasn't very nice, particularly after their coffee the other day and all the time she'd put in getting a system in place for the costumes. Laetitia may have had it organised her way, but it was typically ramshackle and not one the rest of the world could work with.

Aidan turned his head as if he'd lost interest in the conversation. But he wasn't getting away that easily after all the time she'd taken to get ready this morning. She'd bought a new dress specially for today, had worked out what she was wearing for the next few days, too. Megan lowered her voice conspiratorially.

'I heard that Eoin Doyle's been arrested, too. It's all very hush-hush, nobody in Rockfield station is allowed to say anything.'

That did seem to pique Aidan's interest. She suddenly had his full attention again.

'Arrested? Goodness – what for?'

'They think he's the Radio Snatcher.' She kept her voice low and leaned in to him. 'I mean, there was always talk, but they never had enough to prosecute, so I heard. I didn't quite get the whole story, but apparently it's all to do with copper wire. There must be new evidence or something, but I heard he had a roll in the back of his van.'

'Seriously? After all this time?'

328

'Well, I doubt it was the same roll, but who carries copper wire around with them?' Megan opened her eyes wide for emphasis.

'Electricians use it a bit, I'd imagine.' Aidan shook his head. 'He always seemed very nice whenever I've met him. Talks non-stop, but that seems to be his only vice.'

'Apart from killing women.'

Aidan leaned in towards her. 'But how do they know he killed anyone unless they've found a body?'

Chapter 65

CLARISSA SAT DOWN at Tess's desk and leafed through the pages sitting on the keyboard. A movement in the lane beyond the garden wall drew her attention, and she watched for a moment as one of the young gardeners rolled a half-barrel out of the stable yard and set it on one side of the stable yard gate. A moment later he was back with another one. Clarissa smiled. Tess had the whole estate working like a well-oiled machine. The barrels were to be planted with bedding plants, and by tomorrow the whole place would be a blaze of summer colour. Perfect for photographs.

Clarissa watched for a moment longer, running her pearl along its chain. With all the drama of this morning, she was feeling a little jaded. It was at times like this that she was glad she was as fit as she was. She'd amazed the delivery men by moving several stacks of chairs and a trestle table without even thinking about it. But now she was definitely feeling it. She checked the time on Tess's computer screen. Gen would be up in a moment with Malachi and lunch, and she would be able to refuel ready for the afternoon.

Thank goodness Tess was going to be all right. The hospital wouldn't be letting her go anywhere for a few days at least, but Mark was with her for the moment. She'd had her stomach pumped the minute she'd arrived – it had been his quick thinking that had saved Tess's life, Clarissa was quite sure of it.

And Tess's compulsive organisation would save Kilfenora.

Clarissa looked over the pages Tess had laid out on the desk. She always put her current to-do stuff on her left, and things that needed attention, but not immediately, on her right. Clarissa had been most impressed when she'd explained it.

The technical running orders for today and Friday were neatly stapled; the pages were numbered and had been left lying as if they were waiting for her right in the middle of the keyboard. And, weighted down by Tess's *kintsugi* bowl, Clarissa had found a plan for the layout of the craft market. She'd picked up the bowl to look at this; it was a rich liquid blue, the gold a stark contrast.

The bowl was like Kilfenora itself. Clarissa and Mark would be the gold now, holding together the pieces of Tess's plan, making it into something whole.

She'd handed the diagram of the craft market over to the delivery people, who had begun to mutter about the time that everything was taking. As she'd explained the situation, one of them had realised she'd been in a six-part thriller series with Hugh Grant, which had been an unexpected and happy diversion while Gen had been in college, but apparently was enjoying a resurgence on Netflix. They couldn't have been more helpful.

She was quite sure setting everything up wasn't their job, but they'd done it happily, had been treated to lunch in the tea rooms, and the place was starting to take shape. And the AA people had arrived to tell her all the signs were up on all the main roads right up to the gate.

Tomorrow would be the big test, when the vintage cars arrived and everyone came to inspect and prep their stalls ready for Saturday. Some of the stallholders were regulars at markets in other parts of the county and would set up in minutes on Saturday morning, but anyone from the village and surrounding areas would need to sort themselves out well in advance of the doors opening to the public. Mark would be here then and had volunteered to be on site early. Everyone knew him, and they did what they were told when he asked – probably because they were afraid that they'd get barred from The Cross Keys if they didn't.

Clarissa smiled to herself. She was good with coercion, however it happened. And he had the after-party all organised for the cast.

Really, the only thing left for her to do now was to liberate a bottle of 2006 Châteauneuf-du-Pape from her personal collection and decide what to wear to greet the guests and introduce the show tomorrow evening. Tess even had the draft notes for her speech written, so Clarissa knew exactly what she needed to mention. She'd tweak it a bit this afternoon and get it over to the PR company Tess used, to be issued as a press release. Tess had always intended for Clarissa to introduce the play itself, and had a photographer booked who would get the shots to the photo desks with the press release before eleven on Friday night for the Saturday papers.

Everything was taking shape.

Behind her, Clarissa heard a mew. Turning on Tess's swivel chair, she looked at Merlin, who had just sauntered into the office.

'Where on earth did you come from?'

He began to wash his whiskers, which – Clarissa stood up to get a better look – had cobwebs on them.

'How *did* you get into the house?'

Tess was always telling her that he materialised like a ghost. Clarissa hadn't believed her for one moment, assuming that there had to be an open door or window somewhere that he used. He was a master at opening doors; he had long claws to pull them open, and used his full weight to push them. He'd even worked out how to open the catch on her kitchen window above the sink, and she was forever finding it ajar, despite the fact that he had a cat flap in the back door.

'Time to show me where you've been.'

Clarissa knew for sure she'd locked up properly when she'd gone over to sort out the second lot of delivery men, and she'd only just come in through the front door, *and* had closed it firmly behind her. Merlin hadn't been anywhere in sight.

As if he understood her, Merlin stretched and turned around, his tail in the air, and padded into the hallway. Clarissa stepped out of the office and watched him disappear towards the living room. She knew for a fact that she hadn't left the patio doors open.

A moment later she heard scratching and, turning to her left, saw him further down the hall. He'd stopped beside the stairs and was scratching at the wooden panelling below them. Slowly a piece of the wood came away from the wall. He stuck his paw in and levered it open with his nose.

Was it a door? Tess had mentioned something months ago about a draught in the hall, but Clarissa hadn't really taken it on board.

Moving closer to the panelling, Clarissa could see an edge where Merlin had opened it. There was no handle, but as she ran her fingers down it, a catch seemed to trigger and it opened towards her. Pulling it wide open, she felt a resistance as if it was on a spring. Then she saw a flight of steps. She'd need a torch to investigate further, but Clarissa suddenly realised why there might be a draught and where it was coming from – and exactly how Merlin was getting in and out of Tess's house.

FRIDAY

Chapter 66

'HOW ARE YOU feeling?'

Tess opened one eye and winced at the bright light. She was sure she'd heard Mark's voice, but she was in bed. And she felt as if she'd been hit by a truck.

A moment later the room came into focus. She *was* in bed, and Mark was leaning over her, but she definitely wasn't at home. And he had all his clothes on, so the part of her imagination that was panicking that something had happened that she'd somehow forgotten about, began to calm.

'What?' It came out as a croak. 'Where am I?'

'St Vincent's Hospital. You had a bit of a nasty turn.'

A nasty turn? That was the sort of phrase Clarissa used. It covered a multitude of ills. Tess screwed up her face, utterly confused. She felt him rub the top of her arm.

'You're OK. You've had your stomach pumped so you're going to feel pretty rotten, but everything is fine.'

Stomach pumped? Christ.

'What day is it?'

'Friday. It's about two o'clock. And you don't have to worry about anything, Clarissa has everything under control. All the chairs have been delivered and the market's all set up. She's just texted to say that she's getting all the cars parked. I think she's in her element, in all honesty. She likes being in charge.'

Tess smiled despite herself. He was right there.

'What happened? Did I drink too much?'

Everything was coming into focus. There was a pale blue pleated curtain hanging right around the bed and she realised she was hooked up to a drip.

Mark grinned at her encouragingly. 'What can you remember?'

It took Tess a minute, but memories began to fit together.

'I had a couple of glasses of wine, but I wanted to save the rest for Friday.' She screwed up her face as she thought hard. She'd put it in the fridge and then had started to feel really off. 'I felt rotten. I went up to bed.'

She vaguely remembered struggling out of her clothes and falling into bed, but then everything went a bit fuzzy.

'The docs think there was something in the wine. Aconite, to be precise.'

Tess felt her eyes open wide. 'That's lethal.'

'It is indeed. You were blessed you decided not to drink the whole bottle.' He cleared his throat. 'Where did you get it from?'

'It was left on the doorstep. What day did you say it was?'

'Friday.'

'But it's opening night – I need . . .' Tess started to try and sit up.

Mark pushed her down again. 'You're staying here. We have everything under control, trust me. Clarissa will do the introductions tonight. I'll be running everything. It will all be perfect. All the hire stuff has arrived, the AA signs are up.'

Tess looked at him, finally taking in what he was saying, like a row of dominoes falling.

'Who wanted to poison me? I mean, that's what you said would happen.'

Mark nodded ruefully. 'It seems so. I'll call Rockfield station and get them to pick up that bottle. You left it in the fridge?'

She nodded. 'And my glass is on the draining board. Will they be able to find fingerprints or something on the bottle?'

'Let's hope so.'

Chapter 67

GENEVIEVE SAT BACK in her chair in the ballroom, the audience filing into their seats behind her, the babble of conversation rising as they left their champagne glasses and found their places. Clarissa had reserved them centre seats in the front row, best in the house. Gen just wished Tess was beside her.

Making his way down the side of the room, Mark glanced over at her and grinned. He looked pretty amazing in a tuxedo. Gen pulled out her phone and surreptitiously took a photo of him as he checked the lectern and microphone.

Aidan Gaunt appeared from the wings and walked on to the stage, also in a tux and bow tie, and they laughed over something.

'When's it going to start?' Malachi pulled at Gen's arm, interrupting her attempt to lip-read. He was so excited he was jiggling in his chair. It was fortunate that Clarissa would be sitting on his other side as soon as the play began. She'd told Gen that she had a few things to do after the performance – getting changed being one of them – and she'd meet them for the debrief in the stable yard afterwards. The party was such a lovely idea, and would give Malachi a chance to work off his extra excitement before bed. They were both staying in Clarissa's tonight, so Gen could even have a glass of wine – which, right now, she was very much looking forward to. She'd never been so worried in her life as she had been about Tess.

'When's it going to start, Mum?'

Realising she hadn't answered him, Genevieve put her arm around Malachi's small shoulders and hugged him to her.

'Not long now. Nonna's doing the introductions and then she'll come and sit next to you.'

Clarissa had taken him to the theatre in Dublin several times, but this was entirely different. There was a suppressed sense of excitement in the ballroom; it was almost sparking like electricity. The families and friends of the cast mingled with the press, all eagerly anticipating the performance. Their anticipation, Gen was sure, was linked not just to the performance, but to the official opening of the house also, and the weekend of activities that everyone seemed to be involved in.

Beside her, Malachi turned around in his seat to look at the cameraman setting up in the central aisle. Gen could hardly believe that it was all about to begin. It was the culmination of so much work. Right from that day that they'd stood in the hallway huddled in their coats, drinking champagne and dreaming about the possibilities, Tess had given her all to this place.

And for Tess, they hadn't just been dreams. When she had an idea, she made it happen, regardless of how big – or how mad – it sounded. As she was always quoting, unless you aimed for the moon you'd never fall among the stars.

Part of Genevieve was devastated that Tess wasn't here to see everything she'd achieved. She'd brought a basket up to Clarissa at lunchtime, and popped over to the house to see how things looked, and been blown away. The carpenters had been busy building the scenery that Laetitia had designed – abstract shapes that suggested rooms and clouds and storms, and seemed to fit together like a jigsaw. As each scene changed, another piece of ply was flipped into place, changing the entire narrative. It was fiendishly clever, and Gen had felt the tragedy of Laetitia's loss all the more keenly. She was clearly as brilliant as both of her more academic sisters; she should have had such a glowing future.

It had taken all day to get the scenery pieces into place, and the curtains up, Aidan directing operations and making sure everything was in the correct positions. Leaving him to it, she'd gone across to the newly recreated drawing room, salon and dining room, and taken a few minutes to enjoy all the furniture she'd bought, finally in position. It was thrilling to wander through the rooms, and to see it all in one place. She'd brought up a few pieces of china, and Clarissa had suggested laying the dining table with the silver salver and a set of Victorian wineglasses that had been in the shop forever. A screen in one corner and magnificent mirror over the fireplace made the whole room look alive.

As the rows filled up behind her, Gen checked on Malachi again. He'd swivelled around now, and his eyes were glued to the centre of the curtains – swathes of blue velvet that looked like the midnight sky. He was transfixed.

Behind her, Gen heard Tess's name.

'I heard she'd been taken ill. Stress, I'd say. She's done this all on her own, pretty much. And with all the accidents . . .'

Gen kept her eyes on the stage; she didn't want to get into any conversations. Let them think it was stress. The last thing they needed was people linking everything together and the press getting hold of it. There was enough scandal in the village about Eoin Doyle, who had been released again this afternoon, which seemed utterly bizarre to Genevieve.

Suddenly the lights in the ballroom dimmed, just a flash, to indicate things were starting. Malachi looked up, his eyes wide as the lights came on again and then slowly began to dim, a spotlight falling on the lectern. At the side of the stage, Gen could see Mark giving a signal.

A moment later the curtains parted and Clarissa appeared on stage. She was wearing a simple navy dress, her grey hair caught in a sparkling clip that matched her sapphire necklace and earrings, the stone on her hand flashing as she moved. She put both hands on the lectern and in seconds had the audience's full attention. She waited for everyone to fully settle and then she began, her voice filling the entire room.

'Good evening, ladies and gentlemen, and a very warm welcome to Kilfenora House . . .'

Chapter 68

CLARISSA COULD HEAR the sound of chairs scraping and the audience leaving the ballroom, feet loud on the wooden floor, as she picked up the wine bottle. The play had been a resounding success; Liam had remembered all his lines and everything had run perfectly.

Clarissa adjusted her glasses and, holding the dusty bottle at arm's length, inspected the label. The light was dim in these rooms overlooking the front of the house, antique side lamps and standard lamps throwing pools of warm light over the furniture that Gen had styled so beautifully.

This was one of her better bottles, and it was something of a wrench to use it now, but it should do the trick nicely. Reaching for the corkscrew, she opened it with a satisfying pop, and poured out two glasses of wine.

Next, reaching into her evening bag, the movement making the woven silver lamé sparkle in the light from the lamps, Clarissa pulled out a vial she'd borrowed from Malachi's chemistry set. Pulling out the stopper, she tipped a turbid liquid into one of the glasses.

Conscious of time ticking, she slipped the empty vial back into her bag.

Putting the bottle down, she looked critically at the glasses and corkscrew itself. They'd come from Fortune Finds, so would naturally have her fingerprints on them, as would the silver salver that they rested on. This little tableau with the wine and glasses set the scene in the dining room perfectly.

Clarissa glanced up across the table at the huge ormolu mirror Gen had put up over the fireplace. The marble mantel had cracked in the heat of the fire that had devastated this central part of the house, but it was still magnificent, and the mirror finished the room, heavy gilt reflecting the soft lighting. She tucked a stray strand of silver hair back where it belonged and rubbed her lips together to make sure her lipstick was even.

She was ready.

Clarissa felt her heart rate increase slightly as adrenaline coursed through her. This was the moment she'd loved most when she'd been in London – that sense of anticipation and excitement just before she'd gone on stage. And obviously the standing ovations at the end of every performance were wonderful, too, but she didn't anticipate a standing ovation this evening.

In the central salon, she heard the double doors open, the sounds of chatter as the last remaining members of the audience left the ballroom opposite it.

The cast would be downstairs by now in the tea rooms, being royally entertained by Mark, who had set up everything beautifully and ordered a huge delivery from Fabio's. They would love it. There was nothing to beat the high when you came off stage.

In the next room, the double doors clicked closed and she heard footsteps. Then they stopped, as if the visitor was looking around the room wondering where she might be.

'Through here!'

A moment later Aidan appeared at the folding doors that connected the rooms, his face a mixture of curiosity and puzzlement. Before he could say anything, Clarissa swept into her speech.

'That was magnificent – word-perfect, and I have never seen a better performance.' She raised her hands as if in praise to a higher deity and clasped them together in sheer delight. 'I do hope you are thrilled. A standing ovation is not to be sniffed at.'

If Aidan had been unsure about why she'd asked him to cross the hall for a private celebration of the play's success, it was gone as soon as she spoke. He fluffed like a prize cock, then shook his head humbly.

'It was the cast. I'm only one small cog, as you know. They did all the work, under very difficult circumstances.'

'Well, it was wonderful, just wonderful. Which is why I wanted to plan a little surprise for you. When I was in the West End we always used to wet the play's head on the first night with a really good red. Just the director and the leads – it's a little tradition I've always loved. I was going to ask Liam to join us, but honestly I thought Châteauneuf-du-Pape would be wasted on him, and he has quite a fan club waiting for him downstairs. He'll enjoy that far more than celebrating with an old hen like me.'

Aidan laughed. 'He's certainly popular this evening, that's for sure.'

Before he quite finished the sentence, Clarissa smiled and picked up one of the full glasses.

'Here, I've poured to let it breathe.'

Coming around the table, he took the glass.

Raising her own glass carelessly, Clarissa beamed as Aidan checked out the bottle.

'Nice one.'

At least he knew his wine.

'We've got a few minutes before they miss you. I told them you were looking for your phone and you'd follow on. Did you find it?'

'I'll look for it in a minute, it's probably backstage somewhere.'

Clarissa smiled again as Aidan took a sip from the large Victorian crystal glass. She'd selected these specially because there had been one extra to the set of six kicking around the shop for as long as she could remember. The spare glass had turned up in a miscellaneous box from an auction. If one went missing, there would still be a perfect set of six for the display. And they were the most generous size.

Stepping closer to him, she bowed her head slightly as she lifted her own glass.

'To you, and future successes.'

His glass touched the side of hers with a pleasing chink. Clarissa raised the glass to her lips and then, as if remembering something, lowered it. She watched him take a large mouthful and roll it around his mouth, swallowing and taking another.

'You need that. It's such a big job putting together a production like this.'

'There seems to be a bit of sediment for such a great year.'

Clarissa arched an eyebrow. 'Perhaps it's a storage issue. It's vintage. Like me.'

'Oh, but you're very sprightly. What was your last performance? It wasn't that long ago.'

'*Blithe Spirit*. I was Elvira.'

'Oh yes, you said.' He raised the glass to his lips again. 'Great part, great play.'

'It was very well reviewed. I love the Adelphi, such a beautiful theatre.'

He nodded as if he knew.

One more mouthful.

She waited for a moment as he took another swig. The glass was almost empty.

'You can't beat a vintage red, can you?'

He reached for the bottle and topped his glass up.

'Delicious, very thoughtful of you. Definitely beats pints and chips – that was a nice touch for the cast.'

Clarissa took a step backwards and put her head on one side.

'Thank *you*, they put on a fabulous performance. Such a shame, though – you would have had wine like this every day if you'd continued in investment banking.'

He didn't react, just raised one eyebrow. He was a good actor, she had to give him that.

'You can drop the English accent, Aidan – or should I say Adam? I should have realised Aidan Gaunt was a stage name.'

She chuckled quietly to herself. Her own name had given her a lot of fun over the years, her real name of Sharpe a little too plain for the theatre.

But she would always be Sharpe by name, and goddammit, sharp by nature.

'What happened with Conor? Was he off his mark so the light fitting didn't quite hit him squarely? A death on stage would have been the end of the show, it could have prevented Tess from opening at all.'

Aidan took another long sip of his wine and regarded her silently, his eyes hardening.

'Conor was an accident. Such a terrible thing to happen.'

Did he really think that she believed him?

Averting her eyes from him in case her temper boiled over,

Clarissa looked speculatively for a moment at the toe of her nude patent stiletto.

'You might as well tell me everything, Adam. Satisfy an old woman's curiosity. I also know that you won't allow me to leave now that I'm so close to the truth, so why not spill it all? It's quite a magnificent plan, like a production all of its own.'

He didn't answer, but Clarissa could feel him sizing her up. What would he try? If it was her call, she'd go with the bottle over the head and then a 'fall' down the main staircase. A slightly tipsy old lady tumbling to her death would be entirely believable. Another Kilfenora accident.

Just to be on the safe side, she stayed beyond arm's length, ready to throw one of the dining chairs into his way if he moved before she expected. She didn't think he would; the temptation to boast would be too much.

Arrogance had always been his problem.

And that was where he'd come unstuck.

"*Fools that will laugh on earth must weep in hell.*"

Doctor Faustus was such an apt script for him to choose to adapt. She could feel his eyes on her as she frowned.

'Why Laetitia, though? That's the bit I haven't quite worked out. I heard the pathologist had found traces of a tranquilliser in her blood. Leaving the radio on made us all think it could be the Radio Snatcher, but you'd faked her suicide. Why the need to dispose of her at all?'

He shook his head, smirking into his glass, and took another mouthful. Clarissa resisted the temptation to smile. From the amount of powdered aconite root that she'd mixed into that first glass, she knew he had about another ten minutes. Ten minutes in which she was going to find out the truth.

Chapter 69

AIDAN DIDN'T ANSWER immediately, as if he was considering his options.

'Laetitia was foolish. I bumped into her one night in the gardens. She was taking photos for a painting or something, looking at what the darkness did to colour. She never really bought my explanation for why I was picking flowers at midnight, and then she saw me adjusting the lighting rig. Even though I told her I was fixing the spotlights, she put two and two together. I'd worked out the exact time it would take for the bolt to sheer, but even then, it didn't fall when it should have. I had to get him to repeat the speech a load of times. When I went up to see Laetitia that Friday she asked me about it, straight out. She'd happened to be looking my way as the rig fell. I should have looked surprised. That was an oversight.' He cleared his throat. 'I couldn't afford any loose ends.'

'But Katie-Louise? Of all people? How did she get involved? She wasn't even in the play.'

'She heard us arguing. I was explaining that Laetitia had it all wrong. Then doesn't Katie-Lou come and knock on the van door?' He shook his head. 'I had no choice, I didn't know what she'd heard.'

'So, what? You drugged them both?'

It had taken Clarissa a while to work out how two women could have been overpowered together, but then she'd heard about the increase of women being spiked in Dublin nightclubs and the penny had dropped. And the pathologist's report had confirmed it. She'd always wondered what type of men kept date rape drugs handy, and now she had her answer.

He shrugged. 'Had to be done.'

'But you chose to actually kill them in ways that mirrored the tragedies at the house. That feels very calculated.'

'Always good to be prepared. Meg O'Riordan had told me all about the history of the house. I started with Connor – it seemed too good an opportunity to miss.' He smiled, clearly pleased with himself.

Clarissa pursed her lips. He was right. The historical parallels were the type of thing the press loved, and they would feed the rumours about the Kilfenora Curse like a wind fanning flames. If it hadn't been Laetitia and Katie-Lou, it would have been someone else. Megan herself, perhaps, or even Gen.

'Why such a complex plan, though?'

Aidan laughed. 'Because Plan A didn't quite work as well as I'd hoped. A for Adam, and for my new identity as Aidan Gaunt – that bit had gone very well. Acting is the one profession where gaps on your CV are considered normal. I made some contacts in prison, joined an extras agency when I got out, sweet-talked my way from there.' He shook his head as she raised one eyebrow. 'Who do you think passed on the information about the Radio Snatcher? Now that was a gift.' He laughed again. 'You think you're so clever, but you haven't done the maths, have you? I wasn't honestly sure whether my cellmate was just bragging about knowing the location of the bodies, and then, when I saw in the Irish papers that Tess had bought Kilfenora, I couldn't believe my luck. A chance conversation years previously suddenly became incredibly useful. It started it all.'

He looked so smug, Clarissa wanted to slap his face.

She clenched her teeth and drew in a slow breath through a stage smile as he continued. 'Tess Morgan ruined my life. I waited a long time to ruin hers. It was karma.' He chuckled to himself, 'Leaving the radio on in Laetitia's van was a little nod to my "benefactor", a little acknowledgement.'

Clarissa nodded slowly. 'I did have a feeling you might have been at the root of that information. Even if they'd found nothing, the stain would have remained on the property.'

Aidan snorted and took another swig of wine. 'Exactly. It all started there. If it had worked, it might have been enough, but that Lynch guy had other ideas – TV shows and the like. Wanted the glory. That was the real Plan A. But he took too long to do anything about it, so I came up with the play as a way to get in.' He took another sip. 'I wrote most of it in prison, something to keep me occupied. Turned out to be time well spent.' Aidan looked at his glass and chortled to himself. 'I couldn't believe that Lynch *did* actually find a body. That was sweet.'

'But your Plan B was already underway.'

'You could say that. My career was all about risk, while minimising exposure – it's what I'm good at.' He looked at her hard.

'And poisoning Tess was the final part?'

'I wanted her to feel as bad as I had. Slowly debilitating her in the lead up to the opening was a pleasure to watch.' He drew a breath in between his teeth. 'But with the opening still going ahead and so much attention on Laetitia and Katie-Lou, I needed to move things along a bit quicker.' He looked at her. 'Aidan Gaunt is going to vanish tonight, leaving a note for Meg O'Riordan saying how the success of the play has been overwhelming and he needs some time out. I have my plane ticket booked – in my real name, obviously, so if anyone does start looking for Gaunt, the trail will be cold as ice.'

The pieces were falling into place in Clarissa's head, each one like a move in a game of chess. Laetitia had been looking up aconite because she'd caught Aidan picking it, not because she was planning to make it into hand cream. And when she'd discovered what a potent poison it was, she must have asked herself what on earth he wanted it for. Clarissa was desperate to ask what possible explanation he could have given her for wandering around the gardens at night, pulling up plants, but there really wasn't time now.

One thing was clear though: he'd been determined to destroy Tess from the moment his cell door had banged closed all those years ago.

Her face twitched into a smile. 'It's clever, I have to say. Four unrelated killings, if we start with Kieran, four completely different modi operandi, all linked to the house and its history. Quite the mystery. Except one didn't work out. You must have been upset when Conor's "accident" didn't quite go as planned.'

He scowled. 'It just meant I had to step up other parts of the plan. When I was trading, I learned to think fast under pressure. It's something I'm very good at. When Laetitia started questioning me that night, it was the perfect opportunity to continue the historical analogy. '"Murder is easy when it doesn't look like murder,"' I believe is the line.'

'Not quite, but how typical of you to adapt a quote to suit yourself. I always felt the movie worked better than the book,

353

didn't you? I'm sure Agatha was rolling her eyes, but adding Jane Marple held it together so well.'

'She's inquisitive, just like you.'

'So true.' Clarissa paused. 'But why all this, Adam? You were the one driving the car that night. You were the one who was drunk. Didn't Tess pay enough when you killed Kieran?'

'It was her fault. This whole stupid mess was her fault.' He steadied himself against the table. 'My girlfriend dumped me that night because of her. I was going to marry her, and then doesn't Tess say something to her in the ladies about true love, and we had this huge row. It should have been her I hit on that road, not him. If she hadn't been there, none of this would have happened. I'd still be working for Merrill Lynch and making a million a year, have the perfect family. I was almost there, you know, I was their top dealer.'

Clarissa felt her heart harden even more, if that was possible. She gripped the stem of her glass, fighting to keep her rage at bay.

'You should have been convicted of murder, not manslaughter.'

His smile chilled her. 'I was drunk, as you so rightly point out, not capable of premeditation.'

Clarissa deliberately kept her voice relaxed, conversational.

'And when you got out of jail, you tried to track Tess down to finish the job? But she was in Dubai, and not on social media because of her position in the royal household, so you couldn't find her.' She was seeing the whole picture now – and it was worse than even she'd imagined. 'Then when the news broke about Kilfenora House, you found her again.' Something else fell into place in Clarissa's mind; it was all becoming clear now. 'And you trolled her on Twitter. That was you, too, wasn't it?'

'She ruined my life. I ended up on the streets when I got out of jail. It was only those bit parts that got me by, and some X-rated film work. Like I said, acting's one of the few jobs you can do when there are gaping holes in your CV. I could never work in a bank again – my record would have shown up on the first search. How do you think I felt?' His eyes flashed. 'My life changed completely that night. Because of her. Look at me now. Do I look anything like the man who stood in that dock?'

He didn't, that was true. He was vaguely familiar, but he'd lost a huge amount of weight. He must have got fit in jail, and his face had changed shape as he'd aged.

Clarissa sighed. She'd known this would be all about him, had known he wasn't who he professed to be from the moment he'd shown his lack of knowledge about *Blithe Spirit*. No one in the theatre referred to Elvira as 'the wife' – she was the *first* wife, the ghost who was accidentally summoned and proceeded to try to murder her husband so that he could join her in the spirit world. Not that Clarissa had any intention of joining *any* of her husbands in the spirit world: the unfaithful one, the violent one, or Dominic, whose sin had been that while terribly rich, he was also terribly boring. Clarissa just hadn't been ready to give up on life and do boring, and she certainly wasn't prepared to do it in the ever-after.

Clarissa put her glass down on the table and played with the stones in her necklace. The light caught the sapphire on her finger, bouncing it off the huge mirror that reflected them both, sending prisms across the room.

She looked up as Aidan raised his eyebrows. 'So, what am I going to do with you now? You've upset my historical analogy, but I'm sure there must have been someone over the years who . . . what? Had a fall? Those stairs are so smooth I'd imagine they could be lethal.'

Clarissa almost rolled her eyes. *So unimaginative.*

He laughed, half quoting the original line this time. 'You know, murder's easy – *so long as no one suspects you.*'

A smile curled across her face.

'It is rather, isn't it? And you did your research well. Aconitine and the alkaloids found in the aconitum species are highly toxic cardiotoxins and neurotoxins. The roots of the wild plant are *extremely* toxic.' She raised her eyebrows. 'And given its half-life, potentially untraceable.' She glanced at the wine, and back at her own glass, still full. 'Tess wouldn't have had a chance if we hadn't realised.'

He smirked at her, still thinking he had the upper hand.

'She drinks far too much coffee.'

The coffee. Tess had said he was always bringing her coffee.

No wonder she'd been feeling so ill; he had been gradually poisoning her, for . . . how long? Clarissa drew in a breath and held it for a moment, controlling her temper.

This was turning into the performance of her life.

One thing was becoming rapidly clear: Adam O'Donnell *really* deserved everything that was coming his way.

'Strong flavours do rather mask the taste of aconite, don't they?' She paused. 'How are you feeling now? Given the amount you've ingested, the nausea, vomiting, and abdominal pain that Tess has been suffering might be more severe.'

His eyes widened in shock. 'What?'

'"O, Faustus, Now hast thou but one bare hour to live / And then thou must be damn'd perpetually!"' Clarissa smiled triumphantly. 'Though I doubt it'll be as long as an hour. "The time is come."'

Chapter 70

THE SOUND OF laughter rose as Megan followed everyone into the tea rooms. The tables had been moved so that there was space for them all, and Mark Mulligan was standing in the middle of the room, wearing a tux and black bow tie and looking for all the world like one of the Chippendales.

Phew.

'I'll get you a glass of white. Grab me some of those sandwiches.' Beside her, Ally gave Megan a nudge with her elbow. 'Meg, you're staring. Put your tongue back in, please. You look like you're on heat.'

'Me? Just taking in the landscape – nothing wrong with that, is there?'

But Ally had vanished into the crowd, pursued, Megan noted, by the youngest luvvie, who seemed to have taken a shine to her in the past few days. Perhaps he'd discovered she was heading for a first in law, and he was looking for a wife with a proper job who could support his acting career.

Megan looked around, searching the crowd for Aidan. He'd said he'd follow them down, but she couldn't see him. He'd gone looking for his phone; perhaps it was taking longer than he'd thought. She'd texted him to say congratulations, but the signal was so bad around here she wasn't convinced that it would arrive.

Megan scanned the crowd again. Ally had vanished into the melee as the stable yard filled with the sound of classical music. She was sure this lot would prefer country, but there was something wonderfully sophisticated about an outdoor soirée accompanied by violins.

It was perfect, in fact, for her plan. Rather romantic – they could be in Italy in this heat. This evening was her chance, especially after the success of the play, to get Aidan well and truly oiled, and then who knew what might happen? Lots, she hoped. In his apartment, ideally, but she wasn't against a romantic walk around the gardens and a bit of open-air action. Indeed, any action would be a bonus right now. She'd been working hard towards this all summer.

With the cast and their families swirling around her, juggling glasses and baskets of chips, Megan had another look around the interior of the tea room and, forgetting she was supposed to be getting the food, doubled back to see if Aidan was still outside. Perhaps he had been held up chatting. He was, after all, the man of the moment.

Outside, the tables and picnic benches were already filling up, the strings of lights that criss-crossed it attracting moths in the darkness. The place looked gorgeous. Now she really did just need to find Aidan.

Turning, Megan walked straight into Mark, sending the pint he was carrying down his crisp white pin-tucked, very – Megan was sure – expensive shirt.

'Oof, watch out there.'

'Oh, I'm so, so sorry. Here, I've got a tissue.' Blushing hard, Megan started to reach for her bag.

'Don't worry.'

Mark put the pint down and started unbuttoning his shirt. Megan took a step backwards, her mouth open. But he had a T-shirt on underneath – a red one with a lightning flash across it, that was a tiny bit too small. Or perhaps he was a tiny bit too big. In a second he'd stripped the shirt off and balled it up under his arm, bending to pick up what was left of the pint.

He'd been quick enough so the beer hadn't soaked through the thick cotton of his evening shirt. What on earth could she say? He looked as if he'd stepped out of a Marvel movie.

'How can you wear two layers in this heat?'

He grinned at her. 'This isn't hot. Not by Aussie standards. Positively mild.'

He had the most gorgeous smile, and, she noticed, bright blue eyes.

'Oh, oh, right.' Megan flicked her long dark hair over her shoulder. 'Could I get you another drink? I'd love to hear more about Australia. What part were you in?'

Chapter 71

U PSTAIRS, CLARISSA DIDN'T feel the need to watch Aidan's demise. She knew exactly the path from ingestion of aconite to collapse, and she had other things to do.

Wandering through from the dining room to the salon, this was her first chance to properly admire the pieces of furniture Gen had chosen so carefully on her trips to the auctions. The tastefully arranged side tables, scattered with potted ferns and old books, made the whole room look most welcoming. Definitely an improvement on watching Aidan, or Adam, or whatever he called himself now, expire in the room next door. The last few moments were never pretty.

Pausing, Clarissa pulled out her phone and opened the Kilfenora Instagram account. She'd prepared some photographs of the performance, and one she'd taken at about this time last night, of Merlin sitting beside a bottle of champagne on Tess's kitchen table. Setting her location as the Butler's Lodge, she uploaded that one first.

> Such a magnificent evening, definitely a night for bubbles, but off to congratulate the cast first! Faustus will only be showing twice weekly for the next four weeks, book your tickets now!

She'd been wearing her mulberry jacket and navy silk shirt when she'd taken it last night; her reflection was just visible in the glass bottle if you looked carefully enough. And she was sure some people would.

In the dining room, she heard a thump – Aidan falling to the floor, she was quite sure. Aconite had analgesic and local anaesthetic properties that resulted in muscle weakness, tingling or numbness in the extremities, and then paralysis. From the amount she'd put in his wine, she knew he'd have no time to try and leave the room, let alone cry out.

Not that anyone would hear him up here.

Finishing with her phone, Clarissa went into the dining room to find him, as she'd expected, slumped on the floor, face down, vomit trailing from his mouth. She wrinkled her nose in distaste. The only downside to this method of disposal was the vomit. She let out a sigh and put her silver bag down on the table, pulling out a pair of latex gloves. She slipped off her ring and eased her hands into them.

There was an embroidered japonaiserie screen in the corner of the room, and she went over to it now, folding it back carefully. Concealed in the panelling was a door that led to the servants' staircase. Like its mirror image in the drawing room, it wound down to a main arterial passage, and a warren of whitewashed service corridors that connected all the rooms in the house. And significantly, as Merlin had discovered, a passage that Tess hadn't previously found that led to the cellar of the Butler's Lodge.

He was a most useful cat.

And now Clarissa came to think about it, Merlin hadn't liked Aidan Gaunt one little bit from the moment he'd appeared in Kilfenora. They should all have paid more attention.

Opening the door to the staircase, Clarissa took a step backwards to avoid a rope-like spiderweb, grey with dust, that came with it. She had no idea when this stairway had last been used – probably some time in the 1800s, from the look of the detritus on the top step – but that suited her purposes perfectly.

According to the Japanese medical research paper she'd found many years ago, aconitine had a half-life in the body of twenty-four to sixty-two hours. After that it was broken down completely and undetectable.

It would be most helpful if he wasn't found for a few days. Some time on Monday, according to her calculations, would be about right.

"Time runs, the clock will strike."

There was a certain poetry – art, almost – in keeping the historical parallels Aidan had established going. His demise would be the fourth, if you took poor Kieran's death into account. Clarissa had always liked things to be tidy.

Behind her, she heard a muted ringtone coming from her bag. Aidan's phone. Just before the show she'd made quite a performance of bringing him in to see the restored rooms, at the same time slipping his phone from the top of his script notes into her bag. He'd humoured her, but had barely had time to look at the new furniture. He had been so busy when he'd got back, when he'd finally noticed the phone was missing, he hadn't had time to look for it. She'd heard him asking a few cast members if they'd seen it, had had to resist the smile that had twitched across her face.

Turning back to the table, she opened her bag and pulled out the phone. Bobbing down, she pulled his right hand out from under his lifeless body and used his forefinger to open it. As soon as it came to life, she made sure it was switched to silent. It was quite important that no one heard it ringing and became curious.

Standing up, she went to the open door and tossed the phone down the stairs. She heard it bounce off a step or two and then skitter to a stop.

Perfect.

Her mind completely focused on the task at hand, next Clarissa went back to the body. She checked his face to ensure she didn't get any vomit on herself. This was always going to be the difficult bit, but there was a very good reason why she'd worn a jersey dress this evening. Kicking off her heels, Clarissa grabbed hold of Aidan under his armpits and, leaning backwards, used her full weight to drag him across the floor to the door. The polished boards made sliding him much easier than she'd imagined, and she had him at the top of the stairs in a moment.

Which was fortunate, as the next stage would test her.

She needed his body to fall from the top of the stairs so it appeared that he'd taken a tumble, dropping his phone in the process. And that meant hauling him into a standing position, or at least something close to it. She couldn't go down the stairs to pull him or her footprints would show in the dust, but as everyone was always saying, Clarissa was remarkably fit for her age.

She was also fuelled by the most incredible anger. Nobody hurt the people she loved and got away with it.

Taking a deep breath, she straddled him and tucked her hands under his armpits. Thank God she was so tall. Stepping backwards to lift him higher, straining every muscle in her body, she manoeuvred him forwards into the doorway, his head lolling helplessly.

When she could feel the cold stone of the top step under her stockinged toe, she angled herself at the top of the stairs and released his body, giving it an extra shove with her hips, praying his weight would carry him down.

It worked.

Recoiling from the force needed to jettison him down the stairs, Clarissa leaned on the door frame, catching her breath. But she couldn't hang about. Bending down to check she hadn't left any footprints, she closed the door and pulled the screen across it. Returning to where he'd been lying, she checked the wooden floorboards, reaching for her bag to pull out a wipe. There was very little vomit, thank goodness, but she didn't want any stains left behind.

She balled the wipe and latex gloves and slipped them into her bag, picking up her ring.

Next, the glasses and the bottle of wine.

Clarissa tipped her own wine into the plant beside the window. Giving her glass a quick wipe with a tissue from her bag, she put it with the others on the silver salver, which she pushed into the middle of the table. Picking up his glass, she tucked the bottle under her arm and turned to slip on her shoes. She reached for her bag and then realised the lamp was still on.

Clarissa's mind clicked forwards, testing again every element of the scene she'd created.

If Aidan had come in here to find his phone and then gone to join the cast, taking a short cut via the backstairs, he wouldn't have turned off the lights. And as Clarissa had 'gone ahead' of the cast to Tess's house to change, she wouldn't have turned them off either.

Satisfied she had all the ends tied, Clarissa went through the salon and into the drawing room, her heels loud on the wooden floor. In the far corner, she opened the door to the servants' staircase hidden in the panelling. Very few people knew about these passages, and she wanted to keep it that way.

By the time his body was discovered in the stairwell, and the police started digging and discovered Adam O'Donnell was Aidan Gaunt, and tied him to Laetitia's and Katie-Louise's deaths, and indeed Conor's accident, which in turn were tied in to the history of the house, it would be assumed he was one of the people who knew these stairs were here.

After the show, it would be logical to assume that he would be mentally retracing his steps to think where he might have left his lost phone, and obviously he would look in the salon and dining room where he'd been earlier. At which point the pressure of the play and everything that had happened over the past few days, on top of the stress of the missing phone, would cause a significant, if unexpected, heart attack.

Job done.

Chapter 72

HOOKING HER BAG over her shoulder, Clarissa pulled her phone out to use as a flashlight, making sure she still had the bottle tucked firmly under her arm. The stairs were uneven and narrow, with no banister, winding down into the pitch dark in front of her. She had no idea how servants in long skirts carrying coal or trays could possibly have navigated them safely. She had to put her foot sideways, one hand on the wall, her phone and the glass held firmly in the other, to get down at all. She really needed Merlin's eyes at moments like this. In fact, she needed all of Merlin's sixth sense. If she'd had any of it, perhaps none of this would have happened.

She had to give Aidan – or Adam, or whatever his name was – one thing, though. He might not be able to fool a cat, but as far as humans were concerned, his acting skills were top-notch. She'd discovered from her research that an Aidan Gaunt had played an increasing number of small roles in London, having come, apparently, from nowhere. It had taken him a few years by her calculations to reinvent himself, but he'd done a good job. It wasn't exactly as lucrative as trading on the futures market, but he'd brought that on himself.

The narrow stone stairs grew increasingly treacherous as she went further down, but the strong beam from her phone lit her path, her heels clicking on the worn treads. At the bottom she emerged into the whitewashed passage that ran the full width of the house. Hurrying on, Clarissa found the door to the wine cellar. More steps downwards, the temperature dropping as she went deeper. Turning to her right, she followed the main passage through the wooden racks, the air crisp with the scent of wine and mouse droppings. Lord Kilfenora had been renowned as a collector; years ago each bay would have been packed with a magnificent range of fine wines.

Slipping down a narrow passage that linked the sections between the racks, Clarissa hurried into the next aisle. She shivered. It was decidedly creepy down here, especially knowing she was alone in the house.

The ticketing staff who had manned the front desk would have seen the film crew and guests out and already locked the front door. After such an early start, the cameraman had been anxious to leave the very second the play was over – before, in fact, the applause had even died away.

The reception staff would have joined the cast, anxious not to miss any of the free drinks or food. Mark had been keen to lock the stable yard staircase door once everyone was out, conscious of the antiques upstairs. The last thing they needed, on top of everything else, was a robbery.

As Clarissa reached the end of the aisle, she saw the open door that Merlin had been using. She still wasn't entirely sure how he was getting into the cellar from the house, but there could be a broken window or a ventilation shaft somewhere. Whatever route he'd found, he certainly seemed to use it a lot.

The narrow passageway that linked the main cellar to the cellar below the Butler's Lodge was only wide enough for one, and Clarissa had to duck to keep her head clear of the webs criss-crossing the curved brick ceiling. She'd come down here armed with a feather duster, but there had been years of spidery activity.

She was almost there now. Then she needed to make a quick costume change that looked as if she'd taken her time over it, and head across the lane to the party. With Gen and Malachi staying in her cottage, she was going to stay in Tess's house so she was readily on site in case any of the craft people had problems getting to their stalls in the morning. And she'd be the first person in tomorrow, unlocking the house ready for the tours on Saturday morning – giving her a chance to double-check that everything was in order.

Adam O'Donnell really was the most odious individual. She'd been struck at his trial by how utterly callous he was. It was years ago now, and from their conversation this evening, she could see that he hadn't changed a bit.

He'd maintained then that the accident had been Tess and Kieran's fault, that he'd seen them laughing as he rounded the corner, and the next thing he knew, Kieran had gone over his bonnet.

When it had been put to him that he was three times over the legal alcohol limit and exceeding the speed limit by at least thirty kilometres an hour, he'd shrugged it off. His arrogance and inability to take responsibility for his actions had resulted in the maximum sentence available to the judge, who had been as unimpressed as Clarissa.

He was well overdue payment for his crimes.

All of them.

Chapter 73

GENEVIEVE FINALLY FOUND her way through the crowd in the tea rooms and emerged into the prettily lit yard to find Ally deep in conversation with one of the professional actors. Pausing for a moment beside them, Gen smiled.

'You've all done such a marvellous job – I mean, really. And the scenery was amazing, Ally, your parents will be so proud.'

Gen paused.

What did you say at moments like this?

Ally saved her.

'The Buddhists have a theory that there are some people who burn very intensely, but for a very short time. I think Laetitia was one of those. Her art will live on in so many homes.'

'You're right. That's a wonderful way to think of her. She was like a bright light, wasn't she? A very special one.' Gen suddenly felt herself getting emotional again. But this wasn't the moment to burst into tears; she excused herself rapidly. 'Have a lovely evening.'

Scanning the yard, her eyes alighted on a space at the end of one of the picnic benches just as Malachi arrived beside her, pretending he'd swum out of the crowd. There were moments when Gen could see that he had all of Clarissa's theatrical genes. Gen bent down to him.

'Mal, why don't you go and grab that space? Take this basket and I'll bring these over in a second.'

With her hands full of baskets of food and a glass of lemonade, she indicated the picnic table.

'Where's Nonna?'

'I don't know, love. I'm sure she's here somewhere, or she may be getting changed.'

As she spoke, Gen glanced through the stable yard gate to Tess's house across the lane and saw the front door open. Clarissa appeared, her favourite purple raw silk jacket artfully flung around her shoulders, her dress swapped for a navy silk shirt and flowing trousers. Gen smiled to herself. Clarissa had been in all the society magazines during her career, and she didn't let her standards slip for a sleepy Wicklow village. When she'd stepped out onto the stage this evening to greet the audience, she'd looked as if she was announcing the National Television Awards, her fitted dress elegant and perfect for the occasion, her sapphires sparkling.

As Clarissa walked down the garden path, she spotted Gen and waved. Malachi saw her at the same time and, weaving across the yard between cast members like a guided missile, ran towards her. She ruffled his hair when he got to her and he grabbed her hand to pull her along.

'Oh, there she is. Honestly, it takes some women so long to get changed.'

Gen turned to give Mark a look, but she could see from the smile on his face that he was joking. Seeing her expression, he held up both his hands as if she had a gun pointed at him.

'I know, I can't talk. Height of sartorial elegance, me.'

Gen looked him up and down. 'Why are you wearing evening trousers and a Marvel T-shirt? Did I miss something?'

'I had a bit of an accident . . .'

As he spoke, Megan O'Riordan appeared beside them, her black sequinned cami top and crêpe organza trousers perhaps a little glamorous for a stable yard. Gen wondered how truly practical strappy shoes were when you were assisting actors with costume changes, but it wasn't her place to mention it. It looked a lot as if Megan was trying to make an impression on someone. As if answering Gen, Megan smiled broadly, directing her full attention to Mark.

'There you are – I thought you'd run away.'

Mark's face froze for a second and Gen almost laughed out loud. Fortunately Clarissa swept in at that moment, Malachi at her side. Mark's relief at a distraction was almost palpable.

'Here she is, the woman of the moment.'

Clarissa threw Mark a good-humoured withering look.

'Any news on how Tess is doing?'

'Good. The nurse who met us when I took her in has been texting me updates. We've a full-on day tomorrow, so I won't get out to her until the evening, but they'll keep us posted.'

Clarissa nodded and, bending down, whispered something in Malachi's ear. He ran off into the crowd, grinning.

Gen looked at her mother quizzically and Clarissa assumed a mask of complete innocence. Rather than ask what errand she'd sent Malachi on, Gen turned to Mark.

'We'll go in to see her first thing in the morning. I've been worried sick.'

Mark put his arm around Gen's shoulder and gave her a little hug, much to Megan's evident disgust. Gen caught her sniff and averted gaze as Mark sighed, 'We all have, Gen, we all have.'

Clarissa was about to speak when Megan butted in.

'Tess will be so pleased to hear everything went so well. I must congratulate Aidan, he'll be exhausted. He was looking for his phone when I saw him last. Did he find it?'

Clarissa looked surprised. 'I came ahead of everyone to get changed. I haven't seen him. Have you tried ringing him?'

'He's not answering.' Megan said it a little crossly.

Clarissa adjusted the jacket on her shoulders. 'Perhaps he wanted a break. I knew one director who always vanished on opening night. I think he went to get plastered, personally. All the stress of building such an amazing thing hits you when the curtains close.'

Before anyone could reply, Malachi reappeared, concentrating hard on not spilling a glass of white wine as he wove through the crowd, one hand on the glass and one on its stem.

Clarissa's eyes lit up. 'Oh, perfect, I need this.'

Gen shook her head in despair. 'Mother, you cannot send an eight-year-old to get alcohol. I mean, really?'

Clarissa tutted. 'Some things just have to be done. I'm only having one, it's been a busy evening and we've an early start tomorrow, as Mark says.'

She bent down to take the glass from Malachi.

'Nonna, you've got cobwebs on you.'

Malachi delicately reached into her grey hair and pulled one off.

'Thank you, my darling. We might give Tess's house a spring clean before she comes home from hospital, will we? How are you with a paintbrush, Mark? There's the most awful pale blue wallpaper in Tess's office. I didn't realise quite how headache-inducing it was before today. It might be nice to spruce the place up while she's away, perhaps bring in some William Morris. She's put so much energy into the main house she's forgotten to look after herself.'

'I can come over and take a look tomorrow evening when we close.' He took a bow. 'White knight at your service.'

Clarissa looked at him, amused. 'Make sure you do, or I'll send my rook after you.'

Gen looked from one of them to the other in disbelief, suddenly catching up with what they were saying.

'Is he your chess opponent? I mean, really?'

'I am indeed. Always available for games of strategy and cunning.' Mark bowed his head.

Gen opened her eyes wide. 'Honestly, Mum, you're a dark horse sometimes. There's one of the mysteries of the universe solved right there. Tess and I have had bets on just about everyone in the village. We never thought of you, Mark.'

'Should I be flattered or offended?'

Gen laughed. 'You're Kilfenora's best-kept secret, I'd be flattered. Definitely.'

SATURDAY

Chapter 74

WITH MALACHI FINALLY splashing happily in the bath, Gen collapsed onto the sofa, pulling one of the bright velvet cushions that she'd found in a house sale in behind her.

Her back was aching now.

She'd been on her feet all afternoon, taking Mal around the craft market, buying enough bread and cakes in the farmers' market to feed half the village, and then looking at each and every one of the vintage cars as Malachi had asked their owners detailed questions about horsepower and . . . well, Gen wasn't sure what else. Somehow the physics of acceleration had got into the conversation and Gen had been totally lost.

She was glad she'd worn flat sandals and one of her linen dresses. Out beside the vintage cars there had been no shade. Not that the heat had stopped people coming – the place had been packed.

Reaching for her glass of wine, Gen could feel that she'd caught the sun across her shoulders. It was still baking, and she had all the windows in the apartment open to what little breeze might funnel down Kilfenora Main Street.

Tess had looked deadly pale this morning, and she'd been so sleepy when they'd arrived that Gen had been worried about staying, but she'd perked up no end when she'd seen the papers. Mal had clambered up beside her on the bed, asked too many questions about her drip, and then had shown her all the photographs of his nonna and the market and the cars. It was hardly surprising that it had been busy today, given the coverage Kilfenora and the play had had.

Gen took another sip of her wine and clicked to open Facebook on her phone. She hadn't looked at the forum for what felt like days; she was praying the members hadn't run amok with everything that had been happening.

She clicked to open the group.

This is YOUR local forum for the village of Kilfenora and its townlands. Please respect other users, we will not tolerate any abusive posts, comments, bullying, or hate speech of any sort – anything of this nature will get an automatic ban. We support local business wherever we can, no negative comments please. If you have a problem, please resolve it privately. If you are not happy with the way this group is run, please consider leaving. The admins are voluntary and we are all too busy for debate.

Gen scanned the posts, the usual mish-mash of comment and slightly odd requests.

LakeviewBandB
Faustus was brilliant from what I could see, sound terrible at the back though.

> **Trixie Bell**
> LakeviewBandB With your hearing difficulties you should have booked down the front. We could hear everything.

Finn MacCool
GAA practice moved to 2pm tomorrow, so we can all get over the after-show party. Liam was bloody amazing.

LakeviewBandB
Looking for a reasonably priced person to cut high hedges. Any recommendations. Thanks in advance

Meg O'Riordan
Has anyone heard latest on Tess Morgan?

> **Carrie O'Connor**
> Meg O'Riordan Stress I reckon, she's been doing far too much.

Carrie O'Connor
Meg O'Riordan Mark and Clarissa Westmacott were up at the house today. He's excellent at the tours. Knows all the history.

> **Meg O'Riordan**
> Carrie O'Connor I did a project on Kilfenora for my leaving.

> **Tracker Maguire**
> Meg O'Riordan who's running the pub then? we don't want standards to slip.

SharonT
Homes needed for four jet black kittens. Three girls and a boy (currently Dipsy, Tripsy, Lolly and Son of Satan, all names can be changed)

Trixie Bell
Anyone know a good groomer for poms, current one never gets back to me, very unreliable. Thanks in advance.

SharonT
Missing a Ferryman delivery, can everyone check their post? Should be four catnip fish and a feather toy. Supposedly arrived yesterday.

Carrie O'Connor
There's a Tidy Towns meeting tomorrow 4pm in the pub. Doc O'R Wants the whole place spotless before the judging. He's got new window boxes on his house and the surgery. There's more for the church.

Finn MacCool
Carrie O'Connor Who called the Tidy Towns meeting? The Doc needs to stand as committee chair if he's that keen, does he want to take over?

LakeviewBandB
Carrie O'Connor Doc got a job lot probably. He could do with getting some decent chairs in the waiting room before he thinks about flower boxes.

Tracker Maguire
Carrie O'Connor Finn MacCool the Doc wants to run the Tidy Towns committee? Over my dead body.

Gen groaned as she looked at the most recent post. They definitely had more than enough dead bodies in Kilfenora. She hit *delete*.

Chapter 75

TESS WAS DOZING when her curtain was drawn back and a huge bunch of flowers materialised around it.

A face appeared above the flowers, not that Clarissa had managed to appear incognito, with the huge sapphire on her finger catching the light, and her beautifully French-polished nails. Her wide-eyed 'surprise' look made Tess laugh.

'I've only got a minute left before they throw me out. I should have got here earlier, but I wanted to say hello.'

Tess grinned. 'Mark was here, he said you've been mad busy.'

'Was he indeed? Well, that is good news.' Clarissa managed to achieve a look that was both innocent but full of intent. 'Busy, yes, organising that market and the vintage drivers is like herding cats. I think they've realised that they need to follow instructions now, but there have been a few testing moments.' She paused. 'Did Mark happen to mention that he's taken the pub off the market and is looking for a manager so he can concentrate on organising your tours? He's going to stay in Kilfenora.'

'No, really?' Tess couldn't resist a smile. 'That's a huge decision to make. I thought he was desperate to get back to Australia.'

'Well, he was, before all this happened. But I have a feeling he has a reason to stay now.' Clarissa looked pointedly at Tess.

It took Tess a moment to cotton on to what she meant.

'Me?'

'Obviously. Meg O'Riordan's all over him like a rash at the moment, but you should have seen the look on his face when he carried you down the stairs. He was so worried. I think he might stick around for a bit.'

'*Hold my hand.*'

In a distant part of her memory, she'd heard Mark's voice, felt a hand firmly in hers.

And she'd hung on like she was never going to let go.

Tess blushed hard. She could only remember snatches of leaving the house and arriving at the hospital, but was quite sure she hadn't been in a presentable state. When Gen had called in earlier she'd brought clean nightclothes and Tess's wrap and slippers, but the Snoopy T-shirt had gone into the bin. Tess put her free hand to her eyes.

'How utterly mortifying.'

'Don't worry, my dear, he's seen you at your worst, that's a good thing. If you didn't scare him off then, you're on to a winner.'

'Thanks a lot.' A smile twitched across Tess's face again. 'You're starting to sound like me.'

'Irrationally positive?' Laughing, Clarissa came into the cubicle properly, and put the flowers with their reservoir of water down on the bedside locker. 'Well, everything's come together so well, and you're not dead, so what is there to be miserable about?'

Tess shook her head. Honestly, Clarissa was so blunt sometimes. She wasn't dead. But she could so nearly have been if it hadn't been for Mark and Clarissa's quick thinking. She wasn't sure how she could ever thank them.

'How's Aidan? Have you spoken to him? Mark said he hadn't seen him.'

Clarissa shook her head. 'Not recently. We had a great chat on Friday night but nobody's seen him since. I'm sure he'll turn up in the next few days.'

'It's a bit odd, though, disappearing now.'

'He's an actor, darling, many of us have a dark side. Perhaps real success is something he couldn't quite handle.'

Tess couldn't understand that. She was very good with success. Hearing about the play and everything coming together, the queues wanting to look around the house, and seeing the coverage in the papers this morning, she felt as if a weight had been lifted from her shoulders. The public seemed utterly unperturbed by the recent tragedies, or perhaps they were fascinated by them. Tess wasn't sure, but at this stage she was just relieved that they were coming – in what sounded like their droves.

Clarissa came to sit on the edge of the bed. She was wearing one of her trademark Liberty shirts and cardigans, today in a shade of hyacinth that emphasised the colour of her eyes.

'Did Mark tell you they've caught the Radio Snatcher – that they've made an arrest?'

Tess felt her eyes fly open wide. 'Who? Eoin Doyle?'

Clarissa shook her head. 'No, but someone close to him. Turns out that the information that Lynch got from Mountjoy linked to another electrician. He's protecting his sources, but he must have had an epiphany and decided to cough that bit up.'

'Go on.'

'You know how Doyle never stops talking? It turns out that this other electrician – the one who was in Mountjoy – and Doyle used the same wholesaler. A chap called Rick Murphy, who runs his own show over in Tallaght. He's got a very long history of violence against women. Apparently he couldn't get a job working for anyone else with his background, so that's why he set up on his own – about twelve years ago. It seems Eoin Doyle's reckless chatter might have led him to the women who became his victims.'

It took Tess a moment to take it in; something was nagging at the back of her mind. She screwed up her face.

'I think he's the guy . . .'

Clarissa nodded, frowning. 'Mark told me about the security light. It seems it was the very same chap. Which is all helping the guards – Doyle hadn't ordered anything from him, and wasn't expecting a delivery when this Murphy character said he was in Kilfenora. He must have got a surprise when Mark answered the door.'

Tess paused, her head a mess of fear and guilt, images vying for attention: Katie-Louise laughing; Fidelma Hoey's photo in the paper; Jerry Lynch on the hillside.

She could see why women would let someone into their home if he'd said he knew their regular electrician, and perhaps that he was worried about a piece of equipment. She'd been thinking about it since Mark had left. She probably would have let him in, too, if Mark hadn't been there.

Clarissa shifted on the edge of the bed.

'He's been in and out of prison over the last eight years for various reasons. I'd guess he didn't have the time in the gaps to try again. I mean, finding someone who lives on their own in an isolated house . . . it's not that easy. And these things take planning.'

'Are they sure it's him – the Radio Snatcher?'

'They seem to be. Dr O'Riordan seemed very sure, anyway, he has a hot line to the inspector in Rockfield, apparently. I met him outside the shop and he came in for a cup of tea. I think he needed to talk to someone who wasn't quite so caught up in the fabric of the village.'

Tess closed her eyes for a moment. At least Fidelma Hoey's family would see justice now. She just prayed that they found the other bodies.

'Mark told me about Adam O'Donnell, too. About him being linked to Katie-Lou. I can't believe he was in Kilfenora.'

'That was a bit of a turn up for the books. But you don't have to worry about him now. He tried to harm you and failed, and now there are warrants for his arrest all over the place, so I really don't think he'll show up again.' Clarissa sounded very sure. 'He's a warped, screwed-up individual – we knew that from the moment he literally crashed into your life.'

'Gen thinks he could have been the Twitter troll, too, that he saw something in the press about me buying Kilfenora.' Tess took a ragged breath, the tears starting to fall, hot on her face. She tried to wipe them away. 'I brought him to Kilfenora. If it wasn't for me, he'd never have met Katie-Lou. Do they know if he was involved in Laetitia's death?' The words stalled in Tess's mouth. 'I still don't understand what happened.'

'None of it was your doing at all.' Clarissa slipped her handbag off her shoulder and produced a tissue, passing it to her. Tess closed her eyes and tried to fight the feeling of despair that was pulling her into the darkness. Clarissa grasped Tess's hand. 'People like that always come to a sticky end. They get their comeuppance, don't you worry.'

'You seem very sure.' Tess sniffed loudly.

'I am. Trust me. I've been around the block a few times, as they say. Remember, I've had three husbands. Three heart attacks. I could blame myself, but that wouldn't be good for my mental health, would it?'

'But you didn't have anything to do with their fitness – I mean, you didn't smoke or drink them to death, did you?' Tess could feel all the emotion spilling out, all the stress of the past few days welling up inside her. 'God, I feel so bad about Katie-Lou, I mean . . .'

'*It wasn't your fault.*' Clarissa said it emphatically.

Tess looked at her. 'But it was, that's the thing.' Tears began to fall thick and fast again. 'It was all my fault. I've never told anyone, Clarissa, and now all this has happened. I have the most horrible secret, and I've been living with it for so long. It was my fault Kieran died. I pushed him. We were messing and I pushed him and he fell into the road and he died. *All* of this is my fault.'

'Tess, now stop, please. You sound like Mark.' Clarissa shook her head, pursing her lips as if she was considering what to say next. 'This is in absolute confidence. You can't tell him you know, and if he tells you, act surprised.'

'What?' Tess didn't think she could take much more.

'Mark told me that he told his wife that he was leaving her, the day she hanged herself. He's absolutely convinced it was his fault, too. But he didn't put the noose around her neck, and you didn't have a skinful to drink and get into your car. *It was not your fault.* Adam O'Donnell did his own deal with the Devil the moment he started his engine that night.' Clarissa squeezed Tess's hand, her face earnest. 'Guilt is a negative emotion – it tries to elbow its way in where there is no place for it. It does not serve you and it doesn't help anyone. You cannot blame yourself for things you could not control. And honestly, none of this is anyone's business. Some secrets are best left buried.'

FURTHER TRAGEDY AT KILFENORA

Gardaí are not treating the most recent death at the historic Kilfenora House in Co. Wicklow as suspicious after a post mortem revealed that Adam O'Donnell died of natural causes.

O'Donnell, who had been using the name 'Aidan Gaunt' (37), was discovered in the restored property set in the 100-acre Kilfenora estate, on Monday evening.

It is understood that the deceased, who had been living in the area for approximately a year, had claimed to be a scriptwriter and director.

Gardaí have since established that O'Donnell, originally of Howth, County Dublin, was previously an investment banker. However, almost nine years ago he was convicted of dangerous driving following the death of Kilfenora owner Tess Morgan's fiancé, Kieran Murphy, and received a four year sentence. Following his release from prison, he became a film extra in London.

Adam O'Donnell's death comes hard on the heels of two separate murder inquiries into the deaths of local residents Laetitia O'Riordan (20) and Katie-Louise O'Neill (22), and the staging accident that left lead actor Conor Kelly (25) in a six-day coma.

Conor Kelly's condition is now 'stable', according to a hospital spokesperson.

'The state pathologist found that the individual using the name of Aidan Gaunt died of a heart attack,' a garda spokesperson said, adding: 'It would appear he was using the old back staircase from the recently restored dining room, to take a shortcut to the after-show party.'

The spokesperson declined to discuss any of the other cases 'given that they are the subject of ongoing criminal investigations.'

However, a source revealed that, prior to his death, Adam O'Donnell was considered the main suspect in the investigation into the deaths of both Laetitia O'Riordan and Katie-Louise O'Neill.

O'Donnell's DNA was found under Katie-Louise O'Neill's fingernails, the source added.

The West Wicklow Weekender has also learned that a photograph taken on Laetitia O'Riordan's phone a week before her death, shows a mass of flowers from the highly toxic aconite plant, which is believed to have been linked to the collapse of Morgan.

A distinctive ring, worn by O'Donnell is also captured in the shot.

Asked about the recent events, a source believes 'Adam O'Don-nell was intent on destroying Tess Morgan in revenge for his conviction. Talk of a Kilfenora curse is all nonsense. He fooled us all.' The source, who wished to remain anonymous, added, 'The whole village has been involved in the restoration of Kilfenora, Tess Morgan hasn't been here very long but she's transformed the estate and brought business into the area. She has our full support and we hope visitors will continue to come in the same spectacular numbers as were here at the opening weekend.'

Morgan is expected to make a full recovery.

Meanwhile, legendary actress and local resident, Clarissa West-macott, who introduced the play and was hosting the after-show party, was unavailable for comment.

The 74-year-old actress, originally from South Dublin, is a close friend of Tess Morgan's and has lived in Kilfenora village for several years.

THE END

Acknowledgements

The idea for this story started with Amanda Lees' *The Dictionary of Crime* – a brilliant and fascinating book (written by a lovely person, who isn't *too* murderous at all). I read it right through but came back around to the start and aconite with its fascinating properties – I've always loved this particular shade of blue/purple. I can highly recommend it, even if you aren't planning to kill anyone soon.

It also grew from a documentary I saw about Fred West that tried to piece together the last resting places of several of his victims. The programme makers believed they had discovered a link to a piece of land that could have been a burial site, and approached a landowner to get permission to excavate. That got me thinking about what might happen if you owned a similar piece of land, and what a huge dilemma you could find yourself in.

Merlin is the only 'real' thing in this story. Kilfenora House (and the village) is entirely fictitious, based on an amalgam of country houses in County Wicklow including Powerscourt and Kilruddery but also Arreton Manor in the Isle of Wight. Wicklow is the Garden of Ireland with stunning scenery and many beautiful gardens – do visit if you can.

In this story, Merlin plays himself – he's my son Sam's cat, and exactly as portrayed: very hissy and grumpy, and he can open any door, including the door on a spring in our kitchen. And like this Merlin, our Merlin is very particular – he adores Sam, who is the only member of the family who can safely pick him up.

My English teacher at Bishop's Hatfield Girls' School, Mairead McKeever, introduced me to Marlowe, Browning and Blake, and I still have my original, much scribbled on, copies of the texts we used. Thank you for encouraging my love of English – I always knew all those wonderful quotes would come in useful one day.

Huge thanks to my fabulous agent Simon Trewin, whose background in theatre was integral to many scenes in this story, and to my editor, Sarah Hodgson at Atlantic Books, whose experience is invaluable in shaping the text. Without copy editor Steve O'Gorman, several characters' names would be spelled several different ways! I love his attention to detail and meticulous fact-checking.

There are so many people involved in the production of a book, from the cover design to promotion (Gill Hess here in Ireland are fantastic) – it's a team effort and without every member you wouldn't have got this far. A huge thanks to everyone involved, I appreciate each and every one of you.

And I cannot thank enough the reviewers and bloggers who support my books and help so much in bringing them to new readers. You are amazing!

But most of all, thank you to you, the reader, for buying and reading and letting me share my story with you, I hope you enjoyed this glimpse into Tess's world.

Sam Blake

For more gripping thrillers, join the

SAM BLAKE
READERS' CLUB

Get exclusive writing and an insight into bestselling author Sam Blake's books delivered straight to your inbox.

Members are the first to hear all the latest book news, find out when new books are published and have the chance to win books and other prizes in regular competitions.

Plus you'll get a FREE THRILLER by Sam Blake as soon as you join.

Scan the QR code to join or visit:
www.samblakebooks.com

Read on for an exclusive early extract from
Sam Blake's brilliantly twisty new thriller

THREE
LITTLE
BIRDS

SAM BLAKE

CORVUS

Chapter 1

CARLA STEELE ROLLED her chair closer to her desk, her concentration fixed on the screen in front of her – on the damaged eye socket of a human skull. The early morning June sunshine filled her office from the window behind her, dust motes dancing like fractured spirits in its beam. She adjusted the monitor to reduce the glare.

She knew this image like she knew the tattoo on the inside of her wrist: three birds in flight, their wings outspread, the line below it – WITH BRAVE WINGS SHE FLIES – written in script across her pale skin. Across her heart.

Since the week she'd arrived to set up the Forensic Anthropology and Computer Enhancement department, affectionately known as FACE, in Ireland's Garda Headquarters, her days had begun and ended with this image filling her screen – with this case; with the sharply circumscribed semicircular entry wound on the left side of the occipital bone. She moved the image of the 3-D render around with the haptic Phantom lever, VR software allowing her to feel the structure of the skull as if it was in front of her. There was an exit wound at the rear, the bone demonstrating characteristic bevelling created by the direction of a bullet's motion.

Whenever she opened this file, the questions crowded into her head. With only the skull as evidence, she couldn't conclude absolutely that a bullet had been the actual cause of death, or hypothesise that it had been inflicted by someone other than the victim. But given that the skull had been found wrapped in a pale blue crocheted blanket, in a wardrobe, in an abandoned house, it seemed likely that someone had wanted to conceal this death. Someone who knew where the rest of the body was hidden, and exactly what had happened.

From the size of the aperture, the data suggested a medium-calibre bullet, most likely a .32. To Carla's experienced eye, the point of entry suggested an execution.

Carla scowled and flicked to the next screen: the finished render of the girl's face. This had been the first cold case she'd tackled when she'd been invited to set up FACE two years earlier. But despite an extensive media campaign, and her reputation as the woman who had rebuilt a skull mislabelled in the basement of a small museum and given a face to Ireland's famous Pirate Queen, she was no closer to finding out who the victim was.

It nagged at her like the onset of a migraine.

When she'd rebuilt this girl's face, she'd scanned it as she had so many others, using the three-dimensional software to create a model that allowed her to change the girl's skin tone and hairstyle. This was the skull of a teenager of partially Asian descent – one who had had enough anxiety in her life to grind her teeth.

But who? And why? And when?

This girl belonged to someone; she'd had a life, had lived and loved and had died – whether by her own hand or someone else's – violently. Despite the various impressions of her face that had been put out to the media, no one had come forward to suggest a name, or even a history.

Carla twirled her ring, a birthday gift from her cousin Rachel. They'd only met up for the first time this spring, two halves of the family totally unknown to each other until a DNA search had thrown up some unexpected results. They'd connected immediately, had had so much to talk about that Carla was planning a trip to London to visit Rachel and her partner Hunter and stay on their houseboat, as soon as she could get a week off. The ring was the perfect gift – a heavy silver skull, its diamanté eyes flashing in the summer light; Rachel had one just like it. Carla rolled it around her finger, the movement soothing. Deep inside her, she could feel the tragedy of this girl's death as if it was a physical thing. Heavy, like her ring.

Every time she opened the image, anger and sadness and stress and failure blended together, turning her stomach. Because it wasn't just this girl who caused her pain.

She was someone who found answers – it was her job, for goodness' sake – and yet this was another case she couldn't solve.

Carla closed her eyes, an image of Lizzie, her best friend, appearing in her head; the last time she'd seen her, frozen in time like a movie still. Lizzie, turning to wave as she headed off across Dublin's iconic O'Connell Bridge into the night, her red cashmere scarf wrapped almost to her eyes, a pair of brown felt reindeer antlers holding back her crazy auburn hair, flashing with tiny red lights like a warning of what was to come.

It would be her birthday soon.

A knock rang out on her office door and Carla jolted in her chair. She checked the time on her screen. It wasn't even nine.

'Come in.'

The door opened and a man's head appeared around it, followed by the unmistakable form of a Garda detective in plain clothes, whose serious look and creased forehead reminded her of one of the doctors she followed on YouTube. But this guy's eyes were a piercing blue, his dark hair sticking up, as if he fought a daily battle with keeping it flat.

'I was looking for a Dr Carla Steele.'

Carla raised her eyebrows and looked him up and down. His navy sports jacket looked crisp, but the creases in his pale blue open-necked shirt and sand-coloured chinos suggested he'd been driving for a while. His jacket flapped open as he came through the door, revealing the holster on his belt.

'You found her.'

'Oh.' His eyes opened in surprise. He quickly corrected the expression, blushing hard, and opened his mouth – trying, Carla imagined, to find something to say to hide his mistake.

She was never sure whether it was her nose ring, or the streak of white that contrasted so starkly with her long, almost black, hair, that was unexpected. Or the fact that she wore a T-shirt and jeans with Doc Martens to work. It didn't matter; since she'd arrived at Garda Headquarters, she'd been getting all sorts of looks – few of them complimentary. Sometimes she was sure it was just because she was a woman under thirty who had *Doctor* in front of her name. Despite their best efforts, the national Irish police force, An Garda Síochána – the guardians of the peace – was only twenty-five per cent female, although Forensic Services Ireland, where she was based, was closer to fifty per cent. Still not enough, in her opinion.

Suddenly feeling sorry for her visitor, Carla cut in, rescuing him from trying to form a sentence that was clearly taking its time coming.

'How can I help?'

He came fully into her office, a large brown cardboard evidence box under his arm, and pushed the door closed behind him.

'DS Jack Maguire, from Coyne's Cross, Mayo. We wondered if you could help us with this. They catalogued it in reception, said to bring it straight up.'

He proffered the box and Carla could see a printed label had been stuck to one side. Date and case number, the start of the digital trail that would map every item of forensic evidence connected to the contents of the box. It had been stuck firmly shut with brown packing tape.

'Let's see what you've got.' Rolling her chair away, she pulled open her desk drawer and looked for her Swiss Army knife. 'Try this. And sit down. We don't want any accidental slash injuries. It's Friday, and it's the bank holiday weekend. The hospitals will be busy enough with the carnage on the roads.'

Jack Maguire hesitated for a moment at the irony in her tone, but rather than coming back with a smart reply, as she'd expect from some, he sat down and opened the knife, his forehead creased.

He was a serious one. She liked that.

'What's the background?'

Concentrating on the box, Jack answered as he sliced through the tape.

'A couple of divers found it in the middle of Lough Coyne

on Monday. It was really deep. They were looking for a marine video camera that got dropped off a dive boat, some problem with the insurance.'

'Have you got the rest of the body?'

'Not yet. A team's been looking all week, but the lough's tidal. The rest of it could be anywhere at this stage.' He closed the blade of the knife. 'The pathologist took dental casts. He's taken other samples but we're no closer to identification. He thought you might be a better bet.'

Carla slid her chair closer to the desk. 'Extracting and amplifying DNA from bone is tricky on a good day, even assuming you have something to match it to – the environmental conditions can alter its integrity dramatically.'

Jack stood up again and flipped open the lid. Inside was a large brown paper evidence bag marked with the same file numbers as the outer covering. Lifting it carefully onto the desk, he unrolled the neck of the bag and gingerly lifted out its contents. Carla gave him a mental tick; the gentle way he was handling it showed respect for the victim. She'd seen so many who treated skeletal remains like the leftovers from last week's dinner.

Leaning forwards to look properly, Carla tucked a loose strand of white hair behind her ear.

'Did they find anything with it at all?'

'Like clothing, you mean?'

Looking across the skull at him, she nodded.

'Nothing. It was too deep for them to stay down long enough at the time, but they've been over the same area doing a proper search all week.' He hesitated. 'The thing is, we've had a spate of suicides. We were wondering if it was one of them.'

'Your suicides are predominantly male?'

It was Jack's turn to nod. 'They call it Suicide Point, the cliff path. God knows …' He trailed off as Carla reached for the skull.

Picking it up, she turned it gently, inspecting the yellowed cranium, fracture lines radiating across the right side. The mandible was intact, although some of the teeth were missing. She turned it again, looking at the orbital ridges, the same feeling building inside her that she'd had looking at the skull on the screen.

She could hear Lizzie's laughter around her, dancing like the high notes on a violin, infectious, melodious, as if she was standing in the corner of the room. She was always here, but at times like this her presence seemed stronger. Sometimes Carla felt that if she spun around fast enough, she'd see her. She'd tried so many times. Had, she'd thought, occasionally caught a glimpse of movement out of the corner of her eye. But never long enough to speak to her, to ask her where she was, what had happened that night. The night that had changed the course of all their lives.

Carla cleared her throat.

'Come up to the lab, we need to have a proper look.'